The Last Sunday in

Ordinary Time

James McCormack

Dedicated to my sons Jack, Brendan (Oxford comma inserted here for Brendan's benefit), and Patrick. I love them all very much.

The Last Sunday in Ordinary Time

The Last Sunday in Ordinary Time

The Good Son of a Proper Irish Family

The last time I saw Danny Kilnagael alive he sat uncomfortably on the steps of Holy Truth, smoked a cigarette, and predicted his own death. I knew Danny a little, but I wanted to know him better. He waved the cigarette awkwardly, still not comfortable with the habit he started recently after joining the army. I continued to see him almost as if he were a movie star, blinded to his awkwardness by my determination to see him as a hero. His prediction scared the wits out of his sister Colleen, who also happened to be my girlfriend. I watched the two of them with fascination, like an anthropologist studying a foreign culture. In 1966 Chicago was a very Irish city, and Holy Truth may have been its most Irish parish. In my eyes the Kilnagaels were the most Irish people in Holy Truth, a large, wealthy, boisterous family noted for their beautiful children and involvement in the day-to-day life of the church. They were everything I wanted to be.

The only child of the two most boring people in the world, I longed to be a part of a big Irish family like the Kilnagaels. My mother gave birth to me after her fortieth birthday, causing strangers to wonder if she were my grandmother rather than my mother, and me to wonder why God saddled me with the two oddest parents in the parish. In the company of the Kilnagaels I achieved a sense of Irishness that I never got at home.

"Do you consider yourself a lucky man?"

On the steps of Our Lady of the Holy Truth he looked smaller than the six feet, two inches he actually was. He'd lost about twenty pounds since boot camp started, which, when coupled with his military crew cut added to the overall look of a wounded animal rather than the confident young man he seemed to be a few weeks earlier. He never looked up at me when he asked the question, causing me to hesitate before answering because I wondered if he were talking to me or to himself.

"Yeah, I guess I do."

"Not me," he answered. He inhaled on his cigarette, and then let out a long, slow puff of smoke. I never smoked and I struggled to figure why the cigarette seemed so unnatural in his hand. I couldn't tell what he was doing wrong, but the cigarette had the feel of a shirt buttoned wrong, or shoes on the wrong feet. It didn't look right.

"Oh, Danny, come on," Colleen said. "You've always been treated like the prince of the family. You're the only son, and Mom and Dad don't even know that they have daughters when you're in the room. You've had a horseshoe up your butt your whole life."

Colleen Kilnagael was Danny's younger sister, a gorgeous, brown-eyed blonde. They were beautiful people, both of them. The whole Kilnagael family fascinated me, charmed me, and made me long to be one of them. I agreed with Colleen, except that she failed to realize that she shared his luck. They were the Kilnagaels, for God's sake. They were the first family of Holy Truth, and many of their neighbors were star-struck by them. It mattered if you could say you were a friend of the Kilnagaels, and they welcomed everyone to call them friends.

"Coll, you're not the one who gets told what to do all the time. I'm the one who's expected to live up to Dad's standards. Nothing I ever did was good enough. Hell, I joined the army just to show him that I'm my own man. Dumbest thing I ever did though."

"I thought you wanted to be in the army."

"No. Maybe I thought I did. I don't know. I should have gone to Michigan, but Dad was so pushy about Notre Dame that I finally said screw it."

It amazed me to see the two of them living in such a magical world without any sense that it existed. He got to choose between attending a Big Ten school or Notre Dame, and thought this was a burden.

"I actually feel sorry for Dad a little bit, now. He has to act like he's proud of his son for 'serving his country' when the truth is he's mad as hell. And, he's scared too. He ought to be. I know I am."

"What are you scared about?" Colleen asked.

"In a few weeks I'm going to Viet Nam, but I doubt I'm ever coming home. I'm going to die there."

"Danny, don't say that."

"Like I said, I'm not a lucky guy. If I was, I wouldn't be going to war, but I am. I am going to die young a million miles away from home." Colleen sat down beside him, put her arm around his shoulders, and kissed his cheek.

"Daniel James Kilnagael, you are not going to die. Don't you say that to me. I love you, Mom and Dad love you, we all love you, and you are *not* going to die." Danny kept up his casual indifference to the emotion of what he was saying. Colleen pressed her forehead against his shoulder, and held him in an awkward embrace. As far as I could tell, they stopped being aware of my presence. I studied them like an anthropologist who just discovered a new tribe.

"The thing that bothers me most though is the thought of Mom getting that letter: 'We regret to inform you...'"

"Danny," she sort of half screamed, "stop it. Don't say that again. You are not going to die. You are not going to die. You are not going to die." She was on the verge of panic, crying a little, but trying to stay calm.

"I want you to do me a favor." He just kept right on talking, as if he were asking his sister to pick up something from the cleaners for him, acting like he was unaware that he terrified her more with each word. "I want you intercept that letter, when it comes."

"No, Danny."

"It would be better if Mom heard it from someone..."

"No, Danny."

"...she knew rather than..."

"No, Danny."

"Rather than," he said with impatience, "having to read it by herself, alone."

"No. You listen to me, Danny..."

"We'll do it," I said finally. They both looked at me, almost shocked that I was still there.

Colleen had a what-are-you-trying-to-do look in her eyes. "They say a watched pot never boils, right? Well, I figure if Colleen and I keep watching your mailbox for that letter, it will never arrive. As long as we keep a watch out for that letter, it will never arrive, so you won't die."

I don't know where we got the idea that the army sent letters to families to inform them that their sons had died in battle. We must have all watched the same bad movie where a mother reads the letter and then breaks down in tears on the living room couch. No matter where we got the idea, we all had it. When Colleen heard my plan, she jumped at it.

"That's right. We will watch for that letter every day, and as long as we do, you'll be protected. Marty and I will keep you safe. Okay?"

Danny looked at me and nodded his approval. I wasn't sure he bought in to the whole idea that guarding the mailbox would keep him alive, but he got what he wanted. His mother would be spared the horror of reading about his death, and he was relieved from the worry about her being crushed receiving the news in such a cold manner. Colleen, for her part, got to believe that Danny was not so convinced he was going to die in Viet Nam. As for me, I guaranteed myself that I would remain Colleen's boyfriend at least until her brother returned from Viet Nam. I never believed that Danny would die in battle.

The three of us remained there for few minutes more, but Danny had a few friends he wanted to see before returning to the army the next day. As soon as he was out of sight, Colleen kissed me long and hard. She was particularly passionate toward me that night, hugging me tightly, kissing me often, and thanking me over and over again for helping her ease Danny's mind. When I held Colleen in my arms, I pretty much held everything I ever wanted. She wasn't just beautiful. She wasn't just Irish. She was Colleen *Kilnagael*, and she was the girl of my dreams. I knew as I walked home that night that I would see Colleen a lot in the future. I didn't know that I would never again see Danny Kilnagael alive.

The Last Sunday in Ordinary Time

The First Sunday in Ordinary Time

June 5, 1966

I spent my summer evenings alone in my bedroom looking at the fading daylight, listening to the noise other children made, and knowing that life was passing me by. Even at the age of ten my bedtime was 8:30 on school nights, and 9:00 in summer. Literally pressing my nose again the window screen, I listened to other children, some of them half my age, still outside playing with their brothers and sisters, neither of which I had. By the time I turned twelve I came to two conclusions; I was glad I was Irish-Catholic, but I wasn't as Irish-Catholic as the other kids were.

Real Irish-Catholic families were big and loud, having at least four kids, usually more. The Caseys had five, the Tracys had five, the McDonoughs had five, their cousins, the other McDonoughs, had six, the McKennas had seven, the Moriartys had eight, the Daleys had nine, the Reillys had ten. Only we, the woe-be-gone Donovans, had one. Not only did I not have siblings, I didn't even have cousins. It was like I arrived uninvited and unprepared for the world's greatest party.

On Sunday mornings I watched other families stumble manically triumphant out of station wagons in a raucous symphony of "hold stills," "Mommies," and "he started its." We, conversely, arrived in pious silence, wearing our Sunday-best clothes, and exchanging quiet, pleasant good mornings with other older people. My parents were not just dull, they were old and dull.

My father left Ireland when he was thirty-three years old with one suitcase and the address of a Chicago tavern, arrived in Chicago with that same suitcase and a friend he met on the boat, Mickey Riordan, and headed straight to the Lovely Bit O' Blarney Pub. The owner was Charlie Fitzpatrick, a man who grew up in the same Irish town that my father came from, and became somewhat of a legend back home. As the proprietor of a highly successful tavern in America, he was the local boy made good. He was also the only person in America that my grandfather knew, so before Dad left Ireland, Grandpa wrote to Uncle Charlie and asked him to watch out for his son. Uncle Charlie brought my Dad to his new home parish, Our Lady of Holy Truth. Charlie and his wife Bridie never had children of their own, so even though Dad was already in his thirties by the time he got off the train in Union Station, Uncle Charlie treated him like the son he never had.

For Dad, things could not have worked out better. Uncle Charlie was one of the last of the politically connected tavern owners in Chicago, and as such, he had the connections to get his "son" a good job with the city. A few months after arriving in town, Dad was working on a street crew in the department of Streets and Sanitation. Of more importance to me, Charlie and Bridie also knew a nice girl that they wanted him to meet. At the age of thirty-five Dad married Kathleen Brennan, a forty-year-old woman who had come to America in the 1930's. They in turn had one child, me, and so there we were, the Donovans of Our Lady of Holy Truth.

Every Sunday I put on a white shirt, a tie, dark slacks, and black oxford shoes. I sat in the backseat of my father's Chevrolet Impala, and rode to church as silently as I could. Compared to most of my friends, my parents were old, and I already knew who they would talk about, and what they would say. They weren't mean, just boring. Mrs. Donnelly was walking very slowly these days. That fellow over there never removes his hat until he sits down. They knew who arrived late, who left early, and who wore the same clothes every week. They included me in their observations, and I nodded politely while silently begging them not to tell me about the man with the hat again. If I had brothers and sisters maybe I would have enjoyed mass more, but instead I sat alone feeling the same way I did when I looked out my bedroom window.

Like all of the Catholic churches in Chicago, Our Lady of Holy Truth printed a weekly bulletin. Ours was called *Our Lady's Truth*, and it featured a weekly letter from the pastor, the mass schedule, not that it ever changed much, wedding banns, wedding announcements, baptismal announcements, altar boy schedules, various fundraising events, and other odds and ends of parish news. On the back page were advertisements from several local businesses, including Snyder's Bakery, Pfaff's Butcher Shop (A cut above the rest), O'Hearn Funeral Home (The dignity your loved one deserves) among others. The two biggest ads were bought by The Lovely Bit O' Blarney Pub, and Mickey's American Standard, both of which were owned by my uncles.

Although I didn't have any genuine blood relatives in America, I did have two quasi-uncles. Uncle Charlie who owned The Lovely Bit, and Uncle Mickey, who owned Mickey's American Standard, the gas station on Madison avenue, directly across the street from the Lovely Bit. I wanted to view Dad's life story as one great romantic adventure, and sometimes I did although my thinking began to change as I entered high school. He was the precinct captain for our block, a responsibility that he was remarkably unsuited for. Dad hated talking to people. He was a shy man who rarely drank, never smoked, and was content to spend his evenings at home reading the newspaper or making agonizingly slow progress remodeling our basement. But being a streets-and-san man meant that he had to work for the Daley machine in order to keep his job. Not even Uncle Charlie, with all of his clout and connections, could keep a man on the payroll who didn't help get out the vote. Every election Dad had to actually walk up and down the street ringing doorbells and encouraging people to vote Democratic. Whenever I saw him do this, I thought he looked small, like a man who had no control over his own life.

Increasingly I thought he was a drone who married the woman he was told to marry, accepted the job he was given, and generally achieved nothing on his own.

That is not to say that I didn't think he was in love with Mom. To the contrary, I'm certain that he was. Mom, if I do say so myself, was a very pretty woman, and I'm sure Dad was proud to walk into a room and be recognized as the man who won Katie Brennan's hand. But I was an only child. If my dad would have been blessed with a more dynamic personality, maybe I would be one of six or seven children. Maybe he would have been more like Uncle Charlie, a political guy who shook everyone's hand, knew everyone's name, and made everyone feel welcome. Maybe we would have been like one of those big Irish families that populated our parish and I wouldn't feel like I was Irish the way Monaco was a country. I knew that I was Irish, but it felt like I barely qualified.

Uncle Mickey, the man dad met while on the boat from Ireland, remained my dad's best friend, although I was never sure that Dad was his best friend. He actually was everything my father was not. Mick was a gregarious, loud personality, a man who would not be ignored. He stood six feet, four inches with vibrant red hair, and what I thought of as a Hollywood handsome face. Now in his early forties, Mick was still unmarried despite the efforts of my mom and other women to fix him up. He fended off blind dates by winking at Mom and insisting all the beautiful women were already married. He remained his own man in every way possible, usually walking into a room alone, flirting with everyone wearing a skirt, and then leaving alone as well. He quite literally laughed at every joke you told him, if not because they were all funny, then at least because he appreciated the effort that went into the telling.

Years earlier, when Uncle Charlie got a job with the city for my dad, he also offered to get one for Mickey, but Mickey refused his offer. Dad remembered Mickey saying business is what America does, and he wanted to be a genuine American. That philosophy showed itself in every part of Mickey's life. His gas station was a Standard Oil franchise that sat directly across the street from the Lovely Bit on Madison. Like most of the Standards built in Chicago in the forties and fifties, it was a small, square garage that included two bays for car repairs, and a small office/store that sold quarts of oil, newspapers, and a small selection of candy bars, gum, and cigarettes. The building featured brilliant white glazed brick top to bottom, except for a one strip of red glazed brick, and one strip one blue glazed brick that circled the building just above the door. The color pattern matched the red, white, and blue of the Standard Oil sign that stood along Madison, and of the American flag that Mickey flew by the front door.

On Sunday, June 5th, I attended the 8:30 mass like always. We Catholics had just celebrated Pentecost, and this was known as the first Sunday in ordinary time, the period between the end of the Easter season and Advent, the start of the Christmas season. As I sat not listening to the homily I noticed Colleen Kilnagael sitting on the other side of the church. I rarely saw kids my age at mass this early, and never Colleen Kilnagael. I plotted to be sure to get close enough to her to say hello before she left church, something I imagined would not be difficult. When the priest finally left the altar, however, it seemed like a dozen people wanted to say hello to me. I greeted everyone politely while easing toward the door, trying to keep her in my sight. I wanted to call out to her but the church was hardly the place to yell like that, so I followed to the door with my eyes only to have my gaze intercepted by Mickey, who smiled broadly at having caught me staring at her, and gave me a wink.

Mickey, as far as I knew, rarely attended Holy Truth, but seeing him there hardly surprised me. He seemed always to belong wherever he stood, so naturally he belonged here on this Sunday. It surprised me when he decided to join my parents and me at the Silver Cup for breakfast, but it excited me. Breakfast was a treat my parents looked forward to every Sunday after mass, an atypical splurge by a couple who lived a very frugal life. Mickey joining us meant a livelier conversation, and much more laughter. As soon as the waitress laid our plates on the table, Mick tore into his pancakes.

"Mick, are you that hungry? You're gonna swallow a finger thinking it's a sausage if you don't slow down." Mick looked up, speared a sausage off of my dad's plate, and winked at him.

"Never mind my fingers, just pay attention to your own sausages, Billy." He finished his breakfast well ahead of ours, pulled out a pack of cigarettes, lit up, and enjoyed a cigarette with his coffee. I know my parents didn't care for the smell of cigarettes, but it was one of the many sins they overlooked when in Mick's company. His charm overwhelmed any lack of consideration they may have felt he showed.

"Did you hear Pete Harrigan got in a car accident yesterday?" he asked after exhaling a long stream of smoke.

"Did he?"

"Is he all right?" Dad asked.

"I suppose so. I haven't heard anything, so I suppose he's okay. If he was hurt, everyone would know."

"What happened?"

"Tom Murphy told me he fell asleep driving home from work."

"Probably had a few." Dad suggested.

"Honestly, I don't think so. He's been working two jobs, policeman and some construction on the side."

"What's he got, seven kids?"

"Eight," Mom said.

"Well, Pete never could sleep at night."

"Mick, you're terrible," Mom said, letting Mick know she enjoyed his mischief. In my parents world that's what passed as a dirty joke. Actually I was a little uneasy hearing it in front of my parents, but liked that Mick didn't hesitate to say it with me listening.

"So, what's this one doing this summer?" he asked with a nod in my direction.

"We never know what we're going to do with him. It's a wonder we keep him at all." We laughed at her joke partly to be polite and partly because she enjoyed the joke so much herself. I never considered Mom a great wit, but she made a great audience, especially for her own jokes.

"I could use another man at the gas station this summer, if it's okay with you."

"It's a very nice offer, Mick," Mom said, "but I don't think so."

"Mom! What the heck..." She held up her hand to stop my protest.

"Marty, we want you to go to college. Working in a gas station is fine for some, but you have a higher calling."

"Katie, you are absolutely right."

"What's wrong with working in a gas station? Mick works in a gas station."

"No," Mom said while shooting me a look that mixed anger with embarrassment, "Mick owns a gas station. If you want to own a gas station, that's different. You can go to college, get a job that pays lots of money, and then use that money to buy one."

"Your mother is right, young man. She's afraid you'll like pumping gas and ignore your books."

"But it's not fair to..."

"Marty, that's enough." Mom and Dad were ganging up on me.

"Listen. I agree that Marty should go to college. If you don't want him to work in the gas station that's fine, but I can promise you two things: If comes to work for me, he won't enjoy it. I'll make sure he works hard enough to long for the books. And, if he ever does quit school, I'll fire him. He has a job only until he graduates from college."

Breakfast ended that morning with a "We'll see" hanging in the air. As we said our good-byes that morning Mick gave me another wink. For the next forty-eight hours I pleaded, whined, nagged, and relentlessly hounded my parents to let me work at Mickey's. In the end my dad decided that a job would do me some good, and so they relented, although Mom still doubted that it was the right thing to do. After dinner on Tuesday Dad pulled me aside.

"Marty, I talked to Mickey today. We've decided to let you go to work for him."

"Thanks, Dad, really, thanks a lot. I won't let you down, I promise. I swear to God that I won't let you or Mom down."

"I know you won't, but still, you've got to be ready."

"I'll be ready, I promise."

"Marty, just settle down for a moment. I want to tell you something about Mickey. He's a great guy, and tells a funny story, but he works very hard. He's not an easy boss. He's going to give you a hard time. It won't be fun and games working for Mick."

"I'll be ready, I swear." Dad held up his hand and gave me a look of impatience.

"The first summer I was here I worked as a bricklayer's laborer. I happened to be talking to fellow from Cork named Johnny Ryan who had just quit his job as a laborer, because, he said, they blamed him for everything. He said they yelled at him for being too slow, for not picking up the tools fast enough, for not keeping up with the mortar and for God knows what. He said one bricklayer lost a trowel one day, and starting yelling at him because it was the laborer's job to keep track of the tools. Ryan said if anyone had told him that he would be yelled at like that, he would have never taken the job. He lasted only a couple of days before he quit.

"Sure enough, a few days later, someone offered me a chance to be a bricklayer's laborer, and I have to say, Johnny Ryan was right. They yelled at me from minute one to the end of the day, but I had two things working in my favor: I was desperate for a paycheck, and I knew they were going to yell at me even if it wasn't my fault at all."

"So you didn't quit?" Dad smirked.

"No, I didn't quit, at least not until your Uncle Charlie got me in at Streets and San. Now Mickey Riordan is a good man as far as it goes, but he's not one for extending manners too far. He's going to be rough on you. I'm glad you got the job, but you better know walking in that the man is going to test you. I don't want you coming home in a day or two and telling me that you quit."

"Oh, I won't Dad. I promise you."

"I know you won't. I'm telling you you won't, but you have to be ready. Mickey is a man who lives to work. He does his best whenever he does anything. He'll be watching you, and he won't have a good word to say to you. He'll complain about your manners, whether or not you speak clearly enough to the customers, how well you swept the floor. You've got to have a thick skin. He'll be testing you until you prove you do good work even when he's not watching you and the only help I can give you is this. If you feel like he's being too hard on you come home and talk to me about it. If it means you have to put in a long day without complaining, so be it."

This kind of admonition was out of character for my dad. I nodded my understanding, trying not to show how shocked I was that Dad was talking to me this way. While I had always seen him as anything but a tough guy, he was showing me a side of him that I never knew existed.

"Now that you've accepted the job, I expect you to keep it at least through the summer. When school starts again in the fall, if you want to quit, *then* you can quit. But it's still only early June, so you've got June, July, and August to get through."

"Okay, Dad."

My opinion of my dad didn't change that day, but it began to. I viewed him as a man who let life happen to him rather than as a go-getter who made things happen. In his voice, and seemingly in his view of the world, I starting hearing and seeing a resolve that I never imagined before. He offered advice rarely, and the advice he offered never registered with me before. This time, though, it hit the mark.

My first day at Mickey's American Standard started at about ten minutes to six. By 6:15 I was already realizing how good my dad's advice had been. Mick, to be blunt, would not shut up. He taught me how to pump gas, showed impatience if I said I knew something already, and showed impatience if I said I didn't know something already. Our "conversations" were a series of angry sounding questions:

"Do you think you can remember that?"

"You can read, can't you?"

"Did I tell you to touch the oil cap?"

"How long does it take a man to give change?"

For Mickey it was a game, one in which he made the rules, acted as umpire, and took every opportunity to berate me. He told me to sweep out the empty car bay, but to also watch out for cars pulling into the station. He yelled at me when I didn't react fast enough to a customer who pulled in to the second pump. I started watching for cars more vigilantly so he yelled at me to pick up the pace with the broom. When a red Ford pulled I dropped the broom and raced out greet the lady. Mick told me to go pick up that broom before somebody trips over it, forcing me to run back to the garage, and then out to the pump again. When I got back there he said "She's waiting" with a tone of disapproval. I started to open the gas cap, and Mick said "How much does she want?" I rather sheepishly walked over to the driver's window.

"How much would you like?"

"For God's sake, Marty, say hello to the nice lady."

"I took a breath and said, "Good morning, ma'am. How much gas would you like?"

"$2.00 worth."

"Yes, ma'am," I answered and returned to the gas cap thinking 'I got Mick this time.' I inserted the pump into her car, and within just a few seconds heard Mick call "Aren't you going to check the oil?" I ran to the front of the car and stopped in a sudden confusion. My dad drove a Chevy, and I wasn't sure where the latch to open the hood was on a Ford. Under normal circumstances I would have seen it in a few seconds, but knowing Mick was watching me caused me to lose focus and go into a mini-panic. Mick walked over to show me.

"Here, Marty, here. Heaven help us, you'd think you'd never opened a car hood before." I stood before the engine, befuddled a second time while I frantically searched for the dipstick.

"Here it is," Mick said. "If you were Columbus, we'd have never discovered America." I saw him wink at the lady in the car out of the corner of my eye, and realized I didn't have a rag in my hand to wipe off the dipstick. Mick loved that.

"You mean to tell me you don't carry a rag with you? Here, use mine instead of your hand." The oil level was good, but as I returned the dipstick to its tube, Mick called out in a panicked Voice, "Did the pump reach $2.00 yet?"

I looked up to see it was at $1.97 and counting. I ran back to shut it off, but not before it reached $2.08. I assumed Mick had his eye on the pump the whole time, but waited until it was too late for me to shut it off in time. I looked over to Mick who shook his head as if I had made a grave error. He silently mouthed the words "Tell her."

"I'm sorry, but I let the pump run too long. It came to $2.08." The lady had two dollars in her hand, nodded, and started digging through her purse for change until Mick stepped forward.

"That's okay, Missus, we made the mistake. $2.00 is fine."

"I'm sorry," I repeated and took the $2.00.

"Marty!" he yelled in alarm. "She can't very well drive down the street with her hood open, crashing into lampposts and running people over." I returned to the front of the car and closed the hood. When she finally pulled out, I half ran to the office to put the money in the register. I hurried for two reasons: to get away from Mick, and to show him that I was still hustling. Mick, of course, would not pass up this opportunity.

"I'll be out of business in a week with you giving away my gasoline. I think your broom is getting lonely." I started back toward the garage when another car drove in.

"Marty!" And the whole thing started over again.

The Last Sunday in Ordinary Time

By 12:00 I was convinced that a man would have to be hungry to keep this job, but I had made a promise to Dad, so I remained determined to stick it out. I pumped gas, cleaned windshields, checked oil levels, swept floors, emptied garbage cans, and collected money, none of them to Mickey's satisfaction. I quickly learned that the only think he liked better than giving me a hard time was giving me a hard time in front of a customer. I imagined myself proudly serving one of my friend's parents, but Mick had me so self-conscious that I dreaded anyone I knew seeing me screw up in front of him.

Misery surrounded me. I began wishing no customers would drive in so I could get a break from his harassment, but then at 1:00 we experienced a time when no customers came in for about twenty minutes, and I couldn't even pretend to be busy. Mick really tore into me for that. After a few minutes of being alone with Mick, I was begging God to send in a customer. I had to be there until 2:30, but time moved so slowly, I really thought about quitting with ten minutes to go.

At 12:00 another employee showed up, a Polish guy named Sitkowski, which gave me the false hope that I might have an ally. Mick called him Stosh most of the time, or "Polack" when he did something wrong. Stosh worked at the gas station from 12:00 to closing time at 10:00, and he knew Mick's dark side from firsthand experience. After a brief introduction he preceded to ignore me to the best of his ability. I asked him for help a couple of times, but he shrugged and told me to ask Mick. I guess he figured Mick made things miserable for only one guy at a time, and it was better me than him. When business picked up after 1:30, Stosh seemed to find ways to leave me with little to do. He mastered the ability to stay on the boss's good side, and seemed intent on keeping me in Mickey's line of fire.

When 2:30 arrived at last, I wanted to sprint into Mick's office, and then sprint home, but I knew better than that. A woman pulled her car in, and I started walking toward it, but Mick stopped me.

"Marty, let the Polack do that. I'm not planning to pay you for overtime."

For all the misery I experienced that day, it ended on a good note. Mick told me to show up again on Monday, this time at 7:00. I left and crossed the street walking past the Lovely Bit just as Uncle Charlie was coming out of it.

"So how's the working man?"

"Hi, Uncle Charlie. Fine."

"Did Mickey put you through your paces?"

"Yeah, he never let up."

"What'd you do for lunch?"

"I ran down to Pogo's and got a hotdog."

"Hah. You'll never get rich spending all your money at Pogo's. Next time just come here. I'll feed you for nothing."

"Really? Wow. Thanks. That would be great."

"When are you working next?"

"Monday."

"Monday it is. Come over for lunch and Bridie and I will put a burger on for you."

"Great. Thanks Uncle Charlie."

The Last Sunday in Ordinary Time

With that bit of good news, what seemed like a terrible job became a great job. I got to eat lunch for free at the Lovely Bit, and sit at the bar while I ate it. When I told Mom and Dad about it, they seemed a little worried that I was taking advantage of Charlie and Bridie, but then decided it would be ruder to turn the offer down. I assumed that my friends would consider my job at the gas station cool, but being a sixteen-year-old hanging out in a bar was much cooler.

The Second Sunday in Ordinary Time

June 12, 1966

The Bar Fixture

When I looked at Mickey I saw a friend, a hero, and a role model. His charm coupled with my view of him as a role model blinded me to the fact that he actually was kind of a jerk a lot of the time. He seemed to think of himself as a preacher, and he spoke incessantly about our need for faith in the American way, the American work ethic, and the joy of capitalism. He wove bumper sticker sermonettes into his daily criticism of me and my coworkers:

"A man who doesn't work hard is no man at all."

"You'll never get the A unless you do the whole job."

"There's no substitute for elbow grease."

"Start off by working hard, and then finish off by working harder. In between you should also be working hard."

"Never accept a nickel you didn't earn."

"Do it well, or do it somewhere else."

Every one of these statements gave him a great deal of satisfaction, and it showed in the smugness on his face. He owned a business with his name on the door, and there was no greater measure of success than to be an American who owned his own business. It seemed to be a moral imperative for him to preach the need for ambition to his employees, and he did so sometimes with humor, sometimes with a sense of moral authority, but always with a sense of purpose. He knew the right way, and he intended to explain the right way to me at all times every day. Toward the end of my second day there, after Stosh arrived, Mickey decided to congratulate himself.

"Hey, Polack."

"Yeah?"

"How's college going?"

"It's going fine, Mickey."

"You hear that, Marty? The Polack says college is going fine. How about that? Some people say Polacks are stupid, and if Stosh here was the only Polack I knew, I might agree with them. But I know some smart Polacks, so I told him if he wants to keep his job with me, he has to go to college."

"I'd be going anyway, Mickey."

"Would you now? My arse. He quit once 'til his mother, good woman that she is, showed up here wanting to know why he was..."

"Mick,"

"Ah, ah, ah, now. I told her I didn't fire him, he quit because he didn't want to go to college. Well, didn't she lay into him something fierce? I don't speak Polish mind you, but I believe she said something about me being a great man all together, and wasn't it an honor for himself to work for me, and you will work for this great man, and you will go to college."

"That's not what she..."

"Oh, 'tis. I'm sure of it. So, young Mr. Donovan, I'm the reason there's going to be one less dumb Polack in the world, in a year or two. Isn't that right, Stosh?"

"Whatever you say, Mick."

During the first few days at Mick's it continued that way, Mickey going on about his efforts to make us great Americans, unafraid to pursue and achieve success, Sitkowski and me listening to him because our parents gave us little choice. On the plus side, I started eating my lunches at The Lovely Bit.

The Last Sunday in Ordinary Time

The Lovely Bit O' Blarney faced north on Madison with a large rectangular sign hanging over the door. The sign showed the green, white and orange of the Irish flag beneath a large white square with The Lovely Bit O'Blarney in cursive. There were two small windows, three feet high, five feet wide, that sat five feet off the ground. During prohibition all taverns were required to have windows that faced the street positioned so that a policeman could look in to make sure nothing illegal was going on inside. They tended to be as small as possible which frustrated policemen a little, and the children who walked down Madison a lot. With windows that high, whatever happened inside remained a complete mystery to us as we walked past the bar.

In the case of the Lovely Bit, the windows were made even smaller by a green border trim that said "The Lovely Bit O' Blarney" across the top and "A genuine taste of Ireland" across the bottom. Although the windows promised a genuine taste of Ireland, they actually served food that was strictly mainstream American. At all times you could order a hamburger, a hot dog, or chili. On Fridays they served a fish sandwich which was basically an extra wide fish stick on a hamburger bun. Aunt Bridie sometimes made soda bread, or a dozen BLT's, but that was about it. A bar ran the length of the room on the west side. Uncle Charlie spent his days patrolling behind the bar, serving drinks and talking to the customers. Along the east wall there were four booths separated from the bar by an aisle about six feet wide. Beyond the four booths there was a juke box. In between the booths and the juke box there was a door that led to the "banquet hall" next door, a room that consisted of a few tables and some folding chairs. It could accommodate up to eighty people, or so their ad in the Sunday bulletin said. In the back of the Lovely Bit, beyond the juke box you entered a hallway the led to a small store room and cooler on one side, and bathrooms on the other. The cooler had a Meister Brau light on it, and a supply of six packs in it. Uncle Charlie didn't sell much liquor to go, but a few people took a six pack with them when they left.

I remembered a few times Mom brought me to The Lovely Bit on the way home from a shopping or whatever, and sitting on a barstool drinking a Coke while they talked to each other like I wasn't there. I had been in there a couple of times since then, so I was familiar with the fixtures since they never really changed much. This time Uncle Charlie introduced me to a fixture I never saw before. He was an old man named Seamus Touhy. Every time I went into the Lovely Bit after that day, Seamus was sitting at the end of the bar, nursing a beer, and mocking the younger patrons.

The first time I walked in to have lunch Uncle Charlie waved me over and had me sit down next to him. Seamus stood about 5 foot 4, couldn't have weighed more than 130 pounds, but did have a remarkably thick head of white hair. If he brushed it, it didn't show. It gave him a slightly crazy look which eventually I started to believe he wanted. Still, the warmth in his eyes made me feel welcome, and we became friendly right away. He wasted no time starting in on me.

"So, are you Irish, then?"

"Yeah, my parents are both from Ireland."

"Ah. You're not Irish. You're American. Your parents are Irish. Tell me know, Yank, is your Uncle Charlie your mother's brother, or your father's brother?"

"Actually, he isn't related by blood. He..."

"Isn't related by blood? You're sitting here telling me that you're an Irishman who isn't Irish, your *Uncle* Charlie isn't your uncle at all, and now you've come to the bar to have a drink, but it isn't a drink at all, but just a Coke? Is that what you're telling me Yank?"

I tried to answer him but he had me off guard and half laughing, so I was sputtering, struggling to get a word out. This delighted Seamus.

"Tell me, *Unnnncle Charlie,* where did you find this one? No ability to answer a man's question, Irish or not. Be careful serving him a hamburger, now. He might be thinking it's a watermelon or a fire truck." After this initial burst of being a nonstop smart ass, Seamus seemed to settle down a bit. He asked where I went to school, what grade I was in, and a few questions about working for Mickey. I asked him where he was from.

"Well, from Ireland, of course. Sharp as a marble, this one, Uncle Charlie."

"I know that. Which part of Ireland?"

"Ah, the ugly part. All bare feet and crooked teeth. They say the land is beautiful. I was told to take a picture before I left. I didn't bother. Some things I don't need to remember." Mick gave me an hour for lunch, and I didn't dare be late. I got up to leave.

"Thanks for the hamburger, Charlie." Before my uncle could offer the standard "you're welcome" Seamus pounced.

"Charlie is it? Well, now, Charlie I think you've been demoted. When the Yank walked in you were his uncle. Now he hardly knows you at all."

"Marty, you're welcome. I'll expect to see you for lunch whenever you're working."

"Say hi to Aunt Bridie for me."

"I will."

"Oh, he will, he will," Seamus assured me. "Hey, Marty." I stopped as I got to the door. "Since you're so determined to be an Irishman when you grow up, tell me this. Who is Eamon de Valera?"

I shrugged and said "I don't know."

"Go back to work, but don't come back for another free hamburger from your supposed uncle until you know who de Valera is."

Third Sunday in Ordinary Time

June 19, 1966

The Pastor of the Future

In those days the Chicago police department had a policy they called working around the clock. This required policemen to work one month on the day shift, one month on the P.M. shift, and then one month on the overnight shift. I learned this because Mick actually had two policemen who worked part-time for him as their schedules allowed. I had met them only long enough to say hello because Mick didn't need me if either one of them was around. When they worked, they spent most of their time working in the one service bay in the gas station. They were, Mick said, top notch mechanics. For his part, Mick also worked on engines, but only if the two cops were not available that day.

That also meant that I sometimes worked from 8:00 to 5:00, but usually from 2:00 to closing at 10:00, arriving just as one of them left, or leaving just as one of them arrived. On one of my first early starts I got to meet our new pastor, Fr. Francis Connolly because he stopped in the gas station to introduce himself to Mickey. For over twenty years, from 1941 to 1964, Our Lady of Holy Truth had only one pastor, Monsignor Thomas O'Brien. The people of Holy Truth loved him and hated him in equal measure because he ruled with an iron hand. His word was the last word and the only word. In his mind he had the unhappy responsibility of enforcing the changes that came after Vatican II, but he dragged his feet, and clearly never embraced the modern ways. He went into semi-retirement early in 1964, ceding the title of pastor to a younger priest, Fr. John Jaworski, but the monsignor was in no hurry to cede control. A power struggle ensued, and even those who didn't like him tended to side with the older priest.

By June of 1965, Monsignor O'Brien was reassigned, and his forced departure left a lingering bitterness in the parish. Fr. Jaworski was called the holy Polack behind his back. The parishioners expressed their dissatisfaction with the new priest via the collection plate, and Sunday collections fell sharply during the last half of the year. Regardless of his youth and enthusiasm, this new shepherd faced an uphill battle in his efforts to win the hearts of his flock. All hope for his success vanished in November of 1965, again through no fault of his own.

It was common for the police department to send a cop out to direct traffic after the 11:00 mass on Sundays because it was such a crowded mass. On this particular Sunday they sent a colored policeman, and that sent a ripple of outrage across the parish. The last thing the good Catholics wanted was a colored cop pointing them the way out Our Lady of Holy Truth. The phone in the rectory starting ringing immediately, and Fr. Jaworski was told this was unacceptable. He had better get on the phone and let the alderman, or the police department, or whoever, know that this was not to happen again.

The young priest faced a dilemma. He could make those phone calls and probably win a lot of parishioners over to his side but he chose not to do that. Instead he prepared a sermon on the need for love and tolerance of all men, and delivered it the following Sunday. He suggested that, if people were upset by the presence of a single Negro in the parish, they should probably do some soul searching and take the issue to a higher authority. He, of course, meant to ask God for guidance. The parishioners believed the higher authority was the cardinal, and they contacted the archdiocesan headquarters loudly and often. The holy Polack was in more trouble than he realized.

Our Lady of Holy Truth was not the only parish in Chicago that was in turmoil. Rev. Martin Luther King was emboldening Negroes across Chicago, so Holy Truth hardly measured as a big issue in the eyes of church leaders. The church also faced falling revenues due to declining attendance among Catholics upset with the changes brought about by Vatican II. In reality, the shortfall of donations put Fr. Jaworski's job as pastor in greater risk than a little racial dust-up, but that dust-up meant he wouldn't be given the time to turn things around. By March of 1966 we learned that the holy Polack had been reassigned. Our new pastor started his new job, the task of repairing relations between Our Lady of Holy Truth and her parishioners, about two weeks before I started working for Mick.

Fr. Connolly decided to introduce himself to the local businessmen who were kind enough to advertise on the back of the Sunday bulletin, and since Mick always bought one of the biggest ads, he was among the priest's first stops. It was shortly after 11:00 and raining in buckets. I remember that because Mick asked him if he was planning to talk to my Uncle Charlie as well, and when he said yes, Mick sent me across the street to see if he had a moment to spare for the priest.

"It wouldn't look good, a priest popping in to a tavern in broad daylight."

"I suppose it's better than doing it after dark," Fr. Connolly answered with a smile, "but I thank you for your discretion."

I ran across the street and came back with Uncle Charlie. By the time we returned the two of them were talking easily, the good father apparently a man Mick could do business with. Mick introduced the priest to Charlie and me, and then the three of them starting talking about the parish. If it weren't for the rain I would have been sent away, but the rain kept the customers away, and there wasn't much for me to do at the moment.

I realized that I was not the only one that Mickey Riordan enjoyed teaching. He made several observations about Holy Truth, things he delighted in explaining, and in Fr. Connolly he found a receptive audience. Uncle Charlie, ever the silent politician, was always happy to let someone else do the talking. Fr. Connolly came to ask for their continued support, and in doing so, he introduced the subject of money in the parish. It opened the door for the owner of a gas station to explain to the priest how the money flowed in our local parish.

"How do you think the parish works, Father?" Mickey asked.

"Well, I know the school is filled and there's a waiting list, so I know there are a lot of young families here."

"Don't fool yourself. Those families are not sending their kids to Holy Truth because it's a Catholic school. There sending them there because it's not a public school. They're bussing the coloreds into the public schools all over the place, and your parishioners don't like it. Don't waste your energy working to keep the school filled, that's a given. Does the school make money or lose money?"

The priest thought for a second. "It probably breaks even."

"No, it loses money. A lot of money. Most of the young families you speak of are scrambling to keep bread on the table. Paying tuition is a sacrifice parents make for their children. If you raise tuition by more than just a few bucks, you'll have a revolt on your hands." The priest nodded, and seemed to give serious thought to Mick's lecture.

"And," Mick continued, "the parish has a long-standing policy of taking care of those good Catholics with lots of children. One child pays full tuition, the second pays half, the third and fourth pay twenty-five percent, and if a family has more than four kids in the school at one time, the extra kids are free. Several families have five, even six kids in school, but they pay for only four of them."

At this point a Chevy station wagon pulled into the gas station, I ran out in what was now a light drizzle, and popped the hood to check the oil wondering how Mick knew all this stuff. The guy asked for $3.00 worth of gas, but I didn't stop it until it hit $3.35. Luckily the guy wasn't mad and just paid for it. Mick would have been furious if the guy refused to pay the overage. A Buick pulled in, I pumped his gas, and then went back inside the station. Mick must have wanted me to hear what he was going to say next or would have told me to sweep the floor or something.

"Okay, so you know the school needs a new roof, the church has a plumbing problem, and the school itself is losing money. The question is where do you get the money to address these problems?"

The Last Sunday in Ordinary Time

"I'm not sure. How?" The priest acted like a willing student in Mick's business class.

"The biggest mistake Fr. Jaworski made was arrogance. Either that or naiveté. He came in here all full of Vatican II, and ready to teach everyone how to be true Catholics. He focused his attention on the hearts and minds of the young families, but neglected to look in their wallets. If he had, he would have seen that they were empty, or damn close to it. The key to the financial health of this parish, and most parishes for that matter, is the elderly. Everybody thinks that poor old grandma doesn't have two nickels to rub together. She's still wearing the same old dress, Grandpa is fixing the old car he's had for years, and they hang on to every dollar with two hands.

"Don't think for a second that I'm insulting them or that I don't admire them. I do. They survived the great depression, saw sons die in World War II and Korea, and they know poverty and heartbreak. They lived life always a little scared of being poor again, so they saved every dollar they could. They are cheapskates in every way but two: their children and their church. These people lived through hard times when all they had were their families and their church. Their generosity and devotion on Sundays allows the operation of the parish the other days of the week. They love the church. Throughout the heartaches and happiness they always stood by the Church, and the Church always stood by them. When Fr. Jaworski turned his attention to the young, they were insulted. When they decided to tighten their purse strings, they wanted to send a message. They think that Our Lady of Holy Truth needs to respect her elders."

"I see," said the priest. "They need a proper show of appreciation." For his part, Uncle Charlie said nothing, neither agreeing nor disagreeing with Mickey. One of the lasting truisms of Chicago politics was to say nothing but show sincerity. People often quoted the phrase "Say nothing like you mean it" to describe the way Chicago politics worked. Fr. Connolly turned to Charlie and said "What do you think? Is he right?"

"There's a lot of truth in what he says," Uncle Charlie said with a slow, thoughtful nod. I noticed that my uncle never answered the question, but I'm not sure the priest did.

"It's not as simple as that. They don't like what they're seeing and hearing in church these days. They don't like guitar masses, teenagers are wearing blue jeans to mass, and don't forget about miniskirts, T-shirts, and sandals. This whole effort to make the masses more down-to-earth gets under their skin. They like the idea that you go to church, kneel down, and look up toward heaven. They need proof that the church is being true to its core beliefs. They know what it means to be a genuine, devout Catholic, and you need to prove that you know what it means, too."

"Well, you've given me a lot to think about."

"It won't be easy, Father. I know that Rome wants change, but the people who control the purse strings in Holy Truth don't."

"Are you certain that the elderly will give more money if they get their way?"

"The parish is in the middle of a power struggle. A few these people were baptized and married on the altar of Our Lady of Holy Truth.

Still more baptized their own children there, attended the funerals of their parents, and tragically enough, some of those same children there. That church has been the site of their happiest days, and darkest moments. They don't belong to the parish as much as the parish belongs to them. They don't believe you're making changes. They believe you're stealing their church. If you give them the victory in this power struggle, they will show the same concern for their church that they would show for a sick child."

Telling a sixteen-year-old kid like me to throw out the trash hardly satisfied Mick's desire to show the world how smart he was, but that morning with Fr. Connolly certainly did. After the priest left, Mick kind of took the afternoon off, at least as far as yelling at me was concerned. I think he repeated the lecture he gave the priest in his head, probably reveling in the greatness of it. For whatever reason, he went easy on me for the next few hours. The rain picked up again in the afternoon, and Mick spent it quietly working on replacing a starter in a Chevy Impala. My job in between a few random gas fill-ups was to stand there and watch him, and hand him tools as he needed them. It gave him a chance to remind me that I knew darn little about the make-up of a tool box, but for the most part he went easy on me.

I watched him as the afternoon dragged on, and it struck me that he wasn't that good of a mechanic. I thought he would change a starter with all of the ease that I change a light bulb, but he struggled with it. For better than three hours we stood there passing tools back and forth while he Helen-Kellered his way under the hood, making little progress and swearing often. As it closed in on 4:00 he at last asked me to start the car to test it out, but when I turned the key, nothing happened. This time he let out a rather mild-sounding "dog-gone-it," walked over to the pop machine and bought a drink. Actually he bought one for me too.

"I thought you'd be madder," I said after thanking him. He shrugged. "So, how long do you think it's going to take?"

"What do you care? It's not your car."

"No, but, geez, you've been working on it for almost three hours."

"Again, you got someplace else you need to be? All of a sudden you're all worried about time."

"I was just asking." Mick retained his ability to put me on the defensive at all times, so at that point I just shut up. About ten seconds after Mick finished his pop, I made sure I finished mine. He was ready to go back to work, but, thankfully, a woman pulled in and I had to go pump gas. When I got back Mick was reaching under the hood.

"You know, Mortimer, when I was a kid, we used to own this horse. Now, some people will tell you that horses are stupid, but you'd never know it from this horse. My dad always treated his animals kindly, but I remember him standing in the fields just whipping this horse because it quit in the middle of the job. If you allowed yourself to get between it and the side of the stall, it would smash up against you. You had to watch your hands, and always pay attention because he'd try and bite you. At times we teamed him up with another horse to pull a plough, and he would become very lazy, making the other horse do all the work.

"One day my father had me bring the horse into town to get new shoes. Now, normally a horse will stand there peacefully while the blacksmith takes its hoof and removes the old shoe and puts on a new one. I don't remember exactly how long it should take, but I know for this horse it took a lot longer. The horse refused to cooperate. He moved back and forth, wouldn't hold his leg steady, nothing. Finally, the blacksmith had to have his assistant grab it by the reins and try to hold it steady. The two of them worked on that horse for what seemed like hours to me, the blacksmith holding a hoof trying to keep it still enough to work on, and his apprentice trying to keep the horse calm. Eventually, after quite a while, they got it done. As I was leaving their shop, the blacksmith called out to me.

'Riordan, tell your father that a less determined man would not have put shoes on that horse.' Yes, he said a less determined man would not have put shoes on that horse. He is one of the reasons I keep working on this car. I know I can do it, I just haven't finished yet. More importantly for you, he's the reason I hate to see men not trying their best. So if you're ever wondering why I'm such a stickler for details, now you know. I simply expect all of my employees to do their best for as long as they are working for me and long after their done working for me."

By the time I finished that day, Mick still did not have the car started. One of the cops showed up though, and he gave Mick a hand with it. The car was gone the next time I showed up for work.

The Last Sunday in Ordinary Time

The Fourth Sunday in Ordinary Time

June 26, 1966

A Pretty Girl My Arse

Every Sunday the parish bulletin included a reminder of what Sunday it was. On June 26th it reminded us that it was the fourth Sunday in ordinary time. I never needed to be reminded how ordinary that my life was. Those other kids, the ones who lived with so many brothers and sisters, they led the interesting lives. I figured that if I were ever to make it to sainthood, I could be the patron saint of the ordinary, the mundane, of the people like me who spent our lives with our noses pressed against the window, watching other people get to do the interesting stuff. This summer was different though. Working at Mick's and eating lunch at the Lovely Bit put me on the inside for a change.

I enjoyed working for Mickey even though he continued to nag me constantly, and spending time at the Lovely Bit was a thrill. Friends and neighbors stopped into Mickey's a lot, so I got to know people a little more. Inside the tavern I met college kids and neighborhood men I'd never met before. Sometimes I'd be walking down the street with guys I knew and somebody would wave from car or say hello as we passed, giving me a "Wow, you know everybody" reputation. I thought it couldn't get any better than working in a gas station and hanging out in a bar, but it did.

A few days after Mickey gave me the horse shoes lecture, I was standing behind the register when I saw Colleen Kilnagael walking toward the gas station. Mick, as always, watched me watching her, although I managed to forget about his scrutiny. I didn't realize it then, but Mickey recognized her as the girl I was staring at in church a couple weeks earlier. I expected her to keep walking past, but she actually turned in and headed for the office. My nervousness showed because I tried so hard to stay calm, trying to figure where to stand, should I be surprised to see her, or greet her when she walked in the door. She hardly made it through the door when I assaulted her with an overly aggressive "Hi, Colleen."

"Hi, Marty," she said clearly and confidently. "I need two packs of Viceroys." I began looking through the cigarette rack, trying to find Viceroys.

"Marty! Do we sell cigarettes to any child who walks in off the street?"

I looked up, helpless in my ignorance. I didn't know what I was supposed to do, but tried to stay calm. Colleen tried to help me.

"Hi, Mr. Riordan. They're for my mom." Mick raised his hand to stop her from interrupting him.

"Do we?"

"I don't know." He wanted to embarrass me and was doing a good job of it.

45

"You don't know. Well ask the young lady if she has a note from her mother."

"Do you have a note from your mother?"

"Marty, where are your manners? Excuse me, ma'am, do you have a not from your mother?" He gestured toward her, and raised his eye brows. Colleen stifled a smile.

"Excuse me, ma'am. Do you have a note from your mother?"

"I'm sorry, I don't."

I didn't know what to do.

"Mick, is it O.K.?"

"Is what O.K.?"

"Is it O.K. for me to sell two packages of Viceroy Cigarettes to this young lady so that she can bring them home to her mother?"

"Oh, sure," he said. "Colleen comes here all the time to buy cigarettes for her mother. I know her well."

Colleen took the cigarettes from me and handed me the exact change for them. She thanked me and left the gas station, leaving me to stand there in my embarrassment. Mickey continued to enjoy the moment while I waited for her to completely leave the gas station.

"You like her, don't you?" Of course I did, but I tried not to show it.

"What?"

"What my arse? You like her."

"I don't know. She's a pretty girl."

"Ah, pretty girl my arse. You like her. Go ask her out."

"She's already gone."

"Oh, I'm not suggesting that you should ask her out, I'm telling you, you have to ask her out or you're fired." I looked at him to see if he meant it.

"Remember what I said about a less determined man and horse shoes? I won't have you working here growing complacent, afraid to ask a girl out on a date. Here's a pen and paper. I want to see her phone number on this piece of paper. Go strive to be better. Come back with her phone number, or don't come back. I'll know why you're not here."

I took off running after Colleen. I figured I could either catch her and ask her out, or keep running and head for home. I remembered my dad's warning to keep the job or else, and I really did want to ask her out. Besides, I didn't want to fail in front of Mick. I caught up with her about a block away. I wasn't as out of breath as I pretended to be while I tried to find the right thing to say. What if she said no? Would Mickey even believe I asked her? Where would I take her? When?

"Didn't I give you enough money?" she asked.

"Oh, yeah. No, it was right." I was caught off guard by her question. Then I did something completely embarrassing. I closed my eyes for a long three or four seconds and held my hands out in front of me in a sort "Everybody stay calm" gesture, everybody being Colleen and me.

"Colleen, I was wondering if you would like to go out with me."

"Oh, my God. Where did that come from?"

Did she just ask me a question? I wasn't ready for that. I needed a simple yes or no. She wasn't expecting me to ask her out, and that's a bad sign. Crap. What's Mick going to say?

"I think you're pretty and was hoping you'd like to go out with me?" Actually that was a pretty good recovery. If I weren't on the brink of elation or total humiliation, I might have patted myself on the back.

"I'm sorry. Yes, I'd like that."

Holy cow. Talk about winning first place. I wouldn't have to face Dad. I wouldn't lose face in front of Mick, I got to keep my job, and I, one Martin J. Donovan had a date with Colleen Kilnagael. I raised my arms in triumph. I seemed to forget that Colleen was still standing there.

"Yes." I yelled. Colleen, I noticed when I regained my focus, was not exalting. She had a look of bemusement on her face, as if she were rethinking her decision.

"Listen. I've got to get back to work. Can I call you later, and we can discuss the details?"

I handed her the pen and paper and she wrote her name with a smile under the e's to make it look like a smiley face, and her phone number.

"Thanks. Can I call you tonight at 8:30?"

"That would be good. My parents are going out, so I have to babysit my little sister. I know I'll be home."

"Great. Thanks again, Colleen. I'll call you later."

As I ran back to Mick's I went over the moment in my head. Closing my eyes, bad. Holding my hands out, bad. Rushing the question out, bad. The "I think you're pretty," good. She said yes, great, great, great. When I got back to the gas station, Mickey waited with a smirk on his face. I held the paper up over my head with two hands like it was a championship trophy.

The Last Sunday in Ordinary Time

I ate lunch at The Lovely Bit later, sitting next to Seamus like always. I learned from my dad that Eamon de Valera was the current president and basically the George Washington of Ireland. It actually embarrassed me a little that I didn't know that, but when I asked them later, only one of my friends knew it. Seamus was right. For all our talk about being Irish we didn't know much about the place. Our conversations became little Irish history lessons in which Seamus told me a little bit of everything about Ireland, and I listened intently.

Colleen's phone number sat in my pocket like the winning raffle ticket at church bazaar, and I wanted to tell someone, anyone about it. At the same time I worried that if I said anything I would seem like a dork, so I kept fighting the urge to tell Seamus the news. He drifted off of de Valera and on to William Butler Yeats.

"I'll tell you, Marty, it's no small accomplishment. If you ask any man who knows his stuff, an English professor or a brilliant writer, he'll tell you that the greatest poet of the twentieth century is Yeats, and the greatest writer is James Joyce. Hands down. No question."

"My teacher at St. Columba's says that William Faulkner is the best writer since Shakespeare."

"Never mind Faulkner, or Hemingway, or the rest of that lot. The best writer in the world this century is James Joyce. And he and Yeats were both from Ireland. That's something the Irish can be proud of when they're not having more babies than they can feed."

I noticed that Seamus praised the Irish, and then insulted them just as often. Like a battle hardened marine who hated to be seen petting a kitten, he acted like a cynic, but then spoke almost poetically about the

Irish. He seemed to always end his thought with a verbal slap to ensure that no one thought he was getting soft. He also seemed defensive about them. If I or any other American referred to himself as Irish, Seamus would remind them that they weren't Irish, they were American.

"The thing about the Irish is that they are a very friendly people. This, of course, is because they are a bunch of superstitious idiots. Do you know why leprechauns have pots of gold?"

I shook my head.

"The Irish believed very strongly in fairies, and fairies like to do two things: They like to test the kindness of people, so they would disguise themselves as beggars or other strangers, and if you weren't kind to the stranger before you, the fairies might cause a cow to stop giving milk, or put a hole in your roof to let the rain in, that sort of thing. So, out of a sense of superstition the Irish became very kind to strangers. They had the whole 'whatever you do to the least of my brothers that you do unto me" thing figured out centuries before the Catholic Church came sniffing around.

"The other thing fairies like to do is dance. And, since they kept wearing out their shoes from all the dancing, they kept going back to the leprechauns, who were shoemakers. They paid the leprechauns in gold, so, over time, the leprechauns ended up with pots of gold."

Later that afternoon I got one more lucky break. One of my friends, Patrick James, walked past the gas station, and stopped to say hello. He was always Patrick, never Pat, because Mrs. James insisted on it. I called him Pat a few times in her presence, and she always corrected me, and so she trained me and everybody else to call him Patrick. While none of us were particularly adept at picking up girls, Patrick was the closest thing we had to a ladies' man. He taught me, for example, to always pin down a time to call a girl.

"You gotta tell what time you're going to call. Otherwise she won't be home and you end up talking to her Mom or Dad three or four times, and you sound desperate. Or you start to wonder if maybe she's home and doesn't want to talk to you. Always tell her when you're going to call."

I remembered that when I asked Colleen for her number earlier, and I was glad I did. Now I finally got that chance to tell somebody it was Patrick, a guy who could really help me out.

"Really? You asked Colleen out? Good job. She's got a nice rack on her."

"Hey! Hey! Hey," I answered in mock offense. "You're talking about the woman who will be the mother of my children, and we will not refer to her breasts as a rack. Seriously though, now I need to figure out where to take her. A movie, right?"

"No. You go to a movie and you end up sitting next to each other not talking. It's a bad first date. Take her out to eat."

"Okay, where?"

"You really only have two choices. One is the pancake house on Madison. If you want everyone to see you with her, then take her there. Girls are kind of funny. Sometimes they want everyone to know they're on a date, so they don't mind strutting down Madison holding your hand. The other place is Luigi's. Do you know it?"

"That's the Italian place on Kedzie, right? I've never been there."

"There's a good chance that she hasn't either. But that's the thing. If you go there, nobody will see you, so if you're nervous that might be better."

"Is it expensive?"

"Well, more than the pancake house, but not too bad."

That was all of the goofing off Mick was willing to tolerate from me, so I cut Patrick off, thanked him and went back to work. I had a couple of hours to think about it, and I liked the idea of everyone seeing me with Colleen, so the pancake house had its appeal. On the other hand Luigi's sounded more exotic, more grown up, and I kept thinking about how nervous I was going to be. I decided on Luigi's. It proved to be the right choice. When I called Colleen later that night I told her I was thinking about Luigi's.

"Oh, I love Luigi's. We go there all the time. That would be great."

The fact that the Kilnagaels ate at Luigi's all the time was even more proof that they were a more sophisticated family than mine. I worried about whether I possessed enough social grace to match hers, but the fact that I suggested that restaurant gave me some hope. We set a date for Saturday night.

When I worked late, I also ate late. One of Mickey's rules was that you couldn't take your lunch break between 4:00 and 7:00 because that was a busy time. A lot of people stopped for gas on the way home from work or on their way out for the evening. The unintended consequence for me was that I got to spend an hour in the bar after 7:00, which meant I got to meet a whole new group of people. Seamus Touhy still sat in his favorite stool since he usually didn't leave until 8:00, and there were usually a few men who stopped in the Lovely Bit for a couple of beers after work. But then there were also the younger crowd, basically college-aged guys who hung around the bar until closing, usually around 2:00.

Eddie Mulroney, a tall, thin red head (actually his hair was orange) acted as a sort of ring leader for the younger guys. From the first time I met him he had me laughing, buzzing around the bar making jokes and talking fast, and always loud enough to make sure everyone could hear him.

"C'mon. I'll bet you can't throw a dart and hit a bull's eye. If you do, I'll eat a piece of your shit. I swear to God. I will."

The first time he saw me he came right over.

"Seamus, I didn't know you had a son. And here I thought you never got any pussy."

Whenever Eddie started in on Seamus Uncle Charlie or whoever was tending bar would intervene. I had the feeling that Seamus could hold his own if he got into an argument with Eddie, serious or not, but Seamus, for all of his desire to be a smart aleck, never used profanity and was a gentleman at heart. He might laugh at another man's dirty joke, but he never told one himself. Collectively the entire bar viewed Seamus as a mascot, and although they viewed him with affection I did hear a few people grumble that he never bought a round.

Along with the younger guys there were also a few girls who hung around, a fact that was a sore spot among the older drinkers. The older men thought that a bar was no place for a woman, and the Lovely Bit was a place a man to have a cold one without worrying about his manners.

They pretty much all had wives at home, so they weren't out looking for action. For the hours between 7:00 and 10:00, a slight tension existed between the two groups, but the later it got the more the older guys drifted out and the younger crowd took over.

On the Friday night before my date with Colleen, I didn't go to the Lovely Bit until 7:30. I always tried to take my lunch as late as possible because it meant the second half of the workday was shorter. The minute I sat down Eddie was on me, giving me grief about working at Mickey's and then asking me if I was still a virgin. One of the girls slapped him on the shoulder and told him to shut up.

"That was rude," she said as she pulled him away from me. I have to admit, I was a little embarrassed by the question, but then another guy, Brendan Ward, sat down next to me.

"Don't let Eddie bother you. He's just a goofball."

"I take it he's a friend of yours."

"Oh, yeah. I've known him since we were in third grade. We met in cub scouts." Brendan leaned in and signaled Seamus and me to come closer. "He got kicked out because he called our den mother a whore."

We all busted out laughing. I laughed off and on at that story for the rest of the night, and to this day, when I think about it, it still makes me laugh. He sat next to me for the hour I was there, and listened to Seamus tell me a little more about Ireland. When I finished my lunch, Seamus left with me. I returned to Mickey's American Standard, and he walked over to the bus stop to catch the bus home. It was a very pleasant evening, the middle of June, and the daylight lingered, wrapping the entire parish in a soft, peaceful light. In between pumping gas for customers I watched the day fade into darkness, admired the red, white, and blue Standard sign and the green, white, and orange Lovely Bit O' Blarney sign grow more prominent on either side of Madison Avenue. I thought about my date with Colleen and thought about how lucky I was to be living in Holy Truth.

The Fifth Sunday in Ordinary Time

July 3,1966

In the House of the Kilnagaels

During our conversation Colleen and I talked about clothing. Actually she asked me what the dress code was, a question that I never gave a moment's thought to until she brought it up, and my answer was complete silence. It dumbfounded me. After a few seconds she came to my rescue.

"It might be a good idea if you wore a tie."

"A tie? Really?"

"Well, I've seen my dad give my older sister's boyfriends a hard time about the way they were dressed when they came to pick up *his* daughters, so it might make it easier on you."

"Sure, I mean, if you think I should."

"Well, it's better safe than sorry, so wear a tie. It can't hurt."

I rang their doorbell. I stood there wearing a white shirt and tie and felt completely self-conscious. A small fear kept tiptoeing into my head, an image of Colleen laughing at me and telling me she couldn't believe I was dumb enough to dress up for our date. On the other hand if I dressed less formally I would fear being under dressed. Plus, this was the Kilnagaels and I could picture Mr. Kilnagael answering the door wearing a smoking jacked like he was Hugh Hefner or something. They probably expected formality. Mrs. Kilnagael actually answered the door.

"Hi, are you here for Colleen?"

"Yes. Hi, Mrs. Kilnagael, I'm Marty Donovan."

"I know, Marty, I remember you. Come on in. You look very nice. Colleen, Marty's here."

I walked into the house. There was a small foyer by the door, a staircase to the upstairs to my right, a hallway to the kitchen straight ahead, and the living room was to the left. Mrs. Kilnagael walked over to the stairs and called up again. I stood there thinking "You remember me?" Of course I recognized Mrs. Kilnagael because she volunteered at

Holy Truth a lot. There were other mothers there as well, but Colleen's mom had an air of authority, and when if we were goofing around or too loud in school or in the church basement or something, she could put us in our place with just a look or by clearing her throat. I was one of about one hundred and twenty-five kids in Colleen's class, and one of almost one thousand who attended Our Lady of Holy Truth during my time there, so how could she remember me? I tended to be one of the more quiet ones, so I hardly stood out.

"Colleen! Your date is here."

Mrs. Kilnagael spoke as if she were scolding Colleen while she called her. I remembered her being a very tall woman, but now I realized that she wasn't really as tall as I thought, but she carried herself as if she were. She was a thin woman, with a very neat, short haircut, and still very pretty, especially for a woman in her forties. Her daughters all looked a bit like her, which explained why I thought that Colleen was so pretty. Still she maintained a look of importance, a seriousness, a definite presence. She turned her attention back to me.

"Did your mom get her cast off?"

The question took me by surprise. My mom had broken her wrist in a fall a few months ago, and gotten the cast off weeks ago. I hadn't thought about it in a while, but I was complimented that Colleen's mom knew so much about my mom.

"Oh, yeah, a couple of weeks ago. She's fine now.

Mr. Kilnagael came in from the living room to greet me. "Hi, I'm Colleen's father."

"Hi, Mr. Kilnagael. I'm Marty Donovan."

"Right. I've met your parents before. Aren't they from County Mayo?"

"My mom is from Mayo, and my dad is from West Meath."

"Did they meet in Ireland?" Mrs. Kilnagael asked.

"Uh, no ma'am. They met here. Actually my Uncle Charlie Fitzgerald, who owns the Lovely Bit, introduced them."

"Well, now, isn't that something." she said, and then called Colleen one more time. At this point I was ready to start calling her myself.

"Where are you taking my daughter?" Mr. Kilnagael asked this question in the calmest, seemingly friendliest manner imaginable, but there were ominous overtones to it.

"We're going to Luigi's, over on Kedzie."

"Oh, very good. That's a nice place."

"Actually, it's my first time going there."

"Is that so? Well, we like it."

"My parents aren't too big on restaurants that don't serve potatoes, to be perfectly honest with you."

Both of her parents smiled widely at that comment, and then Mrs. Kilnagael turned to call upstairs again.

"Coll..."

Before she could finish calling Colleen's name, her daughter was standing at the top of the stairs. She walked down slowly, and she looked beautiful. She looked every inch like a Kilnagael, and I looked every inch like Gomer Pyle, mesmerized by her, and standing there with my mouth hanging open.

"Hi, Marty. Sorry I took so long." I didn't respond right away, a fact that amused the three of them.

"Oh,... hi, Colleen."

"When can I expect my daughter home?" Mr. Kilnagael asked.

"I'll be home by midnight, Daddio."

"Let's make that 11:00."

"Daaaad."

"11:00 is plenty late enough. Now you go ahead and have fun. It was nice meeting you, Marty."

"Good-bye Mr. and Mrs. Kilnagael. It was nice meeting you too."

Mom and Dad, the two most unromantic people in the world, threw a ton of advice at me while I got ready for the date. I wanted to not even tell them I had a date, but I couldn't borrow the car without explaining why I needed the car, and why I was wearing a white shirt and tie. In the end though, Mom gave me some good advice. She reminded me to hold the car door open for her, something I wouldn't have thought to do on my own.

"I'm sure she'll look very nice anyway, but no matter how she looks, you tell her that she looks nice."

Dad also reminded me to not drive like a madman, and to make sure I filled the gas tank when I was done.

As I held the car door open for her, I told her she looked beautiful. Before she got in the car she gave me a little peck on the lips and said "Thank you, Marty." I thought thank you, Mom. Colleen wasted little time getting comfortable, and she turned on the radio just as I pulled away from the curb, and I tried to act nonchalant about that, but I wasn't really good enough to drive and listen to the radio at the same time. She let out a big, "Oh, I love this song," which scared me half to death although I don't think she noticed. When I turned onto Madison she did hear the horn of a Cadillac blaring as an old man slammed on the brakes to avoid hitting us. She looked at me wide-eyed.

"You *do* have a license, don't you?"

"I do, but maybe we better turn off the radio. I need to concentrate."

Our near accident proved to be a backdoor blessing for me because I no longer needed to pretend that I wasn't a nervous driver. From that point on *we* were driving, and she was helping me keep an eye out for cars and pedestrians lurking in the shadows. We were together in this, and my bad driving became a shared joke. When we arrived at Luigi's, our different reactions to the place supported my contention that Colleen was much more worldly than me. I found the place completely exotic. There were red and white checkered table cloths and a flickering candle inside a green glass candle holder on each table, like something you would see in a movie. We opened our menus and I began looking for something that I recognized, which pretty much began and ended with spaghetti. Colleen, on the other hand, scanned the menu for a moment and then leaned over toward the woman at the next table.

"Are you having the lasagna? Is the lasagna good here?" The woman and her husband looked up in surprise, and then she and Colleen got into a remarkably animated conversation.

"Yes, and it's excellent." They make their own sauce, and you can really taste how fresh it is."

"Does it have garlic?"

"Not too much. Just enough to make it flavorful…" And so it went. The two of them talked about Italian food for what seemed like five minutes, during which her husband looked at me and winked. I smiled back while trying to decipher if that meant "I know you're on a first date," or "You've got a live wire there," or maybe "It beats having to talk to my wife myself." In any event, she finally turned attention back to me.

"So, what do you recommend?" I asked.

"Have you ever had ravioli?"

"No."

"Have you ever had lasagna?"

"No."

"Spaghetti?"

"That I've had."

"Well, I think you should try lasagna." She studied the menu for a few seconds. "Wait. Just wait. Have you ever had pizza?"

"No." I shook my head and shrugged my shoulders as a mild apology at my lack of culture.

"You have never had pizza. Seriously? Never?"

"No. What can I say? I'm a rube."

"Well, then we must order a pizza, my friend."

When the pizza arrived I stared at it like it someone dropped a dead skunk on my plate. I took my knife and fork and picked at it a little, like I was checking for booby traps. She watched me with some amusement before pretending to be offended.

"Oh, God, just taste it. It's not like the world is trying to poison you."

I can't say that I liked pizza from the first bite. My reaction was more of relief that I didn't hate it. Naturally I told her that it was good from the start, but I could see the doubt on her face. It took four or five bites before I relaxed enough to actually start enjoying it, but it pleased Colleen that I did.

"If you live to be a hundred, you will always remember this night as the night you first ate pizza." I looked across the table at her, and saw the flickering candle reflecting in her brown eyes. No, I thought, I'll remember it for something else. But I didn't say it.

"I have to admit, it's pretty good."

To my relief the dinner went well. We talked a lot and the conversation never seemed strained or anything. She was as nice as she was pretty.

"By the way, I want to thank you for telling me to wear a tie. I was extremely nervous, especially in front of your mom, but I was glad that I was at least wearing tie."

She made a face and asked "Why were so nervous about my mom?"

"Are you kidding? She's intimidating, like an army general or something."

"Yeah, I guess she can be that way, but not lately though. Ever since my brother went into the army, she's been, I don't know, different. At first she was furious, but as time goes by she's becoming more and more scared. She's worried to death about Danny."

"Is he in Viet Nam?"

"Not yet, but Johnson's sending more guys there all the time. God help us if goes. I don't think my mother will be able to handle it."

After dinner we still had an hour before she had to be home, so we decided to take a drive by Columbus Park. It was very pleasant evening, and there were quite a few other people in the park, some walking dogs, some high school kids just hanging out, and some couples just out for a walk. The park had a nine-hole golf course, and as we strolled past I mentioned that I wanted to try golfing someday.

"It's a lot of fun, but nine holes are plenty."

"You've been golfing?"

"Yeah. My dad makes us do a family outing here every year. We all play, plus a few of my cousins, and my Uncle Bill. My dad always wins."

I began this date harboring a little fear that she might disappoint me, that no one could live up to the reverence with which I viewed the Kilnagaels. In my eyes they were so beautiful, so charming, and so special that actually getting to know Colleen might cause me to see them as ordinary people. But now, as we strolled past the golf course and I thought about Italian food and family golf tournaments, I knew that I had been right. These were special people, and I was thrilled to be spending time with her.

"Are you having a good time?" I asked her.

She smiled at me and said, "Yes, it's been very nice. You?"

"It's been almost perfect."

"Almost? Why not perfect?" I thought about that question for a few seconds, and then decided to go for broke.

The Last Sunday in Ordinary Time

"In order for this to be a perfect date, I would need two things: A first kiss, and a second date." She smiled, put her arms around my neck, and gave me a kiss I'll never forget.

"Let's make it perfect then."

The Seventh Sunday in Ordinary Time

July 17, 1966

The Last Sunday in Ordinary Time

Colleen was one of seven kids, six girls and one brother, Danny. The girls were named, in order from the oldest to the youngest, Kathleen, Maureen, Eileen, Colleen, Noreen, and Doreen. Danny fell right in the middle, with three older sisters and three younger sisters. When I started dating Colleen the three oldest girls were in college, and Danny was in the army. Even after only a few visits I got used to the idea that there would always be a lot of kids hanging about, mostly college aged, and mostly girls. Compared to the Kilnagaels', my house was like a monastery. Like pizza and golf, the noise and activity reinforced my idea that they lived an exciting and exotic life.

"Our house was always like this," Colleen told me. "My mom likes having our friends over, so our house was like the Kool-Aid house on the block. Our friends stopped by to play, sometimes with our sisters or Danny if we weren't home."

I'd heard the phrase "wearing your heart on your sleeve," but in the case of the Kilnagaels it was more like they wore their shamrocks on their sleeves. Their house brimmed with the trappings of Ireland, or, at least of American Irish culture. A fancy hifi sat in the living room underneath a painting of an Irish landscape. Among the music they listened to were several Clancy Brothers albums, some instrumental collections of jigs and reels, and a few recordings by Irish singers I'd never heard of. There were shamrocks on the curtains in the kitchen, cable knit sweaters hanging in the closets, and photo albums filled with pictures of the girls taking step dancing lessons.

In the basement Mr. Kilnagael installed a bar complete with barstools, a built-in tap, and pint glasses with the family name on them.

The Last Sunday in Ordinary Time

There were signs for Guiness, Harp, Jameson's Irish whiskey, and
Tullamore Dew, and what amounted to an altar dedicated to the worship
of Notre Dame Fighting Irish football. Nobody would out Irish the
Kilnagaels. They decorated their home like it was one giant welcome mat,
and strove to live up to the reputation the Irish had for hospitality.

My mom expressed concern that she never saw me anymore,
between my working at Mickey's American Standard and hanging out at
the Kilnagaels', but that's the way I liked it. The Kilnagaels' house was so
exciting, and my parents' house was so drab by comparison, why would I
want to stay home? I pretended not to notice that I hurt her feelings
when I rushed out of the house as if I were an inmate just given parole,
but that's the way I felt. At home I lived under the constant demand to
turn off the light when I left a room, but at the Kilnagaels' I was part of
the social elite of Holy Truth.

I had dated Colleen for three or four weeks when her brother
Danny came home for a visit, just long enough to say good-bye to his
parents before shipping out to Viet Nam. On July 17 his parents threw a
party, basically a barbecue, in his honor.   Although they were renowned
for their ability to entertain, there was an inescapable tension to this
party, a sense that the playful boisterousness of their typical usual parties
was, this time, a façade. Their son and brother was going off to war, and
all the good wishes and confidence expressed in Danny's certain return
could not hide the fact that his return was not certain. This time the
special magic that seem to surround the family seemed no match for the
hard reality of war.

The Last Sunday in Ordinary Time

I was not the only newcomer to the Kilnagaels' circle of friends. Fr. Connolly attended the party as well, and, as the new pastor of Holy Truth, they treated him as an honored guest. Nobody mentioned anything to me, but I assumed that Colleen's family was one of the exceptions to Mickey's observation that the biggest financial supporters of the parish were elderly.

"So what do you think of the new guy?"

Colleen's sister Maureen saw me looking at Fr. Connolly and came over to join me. She looked quite a bit like Colleen, but was a little heavier, and, therefore, a little sexier I thought. She wore her hair in a ponytail and had on a very tight blouse. I wondered if that was intentional, or if maybe she gained weight and it didn't fit her as well as it was supposed to. Either way, as she stood next to me with a glass of wine in her hand, she looked good.

"Do your parents know you're drinking?" She smirked.

"Yeah. They told me I could have one. This is my third." She barely got the sentence out before she started laughing.

"Fr. Connolly seems all right. I was at his mass a couple of times. His sermons aren't nearly as long as O'Brien's use to be." She nodded at that, and rolled her eyes a bit.

"We used to have O'Brien over for dinner all the time when we were little. Mom and Dad like playing the role of the world's greatest Catholics. I think they even annoyed the priests, to tell you the truth. By the end he was just a guy who smelled like an old man."

"What do old men smell like?"

"B.O. and Old Spice."

"What do you think of him?"

"Connolly? I don't know. He doesn't seem so bad. It's good to have him around though. Mom's losing her mind over Danny going to Viet Nam. She always goes into super-Catholic mode when she's upset. She'll probably take a bath in holy water later. Still, I hope Fr. Connolly can give her some piece of mind."

At that her eyes misted up a little. I realized that the smart ass comments and swigging wine thing were a show of false bravado. Danny's impending action in Viet Nam caused the whole family structure to waver a bit. They were a close family, and the concern they felt for Danny's safety troubled them immensely, but watching their mother start to crack under the strain of worry compounded their troubles.

"I mean, Danny hasn't even left yet, and she's already a basket case. What's she going to be like when he's actually over there?"

"Your mom and dad seem like the kind of people who rely on the church more than most." She looked up at me and nodded.

"I'm glad you're dating my sister. The last guy she dated was a weirdo, but you seem like a nice guy. And you're cute, too." She hugged me, and whispered "Be nice to her."

That was the not so hidden secret at this party. The Kilnagaels did what they always did, hosted a party and made sure everyone felt welcome, had something to drink, and had somebody to talk to. Underneath their social veneer worry and doubt ate away at the normal Kilnagael confidence, and they experienced a vulnerability that was foreign to them. Parties like this one were an effort to make new priests feel welcome both in the parish, and in the Kilnagael home. This time, however, Fr. Connolly was there to give a special blessing to Danny as he headed off to war. Eventually the priest called for everyone's attention, and then said he needed to see the Kilnagael family in the kitchen. At that point Danny, his parents, his sisters, and his sister Kathleen's fiancée all followed the priest into the house. I don't know who I was more jealous of, Fr. Connolly, or Roger Evans, the fiancée. They both got to be a part of the family's inner circle, which was the one thing I wanted most.

Although I never really knew him well, I gathered from listening to his sisters talk about him that Danny possessed a dynamic personality. They spoke as if he were the ultimate charming smartass, able to insult you but make you laugh at the same time. Like his father, he drew people to him and everyone wanted to be his friend. That was not the Danny I met during his visit home. He remained very quiet, and Colleen assured me that he wasn't normally like that. Much to his mother's disapproval, he started smoking in the army, but since she smoked in the house, she couldn't very well forbid her son from doing it too. He went through the motions of extending the typical Kilnagael welcome and friendliness to the guests at the party, but it was an unenthusiastic effort. This radical downshift in his personality caused his family to grow concerned about his army experience.

Whatever doubts the family might have had about their new pastor vanished during that private blessing. When the family reemerged from the house later, there was a noticeable improvement in both their collective mood, and their gregariousness. I asked Colleen about it later and she said that Fr. Connolly rose to the challenge. He expressed his confidence that God had a special purpose for all of us, and that he couldn't imagine that God wasn't sending their son and brother off to war without something special in mind.

"He had us all gather around Danny, placed his hands on my brother's head and recite a prayer he wrote just for Danny:

Dear God make this young man an instrument of your peace.

Through him bring your love and goodness to the people in his life,

To those who suffer under the ugliness of war, and those who

Love him here at home. When your need of him is done, bring him

Back safely to his mother's arms, and allow his family to go forth

Anticipating the joy of his safe return, amen.

"By the time we finished saying that prayer, we were all in tears, even Dad. It was a beautiful moment, and it meant the world to my mom. I think it may have been God's intention to send Fr. Connolly to Holy Truth so he could help my mom get through this."

I didn't say it to her, but I started to think that maybe it was God's intention for me to be a part of Colleen's family as well. If God indeed had a special purpose for all of us, He must have allowed me to become part of the Kilnagael's world for a reason. I just needed to find out what that reason was.

After the blessing Danny carried himself more confidently as well. I wondered if his renewed confidence made the others feel better about his situation, or if he gained confidence from watching his family react so positively to the prayer. I could see that he was the important one in this family, the one they pinned their hopes on. Colleen told me that he was the only son of an only son of an only son, so the future of the Kilnagael name and clan rested on his shoulders. I hoped that she would one day become a Donovan, and if her sisters became Murphys or O'Malleys or whatever, then unless Danny fathered at least one son, the Kilnagaels would be no more. They loved being the Kilnagaels, but without Danny they cease to be a family, Irish or otherwise.

Later that evening Colleen and I went for a walk, and Danny decided to join us. It was during that walk, while he sat on the steps of Our Lady of Holy Truth, that he told us he thought he would die in Viet Nam. When we spoke about that later, Colleen and I decided it would be better not to tell anyone else what he had said. She and I were in this together, and we needed to help keep her mother's spirits up.

The following day the entire family drove downtown to Union Station to see Danny off. It was emotional for all of them, but no one more than Mrs. Kilnagael. After they got home Colleen called me, and we went for a walk, ending up back on the steps of Holy Truth.

"Marty, it was terrible. Mom kept hugging him and saying 'I'm never going to see you again.' It was the same thing that Danny said to us. We were all in tears except my Dad who kept scolding my mother. 'He'll be fine, Peggy. He'll be fine.' But it was no use. My mom was a wreck, refusing to let go of him. 'I'll never see you again.' She kept repeating it over and over. So then Danny says, 'Mom, just pray for me. I'll be all right if you keep praying for me.' Danny shot me a don't-you-dare-say-a-word look, so I remained quiet, but God, I'm so scared for him. And I don't know what to do for my mom."

"Well, we'll just have to keep our promise to him, and keep checking the mailbox. I know it sounds kind of silly, but we promised him."

"It doesn't sound silly at all. We told him we would do it, so we need to make sure we do it."

I leaned against the wall beside the church door, and Colleen leaned hard against me. We sat there for a while, not saying much, but watching as the daylight faded to night. It was very peaceful if you ignored the odd honking of a car horn, the wailing of police sirens in the distance, and the general hum of the city. Even at night Chicago is a very active place, so peace and quiet is a very relative thing. I knew that Colleen was very upset, but I felt needed, and was very excited to have a place in the world of the Kilnagaels.

The Last Sunday in Ordinary Time

The Tenth Sunday in Ordinary Time

Enter Stage Irish

August 7, 1966

A few years ago at the annual parish picnic, I saw a drunken college guy pick up a woman and throw her over his shoulder as if she were a sack of potatoes. The woman screamed, threw awkward punches that fell harmlessly against his back, and kicked to the best of her ability which wasn't much because he had her knees clenched tightly in his left arm. As her embarrassment rose she screamed louder, but to him this was a joke and only caused him to laugh. He then began to pinch her butt which caused her to start pulling his hair and she released a stream of foul language more suited to an army barracks than a church picnic. Finally, with the foul language raining down upon the innocent ears of young children, some men intervened and forced the guy to put her down.

I thought she might start crying at that point, but she reacted in a completely opposite way. She looked around at the crowd watching her, and screamed "What are you looking at?" Her face showed such a searing level of hatred and contempt for the guy who did it to her, and for the people who watched it happen that it made me feel sorry for her. The big jerk caused her to lose any ability she had to remain a lady, and her contorted face, radiating fury and disgust caused her to come across as if she were the bad guy, almost like it were her fault.

I thought about that woman on August 5th when Martin Luther King led a march through the west side of Chicago. He brought his civil rights movement, Operation Breadbasket, to Chicago in an effort to give Negroes access to better middle class neighborhoods, many of them on the west side. Although the marchers moved through several parishes, Our Lady of Holy Truth was not one of them. Already one of the smaller parishes in Chicago, Holy Truth shrank even more when the city tore out houses to make room for the Eisenhower Expressway. Our small size insulated us from the violence and racial tension that we saw in other parts of the city on the evening news, and things continued as normal in our neighborhood.

The images we saw of other Catholics in nearby parishes showed something else. There they stood, Irish and other whites, on sidewalks and front steps screaming at the Negroes and reminding me of that woman. The same rage I saw in the face of that woman at the picnic, the same sense that she was being forced to show this ugly, angry side of herself radiated from the faces of people in nearby parishes. They looked ugly, and they screamed the ugliest things you can imagine at the Negroes who walked stoically down neighborhood streets that didn't belong to them. While watching it on TV we thought the Negroes were acting like the drunk at the picnic, and causing nice, decent people to act in such an undignified manner to defend themselves. Those people, good, decent, hardworking people, didn't deserve to have the Negroes causing such outrageous disruption in their neighborhoods. As far as Holy Truth was concerned, though, in the end the Negro marchers were somebody else's problem.

The following Sunday marked the tenth Sunday in ordinary time. At Holy Truth people lingered after mass and talked about the march, feeling sorry for the white home owners, and agreeing that the marchers were somebody else's problem. They expressed sympathy for the unfortunate people in other parishes who had to deal with those marchers, but remained certain that Holy Truth was safe. Our small parish sat tucked away from other neighborhoods, hard by the highway, but without a nearby exit or entrance ramp. The parish joke was that nobody ever found Holy Truth by accident, and few people ever found it on purpose. The parishioners congratulated themselves because things were not changing in Holy Truth, and our parish remained ours alone.

I sat in the Lovely Bit a few days later eating a hamburger and talking to Seamus and Phil, one of Uncle Charlie's bartenders. Eddie Mulroney and Brendan Ward were there too, this time listening to Seamus, but actually waiting for Charlie to arrive. A fall softball league was starting in a few weeks, and Eddie wanted to know if the Lovely Bit would sponsor his team. Rather than being his usual smart ass self, Eddie sat there almost like a businessman waiting to make a sale. He also was caught up in the story Seamus told about Irish history.

Ever since that first day we met, when he asked me if I knew who de Valera was, Seamus gave me Irish history lessons off and on while I ate. On this particular day he talked about the Easter rebellion of 1916, and about the men who planned it, and the men who died because of it.

The Last Sunday in Ordinary Time

"Now these men had no idea what they were doing. They were supposed to arrive on Easter Sunday, but were so disorganized that they didn't arrive until Monday. They didn't have half the guns or men they thought they would have, but none-the-less, they attacked the Dublin Post Office anyway. Their whole plan was this: They would storm the post office, take a green flag and stick it out the window, and declare Ireland to be a free state. They thought all the farm boys and shop owners would be filled with such great, patriotic pride that they would rush out to the streets, guns in hand, and join the fight to overthrow the British. What happened instead was that the Irish recognized them for the fools that they were, and not only didn't come to their rescue, the Irish people basically laughed at them. The British army, more out of desire to save their own lives and the post office building, decided to starve the rebels out. The rebels had little ammo, little food, and no support. They held out as long as they could, a few weeks I suppose, and then surrendered.

"Now this is where the British made their big mistake. They decided to shoot the rebels for treason, and so they began. Everyday more news came of another rebel executed by firing squad. One day, one man, another day two men. If they would have shot them all at once the story would have vanished like yesterday's newspaper, but they let the story linger. And with each further execution, more of the Irish people grew angry at the treatment of Irishmen at the hands of the British.

"You have to remember, now, that at this time, 1916, England was at war with Germany in WWI. The rebels insisted that what they had done was an act of war, but the British insisted it was an act of treason.

The Last Sunday in Ordinary Time

The anger of the Irish people grew, and they began to argue that if the British captured a German soldier they would not immediately put him to death. Why would they treat an Irishman so much worse than they would treat anybody else? I tell you, nobody knows better than an Irishman what it's like to be mistreated. Eventually the anger of the Irish people over the mistreatment of the rebels at the hands of the British caused the entire nation to boil over with anger, and that led directly to the overthrow of the crown in Ireland."

Seamus's story was interrupted by Uncle Charlie's arrival. He hardly had a chance to get behind the bar when Eddie started his spiel about sponsoring the team. Eddie rattled off the cost of the sponsorship, the jerseys the team would need, and all of the benefits Charlie would get from softball players coming in to drink after the games. The sponsorship would pay for itself Eddie assured him. On the whole I thought that Eddie did a pretty good job of selling the idea to my uncle, but he ran into one difficulty he hadn't planned on, Seamus. Every few seconds Eddie would call out "Don't do it, Charlie," or "It's a mistake, Charlie," "Don't waste your money, Charlie," and so on.

"What's the name of this team?" Charlie asked.

"We were thinking of 'Poig mahouin.'" This was a name that Eddie was clearly proud of, but I didn't get it. I looked over at Seamus to see if he knew.

"It's vulgar, Marty," he almost screamed. "It means kiss my ass in Gaelic. Oh, don't do it Charlie. People running around the neighborhood with the Lovely Bit O' Blarney on one side of the shirt, and kiss my ass on the other. Oh, 'tis vulgar indeed."

"I don't know about that name," Charlie said.

"It doesn't have to be that name. We'll name it something else." Eddie struggled to think on his feet, and Seamus delighted in watching him squirm.

"How about, how about, 'Easter 1916?'" Brendan Ward suggested. Eddie jumped at it.

"Yeah, that's a cool name. How about that? Easter 1916. A good Irish name."

"But you're not Irish," Seamus said. "Besides, you can't tarnish one of the great moments in Irish history by naming a bar league softball team after it. It would offend those who are actually Irish in this neighborhood."

By "those who are actually Irish" I assumed he meant himself. Seamus was obviously well read on Irish history, so I thought he might be actually offended, not just giving Eddie a hard time. Eddie was getting fed up with all of Seamus's smart aleck comments, and he gave him an earful.

"What are you talking about? Of course we're Irish you goofy old man." As always, Charlie stayed out of it, content to let everyone else do the talking.

"If I put a globe in your hand right now, could you even point to where Ireland is? You're as Irish as spaghetti."

"Yes, I am Irish, and I could find it on a globe."

"Ah, you're not Irish, at all. If anything you're stage Irish." Eddie realized that Seamus was continuing to lead him off the subject at hand, and so he turned back to Charlie.

"What do *you* think, Charlie?"

"I hate agree with Seamus, but I don't know if Easter 1916 would be a good idea."

"But will you sponsor the team?" Charlie nodded.

"Yes, thank you. That's great. Thank you."

"I want to know the name of this team before I give you a dollar." For the second time Brendan spoke up.

"How about 'Stage Irish?'" Eddie jumped on that idea right away.

"Yeah, Stage Irish. That's a great name. How about Stage Irish?

"I suppose that will work," Charlie said. "What else do I need to do?"

Eddie pulled a packet of papers out of his pocket. "We've got all of the paperwork filled out. All we need is name, address and phone number of the sponsor, and your signature. And, we'll change the name. I promise you."

Charlie filled in the blanks and signed where Eddie asked him to. Eddie also scratched out the name and changed it to *Stage Irish*. Finally, he raised the last issue.

"We were thinking about green jerseys with white lettering. We need to get fifteen of them, but I'm not sure how much they cost. I'll have to get you a price on those."

Uncle Charlie nodded. He looked over at me.

"What about you? Do you want a jersey too?"

"Sure." I was completely surprised by the question. He turned back to Eddie.

"Get a price on two dozen of them. It might be nice to have a few extras around."

"Absolutely. We'll get a price on twenty-four of them. Great. Thanks, Charlie. Thanks a lot."

"Yes," Brendan repeated, "thank you. We really appreciate it."

The two of them ran out the door as excited as they could be. I got up to leave as well; having stayed a little too long while I waited to hear Charlie's answer, I needed to get back to Mickey's. I wasn't worried about being late because Mick wasn't at the gas station that day, but I didn't want to press my luck.

"Kind of a cool name," I told Seamus.

"Oh, please. It's like a Polish bar sponsoring a team called the Polack Jokes."

The Eleventh Sunday in Ordinary Time

Father Connolly Takes Charge

August 14, 1966

Fr. Connolly took Mickey's lecture to heart. His staff consisted of two other priests and the many men and women who volunteered around the church. He made the parish's biggest contributors his primary focus, and divided the rest of the parish work among the other priests. Fr. Romano took charge of the school and major fundraising events like the winter carnival and annual raffle. Fr. Morris, the newest and youngest of the three priests, took responsibility for coordinating different parish groups, including the Holy Name Society, the Knights of Columbus, the boy scouts and girl scouts, and the youth choir among other things. Almost immediately the parish saw a positive swing in attitude and activity. The elders of Holy Truth liked what they saw, and the Sunday collections increased noticeably. Because he had divided the running of the parish among the three priests, some of the more liberal, more distasteful changes were hidden from the eyes of the elderly. Fr. Ahern might have the teenagers practicing songs for a guitar mass, but the older parishioners never heard them.

I spent more and more of my time at the Kilnagaels' that summer. After all those years of wishing I was a part of a big Irish family, I felt like I was becoming a part of this one. At least I was trying to become a part of it. I tried to be as helpful and friendly as I could be without showing how desperately I wanted to win their approval. I loved being in their house partly because I wanted to spend more time with Colleen, and partly because it allowed me to study everything they did. I wanted to learn what they knew that my parents didn't, and to learn to be like the Kilnagaels, to be a part of a big Irish family. It was that determination to be one of them that kept me going back. I thought most guys would have never lasted through the radical surge in prayer and Catholicism they experienced that year, but I intended to prove myself worthy of their company.

On Thursday, August 18th, I was sitting with Colleen on the front porch of their house when the phone rang. I remember the time and place because it was Danny on the other end calling to tell them he was shipping out the next day, and to say good-bye. It was an emotional moment, made more so because his father and two of his sisters were not at home that evening. Colleen, Maureen, Noreen, and Doreen each took turns saying good-bye, but it was Mrs. Kilnagael who stayed on the phone the longest. She tried to extend the phone call as long as possible, seeming to want still one more chance to say "I love you." She began to cry as she spoke.

The Last Sunday in Ordinary Time

"You are my brave and handsome son, and you're father and I love you very much. Remember that every day when you wake up, and remember it every night before you go to sleep. We all love you. Your sisters and your father and I are all here waiting for you to come home. Okay? Danny? Will you say your prayer with me? Please, Danny?

"Dear God make this young man an instrument of your peace. Through him bring your love and...

"Danny? Danny? I love you, Danny. Oh, dear God. I guess he had to go," she told us after she hung up the phone.

From the very second the phone call ended Mrs. Kilnagael seemed to shrink before my eyes. The commanding presence that tended to intimidate the people around her melted away the instant she cradled the receiver on the phone. She turned and headed upstairs without saying a word to anyone else. Maureen followed her but came back down almost immediately.

"She said she wants to be alone." Maureen said.

"Did he tell Mom 'I love you'?" Colleen asked.

"I don't know" Maureen answered defensively, as if she were saying "Don't ask me."

I never heard what Danny said to his mother, but I knew what he didn't say. He refused to say the prayer with his mother, and he ended the phone call abruptly. I thought it was a mean thing for him to do to his mother, and we wondered if he told her he loved her, or if he even bothered to say good-bye. We couldn't ask her what he said because we feared the answer might cause Mrs. Kilnagael to say aloud that her son refused to say he loved her.   Maureen brought the subject up with Colleen and me.

"What do you think? Did he really have to go, or did he just want to hang up on Mom?"

"Danny wouldn't do anything mean to Mom. There was probably somebody else waiting to use the phone, or maybe he didn't want to start crying, too." Colleen answered.

"I hope you're right."

"God," Maureen said. "She's so helpless. Mom is a woman who likes to take charge, but there's nothing she can do. She's probably sitting up there with her fingers crossed. What else can she do?"

From that point forward we stopped worrying that Danny was going to Viet Nam, and started worrying because he was in Viet Nam. Colleen and I still held to the idea that we could keep Danny safe by guarding their mailbox, and started keeping a daily vigil on it. At least for now, it was easy.   We figured that it would be a few weeks at the earliest before bad news might arrive. In less than a month school would be restarting, and then it would be difficult. Ultimately we decided that we couldn't possibly be there to get the mail before her mother got it, but we could continually check the mailbox for the mail. Colleen decided to check the mailbox every time she entered or exited the house. My job was to check the mailbox whenever I came by for a visit, as long as nobody could see me do it. I wouldn't be able to explain myself if I got caught, and I didn't want to be accused of prying or trespassing, so I became a kind of safety net for Colleen. If she ever forgot to check it, then maybe I could keep up the protection.

The Last Sunday in Ordinary Time

As far as Mrs. Kilnagael was concerned, her tears did not end with that phone call, they began. She became a nervous wreck, crying at the merest thought or mention of Danny. Sleeping proved difficult, and her eyes showed the strain of constant worry that happened without the relief of sleep. From the moment she hung up the phone that day she lived on the edge of heartbreak, struggling to keep from losing her composure at all times. She made it difficult to keep her company, and difficult to leave her alone. The whole family did its best to show her support, but her sorrow suffocated their home, and the usual liveliness seen in Colleen's house disappeared under the weight of their mother's worry.

Fr. Connolly stepped in and again showed me what a capable priest he was. I knew that he made Holy Truth's biggest contributors his primary concern, so it might be cynical to suggest he came to the aid of the Kilnagaels solely for monetary reasons. He might have done the same thing for any other family in the parish, but the truth was, when they needed him, he came through for Mrs. Kilnagael and her family. Colleen and her sisters expected their mom to adjust to the idea that Danny was at war and lighten up a little as time went by. She didn't. She moved lethargically through her daily activities, and spent many quiet hours upstairs in her room, either sleeping or pretending to be asleep. Sometimes one of her daughters would lie beside her, trying to engage her in conversation, but mostly allowing her to stroke their hair, and think of something beside her missing son.

Before he came to see her, Fr. Connolly received a review of her depression and listlessness from Mr. Kilnagael. If there were one positive aspect to Mrs. K's troubles, it was that it forced Mr. Kilnagael focus on his wife, and spared him the burden of worrying only about Danny. In any case, he remained much more stoic about the whole situation. In the absence of Mrs. Kilnagael's role in the house, he became busy keeping the family functioning. He turned to Fr. Connolly to help his wife regain her composure. The priest arrived knowing that she was in trouble, and wanting offer her a way out of it. Colleen told me that he sat with her for a couple of hours after dinner, praying with her and listening to her concerns. I'm certain that he was well aware of the reason for her heartache before she ever said a word, but he allowed her to tell her story, to attempt to unload the burden that Danny's absence placed upon her. Before he left, he gathered the family into the living room where they recited Danny's prayer as a group:

Dear God,

Make Danny an instrument of your peace.

Through him bring your love and goodness to the people in his life,

To those who suffer under the ugliness of war, and those who

Love him here at home. When your need of him is done, bring him

Back safely to his mother's arms, and allow his family to go forth

Anticipating the joy of his safe return, amen.

The Last Sunday in Ordinary Time

Like the last time they said the prayer together, it immediately improved Mrs. Kilnagael's mood and gave at least a temporary boost to the atmosphere in the house. A few days later Fr. Kilnagael made another house call to see how she was doing. This time he iterated her need to place her faith in God, and to lay her burden at His feet. Fr. Connolly asked her to join a group called the Ladies of St. Theresa, a group that volunteered to help clean and maintain the church.

"St. Theresa is a wonderful saint. The church canonized her in 1927, and she immediately became a beloved figure in the Catholic Church. The Church declared her the patron saint of all foreign missions, causing millions of Roman Catholics the world wide, but especially in America, to turn to her for support during World War II. Here in Our Lady of Holy Truth a group of women who had sons serving overseas decided to pray to her to protect their sons. The women would get together once a week to prayer the rosary for all the soldiers overseas, and then spend an hour or two cleaning the church. Some of those same women are still volunteering and cleaning the church to this day."

"I'm rather busy these days..." Mrs. Kilnagael began.

"Now, Peggy," Fr. Connolly said, "I know you're busy, and God knows you've been a great friend to Our Lady of Holy Truth for many years, but I'm doing more than asking you. I'm telling you. You need to allow Our Lady of Holy Truth to wrap her loving arms around you, and see you through this difficult time. The Ladies of St. Theresa's know what you're going through. They've sent sons and brothers off to war, and then leaned on Our Lady to carry them through the darkness."

Mrs. Kilnagael sighed. The priest needed to shake her out of the lethargy she fell into when Danny was sent to Viet Nam, but her sense of surrender was powerful. She lacked the will to fight the tremendous sorrow that engulfed her.

"Peggy, you will go visit these ladies. I expect you to be at the church Tuesday morning at 9:00. Join them, pray with them, and let St. Theresa and God relieve you of your burden."

"I'll go with you, Mom."

"Now see there. Colleen will go with you, so you won't be alone. You need to get out there. You need to keep on living, and remain confident that God will keep Danny safe."

The exhaustion that had come over Mrs. Kilnagael, the heavy, sorrowful exhaustion that kept her from engaging in life as she had before, now caused her to agree to this. She was too tired to fight both the priest and her daughter. She finally nodded.

"Okay, I'll go."

"Wonderful. Wonderful. I'll tell the ladies that you're coming, you and Colleen both. I'm sure this will be a good thing for you."

Later, as he was leaving, Fr. Connolly spoke to Colleen and me out on the front sidewalk. He told us that he knew that the Ladies of St. Theresa would be good for Colleen's mom, and that they wouldn't allow her to remain in such a poor state of mind.

"Prayer and activity are the two things your mom needs most, and those are the two things that she'll get on Tuesday morning. Colleen, I'm so glad you agreed to help your mom. She needs you now, and she'll always be grateful you stood by her."

Before I left that night I asked Colleen a difficult question.

"Do you think Danny told your mom he thought he was going to die? I mean, she's seems so worried, like she knows something."

"I don't know," Colleen answered and wiped away a tear. "I can't ask her. I assume he didn't, and if I tell her what he said, she'll go over the edge. It's so hard on her."

The Fourteenth Sunday in Ordinary Time

The Last Sunday in Ordinary Time

September 4, 1966

I knew that Our Lady of Holy Truth was a small parish, but I never appreciated how small it was until I got to know the Kilnagaels. When they decided to spread news around the neighborhood, they used every means necessary and didn't stop until everyone heard. I bragged to Colleen that Uncle Charlie said he would buy me one of the Stage Irish T-shirts, and she immediately said she wanted one too. I regretted saying anything to her because mine would be less cool if she had one too, but I said I would see if she could get one too. I told her I would ask, but I thought about just saying it was too late, and not mentioning it to my uncle. On the other hand, I started to realize if I didn't get her one, I might have to give her mine. I decided to do my best to get her one and avoid the risk of not getting one myself.

The next day, before I ever got the chance to raise the issue, Colleen and her mother went over to Holy Truth and joined the Ladies of St. Theresa in saying the rosary and cleaning the church. Colleen told me it worked out just the way Fr. Connolly said it would, with the ladies making a point of saying the rosary for Danny, and then offering words of encouragement to Mrs. K. She could see the difference in her mother's demeanor immediately, and thought hearing about what the older women had gone through during World War II had a calming effect. They started talking about putting together a "Good Luck" box of goodies to send to Danny in Viet Nam. Many of them offered to bake things themselves, and wanted to make sure to send a rosary and some holy water. Mrs. Kilnagael decided she wanted to do it, and that gave her a sense of mothering him again.

"They started asking me about things, and (At this point Colleen started talking in a slow kind of sing-songy way) did I have a boyfriend, and I told them 'Yes, I have a boyfriend, and his name is Marty Donovan,' and then Mrs. McNulty says (at this point Colleen started doing an old lady voice) 'Oh, I know Marty Donovan. He's such a nice boy, very handsome,' and I said thank you, and I told them about the baseball shirt you're getting me from the Lovely Bit, and, of course my mom says she doesn't think a lady should be wearing a shirt that advertises a tavern, but then some of the other ladies say maybe it's okay, and then Mrs. Gleason said something very interesting...

"Mrs. Gleason wanted to know if we wanted to a put a shirt from the Lovely Bit in Danny's good luck box. I thought what a great idea. Danny would love that. It would let him know that we all thinking about him back here. So, what do you think? Can we get one for Danny, too?"

I knew that the T-shirts were available because Uncle Charlie had told Eddie and Brendan to get the price of twenty-four of them. When I walked into the bar the next evening I surprised by the size of the crowd because the entire softball team showed up to thank Uncle Charlie and, of course, to drink. Several of the players brought their girlfriends with them, and those girls brought other girls, and so the place was wall-to-wall people. I ended up having to stand, and I was across the room from Seamus, but he was enjoying the young girls who came by to flirt with the old man. I'm sure he didn't miss me.

The Last Sunday in Ordinary Time

I managed to get both Charlie and Eddie's attention, and asked them about getting a shirt for both Colleen and Danny Kilnagael. One of the girls overheard Danny's name and joined the conversation.

"Are you planning on sending a Stage Irish shirt to Danny Kilnagael?"

"Yeah, I'd like to. His mom is sending a good luck box over to Viet Nam, and wants to include one of the softball jerseys."

"I know Danny real well. If you send one, I want to sign it."

"I want to sign it, too," another girl said.

Within a few minutes everyone in the bar knew about this jersey going over to Danny, and they all wanted to sign it. And they all decided they wanted to get one of their own, so the number of T-shirts needed jumped up to over forty. Uncle Charlie asked Eddie if hadn't gotten a price yet, but Eddie said not for forty of them.

"You'd better call that place again and get a price for forty-eight of them, but listen. I'm not going to buy forty-eight of these bloody things, so if your friends want them, you collect the money first."

I told Eddie to mark me down for three of them, and asked if Danny could get the number seven jersey, for good luck. He said yes to that, but said if I knew anybody else who wanted one, try to sell one or two more. Like Charlie, Eddie didn't want to get stuck with the extras either. Later, when I told Colleen about it, she and her whole family were thrilled.

On Friday morning I got a call from a girl named Patti O'Malley, a friend of Kathleen Kilnagael. I didn't know her, but she had heard about the Stage Irish T-shirts, and wanted to know if she could buy one too. I told her yes, and to stop by Mickey's American Standard later, and she could give me the money then.

"Oh," she added. "Do you think I could get number seven, too, like Danny?"

Within an hour I got three more calls from friends of the Kilnagaels, all wanting T-shirts, and all wanting number seven, like Danny. At the gas station people starting dropping by to order T-shirts, all of them friends of Colleen or her sisters, and all of them wanting lucky number seven. I saw Brendan Ward driving past the gas station, and I flagged him down.

"I sold some more Stage Irish shirts."

"Oh yeah. How many?"

"Seventeen."

"Seventeen? Holy crap. Who's buying them?"

"Remember talking about Danny Kilnagael the other night? Well, all of his sisters and their friends want to buy them. I think there's gonna be a lot more sold pretty soon."

"No, that's great. What the heck? Why not?"

"Well, here's the thing. They all want to get number seven. They call it Danny's lucky number. You better get a hold of Eddie and see about buying maybe seventy-two shirts."

Over the next week I kept taking orders for more shirts, but the price I charged was the price if you only bought twenty-four. Brendan took my phone number and Eddie gave me a call about all the T-shirts were selling.

"The more you buy, the cheaper they get. People are overpaying," he told me.

"I don't care. I'm not going to run around giving people refunds, and if we lower the price now, the people who bought them before are going to be mad." He agreed. He said between us we had orders for over eighty shirts.

"The thing is, if we buy a gross of them, at the price were charging, we can pay for 144 shirts if we sell 100 of them, especially if we make them all number seven."

"Are you guys on the team all going to wear number seven?"

"No, I don't think so. Listen Marty. Don't tell anyone the price. I'm going to order 144 shirts and hope that we sell 100 of them. The first twenty-four will be numbered one through twenty-four, and the other 120 of them will all be number seven. If we make a couple of dollars profit, I'll split it with you, okay?"

"Sure, that would be great."

"Hey, Marty, thanks for your help. I really mean it. Thanks a lot."

Eddie placed the order, but people kept on buying. I don't know if sold all 144 of them, but we sold most of them, and I was told not to sell any more. We probably could have sold a few more, but the Eddie had already placed his order, and they were all spoken for.

A few days later the Kilnagaels invited me to stay for dinner, so I got the chance to tell them about all the t-shirts people were ordering in Danny's honor. They were all very pleased with the news, especially Mrs. Kilnagael. I sat next to Colleen in the chair, I was told, Danny usually sat in.

"It's the next best thing to having him here himself," Mrs. K said.

"Well, I really admire your family. You're like the perfect Irish family."

Mr. Kilnagael laughed at that comment and asked what makes them so perfectly Irish. I repeated the story Seamus Touhy told me at the Lovely Bit a couple of weeks earlier, about the leprechauns, the fairies, and the way the Irish developed the habit of making strangers feel welcome so that the fairies would not be offended.

"You guys are just like that. At that big party you had for Danny before he left, I was amazed how you all went around and talked to people and made everyone feel at home. You never make anyone feel like the least of my brothers. Everybody is a welcome friend."

"Well, now, that is as nice a compliment as I have ever received," Mr. Kilnagael said.

"Yes," Mrs. Kilnagael agreed, "it was a very sweet thing to say."

At that point Eileen raised her water glass and said "Here's to Marty Donovan, a welcome friend in our home."

They all raised their glasses to me and toasted my presence there. I could feel myself turning red with embarrassment, but I couldn't have been happier.

"Oh, did we embarrass you?"

They all laughed at my awkwardness, but Colleen leaned over and gave me a sideways hug. I could tell she was glad that her family liked me so much.

The Last Sunday in Ordinary Time

The Sixteenth Sunday in Ordinary Time

Not a Company Man

September 18, 1966

On the picture window in the gas station office were the words
Mickey's AmericAn StAndArd in white lettering with red shadowing. The
A's were all capitalized and had blue stars in the top half of each. It
matched the red, white and blue of the Standard sign on Madison, and on
all of the pumps. At the bottom left hand corner was the phone number,
KEdzie 5-3131, and in the bottom right hand corner was Michael T.
Riordan, proprietor. I watched Mickey as closely as he watched me and
quickly learned how important it was to him that people knew he owned
the gas station. If any doubts lingered, I made the mistake of once telling
someone that Mickey worked for Standard.

The Last Sunday in Ordinary Time

"Marty, I don't work for Standard. Standard Oil works for me."

That independence meant everything to him. He took pride in his business however humble I thought it might have been, and expressed genuine admiration for anyone else who also owned his own business. Among those he liked and admired was an Italian man named Mario Rizzo, an Italian immigrant who delivered gasoline to the station. Like the gas station itself, his tanker had Standard Oil logos all over it, but, as Mickey pointed out to me one day, not on the cab. The doors both had Rizzo and Sons Trucking stenciled on them. The two of them, Mickey and Mario, were kindred spirits, funny, charming and fiercely determined to own a part of the American business world. The first time I met Mario he began by insulting me.

"Hey, Mick, is this your son? He looks like a chip off the old potato."

"Oh, listen to the dago talk. Marty, you know why Italy is shaped like a boot? Cause you couldn't fit all that shit in a shoe."

Mario's visits typically started with insults, Mickey calling his friend "Spaghetti," and Mario referring to Mickey as Mr. Potato Head, although, in his thick Italian accent it sounded more like Patata head. He asked me if I knew what an Irish seven course meal was. Actually I knew the answer but pretended I didn't just to be polite.

"A six-pack and a potato." I laughed even though I thought we both knew that it wasn't that funny a joke.

"Mario," Mick protested, "did some dinosaur tell you that joke. Marty, tell him you're wearing Italian shoes; where you go, dey go." I realized that Mick's joke was an old one too, but I had never heard it before, so I laughed pretty hard. Eventually their conversations became a little more business-like, and they compared notes on what they heard about things at Standard, or things in general. One day they talked about a man named Ebersol who left Standard under suspicious circumstances. They weren't sure if he quit or was fired.

"I heard he got a job in St. Louis for another oil company, Sinclair I think."

"I don't know, Mick. Standard will fire a guy for no reason. They ask me to work for them once, but I told them no. If you go to work for them, they act like they own you."

Even while he talked, Mario kept busy hooking the truck up the underground tanks, keeping an eye them, completing paperwork. Like Mick, he took his work seriously, and made sure he did his job well. Salesmen used to stop by sometimes and try to get Mick to hang a sign for Viceroy cigarettes, to place a Chicago Daily News rack in the office, or put another vending machine in. Although Mick listened respectfully to all of them, they worked for somebody else, and, in Mick's eyes, were less accomplished than a guy like Mario who actually owned his own business.

Eddie Mulroney came across the street with a stack of Stage Irish T-shirts and a list of who ordered what. He had a lot of names, but not many addresses or phone numbers. We sorted through the names and I ended up taking almost sixty of them to deliver to the Kilnagaels. Some of the names meant nothing to me, but I recognized them as friends of Colleen and her sisters. Like Eddie, having that many shirts made me nervous that I would lose some, so I called Colleen, and she and her sister Maureen drove over and picked them up. I didn't dare put mine on, or mix it up with the others. Colleen and the others all had number seven, Danny's lucky number, but I had eighteen. I originally asked for number ten, Ron Santo's number on the Cubs, but it was taken. Then I asked for number nine, Randy Hundley's number, but that was taken, too. Finally I settled for eighteen, like Glenn Beckert, the Cubs second basemen.

Across the street at the Lovely Bit the guys talked about their first Stage Irish game coming up against Gambler's Pub. The guy who printed the shirts agreed to put Danny's name on the back of all the number seven shirts at no extra charge because the order was so big, and to show support for a "war hero." It surprised me to find out how much this rankled the older guys at the bar who were expressing some weariness at all of the attention being paid to Danny Kilnagael.

"Hey, Joe," Mr. Hanley called out to Joe O'Grady, "what did you do with the T-shirt they gave you for fighting in Italy?" Mr. O'Grady smirked and waved him off in kind of a forget-about-it manner. John Lally, maybe the only regular at the bar older than Seamus Touhy, picked up where Mr. Hanley left off.

"You'd think no one had ever joined the army before."

"This lot thinks there never was a war before this one," Mr. Hanley continued. "I know I never heard so much talk about heroes."

One of the girls who hung out with the softball team said something to them in defense of Danny, although I didn't hear what it was. This started a heated exchange back and forth until a couple of softball players stepped in between. Mr. Hanley kept talking, pretending to be talking to the older men, but making sure he was loud enough for the girls to hear.

"I remember a day when a man could sit at the bar and have a cold beer without watching his language because they were no ladies around. Thankfully, there still aren't."

The younger guys let that comment pass although the anger was apparent. Things settled down a bit, but the resentment lingered. The younger men were bringing more women around more often, something I thought the older men wouldn't mind. But it changed the dynamic of the bar as a place for these men to get away from their wives and drink a beer in peace. The older men honestly believed a bar was no place for a woman. They always let the occasional flurry of women in the bar pass without comment, but this became a trend rather a single episode.

Over the next couple of weeks as September turned to October and we returned to school, it became hard to walk down the street in Holy Truth without seeing a Stage Irish T-shirt. They became both a fashion statement and a status symbol. The Kilnagaels' popularity in the parish added to the cachet of owning a T-shirt, marking the person wearing it as a friend of the family. Conversely, some people grew to resent the Kilnagaels for forcing their so much attention on their son. Danny was not the only guy from the neighborhood serving in Viet Nam, so why didn't the other guys merit some attention? It struck me that the Kilnagaels became self-absorbed, concerned only about Danny and their mother's constant worry about him. When coupled with the natural tendency of people to express only kind thoughts and wishes to them, the family remained blissfully ignorant of the smoldering resentment of Danny's prominence in the thoughts of the parish.

The Last Sunday in Ordinary Time

The Nineteenth Sunday in Ordinary Time

A House of Prayer

My mother taught me to say the rosary. We knelt in the living room, using chairs to support us, and facing the crucifix that hung above the doorway. Since there were only two of us (Dad rarely joined in), Mom always led on the first, third, and fifth decades, and I led on the second and fourth decades. Among the guys I knew in school, and even among the girls, I was probably the one who prayed the rosary the most. I hesitate to say that I hated praying the rosary, but, God help me, I did. I was at the mercy of Mom's whims, and anytime she decided she needed to say one, usually after dinner, I got stuck doing it, too.

The Last Sunday in Ordinary Time

The Kilnagaels never said the rosary with the regularity that we did, but when they did say it, there were more of them to share the load. Nobody except Mrs. Kilnagael had to take a turn every time, and sometimes Colleen or one of her sisters got through it without having to lead a decade. As Colleen's mom leaned more and more heavily on the church for support, saying the rosary became a regular part of the family's life. At these moments she returned to the domineering woman she typically was. She invited everyone at the house to join her, but an invitation from Mrs. Kilnagael sounded like an order. The thought of getting stuck kneeling in the living room saying the rosary caused many of their friends to keep their distance from the family's house. Maureen told me that her friends even asked her to call them when it was over so they didn't get roped in to saying it, too.

Unlike the others, I wanted to pray the rosary with them. The Kilnagaels still treated me warmly, and joining them encouraged me to believe I was part of the inner circle, and I wanted as much of that as I could get. If praying the rosary with them would help me become more like them, I was all for it. Praying with them was also easier. Like in my house, we would gather in the living room and kneel on the floor with our arms resting on the seat of a chair or the couch, essentially with our backs turned to each other. Mrs. Kilnagael began reciting the Hail Mary's of the first decade, and we joined her at the halfway point:

Mrs. Kilnagael: Hail Mary, full of grace, the Lord is with thee. Blessed are

Thou amongst women, and blessed is thy womb, Jesus.

The Last Sunday in Ordinary Time

All of us: Holy Mary, mother of God, pray for us sinners, now and

At the hour of our death, amen.

Unlike the quiet boredom of saying it with my mom, the Kilnagaels were much livelier, especially when joined by other teenagers. As each decade of ten Hail Mary's passed, they got antsier, and sillier. At one point during her decade, Colleen got confused and reached the halfway point by saying, "...thy womb, Jesus. Amen." This stray amen caused everyone to develop a case of the giggles while Mrs. Kilnagael tried to get everyone to be serious.

Doing things to make other people laugh without getting caught became the game they all played. The girls would make faces at each other, poke each other, and try almost anything to make the others break up. One time Noreen farted, causing absolute pandemonium while she turned red because I was there to hear it. Despite all of the laughter, Mrs. Kilnagael continued on, determined as always to finish.

For all of the fooling around though, the girls all agreed to return night after night to pray with their mother. I wasn't there every night, but I was there often enough to see how much they cared for her. I usually took the same chair in the corner so I gained an angle where I could watch them. Amid all of the faces and barely contained giggles there was the sweet warmth of a family that gathered around to support their mother. I must admit, my angle also allowed me to spend my time checking out Colleen, her older sisters, and their friends. Seeing those girls kneeling, slightly bent over like that was sexy, and made the whole thing easier to sit through.

Mr. K joined the ranks of those who made themselves scarce when the rosary started. Colleen thought her father acted cruelly toward her mother, failing to recognize how much she needed him at the moment. Fr. Connolly actually came to Mr. Kilnagael's defense during a conversation with Colleen and me, telling us that some people needed to talk about these things in order to deal with them, and others, like Colleen's dad, needed not to talk about them. He encouraged Colleen not to be too hard on her father, an old army man who learned the army way to deal with difficulty, which was to say little and keep a stiff upper lip.

Everything Fr. Connolly did impressed me. He stopped in to pray with Mrs. Kilnagael at least once a week, and remained a steady and caring friend to her. He also became her confidant and shoulder to cry on. When he came he made sure they said Danny's prayer along with the rosary. I never watched a priest in action before other than in church, but he lived up to the stereotype of what a parish priest is supposed to be. He honestly cared about Mrs. Kilnagael, and he made sure she knew her welfare was part of his weekly work at Holy Truth. He also massaged the subtle cold war that waged between Colleen's parents.

The Kilnagaels prided themselves on being a modern, sophisticated couple. They followed the trend of prosperous Americans in the 1960's, and made a point of enjoying a martini and a cigarette before dinner, and joining friends at a classy restaurant at least once every couple of weeks. Like all things they did, their socializing impressed me greatly. Like martinis glasses that somehow got mixed up with beer steins and shot glasses, they lived their lives to a sort of suburban ideal, but they managed to do it in our mundane city parish. Holy Truth may have been a lot of things, but hip wasn't one of them. The Kilnagaels seemed to possess all of the great things about being Irish in Holy Truth and transcend them at the same time.

In Danny's absence that started to change. Mrs. Kilnagael started to forgo the ritual martinis and lost the desire to engage in the fashionable social life. Mr. Kilnagael, conversely, wanted the martinis and social life more than ever, and started pursuing it on his own. He started enjoying his afternoon cocktail on the way home from work so he wouldn't have to drink alone. Even when he did drink his martinis at home it was not unusual to find him sitting alone in his dark basement bar, smoking cigarettes and listening to Frank Sinatra records on the hifi, sometimes while the rest of us were upstairs praying.

We all became invested in Mrs. K's welfare and watching her was like watching the stock market, up one day, down another. The attention, the volunteer work at the church, and the group prayers all seemed to help, though, and her mood slowly began to moderate. She came closer to the confident, take-charge woman she had been before Danny left, although she never fully regained the full presence she once possessed. Down at the Lovely Bit people asked about her sometimes, but rarely asked about Mr. Kilnagael. They assumed that men instinctively knew how to handle life's problems, and since he, like many of the men of his generation, fought in World War II, he possessed a hardness that protected him from life's difficulties. As far as I could tell, Mr. K was determined to live up to that reputation. Colleen told me he insisted that she and her sisters take care of their mother, but he was apparently on his own.

The Last Sunday in Ordinary Time

Even away from the Kilnagaels' home I could not get away from them, a fact that pleased me immensely. At the Lovely Bit Stage Irish continued to hang around on game days and in between. Many more people wanted Stage Irish T-shirts than were available, and so they remained quite the fashion statement. It meant something to own one. They also kept Danny's name in daily conversation, for better and for worse. While I, along with most of the younger crowd enjoyed celebrating "Danny the Hero," the older men grew increasingly tired of the attention he received. The girls who hung around the team made a point of asking me about how Mrs. K was doing, and did they hear from Danny, and so on. When anybody gave me a hard time they rose to my defense, commenting on what a cute couple Colleen and I were. I have to admit my favorite one was Nancy Tobin, who made a point of leaning against me when she talked, pressing her large breasts against my arm or back while asking me about Colleen. At first I assumed she didn't realize what she was doing, but eventually caught on to the fact that she enjoyed my awkwardness about it. If she was ever in the bar and no one was paying attention to her, she became very flirty. I was not the only guy who wished she would stop and, and the same time was glad that she didn't.

"Colleen? Colleen is it?" Seamus said with mock confusion when he learned her name. "What kind of a name is Colleen? It's not a name at all."

"Oh, stop," Nancy said in my defense. "It's a pretty name for a pretty girl, right, Marty?"

"But it's not a name at all. It's... it's... it's like having a son and naming him 'Boy.' It's a word that means girl."

"I think it's a beautiful Irish name."

"But it's not at all. Do you think in Ireland they are in the habit of calling girls 'Colleen?' They don't give girls silly names like that one."

"It doesn't matter what you think," Nancy said pleasantly, but defiantly. "Colleen is a beautiful Irish girl with a beautiful Irish name. Right, Marty?"

"But, she's not Irish. She's American. Charlie behind the bar, here, is Irish. Marty's mom and dad are Irish. But his girlfriend, she's a Yank all the way."

"I say she's Irish, and that's all that matters."

"There's no use in talking to you Yanks. I'll tell you right now, the surest way to tell an Irishman from a Yankee is by the names they give their daughters. You'll never meet an Irishman with daughter named Colleen."

For Seamus it proved to be a useful little nugget of grief he could give people. There were two girls named Colleen who sometimes hung around with the Stage Irish crowd, and Seamus amused himself by insisting he knew they were colleens, but he wanted to know their names. He enjoyed mentioning that I had a supposed uncle in Charlie, a supposed girlfriend in Colleen, and that I was a supposed Irishman myself. He'd tell me to finish my supposed hamburger, cross the supposed street, and get back to my supposed job.

In late October Charlie put two posters in the window, one for the reelection of Mayor Daley, and the other for the reelection of Alderman

John Patrick "Mugsy" O'Bannion. There was an election coming up on the first Tuesday of November, and the political signs were sprouting on lawns throughout the parish, typically in pairs, always one for the mayor, and usually one for somebody else, the state's attorney, a candidate for judge, or the alderman. I assumed that no doubt existed that the local Democrats would win everything like they always did, but to my dad and Uncle Charlie, it was serious business. Mick put the signs up in his gas station as well, but Mick insisted that he was not a political man, he was simply avoiding trouble.   To openly defy the Daley machine invited a city inspector to stop by and determine if the gas station had any code violations. The truth was, your business had political signs or it had building code violations, so it was cheaper to put the signs up than to pay the fines.

Mayor Daley, I learned, always ran scared. Every election offered the mayor something to worry about. This year the trouble emerged in the person of Richard Ogilvie, a Republican running hard for Cook County state's attorney. If the state's attorney's office fell into Republican hands, the Republicans gained the ability to investigate Mayor Daley's Democratic machine. The mayor, therefore, leaned heavily on the local committeemen, like Charlie, to get the vote out. And the committeemen leaned heavily on the precinct captains, like my dad, to ring doorbells and remind their neighbors to vote democratic. As the election neared, Daley demanded that his machine retain control of the county's legal system. Having stood up to Martin Luther King and the coloreds who had so rudely marched through White neighborhoods, the mayor now wanted to fend off the Republican Party.

The Last Sunday in Ordinary Time

Despite the strength and organization of the Daley machine, all of the politically active people worried about breaking one of the timeless political adages "say nothing like you mean it." The idea was to express concern for the voters sincerely, but to not actually say anything meaningful or to make any concrete promises. Daley managed to keep the aldermen in line during the summer of Negro marches through White neighborhoods, so it was generally felt that the danger had passed. There were no angry outbursts by politicians, and the general impression was of reasonable men who remained calm in the face of a difficult situation. The local Democrats managed to avoid saying anything that might inflame the situation, or give the protestors any additional sense of purpose, but then Mugsy O'Bannion said something.

When asked about the fact that none of the marches actually went through our ward, he tried to convey the idea that the people of our ward had no racism in their hearts, and so the Negroes never felt any need to protest in Holy Truth. What he actually said was this:

> "Martin Luther King and his followers knew better than to waste their time marching here. The people of this ward aren't going to change because they don't need to change. We are happy with our ward the way it is."

Just when the political atmosphere seemed to settle down, this quote proved irresistible to the press. The Chicago American ran a front page story with the headline "O'Bannion: Negroes Afraid to March in Ward." Some reporters raced to the mayor's office for a comment on the comment, while others worked the parish, asking people if they agreed with the alderman. To the horror of the mayor, many of them said they did. Months of carefully orchestrated silence now exploded in an election rattling noise that terrified the party. If Mugsy O'Bannion's name could have been removed from the ballot, it would have been, but it was too late for that. Instead the Democrats began high level damage control.

My dad, along with all of the other precinct captains across the city, was called to emergency meetings to discuss the problem. They were instructed first of all, to not talk to reporters. Anyone who so much as said hello to a reporter put his job at risk. Dad said they were told to follow another old Chicago adage, "Don't say anything. If you gotta say something, don't say nothing." Secondly there were told to quietly agree with whatever the voters told them on the doorstep. If a man complained about Coloreds not knowing their place, agree and say we just have to wait them out. If someone expressed sympathy for the plight of the Negro, the precinct captains were to nod and say the party was striving to find a solution that was fair to everybody. The bottom line was to never argue with anyone, and to avoid talking to reporters at all times.

The strategy seemed to work. The reporters kept trying to bait the politicians into making more comments on the racial situation between Negroes and Whites, but the machine men proved well-disciplined. The fear of losing their jobs kept their tongues still, and the news people moved on to other stories.

For weeks, since Danny's phone call telling his mother he was shipping out, Colleen and I maintained the vigil on their mailbox. At times it struck me as a useless, silly thing to do, but it mattered to her, so it remained a priority with me. During the warmer weather the windows and front door of the Kilnagael's house were wide open, so I sometimes refused to check it for fear that I would get caught. As the autumn progressed, I rarely got to their house before 7:00 in the evening so the mailbox was always empty if I checked it. As the weather turned colder in late October, their front door was usually closed when I arrived, so I could check the mailbox without getting caught. Imagining myself explaining why I was nosing around in their mailbox filled me with such dread that I preferred to skip it than risk being seen. Keeping our secret gave me a constant good excuse for not checking it, but pleasing Colleen gave me a good reason to keep checking it. Besides, the apparent success of our vigilance guarding the mailbox appeared to work since they had not received any bad news about Danny. I actually started to believe that our little covert operation made a difference. Under the cover of cooler weather and growing darkness, I grew more steadfast in my mailbox duties, and missing an opportunity to check it bothered me a bit. If I couldn't make it to check the mailbox, I called Colleen to remind her to do it. She didn't need the reminder but I brought the same sense of urgency to my campaign to romance Colleen that the mayor brought to his campaign for reelection.

While all of this was happening, across town in an Italian neighborhood, a little girl ran into the street chasing a ball. A Chevrolet Impala struck Diana Rizzo, sending her tiny body flying through the air, and slamming it into the side of a parked car. The six-year-old daughter of Mario Rizzo, the Italian man who delivered gasoline to Mickey's American Standard, died on the street in front of her home.

The Last Sunday in Ordinary Time

On the fourth Tuesday evening in October my father left the house wearing a suit. A supervisor at Streets and Sanitation, he never wore a suit to work, reserving the lone suit he owned for Sunday mass, weddings, funerals, and those rare occasions when my parents actually went out on a date. When I asked why he was wearing a suit, he confirmed that he was indeed attending a wake that night for the father of one of his coworkers. A few minutes after he left, Mick called looking for him.

"Marty, put your suit on. You're coming with me. I'll be over fifteen minutes."

Mickey learned of the death of Diana Rizzo only a little while earlier, and feared that the turnout at her wake might be too small. Because Mario was an immigrant, Mickey wondered how many people would know Mario well enough to attend, and had intended to ask both my dad and me to join him in attending the wake. My mom, on hearing the sad story of the little girl told Mick he was doing a nice thing, and told me to go say a Hail Mary for the little 'girleen.' While Mick and I drove over, he discussed a few possibilities.

"If there's not many there, Marty, we will stay a while. I don't think Mario should have to be without friends at time like this. Maybe he has a lot of friends, I don't know. If he does, we'll stay long enough to be seen, and then leave so his crowd can do their thing. I don't know what to expect. If there's a long line to file pass the casket, say a quick Hail Mary, and move on. If there isn't...well, linger a bit and say a prayer or two for Mario as well as his daughter."

The Last Sunday in Ordinary Time

Mickey needn't have worried. The funeral home filled to overflowing, seemingly hundreds of people, many speaking Italian, most of them red-eyed, crying or on the verge of tears. Mickey and I got in the long line of people waiting to pass by the casket, two of the very few non-Italians in attendance. We were not yet in the main room because the line snaked down the hall and nearly out the front door. A young woman in front of us asked how we knew the family.

"I work with Mario Rizzo," Mick told her. "He's a lovely man. I'm heartbroken for him."

"Me, too. She was a delightful little girl, just beautiful. She was in my son's kindergarten class."

"Do you know the family well?"

"Sometimes her mother picked her up from school, sometimes her grandmother did, and sometimes they both did. To see the three of them together..." The woman stopped to regain her composure. "They were just the cutest..., the three of them together."

"Was it her grandmother on the mother's side, or the father's?"

"That's her brother there, that teenager. Poor thing."

We all watched as the boy, about my age, left the salon and headed downstairs, pursued by a man I assumed was his uncle. It looked, from our distance, like he raced to get to the family room before he broke down in front of everyone.

"The grandmother is the mother's mother, I think," she continued. "It must be so hard. On all of them."

It took about fifteen minutes just to reach the doorway into the viewing area. A sign by the door said "Salon A, Rizzo." I had attended

117

only a few wakes before this one, but knew the routine pretty well. The others all were for old people, lying in their embalmed stillness, and, to be honest, not stirring much emotion in me. Nobody I was really close to ever died, so my visitations were more out of good manners than out of mourning. In this room, however, on this night, the sadness enveloped everyone in attendance. As we turned the corner and edged into the salon, the eeriness of the mood grew.

The casket was closed. I guessed that the damaged to her was too great to allow for viewing. The most striking thing, though, was its size. In both length and width, it measured about half of what a normal casket measures. The smallness of it underscored the innocence of the child inside. From across the room it appeared almost small enough to be a baby's.

"Oh, dear God," the woman whispered.

"If that tiny speck of a casket wouldn't break your heart, you don't have one," Mick said.

I could see Mario, handkerchief in hand, gamely greeting those who stopped to say a few words to him. He too looked small. I could see him nodding, shaking hands, accepting hugs, but looking utterly defeated. His wife sat a few feet away, almost hidden among a circle of women who sat by her side, whispering condolences to her. There were other women nearby, grandmothers being tended to by women closer to my mom's age. Mrs. Rizzo sat stonily among the crowd, looking as if she were unaware that anyone else was in the room. Like virtually everyone near the casket, her eyes were red from tears, but her body language otherwise suggested a lack of emotion, a state of shock. So distant did she seem that most of the mourners whispered their condolence to Mario, but left her undisturbed on her island of grief. As the line progressed, I saw another boy run up to Mario, his other son the woman in front of us said. It was an overpoweringly sad picture, and I dreaded having to pass through it. The line continued to edge us closer.

Mick and I took our turn kneeling before the casket. A picture had been placed atop the casket, and it showed a baby-faced little girl with beautiful brown eyes, and two front teeth missing from her smile. I said a Hail Mary and a prayer for the lately departed that Sr. Mary Agnes taught us back in fourth grade, when Katie Walsh's mother died. It had been years since I said that prayer, and I surprised myself a little that I remembered it at all.

> Absolve, we beseech Thee, O Lord
>
> The soul of Thy servant Diana
>
> From every bond of sin,
>
> That being raised in the glory of the resurrection,
>
> She may be refreshed among the Saints and the elect
>
> Through Christ our Lord, Amen.

I waited for Mick to rise and followed him over to Mario.

"Mick." Mickey held his hands out in front of him.

"Mario, my friend, I am so, so sorry for your loss." At six feet, four inches tall, Mick towered over Mario. He moved closer and hugged the grieving father, holding him in his embrace for what seemed like a minute. Much of the crowd took note of it, wondering, I supposed, who this Irishman was. "You know that you and your family are in my prayers."

"Thank you. It was good of you to come."

"You remember, Marty." Mario nodded.

I shook his hand and told him I was sorry for his loss. I hesitated momentarily, expecting him to acknowledge me a little more, but his nod notwithstanding, I realized that he probably didn't recognize me. We moved on and walked to the rear of the room. Mick said we'd wait a moment or two so it didn't look like we were racing out the door. It pleased me that I came. Being there to say a prayer for the soul of little Diana Rizzo was at least a small act of kindness, and may have, in some way, eased the family's grief. It moved me to see all of these people milling about the room, seeming almost desperate to do *something* for Mario or his family. I wished I could do something, but all we could do was be there.

A priest approached the Rizzos, speaking softly to Mario, and then to Mrs. Rizzo. He then turned to the crowd and announced that we would all say some prayers for the repose of the soul of Diana Rizzo. We all made the sign of the cross, and then he began with the Prayer for the Faithful Departed:

O Lord Jesus Christ, King of glory, deliver the souls of all the

Faithful departed from the pains of hell and from the
Bottomless pit; deliver them from the lion's mouth, that
Hell swallow them not up, that they fall not into darkness,
But let the holy standard-bearer Michael bring them into
That holy light which Thou didst promise unto Abraham

and

His seed.

After other wakes I heard people mention that they tried to leave before the prayers started. Once the priest started leading the prayers, those in attendance were stuck until the priest finished, which all depended on the priest. Sometimes they kept the mourners praying for ten minutes, which didn't sound like a lot, but felt like an eternity if you wanted to leave. On this night, however, people welcomed the chance to pray. The priest began an Our Father, and we all joined in just like during the rosaries at Colleen's house. Then he led us in a decade of Hail Mary's. As we prayed I looked around the room and admired the level of concentration the people showed. All of these people wanting to show the Rizzos that their friends and neighbors shared their grief, and this moment of prayer offered the proof. I was never more proud to be Catholic than at that moment. The Church, I thought, really was there when people need it most.

The priest standing before the casket reminded me of Fr. Connolly a little bit, not physically, but by his presence. He showed both a take-charge attitude, quite literally leading us in prayer, and also a level of compassion that I found comforting, and I assumed that it comforted Mario's family as well, at least a little bit. I found myself, as time when by, more and more impressed by the way priests handled themselves. A couple of weeks earlier I ate dinner with Fr. Connolly at the Kilnagael's house. Mr. Kilnagael asked him if he had ever met Monsignor O'Brien, the long-time pastor of Holy Truth.

"I did actually meet him once. I was with another priest, Fr. Gerald McGovern, an old friend of the monsignor's. Fr. McGovern introduced us. Afterward I remember him saying 'Monsignor O'Brien is the real McCoy. He's what a Catholic priest is supposed to be.' He was, too. He had the twinkle in his eye, and the charming smile."

"Don't let that smile fool you," Mr. Kilnagael said. "He knew how to throw his weight around, and if you got out of line, Msgr. O'Brien would take you out to the wood shed."

"I'll bet he would. Even in the few minutes I spoke to him I could see beyond the humble parish priest routine. He might kick his toe in the dirt and claim all humility, but you knew he was a man who was definitely in charge. Fr. McGovern was right. Msgr. O'Brien was the type of priest we all wanted to be; the kindly but stern master of his parish."

Watching this other priest now, I thought he also seemed like a proper priest, like what a priest was supposed to be. I thought that if I ever became one, he was the type of priest I would want to be.

During the prayer session an Italian woman eased her way through the crowd so that she ended up standing just a few feet in front of Mickey and me. While the prayers continued, I had the chance to get a good look at her, and thought she was beautiful, one of the most beautiful women I had ever seen. She wore, like virtually every other woman in the room, a black dress, and high heels. Her dress, though, was rather tight, and showed what a great figure she had. It wasn't that it was low cut or anything like that, and on another woman it would have revealed only a small area of skin below her neck, but on this woman it did offer a tiny glimpse of the top of her rather large breasts. In all honesty, she could have worn a potato sack and still looked sexy. I needed to make an effort not to stare. When the prayers were completed she turned to Mickey.

"Are you a friend of Mario's?"

"Yes," Mick answered, "I'm Mickey Riordan. I own one of the gas stations that Mario delivers to. This is my nephew, Marty."

"Hello, Marty, hello, Mickey, it's nice to meet you. I'm Tina Avelini, one of Mario's cousins. It was very thoughtful of you to come."

"Well, I've worked with Mario for a number of years. He's a good man. I can't believe how awful this all is."

As the two of them talked, we could sense the eyes of others around the room looking at us. Apparently they appreciated our willingness to mourn the loss of Mario's daughter, but that didn't give Mickey license to talk to their women. An older man joined us in our little group.

"Tina, who is your friend?" the man asked.

"Papa, this is Mickey Riordan and his nephew, Marty. He came by my office a few weeks ago. He's thinking about buying a house in Elmwood Park." As she said this she rested her hand on Mick's stomach, a move that her father definitely noticed. Mick and I knew she was lying, but we went along with her, and said nothing. "I didn't know that he knew Mario, and I was thanking him for coming tonight."

At that point her father said something in Italian which I guessed was keep your hands to yourself. She made a face and said something back to him. She then turned her attention back to Mickey and me.

"I think I may have found the house you're looking for," she said, and reached into her purse for a pair of business cards. "Now, I want you to call me and let me show it to you. It's perfect for you." She handed a card to Mickey, and one to me to polite I guessed, which was odd because handing out business cards struck me as a rude thing to do at a wake. "And, thank you for coming tonight. It was very kind of you."

Even after she walked away the crowd kept looking at us. Mickey suggested it was a good time for us to leave. As we walked out the door I read her business card. *Avelini Real Estate   We'll make you right at home.*

"Are you really looking for a house in Elmwood Park?"

"No." Mickey said it in a tone that suggested it was a ridiculous question. "I don't know what that was all about. I guess the Italians like to keep a tight rein on their daughters. She probably had to make up a story just to placate her father."

We both remained very quiet on the ride home. I don't know what Mickey was thinking about, about I was thinking about Mrs. Rizzo and Mrs. Kilnagael. Up until that moment I never gave much thought to the idea that Danny Kilnagael might actually die, but now I thought, "What if he does?" Seeing the paralyzing grief, the devastating sense of loss that Mrs. Rizzo experienced at the loss of her daughter made me fearful for Colleen's mom. I also thought about Fr. Connolly, and all of the attention he paid to her. Seeing the priest at the wake tonight and Fr. Connolly at the Kilnagael's house gave me a new perspective on how important priests could be to people in their times of need.

At the beginning of the school year, Br. Timothy O'Toole called me and five other guys down to his office to discuss whether we had a vocation, a calling to either the priesthood or the brotherhood. It was kind of an awkward discussion since none of us really wanted to be priests, but we also didn't want to insult him either. After carefully tiptoeing around the subject of celibacy for a while, Charlie Finnegan finally decided he had enough.

"I'm sorry, Bro," he said, "but I've gotta have some pussy."

There was a momentary look of shock on all our faces, but then Br. O'Toole smiled, and we all erupted in laughter. Obviously I shared Finnegan's attitude, and I left that meeting thinking that I had left any thought of entering the priesthood behind me. Apparently I gave more thought to the priesthood than most guys did. Later I talked to Finnegan about it and congratulated him on having the guts to say what we all were thinking.

"Yeah," I said, "I may have considered the priesthood a little bit, but I plan to have a beautiful wife, a dozen kids, and one of the biggest houses Holy Truth."

He scoffed and said "Are you planning to stay in Holy Truth? I think I'd rather become a priest. At least they'd send me somewhere else."

"What's wrong with Holy Truth?"

"The rest of America lives somewhere else. Why would you want to stay here when there is so much more out there."

"Not for me. I think Holy Truth is a perfect neighborhood, and I can't think of a better place for to live."

"Oh, please. Holy Truth is the place where Satan farted. I'm planning to live somewhere else, California maybe. Any place is better than here."

It shocked me to learn that everyone didn't share my romantic view of what a great place Holy Truth was. The meeting with Br. Timothy did cause me to think about becoming a priest for a few minutes. It wasn't that I suddenly changed my mind, and suddenly desired to be a priest; it was just that the decision wasn't quite as one-sided as it had been.

In any event, during the ride home I decided to make more of an effort to concern myself with the Kilnagael's welfare. I wasn't going to become a priest, but I would try to think about them a little more. Most of the actions I took with the Kilnagaels were for my benefit, but now I resolved to be less selfish, and more genuine in my concern for Colleen's family.

The Last Sunday in Ordinary Time

The Twenty Second Sunday in Ordinary Time

If You Can't Stand the Cold, Stay Out of the Ward

October 30, 1966

The church bulletin, *The Holy Truth,* added a new wrinkle in October. It may have been done to please the Kilnagaels, or it may have been done to please those who were growing tired of the Kilnagaels. For whatever reason, the bulletin now asked parishioners to pray for the men who were in the military during a time of war. Actually, the government remained reluctant to call it a war up to that point, but that's what we all called it. The first time the item ran five names appeared, a fact that surprised me a bit since I thought Danny Kilnagael remained the first and only guy from our parish in the army. That common misconception contributed to a building resentment others held because they believed Danny garnered too much attention and sympathy at the expense of others. The second week it appeared, the list of names grew to eight, including, to my surprise, Brendan Ward, one of the guys on Stage Irish. The next time I saw Eddie Mulroney I asked him about it. He told me that Brendan kept it a secret until the last minute, so everyone was surprised. Brendan left for boot camp a few days earlier, and hadn't even been gone two weeks yet.

In mid October the weather turned mild again, and the Stage Irish t-shirts with Danny's name remained a common sight. Uncle Charlie called over to the gas station and asked Mick if he could borrow me for a few minutes. Mr. Lally, one of the older men who frequented the bar had too much to drink and needed a ride home. Charlie wanted me to drive him home, so Mick sent me over, and Charlie and I helped him to Charlie's car in back. Mr. Lally turned ugly, verbally abusing anyone who said anything to him, even my uncle. When I arrived, he tried to pick a fight with me.

"To hell with Danny Kilnagael, you hear me, to hell with him."

"Come on, John," Charlie said, "let's get in the car. Atta boy. There you go."

"He's not so special. Act like he's the only guy who ever joined the army. To hell with him."

We worked to guide him to the front seat, but he kept stopping, intentionally hesitating, insisting that he was okay. We finally got him to the door, but he stood there, certain that he needed to add something to what he had already said. He repeated that Danny Kilnagael was not the only guy to join the army, and was telling us Danny could go to hell one more time before we finally got him in and shut the door. Uncle Charlie gave me his address, and told me to deliver him to the back door. His wife called for him to come home, and didn't want him making a scene in front of the neighbors.

"I'll tell you this, Marty, I'll tell you this right now. Nobody ever gave Jimmy a t-shirt. Where's Jimmy's t-shirt?"

"Who's Jimmy? Is he from Holy Truth?"

"See." He said. "You don't even know who Jimmy is. Jimmy was a good boy." He nodded very knowingly, like he had put me in my place.

The Last Sunday in Ordinary Time

"Jimmy was a good boy." He repeated that Jimmy was a good boy several times during the short ride home until we reached the alley behind his house, but never told me who Jimmy was. I walked around the car and helped him to his feet. By this time his mood changed and he became much more mild. I put his arm around my shoulders and the two of us walked toward the backdoor, where Mrs. Lally waited impatiently. She wanted him inside before the neighbors got too much of a show.

"You're a good boy, too, Marty. A good boy too."
The closer we got to the back stairs, the weaker he became, but we made it. I tried to help him up the stairs, but he refused my help, insisting that he was okay now. He wasn't. There were five stairs, but by the time he reached the top one, he was crawling. His wife held the door open for him, and he actually crawled through it like a baby. I made eye contact with her, and could see that she was humiliated. She thanked me for bringing him home. I wanted to assure her that I wouldn't tell anyone, but thought it would only make things worse for her. I said you're welcome and left quickly.

When I got back to the car I thought about "Jimmy," and who that might be. Out of curiosity I drove by Our Lady of Holy Truth, and stopped in front of the war memorial there. Erected at the end of World War II, the memorial was a statue of St. Joseph above a plaque that listed the name of every parishioner who died in World Wars I & II. I scanned the names and there it was: James Lally, 1944. Jimmy was the son he lost twenty-two years earlier. Until that moment I never realized that people like Mr. Lally still mourned the loss of sons and brothers, maybe even husbands, who died during World War II. No wonder they resented the attention we paid to Danny Kilnagael. Like Mr. Lally said, he wasn't the first guy to join the army.

If Fr. Connolly was trying to balance things out between the people who supported Danny and the people who resented him, I figured that the bulletin list was good start. I also knew that the Kilnagaels made themselves heard in all situations. Mrs. K continued to join the Ladies of St. Theresa every week, and, as one of the younger women in the group, began taking a larger role in their activities. With each passing week she reclaimed much of the assertiveness that disappeared when Danny shipped out. She joined them at Fr. Connolly's request with them knowing she needed their support to get through a tough time. After a while it became hard to tell if the others were giving Mrs. Kilnagael more authority, or if she were taking it. Like the situation with Mr. Lally, resentment grew as some began to feel that she failed to realize that they all had sons who also went to war, but not all of them saw their sons return.

The Kilnagaels possessed strong personalities, and despite the seeming helplessness of Mrs. Kilnagael at the start, she remained a woman who generally got what she wanted. Colleen also knew how to get what she wanted. I realized that she manipulated me sometimes, but I didn't mind because I wanted the acceptance of the Kilnagaels more than anything else. I wondered if Fr. Connolly thought they manipulated him. He certainly gave them a fair amount of attention, and seemed pleased to do so. Did he hear the same complaints about Danny Kilnagael that I heard? Whatever choices he made, they seem to be the right ones. As a pastor he enjoyed much more respect and approval than the Polack priest ever received, and managed to avoid angering any significant group within the parish.

He put his balancing act between doing what he thought he should and doing what the parishioners wanted to the test on October 30th, the twenty second Sunday in ordinary time. The Chicago American's star columnist, Roy Cannon, wrote a series of columns criticizing the people of our ward. Cannon enjoyed his reputation for stirring things up, and making everyone, from Mayor Daley down to the average blue collar Joe Six-pack, angry. Generally he sided with whoever possessed the least amount of power, but he primarily aimed make the most people complain. Even though most of the press moved on from Mugsy O'Bannion's comments about the Negro marchers, Cannon couldn't let it rest. In his column, "Cannon Fire," he wrote about the people of our ward under the title, "If You Can't Take the Cold, Stay Out of the Ward."

Mayor Daley orchestrated an almost universal silence about the idea that the marchers being too afraid to march down the streets in our parish. No aldermen or precinct captains said so much as a single controversial word about racial tension, so the issue dried up, or so we thought. Cannon sent his researchers into Holy Truth to "find out what the people thought." The responses were all over the map, some people being very careful about what they said, and others speaking with a defiant bravado. The column told of the man who said "I ain't prejudiced. I just hate Coloreds," which caused a great burst of laughter among the crowd gathered around. Others never tried to be light-hearted, avowing "We don't want those people here. They don't belong." Several people offered that they weren't bigots, but..." Those buts were followed by comments that strained to explain why it wasn't fair that their homes and neighborhoods should be violated in this way. What did we ever do to the Negroes? The column made it seem that everyone in the ward thought the Negroes were picking on us, a neighborhood of hardworking people who were just doing their jobs and wanted no trouble. Cannon saved his favorite comment for last. One man said with confidence that the "Coloreds won't come march here because it's too cold, and they don't like the cold." This was his chance to mock the people he wrote about, and praise the courage of the Negro marchers.

They haven't backed down from fire hoses and attacking police dogs

in Alabama, Ku Klux Klansmen in Georgia, or rock throwers in Chicago.

If you think they're afraid of a little cold weather, you're out of your minds. With only a few days left before the election, there isn't

time to plan a march through O'Bannion's ward. Besides, it's never

that cold on the first Tuesday in November anyway.

Now, the Saturday before Christmas, that's another story.

This year Christmas falls on a Sunday, which means that last shopping

day of the year is Saturday, December 24th, Christmas Eve. I bet no

matter how cold it gets, it won't be too cold for Chicago's Negro-Americans to take a leisurely stroll along Madison Avenue.

The Last Sunday in Ordinary Time

That Sunday Fr. Connolly began his homily with a Jewish joke.

"One day a Jew walked up to the counter and asked for an order of bagels and lox. The man behind the counter says 'We don't have any bagels and lox.' The next day the same Jew walks up to the counter and again asks for bagels and lox, and the man again says 'We don't have bagels and lox. The third day the Jew again walks up to the counter and orders bagels and lox, and again the man says 'We don't have bagels and lox. Finally, on the fourth day the Jew again orders bagels and lox, and the man behind the counter says 'We don't have bagels and lox.' The Jew says 'I come in here day after day and ask you for bagels and lox, but you never have it. Why don't you have bagels and lox? Do you hate Jews?'

"The man behind the counter says 'We don't have anything against Jews. The problem is that this is a hardware store, not a deli.'"

The joke got a pretty good laugh, though most of it was more out of politeness than because it was not all that funny. When a priest told a joke, we generally gave him points for trying.

"Today's gospel," Fr. Connolly continued, "told the story of the servant who owed his king 10,000 talents. In order to settle the account the king ordered the man, his wife, and their children to be sold. The servant begged the king for patience, and promised he would repay the debt in full. The king, moved with compassion, released the man from his debt. Later the man who received the compassion met a fellow servant who in turn owed the original servant a lesser amount, but when the fellow servant asked for compassion and more time to repay it, the request was refused. The lucky man who had been forgiven a large debt refused to extend that same compassion to another man, and had his fellow servant thrown into prison. When the king heard of this hypocrisy, he rescinded the order, and had the man and his family sold to repay the 10,000 talents.

"Jesus tells us that Our Heavenly Father is like that king. He is kind and merciful to us, and he expects us to be kind and merciful as well. Our ability to be kind and merciful will soon be put to the test. In the news recently there has been talk of Negroes considering a march through Our Lady of Holy Truth. People, good people who would otherwise not raise a hand in anger at another human being, are talking of 'defending' the parish from these marchers. Now we are like the man who works at the hardware store. Even if he wanted to please the unfortunate Jew, he didn't have the ability to do so. Likewise, we may soon have Negroes marching through our neighborhood looking for...looking for...well, to be honest, I'm not sure what they're looking for. But what can we give them? You'll notice that the man in the hardware store did not call the Jew a fool, he did not get angry, and he most certainly did not have the man thrown out of the store. We have nothing to give these marchers, except,..." At this point the priest pointed his finger in the air to emphasize the importance of his next word. "Patience. If we remain patient, they will realize they can't find what they're looking for here and move on.

"So," he continued, "I urge you to relax. Remember Jesus's advice about casting stones. No one here should be the first to hurl an insult, let alone cast a stone. If we ignore them, they will go away."

The Last Sunday in Ordinary Time

It was a well-received homily. As for the joke, a few people said they heard that same joke as a Polack joke about a pair of shoes. We did have some Polish people living in the parish, so he probably changed it to a Jew to keep from offending anybody. In any event, unlike the "holy Polack" who aggravated the parish by lecturing about tolerance, Fr. Connolly spoke of what *we* needed to do. He was one of us. For my part, my admiration for him grew. Every time I saw him in action, whether at the Kilnagael's house, running the parish, or giving a homily like the one he gave that Sunday, he struck me as a very capable priest.

The Twenty Third Sunday in Ordinary Time

Exit Stage Irish

November 6, 1966

With the end of October came the end of the softball season. The

decision to sponsor Stage Irish proved to be a profitable one because of all the business the team brought to the tavern. Eddie Mulroney and his friends frequented the Lovely Bit of Blarney and spent a lot of time and money there. They apparently spent very little time practicing because they finished second to last in an eight team league. Eddie brought in a small chalk board on which he updated the league standings after every game.

Della's Fellas	16	0
Plumb Crazy	12	4
Hitless Wonders	11	5
Long Doggies	9	7
Curly Buthair's	7	9
CLAP II	5	11
Stage Irish	3	13
Booze Train	1	15

Della's Fellas, the team sponsored by Exton's Tavern, defeated Plumb Crazy in a best-of-three playoff for the championship. Plumb Crazy was the only team not sponsored by a bar. The father of one their players, a guy named Barnicle, talked his father into sponsoring the team, so they had Barnicle Plumbing on the back of their shirts, and Plumb Crazy on the front. The name I really liked was Curly Buthair's. They actually wanted to spell it 'Curly Butthair's,' but the league had a fifteen letter limit on names, including spaces and apostrophes. They were sponsored by Curly's Tap, but Eddie told me the owner actually wanted to call the place Curly Butthair's Tap. The alderman decided that name was too vulgar for public display on a sign, so he held their liquor license up until the name was changed. Their t-shirts featured a little cartoon picture of Curly. The last place team, Booze Train, got their only win by forfeit against the Hitless Wonders, allowing Plumb Crazy to finish in second place.

No one took greater pleasure in Stage Irish's ineptitude than Seamus Touhy. When they returned to the Lovely Bit after yet another loss, Seamus made a point of asking every one of them what the score was. He wanted to know if it were too late for Charlie to get his money back, asked about the slaughter rule, and insisted that the White Sox were on the phone right now, asking if any of the Stage Irish players were available to play on the South Side. The guys took it all in pretty good spirit I thought.

As the weather cooled, we saw fewer and fewer of the Stage Irish shirts around the neighborhood, but Danny Kilnagael remained an unofficial hero of the neighborhood. If anything, both his popularity and the animosity toward his popularity continued to grow. His mother, with the help of Fr. Connolly's friendship and guidance, regained her take-charge personality, but now she started using it to keep Danny in the minds of the other parishioners. The listing of the active soldiers' names in the bulletin continued, and Fr. Connolly named her as the contact point for adding names. It was quickly noted that Danny's name was listed first, and all others were in alphabetical order. My mother told me she heard a woman complaining that Mrs. Kilnagael started thinking she was Our Lady of Holy Truth herself.

At about this same time Colleen started complaining that I never went to church with her. I explained that my parents expected me to attend church with them, so it was hard for me to ignore them to go to mass with her. Colleen sang every Sunday at the 9:30 teen mass which was held in the church basement. It was the "cool" mass that the high school and college kids attended, featuring guitars instead of the organ, and the young people's choir that she sang with. She wasn't buying my story.

"Oh, come on, Marty. You're sixteen for God's sake. Quit being such a mama's boy." She said this in front of her father, who smiled and winked at me.

"Don't look at me. Any guy who isn't at least a little bit afraid of his mother is either a liar or a fool."

It was the way of the Kilnagaels. Colleen wanted me at that mass, and she wouldn't stop pushing until she got what she wanted. Like her mother, Colleen and her sisters had pushed the cause of Danny to be a part of the teen mass, and forced everyone else to belatedly add the names of others. Most of the time, what the Kilnagaels wanted paralleled what others felt was good for Holy Truth. The desire to make praying for Danny such a high priority, though, struck many of their fellow parishioners as a little self-serving. It also struck me that, for maybe the first time in their lives, they, as a group, faced grumbling from others in response, but the Kilnagael sisters were deaf to it.

Colleen gave me an ultimatum. The young people's choir received an invitation to sing at all of the regular masses on Sunday, November 16th. She told me she expected me to be at the 7:00 mass that Sunday to hear them sing or, if not, maybe we should stop seeing each other. I tried not to panic, but I couldn't see how I could tell my parents I was going to church without them. The "mama's boy" comment struck a nerve with me, and made me think that sneaking out of the house early would prove that I really was a mama's boy after all. The one thing I knew for certain was that I wanted to keep dating Colleen, so I had to be at the 7:00 mass, and I had less than two weeks to figure out how.

The election took place on Tuesday, November 1st. Because Illinois law forbade the sale of alcohol on Election Day, The Lovely Bit O'Blarney was closed. My dad told me that election days also served to let you know where you stood in the Democratic Party by the invitation you got to drink in somebody's house. The highest honor, of course, was the invitation to join Mayor Daley in his home while you waited for the election returns. Only the most inside of insiders got invited to do that.

Below that on the pecking order were ward committeemen, county office holders, alderman, judges, and various high level city workers. My dad always got invited to Uncle Charlie's because for family reasons as much as political ones, but most precinct captains like him usually had to work on several elections before receiving a first invitation. If you wanted a job with the city you had to pay your dues as a precinct captain for a few years, or get very lucky. Many men grew tired of waiting for the job offer to come, so quit acting as precinct captains long before an election night invitation came.

On that Tuesday I ran into Seamus Touhy on Madison as I got off the bus from school. With the Lovely Bit closed for the election, he was a man with nowhere to go, and nothing to do. He didn't say as much, but I got the impression he came by the bar even though it was closed, hoping to run into my Uncle Charlie, and get invited to the party.

"Seamus, did you do the right and proper thing and vote Democratic?"

"I can't vote. I'm not a citizen."

"Really?" I regretted the level of surprise in my voice immediately. It sounded like I accused him of doing something wrong. I tried to soften it, and give him a graceful way out. "Too much love of the auld sod, huh? You couldn't break ties with Mother Ireland?"

"No, nothing like that. I haven't too many fond memories of my youth. It was a nasty place back then. I couldn't wait to leave, to be honest with you."

"I thought you loved Ireland."

"When I left there, Marty, 'twas terrible with civil war and poverty. People shooting each other over the most minor things. I thought it would never change. I left forty-five years ago, as quickly as I could. We use to say about Mayo, "'Tis beautiful. Take a picture before you leave.' I haven't been back since. I suppose it's changed enough, now, but still, I have no desire to go back."

As we walked along he asked if I had seen my Uncle Charlie, and of course I hadn't because I was in school all day. He looked uncertain that day, which was unusual for him, and seemed lonely. I felt sorry for him because he seemed like a man without a country, not wanting to be an Irishman, and never becoming an American. I waited with him at the bus stop and we chatted a little while longer until the bus came. It dawned on me as the bus pulled away that he rode the bus out of the parish. He wasn't even a member of Holy Truth. When I mentioned that to my mother later she said "He sure sounds like a lost soul, doesn't he?"

The Last Sunday in Ordinary Time

The polls closed at 6:00, but my dad, like all of the polling place workers, stayed to finish paperwork, count the ballots, and turn in the totals. He stopped in at home about 9:00, but stayed only long enough to eat dinner. His next stop was at Uncle Charlie's house to report the vote totals at his polling place, and to wait for the overall totals, and to celebrate the end of another election day. The news, he told Mom and me, was not good so far.

"Ogilvie is running very strong. They don't want to turn the state's attorney's office over to the Republicans. Everybody is sweating their jobs. Ogilvie only got 10% in my precinct, thank God."

If I had been talking to my Uncle Charlie, he would have said, "*We* don't want to turn the state's attorney's office over to the Republicans." My dad always said *they*. Even though his job depended on the continued success of the Daley machine, Dad always maintained a sort of psychological distance between himself and the harsh political reality of his low place in the party. When I was younger I used to hope that they would ask my dad to run for office someday, imagining him becoming Alderman Donovan or Commissioner Donovan, but eventually I realized that he was a peon. He did what he had to do to keep his job, but never stuck his neck out, or showed any ambition. As he walked out the door I couldn't help but think that neither Mickey Riordan nor Mr. Kilnagael would have allowed themselves to be pushed around the way my dad was.

For example, a few days earlier, I heard Mickey telling a man from Standard Oil to "get the hell out of my gas station." The company man had come by and told Mickey that campaign posters were not to be displayed in Standard gas stations. Mickey told me he put posters in his gas station window for years, and nobody ever said a word to him. Now, all of a sudden, it violated company standards. The complaint actually had nothing to do with politics, and everything to do with money. The franchise agreement with Standard Oil dated back to 1925, and ran for fifty years. Mickey bought the building and the franchise from the original owner in 1954, and now learned that Standard really didn't want to renew it or wait for it to expire in 1975. A change in management philosophy called for the company to own as many stations as possible outright, and they stopped issuing new franchises many years earlier. The issue about the campaign posters struck Mickey as a phony one, the first step in making a case for taking control of Mickey's American Standard.

Not more than ten minutes after that guy left, Mickey was on the phone with the local contacts for Sinclair, Gulf, and Clark, three other oil companies who might extend a franchise to him. In a more muted anger he told me "I never needed Standard more than they needed me." I didn't take it too seriously because I couldn't imagine the gas station being anything other than a Standard.

Colleen and I stood outside Galway Lady Irish Imports looking in the window. Mom's birthday was in a couple of days and I needed to get her a gift. My parents were very plain people, so the Irish import store became my failsafe place for buying them presents. If I couldn't decide on anything else I always got Mom a tin of Irish cookies or some little trinket for the kitchen for her birthday. I bought Dad cookies or boxes of loose tea for his birthday. My parents, as kind of an act petty snobbery, refused to use tea bags. I assumed they never used them growing up in

Ireland and so refused to use them here. Over the past couple of years I started drinking tea after dinner just like my parents did, but I never got used to the tea leaves that ended up in the bottom of my cup. The tea leaves never seemed to bother Mom or Dad, but I hated having to spit them out if I didn't pay attention. One day at the Kilnagaels, they served me tea without either tea leaves or a tea bag. They actually had these little round metal balls that were covered with holes. They filled them with loose tea and put them into the bottom of the teapot. The tea was great and I didn't have to worry about tea leaves. I knew right away that I was going to get Mom for her birthday. I kept calling them those "tea leaf thingies," but Colleen corrected me, telling they were called infusers. We decided to walk over to the Irish import store because I was sure they'd have the tea leaf thingies there.

It was a tiny store that had things jammed into every available space. Along one wall there were record albums, mostly the Clancy Brothers, the Chieftains, and collections of fiddle music, jigs and reels. There was also a small selection of ash trays, tea cups, coffee mugs and decorative plates. I picked up a wooden ash tray that featured a picture of the Irish countryside on it, but when I looked at the bottom of it, a sticker said 'Made in Japan.' Most of it was novelty stuff, with sayings like "You can always tell an Irishman but you can't tell him much." Behind the counter they kept some Waterford crystal and Belleek china, very expensive stuff that some people liked to collect. I paused to consider getting her something like that, but they all seemed like old lady gifts.

I told the lady behind the counter what I wanted to get for Dad and she walked us over to a spot where they sold tins of cookies, boxes of tea, orange marmalade and other jars of jelly all imported from Ireland. She also had a couple of kettles and a couple of teapots. There, in the middle of all of that stuff were the tea leaf infuser things, packages of two holey metal shamrocks with short chains that allowed you to drop them into the teapot and then use the chain to pull them out when the tea was strong enough. They were exactly what I wanted.

Colleen was looking through some t-shirts when she held up one that said *Kiss me, I'm Irish*. She told me to ask the lady if they had one that said 'Forgive me, I'm Irish,' and while she went back to looking at the rest of them I could see her laughing at her own joke. She really got a kick out of it. I wandered over to the register to pay for some tea leaves, cookies, and the infusers. Because I was now a working man I could afford to be a big spender and get Dad all three of them. Colleen joined me at the register and commented on the cable knit sweaters that were stacked on a shelf behind the counter below a sign that said 'Hand knit in Ireland.'

"I love those sweaters," she said.

The lady pulled one of the sweaters down and unfolded it on the counter.

"They're lovely, aren't they?" she said. "Hand-knitted in Ireland."

She pulled down a second one and unfolded it as well.

"Do you see how different they are? Each one has a different pattern. Years ago in Ireland, each family had its own pattern. They are a lovely, quaint piece of Irish tradition. There are stories of drowning victims washing ashore, and they could only be identified by the sweater that was still on the body, that's how important they were. A sweater like this will not only keep your sweetheart warm, it will always remind her of you."

With that she looked at me and winked. I looked over at Colleen who was running her fingers over the thick wool of one of the sweaters. I immediately knew what to get her for Christmas. The sweaters were expensive, but I was convinced that one of them was the right gift for her. The more I studied it the more I convinced myself that it was. I pictured her standing in front of a Christmas tree wearing one, and telling all her friends I bought it for her. I liked the idea of people seeing as Colleen'

The Last Sunday in Ordinary Time

The Twenty Fourth Sunday in Ordinary Time

All of the Drama of an Italian Opera

The Last Sunday in Ordinary Time

November 13, 1966

A taste for higher culture separated the Kilnagaels from the ordinary people in Holy Truth, at least in my eyes. For example, Mrs. Kilnagael purchased season tickets to the opera every year, and then attended it every month throughout the winter. Mr. and Mrs. Kilnagael attended the opening show, and then she took a different one of her kids to each new opera as the season went on. Maybe more than her sisters, Colleen actually liked the opera, and the pomp and circumstance that went with it. On opening night some of Chicago's wealthiest or more famous people stepped out of limousines dressed in tuxedos and elegant furs. The women wore expensive jewelry and formal gowns, delighting in walking the red carpet the way Hollywood stars did on Oscar night.

For Mrs. Kilnagael a night at the opera included dinner downtown, so she and one of her children dressed up for the occasion and dined at a very nice restaurant downtown. From there they took a taxi to Orchestra Hall and watched some of the beautiful people step out of Cadillacs, hand their car keys to the valet, and then make a grand entrance. The women, Colleen told me, played dress up for every performance, but the men usually only wore tuxedos on opening night. I assumed that neither Mr. Kilnagael nor Danny ever enjoyed the "fashion show" as much as the girls did, but Mrs. Kilnagael always insisted on staying outside long enough to admire the outfits the people wore. They went inside and found their seats only after the parade of beautiful people slowed down.

"We're standing there," Colleen told me, "and this beautiful, long, black Cadillac Coupe de Ville pulls up, and this Italian woman gets out. Let me tell you, she was beautiful. As she swung her legs out her dress rode up a little so she was showing a lot of leg as she stepped out of the car, and I'm sure all the guys watching were getting an eyeful. She stands up, and she's incredible. She must have been about five-foot-nine to begin with, but she's wearing some serious high heels, so I figure she's got to be six feet tall. And she's wearing kind of a low cut dress, showing off her big boobs, like people wouldn't see 'em anyway. If you were standing next to her and she turned suddenly, she might poke your eye out with one of those things. I honestly think she might have been the most beautiful woman I've ever seen. Then my mom goes 'Isn't that Mickey Riordan getting out of that car?' "And it was! Mickey Riordan drives a Cadillac and is dating this insanely beautiful Italian woman."

"I think you're wrong. Mick doesn't own a Cadillac."

"I'm not *wrong.*" When Colleen felt I didn't take her seriously, she put me in my place in a hurry. She exaggerated the word wrong in a way that accused me of being rude and disrespectful.

"I'm telling you," she continued, "I saw Mickey Riordan at the opera. He was driving a black Cadillac, and his date was this stunning Italian woman."

"Tina Avellini."

"You know her?"

"Well, not exactly. Remember a couple of weeks ago Mickey and I went to that wake for the little Italian girl? At that wake this woman walked up to Mick and introduced herself. She was the girl's aunt or cousin, or something."

"Oh, that's very nice. Poor parents are heartbroken over their poor child's death, and Mickey Riordan's using the wake to pick up women."

"He didn't do anything like that. She approached him. Her family started watching them like the way your father might react if a Dago came into your house and started talking to one of your sisters. She ended up giving Mick and me one of her business cards. She's a real estate agent. That's how I remember her name."

"Well, he's dating her whether her family likes it or not."

I wasn't the only one Colleen told about Mickey and the Italian woman. The Kilnagaels spread the word spread quickly, and everyone was talking about it. The news about Mick dating an Italian was too exciting not to share. The following Saturday evening I took my lunch break and stopped in at the Lovely Bit. The minute I walked in the door Eddie Mulroney was on me, wanting to know if it was true.

"What does she look like?"

I cupped my hands in front of my chest to indicate she had big breasts.

"I knew it," Eddie said. "Those Dago broads, that's the way they are, I swear to God. They all got big noses and big boobs. Hey, Mr. McCarthy, you were in Italy in World War II. You ever nail a Dago broad?"

"If I did, I wouldn't tell you."

"You did, didn't you? I knew it. What's going on here? Mick's nailing an Italian broad. Mr. McCarthy was nailing Dago chicks back in World War II. I mean, come on. Italian broads?"

A discussion broke out about the relative attractiveness of Italian women. Somebody mentioned Sophia Loren, another guy mentioned Claudia Cardinale, and everyone pretty much agreed that there were some very sexy Italians. Mr. Tracy wondered if Raquel Welch were Irish, but Eddie said no, she was "Spanish or something."

"If you had to, would you rather nail a Polish broad, and an Italian broad?" He looked at me.

"I don't know," bewildered by the question.

"The thing about Polacks is they tend to be too skinny. You're like, hey, babe, eat some more kielbasa, or something. So on one hand, you got your dago, big nose, big boobs, and probably a big butt too. On the other hand, you got a good looking, flat-chested Polack, but she probably has blond hair and blue eyes, which I kind of like. I don't know."

"I wouldn't worry about it if I were you, Eddie," Mr. McCarthy said. "There probably isn't enough vodka in Warsaw to a get a girl drunk enough to want to have sex with you."

"Is that why you come in here, Marty?" Seamus asked. "To listen to drunken Irishmen talk about Dagos and Polacks and other women who wouldn't so much as kiss them?"

"Eddie's not Irish, he's American."

"True enough, but it doesn't explain why you come in here. It doesn't explain why you come in here at all."

I pointed to the front window.

"I just want a genuine taste of Ireland, like it says on the sign."

"Well, that makes sense. The Irish kid who's not really Irish at all, but an American, visits his uncle's bar, who isn't his uncle at all, to have a drink which isn't a drink at all but only a Coke, and then dates his Irish girlfriend who isn't Irish at all, but an American, a girl, mind you whose name is Colleen which isn't a name at all, and then eats a hamburger of all things because he wants a genuine taste of Ireland, but doesn't have the sense to at least put a slice of raw onion on it to make even the tiniest bit Irish. Do I have that right, Marty? Or maybe Marty isn't your name at all, you just think it's your name?"

"I think you pretty much have it right," I said.

"Uncle Charlie," Seamus called with glee. "Young Marty here, your supposed nephew, would like a genuine taste of Ireland. Do you have a plate of spaghetti for the man? He wouldn't know the difference between a potato and a pineapple, and he thinks hamburgers are Irish."

"In the Lovely Bit O' Blarney Pub, hamburgers are Irish," Charlie told him.

"Now that is a most unusual name for a tavern, isn't it? The Lovely Bit O' Blarney Pub. How did you ever come up with a name like that?"

"It comes from something my grandmother told me years ago in Ireland. My grandfather was a bit of a silver-tongued devil, quite the ladies' man in his day, I was told. He was always going on about how beautiful my granny was, 'the most beautiful flower in all Ireland' he called her, especially when she was in a foul mood. One day when I was visiting them just before I left for America, Granny was fierce angry at him, going on and on about something he did. He responded with his usual flattering, telling her how beautiful she was, she looked the same as the day he first met her and so on. Finally she ended up chasing him out of the house with a broom.

"When she came back in the house she looked at me. 'He's a divil, that one,' she said. ''Tis all blarney.' She winked at me, smiled, and said 'But what a lovely bit o' blarney it is.' I always liked that phrase: What a lovely bit o' blarney it is."

"She was a clever woman, your granny. She knew better than this lot. They all call the place the Lovely Bit. They all come in to drink their Irish Meister Brau's, eat their Irish hamburgers, listen to Irish Frank Sinatra on the juke box, and enjoy a genuine taste of Ireland. Never mind the blarney. They're too busy enjoying the lovely bit to remember that it's all blarney."

For Fr. Connolly it proved to be a very successful summer. He followed Mickey's advice about paying more attention to the elderly while at the same time allowing Fr. Doyle to work with the younger parishioners. One example of the Fr. Doyle's success emerged from the very popular young people's choir, a success partly due to the Kilnagaels. Both Colleen and her younger sister Noreen joined the choir, and their popularity caused other girls to join as well. The high concentration of the more popular girls in the parish inspired some of the guys to join, so the choir became the place to be. As a reward for the success of the choir, they decided to ask the teenagers to sing one song at every Sunday mass to let everyone see how well the choir was doing.

The Last Sunday in Ordinary Time

Part of the reason that Fr. Connolly enjoyed so much success arose from the fact that he followed the biblical advice to not let one hand know what the was doing. His solution to the growing unrest among the parish elders revolved around the idea of dividing and conquering. As long he kept the youthful parishioners engaged but generally separated from the older parishioners, everyone got to be the kind of Catholic they wanted to be. The decision to allow the choir to sing at all the masses violated the strength of that strategy and proved to be a big mistake.

Colleen asked me to attend all the masses with them, but I refused that offer. One mass on Sunday morning lasted long enough, but six of them? I did agree to go to the 7:00 mass to hear her sing, and then I had to head back home to go to church with my parents. I thought about skipping church with Mom and Dad, but she already complained so much about how all the time I spent with the Kilnagaels anyway that I chickened out. When I told her that I would meet them at church she disagreed with me.

"No you won't. You'll come back home and we'll go to church like a proper family."

If a stranger came to Our Lady of Holy Truth and attended only the early Sunday mass, he might come away with the idea that Holy Truth had no parishioners under the age of fifty. I sat near the back and marveled at the collection of balding men and graying women in front of me. The teenage choir sat in a couple of pews off to one side of the church while the main choir sat up in the balcony. They decided that the young people's choir would sing the offertory song which meant I needed to stay for the entire mass. Had they sung the opening hymn I could have snuck out when they finished, but now I had to stay.

At last the moment came and the choir stood up to sing. It proved to be another moment when the Kilnagaels abused their influence because instead of singing a regular church song, Colleen and Noreen convinced them to sing a song in Danny's honor:

> Oh Danny Boy
>
> The pipes, the pipes are calling you...
>
> *From glen to glen*

A murmur went across the room like a wave. The elders looked at each other expressing a "Do you believe what we're hearing?" sense of outrage. Mr. Lally stood up.

"God damn it," he shouted.

He made sure his voice carried loudly over the choir. He made his way to the center aisle and headed for the door with a look of absolute fury on his face. A few of the others began complaining and telling the choir to stop singing.

"That's not a church song."

"That's not an appropriate song for mass."

"Father, tell them to stop. They need to sing something else."

"There are other boys off at war."

The comments grew so loud and so frequent that any chance the choir had to continue ended abruptly. One of the girls in the choir let out a "That is so rude," which drew an immediate verbal backlash from the rest of the congregation. The teens were absolutely dumbfounded by the anger directed at them, and the elders were furious that anyone would be so oblivious to something so obviously inappropriate for mass.

Fr. Doyle motioned to the choir to be seated and announced that he would speak to them after mass. He then apologized for not being more aware of what the choir intended to sing. He agreed with the elders that 'Danny Boy' was not a song that should have been sung. The tension subsided somewhat, and the mass continued. I could see how angry Colleen and the rest of the choir were though, and that she didn't believe that she had done anything wrong.

After mass several of the elders took the time to admonish the people in the choir, telling them

they should have known better. Fr. Doyle found himself surrounded by men and women who made sure they expressed their displeasure with him, putting him on the defensive, and he repeatedly apologized for the mistake. Colleen and the others watched him distancing himself from the choir and seethed. She made sure I knew that Fr. Doyle himself approved the song.

"That little kiss-up. When we told him that we were planning to sing 'Danny Boy' he agreed right away. I know he thought Fr. Connolly would be pleased if we sang a song that would make my mom feel better. He was trying to impress his boss. And then, and then... when all the old farts start complaining he stands up there like he didn't know a thing. He knew. He's just a coward. A hypocrite."

Fr. Doyle decided to cancel the rest of the scheduled singing at other masses and that made the choir angry as well.

"We know other songs. We don't have to sing that one."

A couple of the other kids told me that they felt a little weird singing 'Danny Boy,' but worried about offending Colleen and her sisters if they argued. I wasn't the only one intimidated by the Kilnagaels. Under different circumstances it might have been nothing more than a momentary flash of anger, and to Colleen and the choir I think it was. For the older congregation, however, it became part of the bigger power struggle going on within Holy Truth. A number of parishioners, many of whom did not even attend the 7:00 mass, contacted Fr. Connolly to voice their complaints. They believed they wrested control of the parish away from the disrespectful, liberal wing of the church, and they had no desire to give it back.

The Last Sunday in Ordinary Time

November 20th, 1966

Christianity Ain't Beanbag

Like always, I watched Fr. Connolly closely. I remembered that night at the Kilnagael's dinner table when he talked about Monsignor O'Brien, and how he always thought the most remarkable priests were those who served one parish for so many years. I assumed that he wanted to be a priest like Monsignor O'Brien, and remain in charge of Holy Truth for thirty or forty years. After roughly six months in charge of Holy Truth he made remarkable progress. The elderly returned to their previous level of giving to the church, and the parish finances stabilized. The younger parishioners embraced the changes Vatican II brought to the Church, and saw Fr. Connolly as a breath of fresh air, a progressive priest who got things done. In a short time the priest managed to bring an air of stability to the parish that caused everyone to think "He's on my side."

That all ended with the *Danny Boy* debacle. All of the work he had done to bring peace to Holy Truth now seemed to unravel in just a few, short days. I wondered what he planned to do to regain his reputation as a leader within our parish, and figured his back was against the wall. On the way into church I heard some people still complaining about the outrage, and the disrespect teenagers showed for the Lord. "Msgr. O'Brien would never tolerate that kind of thing. He'd put his foot down and stop it right there." Fr. Connolly must have heard the same thing. Half the congregation wanted an old-time pastor who acted as the undisputed leader of the parish. The other half wanted a more modern pastor, one who listened to and gave great consideration to the voices of others. They all seem to watch Fr. Connolly closely, wanting to know whose side was he on anyway. I decided to put my faith in Fr. Connolly, and I sat in the pew listening to him with the same high level of attention that I gave him at the Kilnagael's house.

Like every Sunday in ordinary time, Fr. Connolly wore green vestments. I learned in school that the priests wore green to represent rebirth like we see in the resurrection of Jesus, and in the return of green grass and trees in spring. Of course I also saw some semblance of the Irish factor in the choice of green, a reflection of how devoted we Irish were to our church. Either way, this was the last Sunday the priests would wear green for a while, with ordinary time ending and Advent beginning.

We all stood for the gospel which our Sunday missals told us would be a long one, Matthew 24, 15-35. Fr. Connolly chose a different reading.

"The Lord be with you," he began.

"And with thy spirit," we answered.

"A reading from the gospel according to Luke."

"Glory be to Thee, O Lord." As we said this we made the sign of the cross on our foreheads, lips, and breasts. We made these motions and said these words mechanically, without thought. We were well trained, and we knew the correct responses, we knew the prayers, and we automatically followed the priest as he led us through the mass. This, however, was very unusual.

In the pews people began turning pages in their missals, wondering if they had turned to the wrong page. People exchanged glances. Did the priest understand that he was wrong? He was reading the wrong gospel, but what was the protocol? Is it permissible for a parishioner to call out the priest publicly, and point out his mistake, or should we just ignore it and tell him quietly later? Even the older parishioners, those who confronted him about the *Danny Boy* issue, chose to remain quiet now. Correcting a priest during mass seemed like too much of an indiscretion to attempt lightly. It was a line that none of us wanted to cross. Fr. Connolly continued, uninterrupted.

> I am come to cast fire on the earth; and what will I, but that it be rekindled. And I have a baptism wherewith I am to be baptized: and how am I straitened until it be accomplished? Think ye that I come to give peace on earth? I tell you, no: but separation. For there shall be from henceforth five in one household divided; three against two and two against three. The father shall divided against the son, and the son against the father; the mother against the daughter and the daughter against the mother; the mother-in-law against her daughter-in-law and the daughter-in-law against her mother-in-law.

"The gospel of the lord."

"Praise be to Thee, O Christ," we all responded in unison.

We all sat back in our seats. Years of attending Sunday mass allowed us to go through the motions without giving them a second thought. Amid all of our rote actions, however, a distinct sense that something was wrong distracted the congregation. Our confusion seemed to please Fr. Connolly as far as I could tell, but he never let on that he even noticed it.

The Last Sunday in Ordinary Time

"There is an old saying in Chicago, 'Politics ain't beanbag.' It means that politics isn't easy. It's not a kid's game. It is not for those who lack the toughness it takes to survive in it. Jesus tells us in today's gospel that Christianity ain't beanbag. It takes some determination to follow Jesus. Our gospel this morning is not a friendly one. Jesus tells us that the salvation he offers is an invitation, but it is an invitation with strings attached. And we, those of us who so willingly dip our fingers in the holy water and make the sign of the cross as mass begins and ends, carry with us a heavier burden than others do. We, the people of the Holy Roman Catholic Church, are the direct descendants of the first followers of Jesus Christ. It is our duty to serve the Church, and in so doing, serve God Himself.

"Almost two thousand years ago God sent His only son to save us. He did not choose to make His son an Irishman or an American, but a Jew. When choosing an Earthly father for the Son of God, our heavenly father chose not a king, not a wealthy man, but a common working man, a carpenter. The mother of Jesus was likewise not a queen, not a member of the wealthy upper class, but a common girl-next-door.

"If the humble nature of His earthly parents were not modest enough, His Father arranged for Jesus to be born in a manger, desperately poor, and in the company of farm animals. God's great gift to us did not come wrapped in fancy paper. He came to us in the quiet cold of the night, not much noticed by the people on Earth.

"Our Jewish brethren have long described themselves as the chosen people. And they are right. But, and I can't stress this point strongly enough, they are not the only chosen ones. At the time of Jesus' birth the Jews believed that Judaism was an exclusive club, a faith that you had to be born into. Salvation was open only to those who were lucky enough to be born Jewish.

"As St. Paul began his life as an adherent of Jesus Christ he found himself speaking initially to Jews who had converted to Christianity. These converted Jews brought with them some baggage. They wanted to believe that Christianity was a new form of Judaism, open only to the chosen people who wished to convert from Judaism to Christianity. Paul informed them, however, that Jesus Christ was a gift from God to all people, an invitation to find salvation through His Son that was extended to everyone. We cannot make the mistake of believing ourselves to be the chosen people. We are no more chosen than an illiterate Chinese farmer, an African Tribal chieftain, a skid row bum, or a protestant American president. Nor are we less chosen than the pope himself, the martyred saints, or the most devoted of our fellow Catholics.

"In declaring ourselves Catholics, however, we are declaring ourselves to be leaders. When we genuflect before His altar, when we dip our fingers in the holy water and make the sign of the cross, we have an obligation to serve as examples of how proper Christians should comport themselves. We have an obligation to extend God's invitation to Protestants, Jews, and all of the other false religions that place barriers between God's people and their salvation.

"What does the Lord say to us in today's gospel? This is not a happy message from a friendly God, is it? Jesus tells us that he did not come in peace. He even asks us 'Do you think I come in peace? I tell you no.' Our savior, the one we call the Prince of Peace tells us that he does not come in peace, but instead he comes to divide us. Fathers against sons, mother against daughters, even in-laws against in-laws. Any reasonable man would ask why. Why would our Lord come to divide us? Why would he desire to cause friction and anger between family members?"

"A better question to ask is 'Jesus, what do you want from me? From us?' The answer, I'm afraid, is that he wants our absolute loyalty. Our faith in Him must be unwavering. Our devotion to Him must be foremost in our hearts. We must love Jesus with all our heart, and all our soul. We must place our love for Jesus above our love for all others.

"How do we show our Savior our devotion to Him? It is our responsibility, our duty, our requirement to serve Him by serving the one, holy, Catholic, and apostolic Church. Whatever emotions, moods, or passions we experience during our lives, must be of secondary importance to our love for Jesus. We must serve His church, and, in so doing, serve Him first and foremost.

"Recently, as I am certain that you know, I asked the young people's choir to sing one song at all of our Sunday masses as a way to showcase what a fine choir they had become. But I, as the leader of Our Lady of Holy Truth, failed to maintain a proper level of supervision over the choir, and they chose a song that really wasn't appropriate for a Sunday mass. While the song *Danny Boy* is a fine, lovely song as it goes, it definitely is not, in any way or by any measure, a holy song, or even a Catholic song. All songs that are sung in this church should be Catholic songs, written by devout Roman Catholics in order to honor our Lord. By this reasonable standard, the song does not meet our requirements for a song to be sung in church.

"Allowing this song to be sung was clearly my mistake. And while I apologize deeply and humbly for my mistake, I need to tell you that I am not the only one that erred. There have been a number of issues, let's call them indignities, that have been perpetrated upon this house of worship. In that light I have to let you know that it is my intention to put an end to these indignities, to make sure that we again bring a proper level of respect and dignity to this church.

"My first issue is the state of dress that I see coming into the Lord's house. I see young people attending mass wearing blue jeans, gym shoes, and skirts that are scandalously short. This will not continue. In order to show the Lord proper respect, you must dress respectfully."

At this point a large wave of applause swept across the church. Not everyone was applauding, but many of the elderly were.

"Stop. Stop that clapping right now." Fr. Connolly spoke with a genuine anger in his voice. "This is not a baseball game. This is a Roman Catholic mass. We do not *applaud*. We sit in quiet reverence, and we certainly don't make vulgar shows of approval when we hear something we like, nor scream obscenities when we hear something we don't like. It is very nice to sit here and mumble that young people don't know how to behave in church, or to sit here and complain the old fogies who run the Church are too inflexible. Our mission is always to strive to make ourselves the best Roman Catholics we can be. We can't spend our lives worrying that everyone else is practicing their faith in ways that we or I don't approve of, or that they are not Catholic enough.

"It is not enough that I stand before you and apologize for being lax in my duties. I need to let you know what actions I plan to take to address the problems taking place here at Our Lady of Holy Truth. I assure you that we, all of us, will be adhering to the traditional standards of the Roman Catholic Church. I know that many changes have come to the Catholic Church because of Vatican II. These changes seem to have given some parishioners the idea that the old rules do not apply. They seem to think that we no longer honor the holy days of obligation, that confession is now a voluntary sacrament, and that our relationship with Jesus is a casual thing. It is not. These misguided attitudes will not be tolerated here in Our Lady of Holy Truth.

"I recognize that these things are not easy. Remember, Jesus told us that he came not in peace, but to divide us. This is what he meant. Being a Christian, being a devoted servant of our Lord, is not easy, but there can be no compromises. You will be separated if you choose to be disrespectful to our Church, and, therefore, to our Lord. This is not the first time the Roman Catholic Church has seen turmoil within. Nor will it be the last. But remember Jesus warned us all. Your commitment to Him must be your first choice always, even over family and friends. Adhering to the teachings of Jesus may cause divisions within families, like the divisions we are currently seeing here in our family at Our Lady of Holy Truth, but that is part of God's tough love. Everyone here is expected to obey and serve the Church. If you don't like it, you know where the door is. We will not offer exceptions nor lower our expectations. Whether the mass is said in Latin, English, or any other language, it is still the mass. Despite a few minor changes in the Church, it is still the Church. It is not enough to call yourself a Catholic. You must become and remain the right kind of Catholic, and adhere or you are not serving God at all."

Some people, my parents included, said it was the kind of sermon that Monsignor O'Brien used to give, a no-holds-barred, uncompromising demand for more commitment to the faith. The elders seemed a bit smug, believing that they succeeded in holding Fr. Connolly to their standards of the way a parish should be run. And even Fr. Connolly himself carried himself with a bit of bravado, feeling like he successfully reasserted his authority. After mass he stood by the front doors of Holy Truth accepting the congratulations of those who admired his sermon. Like always, my admiration of Fr. Connolly continued to grow. He faced an angry congregation and turned their anger into support while at the same time making sure that everyone knew he was now more than ever, the man in charge.

The Last Sunday in Ordinary Time

November 24th, 1966

They Don't Deliver Mail on Thanksgiving

We all knew and dreaded those times when a priest chose to get tough with us. Sometimes it blindsided us, like when a priest gave out particularly harsh penances after we made confession. Usually a confession ended with instructions to say a few prayers or maybe the entire rosary and then our sins would be forgiven. Once in a while a priest heard our confessions at a bad time or maybe he thought we, as a parish, were not taking our faith seriously enough so he would take steps to correct it. If the parish organized a novena, meaning people were invited to come to the church and pray a special series of prayers for nine evenings in a row, the priest might make that our penance. If someone happened to be walking past the church just as a benediction service or a novena started, a priest might order us inside to participate. They had that kind of random authority, especially over children. I could hardly go home and complain to my mom that a priest ordered me to attend the benediction because she most likely agreed with his decision. Those moments always gave my Catholicism a heavy, unpleasant air of oppression.

Nothing reinforced the church's control over us like the smell of fish. We were not allowed to eat meat on Fridays, and Mom fried fish for our Friday dinners, if not every Friday, then probably half of them. The whole house reeked of the heavy, unpleasant smell of fish, and I always associated that smell with the Church's authority to tell us what to eat on Friday or to order us in off the street to attend a novena. I imagine many people realized that, now that Fr. Connolly stated a new get-tough policy about our devotion to the Church, it meant we needed to stay out of his line of fire. Now we needed to avoid walking past the church just before an evening service started in case he was looking for "volunteers."

He barely finished his big promise to the elderly of Holy Truth that he would uphold the traditional decorum of the Catholic faith when news came out of Rome. The Vatican decided that it was no longer necessary for Catholics to abstain from meat on Fridays. For centuries we were forbidden from eating meat on Fridays, meaning we all typically had fish or some combination of potatoes and eggs. Now, just as Fr. Connolly promised to make us adhere to the traditional standards of Catholicism, the Vatican undercut him and told us that we didn't need to do it. I thought of my religion teacher who told us that "men make plans and

God laughs." It was like God was laughing at our parish priest, telling him not to get too big for his britches. I almost felt bad for him, but it thrilled me to know that I wouldn't have to live with that awful smell of fried fish nearly as often. Whatever embarrassment he may have felt about that contradiction to his authority, it quickly became insignificant. A whole new challenge emerged and this one was far more important.

I remember the moment so clearly. It was Thanksgiving Day shortly after 11:00. Colleen and I had gone out for a walk and strolled back toward her house very casually. On the porch Colleen stopped to look in the mailbox, maintaining our vigil to prevent bad news about Danny from arriving. While we may have joked about it from time to time, checking the mailbox carried a solemnity that we took seriously. There were times when I felt guilty for having missed a day. If I thought about it rationally I understood the mailbox neither blessed nor cursed Danny, yet my belief that his safety required our vigilance continued to grow. Colleen and I were the only ones who knew about it, and it drew us closer.

"There's no mail on Thanksgiving, so you don't have to check it today." Colleen turned to me and raised her eye brows.

"Are you daring to question my actions?" she asked in a fake how-dare-you voice. "I check the mailbox as I please, and you are not to question my actions or motives." Nonetheless, she never looked for mail that day.

We walked into the house smiling and saw Maureen, Noreen, Josephine, and Eileen sitting on the couch in the living room definitely not smiling. Maureen sat with her arms crossed and her hands in her armpits as if she were cold, rocking back and forth with a look of dread on her face. They all looked scared and nervous at the same time.

"What's wrong?" Colleen asked.

Eileen stood up and came over to us, speaking in little more than a whisper.

"We got a telegram from the government."

"What does it say?"

"We didn't *open* it. It's addressed to the parents of Daniel J. Kilnagael."

"Eileen!" Colleen said, dragging out the een for emphasis.

"I know. I mean, I don't know, but..."

"You don't know anything for sure," I said, trying to stay positive.

"Where are Mom and Dad? Do they know about it?

"They're not here."

"We don't know where they are," Kathleen said. She walked in from the kitchen.

"I'm scared to death for Danny," Eileen said. "What if Danny is dead?"

"Shut up, just shut up," Kathleen ordered. "We don't know anything. Maybe he's just hurt. Maybe a lot of things, but we *don't know.*"

She said those last two words very slowly, very deliberately.

"They said they were going to the liquor store, but I think they may have stopped somewhere else, too," Eileen said.

"We have to find them. Marty, can you call your parents and ask them to check the liquor store?" Maureen asked.

"Sure." I went over to the phone and started dialing. "Wait, what do I tell them?"

"Just tell them, it's an emergency. They're needed at home."

I called home and my dad answered.

"Dad, it's Marty. Um...there's kind of an emergency here at Kilnagael's, and Colleen's parents aren't home."

"What's wrong?"

"I don't know. It's hard to say, just, they need to get home. We think they went by the Commonwealth liquor store. Can you drive over there and see if they're there?"

"What's going on, Marty?"

I worried about saying the wrong thing and getting yelled at by Kathleen, like Eileen did. I wanted to tell him, but didn't know what to say.

"Nobody's in any danger, Dad. It's just that...well, they need to get home. Can you go get them?"

"Marty..."

He didn't finish because I cut him off.

"Dad, please. I'll explain it later. Trust me, there's a good reason. We need to find them."

I returned to the living room and received thank yous from everyone. Obviously they all heard me talking to my dad, so I was glad I didn't say anything that would upset them. There was a quiet awkwardness in the room.

"Do you guys want to say a rosary?"

The Last Sunday in Ordinary Time

There was an explosion of "good ideas," and "thank you's again. We all positioned ourselves by various chairs and the couch, and I took the lead. The chance do something, anything, was a welcome relief for the girls, and actually praying was probably the best thing for them to do. The rosary we said that afternoon was very emotional, and despite Kathleen's insistence that we not think of Danny as dead, the feeling in the room was very sorrowful. I needed to lead because they struggled to say the prayers without breaking down. We finished saying it, but their parents still weren't home.

"Thank you, Marty. I feel better for having done that," Kathleen told me.

We continued our waiting. When the telegram first arrived they put it on the coffee table in the living room, and it sat there like a snake coiled up, waiting to strike at anyone who came near it. Colleen and I sat near the front window, repeatedly looking out for their parents and glancing back toward the telegram. We stayed that way for about another few minutes, saying very little and trying not to make eye contact. Finally we heard Mr. and Mrs. Kilnagael coming in the back door. All of the girls ran to the kitchen. I stayed back and listened to the panicky cries they made as they all tried to explain it to their parents.

"Everybody just calm down," I I heard Mrs. Kilnagael say loudly.

She came rushing into the living room, but stopped suddenly when she saw the telegram. She immediately started shaking. It was as if the telegram did not exist until she saw it for herself. She gasped and placed her hand over her mouth as if she couldn't believe what she was seeing. She sat slowly in a chair and spoke in an even tone.

"Peter?"

Mr. Kilnagael arrived in the living room and made eye contact with his wife. She looked at him and spoke without emotion.

"Peter, would you please read the telegram?"

She almost had it. Her tone of voice was perfect. She sat erect with her hands on her lap. The only thing that betrayed her total fear was the look in her eyes. She looked directly at her husband, but her eyes watered just a little. She looked to be on the verge of either complete composure or a complete emotional breakdown. Her eyes suggested that the slightest nudge in either direction would determine her next move, but for the moment she remained calm.

"Okay, Peggy, stay calm. Let's find out…"

"Don't tell me to calm down." She raised her hands defensively in front of her. "I am calm. Just please read the telegram."

Mr. Kilnagael picked up the envelope and opened it.

Eileen ran over to her mother and offered her hand, which Mrs. Kilnagael took gladly with two hands, pressing it hard to her chest. Colleen moved closer to me and took my hand. All eyes turned to Mr. Kilnagael who clumsily pulled a piece of paper out of the envelope, hesitated, and then took a deep breath to calm himself.

"It's from the Secretary of Defense. 'Dear Mr. and Mrs. Kilnagael, we regret to inform you that your son…," He stopped and whispered "Oh dear God." He shook from head to toe, his hands almost violent in their unsteadiness. His voiced quivered as he continued. "…that your son, Private Daniel J. Kilnagael, was killed in action in South Viet Nam."

"Danny!" Maureen said almost in a shout.

The Last Sunday in Ordinary Time

"My baby, my baby, my baby...oh my baby..." Mrs. Kilnagael said in a voice sounding both small and wounded.

Colleen ran to her father as did Kathleen. The other girls went to their mother and anxiously piled on the couch near her, desperate to touch their mother. It was the most human of reactions I thought as I stood there watching them. When someone in a big family dies, all the other members of the family close ranks, seek comfort in each other, and extend their arms into a family embrace. The children rush to offer their parents some solace, some measure of shared mourning. I felt sorry for them but I also envied them. If it had been me, there were no brothers or sisters to mourn me or comfort my parents. The Kilnagaels, despite the death of their son and brother, were the lucky ones. The awkwardness of my presence struck me. They didn't need me there, so I began moving slowly toward the door. Mr. Kilnagael continued reading softly.

"Pvt. Kilnagael engaged with the enemy in Tay Ninh province, and despite the courageous efforts of his fellow soldiers, he was mortally wounded. Your son showed the highest level of bravery and dedication to his country. We wish to extend the condolences of your president and a grateful nation for his service to his country. He was a brave soldier who made the ultimate sacrifice for his nation and his fellow soldiers. We are sorry for your loss."

"Marty! You're not leaving, are you?" Colleen called.

She came quickly around the corner as I turned to answer.

"No, of course not," I said. "Not if you want me here."

She hugged me tightly, put her head on my shoulder and said softly "I do."

The Last Sunday in Ordinary Time

The Kilnagaels all remained in the living room except for Colleen and me. As we stood in the hallway the phone rang and I went to the kitchen to answer it. None of them was ready to talk to anyone as their sense of loss grew more profound. I, on other hand, was elated. It's not that I didn't feel a sense of sorrow, and I was absolutely aware of how devastated they all were. It was just that I was there, in the Kilnagael's house, like I was one of them. I wanted to be like the Kilnagaels more than anything else in the world, and here I stood with Colleen actually asking me to stay during this special time for the family.

"Hello, Kilnagael's residence," I spoke.

"Marty?" My mom asked.

"Oh, hi Mom," I answered almost like it was a question, as if I were completely baffled by the fact that she would call.

"Is everything all right over there? Your father never found Colleen's parents."

"Um...no, actually. We just learned that Danny was killed in Viet Nam." The emotion I felt as I said it surprised me. I almost broke down saying it out loud.

"Oh, I'm sorry. Oh, that's too bad. That's a shame."

"I know. They're all in the living room now."

"Well, it's a family time. Maybe you should come home now, and let them be."

"But Colleen asked me to stay. I think I'm needed here."

My mom brushed that thought off almost like I didn't say it.

"Did Colleen's parents make it home yet?"

"Yeah, Mom. They're here. They got home a few..."

"Then you don't need to be there. That's what family is for. I want you to come home."

"Look, Colleen *just* asked me to stay. I can't go running out the door."

"Marty," she said with some impatience, "has anyone called Fr. Connolly yet? I know that he is close to Mrs. Kilnagael."

"No, I don't think so, not yet."

"Well, then you call him now. You can stay a little while longer, just to be polite, but it's a family time. You're only in the way. If Fr. Connolly comes over soon, that will give you a good reason to leave. If he doesn't, you can stay a little while longer, but you need to come home soon. You need to spend Thanksgiving with your family, and let Colleen's family have some privacy."

"Okay, Mom, I will."

I wanted to say "but Mom, I want to be here, with this family," but I held my tongue. We said our good-byes and I called Holy Truth, and asked for Fr. Connolly.

"Fr. Connolly?"

"Yes."

"It's me, Marty Donovan. Um,...I'm over at the Kilnagaels. They got some bad news. Danny was killed in Viet Nam."

I said it quickly. It came out in a rush because I was trying to stay ahead of my emotions, and saying it was harder than I thought it would be.

"Merciful Jesus. When did this happen?"

"I don't know, sir. We just found out, and they're too broken up to hear any details. Everyone here is in tears. I was hoping you could come by."

"Of course. Of course I can. I will be over in a few minutes. Thank you for calling, Marty."

As we hung up Colleen came into the kitchen looking for me. She heard that it was my mom on the phone, but didn't realize I had called Fr. Connolly. She was glad that I did, and when we returned to the living room she made the announcement.

"Marty called Fr. Connolly. Wasn't that thoughtful of him?"

They all agreed that it was nice of me, and thanked me for being so thoughtful.

"He said he was going to come over soon."

Mr. Kilnagael looked up at me, eyes full of tears, and nodded his approval. Mrs. Kilnagael had been crying loudly, as her husband and her daughters tried to console her. There really wasn't anything anyone could say at this point, and no purpose in trying to convince her that it wasn't so bad. It wasn't just bad, it was the worst thing that ever happened to this family and crying seemed like the only thing to do at this point. I sat down and Colleen sat down on my lap, put her head on my shoulder and wept. We made eye contact and that was enough to make me cry as well. Crying with them made me feel like I crossed some sort of threshold, like I was formally entering the lives of the Kilnagaels for the first time.

"Marty, did Fr. Connolly say when he would get here?" Maureen asked.

I shook my head, unable to speak, ashamed and proud of my tears at the same time.

"God, why did this have to happen? Why? That's what I want to know," Kathleen said.

Colleen walked over to Noreen to see if she were all right. The girls took turns hugging, comforting each other, and breaking down into tears again. Each new hug elicited a new burst of tears, and I admired the love that the sisters shared. Again I thought about if I had died in Viet Nam only my parents would have cried. The shared emotion of siblings was so powerful that I regretted being an only child now more than ever. But the girls included me in their hugs, and that gave me a mixture of joy with the pain of Danny's death. Was this what it was like to be in a big family?

A little later Fr. Connolly arrived. It had been less than an hour since we learned of Danny's death, and the hurt was still fresh. When the priest arrived Mr. Kilnagael went to the door to meet him. Colleen's father shook from head to toe. Fr. Connolly took Mr. Kilnagael's hand with two hands, and Mr. K responded in kind.

"Peter," the priest said barely above a whisper, "I'm so sorry."

Mr. Kilnagael nodded gamely. "Yeah, me too."

The girls, much to my admiration, watched carefully, hopeful that Fr. Connolly could bring some comfort to their father. They were undoubtedly heartbroken themselves, but their first concern was for their parents. The look in their eyes pleaded for the priest to do or say something to lessen their parents' pain. Fr. Connolly went immediately over to Mrs. Kilnagael, knelt beside her chair and hugged her.

"Peggy, I'm so sorry for your loss."

Mrs. Kilnagael didn't say a word, or even move in the slightest. It was a one way hug, and she sat so still, it was as if the priest wasn't there at all. Fr. Connolly held that hug for a few seconds, but it quickly became more awkward that comforting. I got the sense that she really didn't want him there, that he had somehow failed to protect her son like he promised. Fr. Connolly stood finally and turned to everyone else.

"Perhaps we should pray the rosary, pray for Danny's soul," he said.

There were several rosaries in the room already because we had said one before Colleen's parents got home, but no one knew what else to do. Colleen ran upstairs to get her mother's rosary from the bedroom while the rest of us picked up the ones we had used before. Mrs. Kilnagael continued to be the center of everyone's attention, even Mr. Kilnagael's. If his heartbreak were as great as his wife's, it went unrecognized for the moment. No one knelt this time. We all sat in a circle and Fr. Connolly led us in the rosary. The soft murmuring of the repetitive Hail Mary's continued amidst repeated sobs and awkward glances. We said this prayer as a way to simply to let a few minutes pass while we tried to figure out what to do next. We completed the rosary with a mix of relief that it was over, and dread because now we didn't know what to do.

"Why don't we go around the room," Fr. Connolly suggested, "and let people say what they loved and admired about Danny."

"No, let's not," Mrs. Kilnagael snapped.

The Last Sunday in Ordinary Time

"I'm sorry, Peg. It's too soon for that. I should have known better than to say that."

The silence returned. We all squirmed in our chairs, everyone afraid to move, and afraid not to. Everyone in the room, Fr. Connolly and I included, sat awkwardly trying to figure out what to do. It became unbearable for me.

"I have something I would like to say. I was not blessed with any brothers or sisters, and you and Danny have been the closest thing I ever had. I know that your hearts are breaking much more than mine is, but I also can't believe how much this hurts even me. But what if God had come to me before I ever entered this house and offered me a deal? What if God told me that I would find more happiness here, and that I would love being here as much as I ever loved anyone or anything else in life, but after six months I would feel the pain I feel right now? If God told me that I could avoid feeling all the pain I feel right now, but I would have to live without all of the laughter and joy I experienced in this house, what would I do? I just want you all to know that all of the pain that Danny's death has brought to this house is far outweighed by the joy that his life brought to this house, and I'm glad I got to be a small part of it."

They all looked at me with astonishment. I was astonished myself. I liked what I said. It came out so well, I could hardly believe it. Finally, Maureen spoke. She pressed her hand against her chest.

"Oh my God. Oh my God, that was so sweet."

The girls rushed over to me to hug me. In the background I heard Mr. Kilnagael say that it was very nice. Mrs. Kilnagael didn't say a word, but she stood up and headed upstairs almost running. When she left it was as if everyone else had been granted permission to move. All of the girls including Colleen followed their mother upstairs.

"That was beautiful, Marty," Fr. Connolly said finally. "Thank you for saying that."

"Yes, Marty, it was beautiful," Mr. Kilnagael said. He then turned his attention to the priest.

"Listen, Father. I don't know the right or wrong thing here, but I think we just need some time to do some mourning on our own. It might be better if you left us for a while. I don't know, maybe in two hours I'll be calling you and asking you to come back. I don't know."

"Of course. I understand, Peter. If you need anything, anything at all, you call me. In the middle of the night, call me if you need me. I'll check in with you tomorrow, regardless."

Mr. Kilnagael walked him to the door and they said their good-byes. Then Mr. Kilnagael headed to the kitchen and started dialing the phone. All of her sisters were upstairs with their mother, and I sat in the living room as an eerie quiet settled over the house. I could hear her father speaking in the kitchen.

"Hello, Bill? Yeah, it's Pete. I have some bad news. We just got word that Danny was killed in Viet Nam." At this point he broke down. "Yeah, yeah, we're all in a state of shock here. No, I think it's best that nobody come by today. We're not ready..." Again his voice faltered, and he struggled to continue. "Obviously the thanksgiving dinner is out. Yeah, no, I don't know. We'll do something. No, Mom doesn't...Mom doesn't know yet. I'm not sure I can..."

He went quiet at that point. I could hear his sobs faintly.

"Would you? Would you and Alice...Yeah, go ahead and tell anyone who needs...Okay, thanks Bill."

With that he hung up abruptly. He hesitated a moment and started dialing again.

"Hi, Mary. Is Don there? Happy Thanksgiving to you too. Is Don there?"

I imagined that Mary, whoever she was, must have been surprised by the second of the "Is Don there's?" Mr. Kilnagael was normally very chatty and polite. To cut her off like that was unusual.

"Don? Hi. Listen. I won't be into the office for a few days at least. We just got word that Danny...that Danny...Danny was killed in Viet Nam."

He broke down as he said it. Saying it, I thought, that's the toughest part. Thinking about it was bad enough, but when I said it to my mom, I was the same way. Saying it out loud, that was tough.

"It's terrible, Don. It's a son-of-a-bitch, that's what it is. A son-of-a-bitch." He said that last part with anger. "God, I'm sorry, Don, but you know...well, anyway, tell the guys at work for me, would you? Thanks buddy. I appreciate it."

Two phone calls were his limit. After he hung the phone he headed downstairs, I assumed to get a drink. I sat in the quiet of the living room caught between two competing thoughts: I should leave, and I want to stay as long as they let me. Eeriness filled the house and I increasingly felt that I didn't belong there. I decided to follow Mr. Kilnagael downstairs to see if there was anything I could do for him.

He was sitting at his bar, surrounded by the various Irish whiskey and beer signs and mirrors, an open whiskey bottle on the bar, and a glass with two fingers worth in his hand. He was lighting a cigarette as I approached. His eyes were red, and although he wasn't full out crying, the odd tear escaped and slid down his face.

"Mr. Kilnagael, is there anything I can do for you?"

"No, Marty, there's nothing anybody can do for me now."

I remained for a moment or two, growing increasingly uneasy as I sensed he really wanted to be alone. Just as I was about to leave he started to speak.

"Kilnagael. It's a grand old Irish name."

"Yes, it is."

"You know, when my father first arrived here from Ireland, they advised him to change it. The guy on Ellis Island told him that it would be easier if he shortened it to Nagle, but my dad refused. Then he suggested Kilnagle, or even just Kilna, but my dad refused. He was proud of his name and wouldn't change it. Look at me now. I'm the last of the Kilnagaels. I'm the only son of an only son of an only son. And now...my only son is gone." He hesitated for a moment and then continued. "My daughters will marry, take their husbands' names, and the Kilnagaels will be no more."

"There will still be Kilnagael blood running through the veins of your grandchildren," I answered.

"There will be, but it's not the same."

Colleen once told me that her father liked to open telephone books when he travelled to other cities, and check for anyone named

Kilnagael. He never found another, not even in Dublin, Cork, or Belfast. "Do you see how unique your name is?" he'd say to his kids. He always believed that Danny would continue the line of Kilnagaels for at least one more generation, but now that wouldn't happen. Soon it would not be a unique name, it wouldn't be a name at all.

Colleen, Eileen, and Maureen came downstairs and joined us. Maureen picked up her father's arm and placed it around her shoulders. Mr. Kilnagael bowed his head, pressing his forehead against the top of hers.

"Daddy, I know that Danny was your favorite one. I'm sorry..."

"Moe, you're all my favorite one."

The three girls surrounded him, each pressing their faces hard against him. It was my observation that Danny was more his mother's favorite than his father's favorite. As Colleen noticed long ago, daughters will continue to crawl onto their father's lap for years after sons refuse to do so. They all took turns being Daddy's little girl, and they showered him with small shows of affection, hugs and kisses that he never received from his son.

His mother, conversely, was subject to bear hugs from Danny at any given moment. Once he got taller than his mother he liked coming up behind her, wrapping his arms around her, and giving her a big squeeze. "She complains like she doesn't like it, but we all know she loves it," Colleen told me. At the same time she could straighten his hair, fix his tie, place her hands on his shoulders while he sat at the kitchen table, or show affection in a dozen other ways just like she did with her daughters. While her daughters wanted to pick out their own clothes, Danny received

The Last Sunday in Ordinary Time

Christmas and birthday presents with gratitude, gladly allowing his mother or older sisters to do the choosing for him.

Colleen once expressed some jealousy over the way her mother fawned over Danny.

"I swear to God," she said, "once Danny walks into the room it's like we don't even exist anymore. 'This is my *son* Danny. Able to leap tall buildings in a single bound. My daughters know how to do the dishes, but my son...' It's like we don't even exist."

All of that was forgotten for the moment. Eileen went behind the bar and started opening bottles of Coke, handing one to Maureen, Colleen, and me. We all joined their father in a drink, an image that he found somewhat amusing, a moment of levity that was much needed. The little conversation that we engaged in came in short bursts followed by long, lingering silences. One such moment was interrupted by the doorbell.

One of the girls upstairs answered it, and we heard a loud "Grandma!" Everyone moved upstairs and a new round of tears and "I'm sorry's" started. Mr. Kilnagael's mother arrived with his sister and brother-in-law. As they all hugged and carried on I pulled Colleen aside.

"Coll, I think this might be a good time for me to go."

"Yeah, I suppose so," she said. "Thanks for staying. Thanks for saying what you did. Thanks for everything, Marty. I love you."

"I love you, too, Colleen." We kissed by the back door, and I left quietly.

I should have gone straight home but I knew what waited there; Thanksgiving with my parents, Uncle Charlie and Aunt Bridie, the five of us sitting alone in the house making little conversation while I heard nothing but the ticking of the kitchen clock. On a good holiday Mickey Riordan joined us, and at least there was better conversation, but I wasn't sure Mickey was coming that day. After what Colleen said to me at the door, I wanted the good part of the day to last longer. It was almost 4:30 as I approached the Lovely Bit and figured I should stop in and tell them the news about Danny.

There weren't many people in there, but Eddie Mahoney and a few of the guys from Stage Irish were sitting at the bar. Liam tended bar. I never knew his last name, and never saw that much of him because he usually only worked hours when I wasn't there. He eyed me suspiciously as I entered.

"Marty, you shouldn't be in here right now. You need something?"

"No, I just have some news to tell the guys."

"What's up, Marty?" Eddie asked.

The few guys at the bar all turned their attention to me while Liam muttered a "Make it quick."

"I just left the Kilnagaels. Danny got killed in Viet Nam."

They all reacted at the same time, a series of "What's," "No way's," "Oh, my God's," and similar things.

"When?" Eddie asked.

"I don't know. They didn't get a lot of details. Everybody's over there in tears, basically in shock I guess. A telegram from the army arrived, said he died in battle and they were sorry. Mr. and Mrs. Kilnagael were so broken up that we didn't go into details."

Liam put a shot glass in front of everyone at the bar and grabbed a bottle of whiskey.

"That stinks," somebody said. "He was a great guy."

"In honor of lucky number 7," Liam said, and poured a shot of Seagram's Seven Crown for everyone at the bar except me of course.

"Here's to Danny."

"Here's to Danny," they all repeated in unison.

"Man," Eddie said, "I knew he was at war and all that, but, honestly I never thought he was going to die. I mean, crap. His poor parents must be crushed."

"They are," I said.

"When's the funeral?"

"I don't know anything about that. I'll let you know when I find out."

"You do that Marty. Let us know. And, when you see any of his sisters, tell them how sorry we are?"

"I will, I promise."

"Marty, I hate to kick you out, but you're too young to be in here. You can't be in here."

"Yeah, I know, Liam. That's okay."

I finally reached my house knowing I was in trouble. I was barely in the door when my mom pounced.

"Where have you been?"

"The Kilnagaels'. You know that."

"Marty, didn't your mother tell you not to stay long?" Dad asked.

"What was I supposed to do? Colleen asked me to stay. I couldn't just walk out like I didn't care."

"Well come in and greet our guests. We have company you know."

It relieved me when Mom changed the subject, but there was a "We'll talk about it later tone in her voice. I walked into the living room and saw Charlie, Bridie, Mick, and Tina Avelini. I did a double take when I saw her. Uncle Charlie let out a loud "There he is" in an effort to get me out of trouble, and then Mom rushed us to the table. She was apparently holding dinner until I got there. I said my hellos while we walked into the dining room, actually relieved to have more company than I originally expected.

"So," Uncle Charlie started, "Danny Kilnagael was killed in Viet Nam?"

"Yeah. The telegram said he died in battle."

"His poor parents, to lose a child like that. God help them."

"Everybody over there was crying."

"Is he a family friend?" Tina asked.

"He's the brother of Marty's girlfriend," Mick told her.

I loved the way that sounded. The sadness of the news notwithstanding, it allowed us to get past the strangeness of Mickey bringing a date to our house, and Italian woman at that. Danny's death and the war gave us a nice, safe topic that allowed us to ignore that she was a Dago. I knew my parents didn't like having her in their home, and only their affection for Mick made it possible for them to mute their displeasure.

"Father Connolly came by and we all prayed a rosary for him."

"That was kind of him," Mom said.

"Sometimes that's all you can do," Tina said. "I'm sure there's nothing anyone can do to make the pain go away."

An awkward silence came over us. I wondered if Mick was aware of what the rest of us were thinking, but we all wondered about having a Dago at the table. I held no memory of any actual Italians in our house before, but I wasn't sure who was or wasn't Italian. Tina was not just an Italian, but a beautiful, sexy one, and she seemed to dress like she wanted everyone to see her that way. In the two times I had seen Tina everything she wore seemed just a little tighter than the young Irish women I knew wore their clothes, never mind my mom and Aunt Bridie. I assumed my mom was thinking she had a tramp sitting at her dinner table, but Tina was Mick's girlfriend, so Bridie and Mom both kept quiet. Mick asked Tina if she would like something to drink and she asked for a glass of wine.

"That's a tall order. Katie, do you have any wine in the house."

"I'm sorry, Tina, I don't. Would you like a high ball, or maybe an old fashioned?"

Tina looked at Mick and said "A 7-UP?"

"Those we have," Mick said, and then added, "Right, Katie?"

We did have 7-UP, so Mick was able to take care of his girlfriend, but for the rest of us, an awkward silence descended on the table. We sat there with this Italian woman, not knowing what to say to her.

"Well, it looks like the Coloreds are coming to Holy Truth," Uncle Charlie said finally.

"What?" Mick asked.

"The Coloreds. Remember that thing in the paper about them marching down Madison the Saturday before Christmas? Well, they're coming. Going to march on that Saturday."

"I don't know why those people can't stay in their own neighborhoods."

"I heard they want better houses," I said. Mom gave me a look of impatience.

"We all want better houses, Marty. Some of us are just more willing to work hard to get them."

"That's right, Katie. All these people who made a down payment and then spent years paying their mortgages, taking care of their houses, making Holy Truth a nice place to live in, and now Rufus and Willie want for free what we had to pay for." Uncle Charlie spoke with some anger in his voice.

"They marched through our parish this summer," Tina said. "They were all wearing their suits and ties, but they weren't fooling anybody. All that stuff about nonviolence. There were fights all over the place, and we weren't the ones who started all of them. I heard they even tried to drag one girl into an alley, but some neighbors heard her scream and stopped them."

"They should stick to their own neighborhoods, and their own people, never mind trying to take what's ours. And the poor store owners..." Aunt Bridie added. "One of the busiest days of the year and those people come marching in, ruining everyone's business. How's a man supposed to make a dollar with an unruly mob in the street."

The Last Sunday in Ordinary Time

"It's unfair," Mick agreed. "Herbert Feingold's been in business for twenty-five years. A nice man, never hurt anybody, and now they're going to ruin his business right before Christmas?"

"My teacher said he thought the Coloreds had a good point. He said that white people have been treating Coloreds badly forever." Mom shot me another look.

"To think," Mick said, "that we all celebrated the day that one learned to talk."

They all laughed at that, and I sat there a little embarrassed though I didn't think I had done anything to deserve it. I look over at Tina to see if she was laughing too, and she made eye contact with me, smiled and winked. Like with everything else she did, she was sexy when she winked.

"Your father went out and earned his paycheck. Nobody handed him anything," Mom told me in a tone of voice that suggested there would be no arguing with her. "If these people want to buy a house like ours then they should go out and find a job like your father did."

I said nothing. I sat there like a dog that had been swatted with a newspaper, but I thought about saying "Uncle Charlie handed Dad a job. He didn't have to go looking for a job; Charlie sent a job looking for Dad."

The one thing that came out of the conversation was that Tina was now one of them. They were united in their belief that the Negroes who planned to march through our neighborhood were hypocrites who acted innocently but were really trying to steal our parish from us. They talked about how we should handle it. Charlie suggested that if we ignored them, they would go away, but Tina said the TV people would be there filming it all for the 5:00 news.

"Even if we ignore them, the television newsmen make them out to be heroes."

"And they know it, too," Bridie added.

"It's un-American," Mick said. "America is the land of opportunity. You don't wait for the government to give you things, and you don't demand that the government give you things. You go out and you make it happen yourself. That's what real Americans do."

"That's why the Italians started the Mafia," I said. Mom looked at me like she was mortified, like I had insulted our Italian guest. "What? My history teacher told us that Al Capone once said 'I tried to go legit, but they wouldn't let me.' So he and the other guys started doing all that Mafia stuff."

"Actually, Marty's right." Tina came to my rescue. "There's a lot of mixed feelings about the Mafia in my family. They make us all look like crooks sometimes, but they also helped open a lot of doors for Italians here."

"And don't forget, they named the paddy wagon after the Irish," Mick added. "We used to get arrested a lot."

"They called them paddy wagons because there were so many Irish policemen, not Irish criminals," Charlie said.

"Same thing, most of the time," Mick answered, which caused Tina to start laughing.

"What were you doing all afternoon? You didn't seem to be in too much of a hurry to get home?" Everyone looked at my mom, fairly shocked by the question. "I mean if Fr. Connolly was there what were you doing there?"

"I don't know, holding Colleen's ha..."

"Katie," Mick said, "I don't think..."

"I'm just wondering," Mom said, undeterred. "I'm sorry Peggy Kilnagael lost her son, but she can't have mine as a replacement."

"Mom, nobody's asking me to take Danny's place."

"You certainly spend enough time over there. They see more of you than we do."

"Okay, that's enough," Dad said. "We'll talk about that later."

The Last Sunday in Ordinary Time

I Knew a Guy Who Knew a Guy Who Knew a Guy

The Kilnagaels knew their son was dead. They had a piece of paper that said so, but, beyond that they knew almost nothing. On Friday morning I talked to Colleen on the phone and she told me that her parents were upset by how little they knew about Danny. The Kilnagaels spent Thanksgiving night in a helpless sense of mourning. It would have helped to be able to do something, anything to address the situation, but all they had was "that stupid piece of paper" as Colleen called it a few times. They wanted to know when his body would be returned, if they needed to pay for the funeral, did they need to buy a casket, and I'm sure few dozen more questions, but they didn't know where to ask or who to ask.

I arrived at Mickey's at 1:00, and he asked about the Kilnagaels. I told him about the sense of helplessness they felt, and he told me to ask Uncle Charlie.

"Look, Marty, you've got a war hero who died serving his country. Politicians go crazy for the chance to show how much they care in times like these. If you ask Charlie to make a phone call, I'm sure he'll get things done."

Mickey was right of course. My dad used to comment about how people he knew would go into a frenzy for the chance to please the mayor. Politics in Chicago created a counter intuitive reality. People generally thought the senator was more powerful than the representative, who was more powerful than the governor, who was more powerful than the mayor, and so on. In Chicago, though, the mayor's office was where the power began and ended. A lot of people claimed to have a connection to Mayor Daley, as if they could pick up the phone and talk to him any time they liked. In reality, very few people had the clout to actually get a phone call through to the mayor's office. Uncle Charlie, being the successful ward committeeman that he was, did have that clout, so when I asked him to see what he could do for the Kilnagaels, he said he would. He also told me to call the Kilnagaels and have them sit near the phone.

Any Democratic office holder in Illinois, whether it was the United States senator or the local alderman, owed his position, at least in part, to the Chicago mayor. After I spoke to Charlie, he got the wheels of the Democratic machine moving. Word travelled quickly, reaching Mayor Daley in a very short time. The mayor, sensing an important public image opportunity, immediately sent word to Washington requesting information about the death of Danny. Every Democratic congressman from Illinois began making phone calls to the Pentagon or to whatever military contacts he might have. The situation surrounding Danny's death offered a rare chance to be the guy who got something done for Mayor Daley. It was the kind of thing, Dad told me once, that guys killed for. Of course Dad was no good at it, which is why he was destined to be a low level political hack his whole life. The more ambitious guys, the ones who actually used their place in the party to advance their careers and run for office, pursued this opportunity the way a lion pursued a zebra on the open plain. The right phone call, the right answer and suddenly one man would emerge as the guy in Washington who could get things done. Within a few hours, flowers arrived at the home of the Kilnagaels expressing condolences from the office of the mayor, the Chicago Democratic Organization, and the people of Chicago.

About a half hour later the Kilnagaels received a phone call from our representative's office. Like Charlie, he was a part of the Daley political machine, so when a voter called with a problem like this one, the machine responded. The man on the phone spoke to Mr. Kilnagael and asked some questions about Danny and then promised that the congressman and his people would get some answers. Colleen called the gas station thanking me for what I had done. Mrs. Kilnagael got on the phone.

"Marty," she began, "I can't begin to thank you enough for doing this. Congressman Rooney's office called and...well, thank you Marty."

"I really didn't do anything, Mrs. Kilnagael. I just called my..."

"Oh, but you did, Marty. No one was helping us, but now, because of you, they are. I am so glad that you took the time to help us. Thank you, Marty."

After a few more thank yous Mrs. Kilnagael finally handed the phone back to Colleen. She gave me an "Oh my God, Marty" and proceeded to tell me how much her whole family appreciated what I had done. As if Danny's death were not bad enough, without more information they were unable to plan a funeral or anything like that, so it was as if they couldn't even begin mourning yet. The call from the congressman's office broke through the sense of paralysis that had come over the house. It finally felt like things were moving again a little bit, so they could anticipate the wake and funeral that were to come. Colleen needed to get off the phone in case another phone call came in, so I hung up without knowing anything more.

In Holy Truth the news of Danny's death spread quickly and a few people stopped by Mick's to talk to me about it. I still didn't know too much, but I repeated what I knew, when the telegram arrived, about how everyone cried and how devastated they all were, and that sort of thing. I promised to pass messages along and accepted some condolences myself as if I were one of the Kilnagaels. Enjoyed was not the right word, but I did feel a sense of worthiness at hearing those things said, like I had become a pillar of Holy Truth because I was so closely tied to Colleen's family.

Mick noticed how much time I was spending not working but chose to look the other way. The circumstances were unusual and I guessed he felt it would be disrespectful to not allow me to talk to people who wanted to know about Danny and his family. He did reach his limit later though, when Colleen called the gas station again, this time to tell me about the flowers from the mayor and another phone call, this one from Congressman Rooney himself. He handed me the phone and said "Make it quick," and then stood by as I talked, ensuring that I had no privacy during the call. I listened to Colleen but said very little, trying to find a way to end the conversation gracefully.

"Colleen, I have to go."

"Okay, but wait. I have to tell you about..."

"Colleen, I can't talk right now..."

Colleen refused to hang up until I promised to come to her house the next morning. I didn't have to work at Mick's that Saturday, so I promised her I would be there. She started thanking me over again, continuing on so long that I finally had to say good-bye and hang up without waiting for a response. I gave Mick a kind of a "Happy now?" look, but he just pointed a Chevy that was pulling up to one of the pumps.

Later that evening I crossed the street to have dinner at the Lovely Bit. There were a few people in there, including Mr. Lally. He asked me about the news, and I told him it was true, that Danny had indeed died in battle.

"That's too bad," he said quietly.

"Mayor Daley sent some flowers to their house. And Congressman Rooney called." I thought that he would be impressed by that, but he seemed troubled. He gave me an odd look, like he was almost angry to hear it.

"Well," he said after a few seconds, "It seems like the wrong thing to say in their time of sorrow, but his parents are lucky."

"You think so?" someone else asked.

"Hell, when my son died in World War II, nobody sent my wife any flowers. Jimmy died on an island in the South Pacific, and I can never go visit his grave. I don't even know if he has one. We never got to give him a proper funeral. When my boy died, nobody in the world knew except his mother and father and a few of his buddies in the army. Now the Kilnagaels have politicians calling them, offering condolences? I feel bad for anyone who loses a son in battle, but still, the Kilnagaels are lucky. Apparently their son is a hero. My son was just a poor, dumb bastard who died a million miles from home. Well, he's still my hero, I tell you that."

At that point he finished his beer, stood up and left the bar. He looked suddenly tired, as if defending the honor of his own son drained him. I guessed Danny's death caused Mr. Lally's loss to reverberate within him, stirring the painful memories of the grandchildren he never had, the family that never recovered, and the empty chair that still haunted their dinner table. We remained quiet for a few moments, watching him walking out to his car.

The Last Sunday in Ordinary Time

"Geez, I guess the pain never goes away, does it?" Seamus said.

"It's over twenty years since his son died, and it hurts like yesterday."

The First Sunday in Advent

November 27th, 1966

Father Marty

When I got to the Kilnagael's house that Saturday morning Mr. and Mrs. Kilnagael were gone, having made an appointment to meet with Fr. Connolly and make arrangements for Danny's funeral. Friday evening they learned that his body was on its way to Japan where it would be embalmed before being loaded onto a plane to San Francisco, and then flown to Chicago. Their son would be returned to them on Thursday, December 1st just one week after they learned of his death, and they were determined to do everything right.

The girls had been assigned the job of cleaning the house, getting it ready to receive guests. Kathleen's fiancée Roger was also there, and Kathleen decided they could put our muscle to work, so we carried chairs up from the basement, moved tables, couches, beds and dressers so the floors beneath them could be cleaned, and whatever else they asked us to do. They threw themselves into the work, glad to have something to do to distract them from the sadness of their brother's death. Kathleen told me the least they could do was make sure Danny came home to a clean house. I wanted to say that he wouldn't actually ever be in the house again, but I said nothing. If cleaning made them feel better, so be it.

By late afternoon the house was about as clean as it was going to get. I found myself in the odd position of being a father-confessor of sorts, listening to various sisters admit that they had been terrible to Danny from time to time. I listened patiently, assured them that it was typical kid stuff, and that I was sure Danny knew they loved him. The girls were exhausted. Forty-eight hours of mourning coupled with a lack of sleep left them in a suddenly giddy mood. It started when Eileen declared that she was the sister that Danny loved the most, so she deserved his bedroom. Colleen reacted angrily but her "How dare you" was cut off by Maureen.

"Don't think because you're acting holier-than-thou that you're getting it."

We were suspended between horror and laughter.

"I can't believe you guys," Josephine said.

"Maybe we could turn it into a shrine. St. Danny's room," Eileen suggested like she was daring her sisters not to laugh. I didn't risk joining in, so I remained quiet. This was their moment, their heartache, and I could only insult them by making jokes.

"We'll have to put his report cards up, and his Boy Scout merit badges." Maureen's comment caused a collective gasp among the sisters. They were staring at each other, mouths agape.

"Shut up, you guys, shut up." Colleen was refusing to surrender to the moment.

"And..." Kathleen said slowly, "that poem he wrote for Mom in fifth grade."

With that the dam burst. They were in hysterics.

"We'll have a tape of Mom saying "Don't make fun" any time somebody doesn't show enough respect."

"We have to make his bed."

"Why? He was a slob. It would be more realistic if it weren't made."

"Remember, cleanliness is next to Danliness."

This last line caused full-bore hysterics. The sisters were helpless in their laughter, regaining their composure only long enough to insist "You guys are terrible," or "That was not nice," or something similar. As we stood there and watched them, Roger and I laughed a little ourselves, but refused to cross the line between family and nonfamily. Roger was actually a little closer to being family because he was engaged to Kathleen, but still, Danny was not our brother, so we treaded lightly. As hard as it was to watch them laugh and not join in, we both chose not to intrude. After a couple of minutes the laughter subsided and the true sadness of the situation reasserted itself. The girls avoided making eye contact, and seemed as ashamed now as they were amused a few minutes earlier.

"We shouldn't being doing this," Maureen said finally. "What would Danny think if he were here?"

"I don't know," I offered. "I think he loved you most when you were laughing. They say laughter is good for the soul. I think your laughter is probably good for his soul."

"God, Marty," Eileen said, "You say the most amazing things sometimes."

"You do," Kathleen insisted. "It's so good having you here. You've been a big help."

"He's like a priest," Noreen added. "Really, did you ever think of being a priest?"

"Seriously. You'd be a good one," Maureen said. "Fr. Marty."

With this comment they exploded into laughter again. Unable to stop them, I made the sign of the cross with my right hand as if I were blessing them.

"Forgive them Lord, they know not what they do."

Even though we got back to doing some chores around the house, finishing up some last details, the girls insisted on calling me Fr. Marty for the rest of the afternoon. I didn't mind that they teased me like that, and the fact that the little game they were playing distracted them from their grief. It also made me feel more like a part of the family. I doubted that Roger was aware of it, but I allowed myself to enter into some bizarre competition with him, trying to prove which one of us was more of an insider in the Kilnagael's household.

As it got later in the afternoon, the girls began to wonder what had become of their parents. It shouldn't have taken that long to make the funeral arrangements, but they had been gone all day. When Mr. and Mrs. Kilnagael finally did return home, they had exciting news. Among the other people the Daley machine had contacted was Phillip Hendrickson, the star columnist of the Daily News. One of his researchers had contacted Fr. Connolly and met with the Kilnagaels at Holy Truth while they visited the rectory to discuss Danny's funeral. The following Monday the Daily News was going to run a big story about the death of the war hero, and the family that now made plans for the return of his body.

Colleen's parents spent the afternoon being interviewed for the article, and telling stories about Danny's childhood. It was going to be a front page story.

I thought of Mr. Lally and his sense that nobody cared about the death in battle of his son Jimmy, and how this appeared to be one more way in which the Kilnagaels received special treatment.

At the Lovely Bit there did seem to be a generational divided among the people there when Mr. Lally spoke. The older men seemed to hold a little resentment that so much attention continued to be showered upon Danny, and the younger guys seemed to want to stick up for one of their own. I didn't say anything right away, but I did say something later to Colleen, her sisters Maureen and Eileen, and to Roger. I told them about what Mr. Lally had said at the Lovely Bit, and how the other people reacted to it.

"There may be some people in Holy Truth who may resent that Danny is getting so much attention."

"Hey, we didn't do anything wrong," Colleen shot back. "It's not our fault about his son."

"I'm not saying it is. I'm just letting you know that not everyone will be as excited about that story in the Daily News as we are."

As I walked home that night I feared that they took what I said the wrong way. Some of the resentment I sensed at the Lovely Bit probably wouldn't have been as strong if it were for a family other than the Kilnagaels, but it also seemed like any other family wouldn't have gotten so much attention. The attention they got from Fr. Connolly, from the Stage Irish t-shirts, and now from the Daily News reinforced my thoughts that the Kilnagaels were a charmed family. It was as if even in the worst of times, like the death of their son, good things always happened for them, like Monday's big story in the newspaper. If there were already some resentment that Danny's death was being over-glorified, what would it be like after the story appeared in the paper?

There were two major afternoon newspapers in Chicago, the Chicago American and the Chicago Daily News. The Daily News courted the blue collar readers like those in Holy Truth. In Danny Kilnagael the Daily News had a perfect story, a genuine working class kid from a working class neighborhood who died valiantly in battle serving his country. The following Monday the Daily News ran the story about Danny, complete with pictures of him in his Holy Truth school uniform from sixth grade, and one of him in his army uniform. In our parish we took pride in the story of heroism by one of our own, and it became the talk of the parish. Along Madison Avenue signs appeared in the windows of businesses that read "Daniel Kilnagael Rest in Peace." Danny's profile as a war hero rose ever higher.

Two contrary opinions that simmered under the surface boiled over as I sat in the Lovely Bit that Monday afternoon. After school I stopped by the Lovely Bit before starting work at Mick's and watched as a fist fight almost broke out in the bar. There were only about eight people in the bar, six men who had stopped in on their way home from work, two college-aged guys I wasn't familiar with, and Seamus Touhy of course. Like everyone else in Holy Truth, they were talking about Danny.

For a few moments they were in agreement that the dead soldier was getting too much attention. The older guys talked about all the other men in the parish or in their families who had served in World War II or in Korea. It wasn't like Danny was the first local guy to die in battle. The younger guys were nodding their heads like they were in complete agreement.

"Besides," one of them said finally, "he was more of a fool than a hero."

This comment caused all of the conversation to stop for the moment.

"What do you mean?" Seamus asked.

"Well, during World War II we knew Hitler was the bad guy, we were the good guys. It made sense. In Viet Nam, nobody knows anything. Hell, the Vietnamese don't want us there. You'd have to be an idiot to go to Viet Nam."

"Hey," one man shot back, "nobody said he was an idiot. Any man who has the guts to go to war and serve his country deserves our respect. He is still a he..."

"He's not fighting for his country. He's fighting for someone else's country. And even that country doesn't want him there."

"Wait a minute. This is still the U.S.A., the greatest country on earth. We're over there protecting those people's freedom. It's important, heroic work."

The argument escalated into a shouting match. By the end of it, men who had been critical of all the attention Danny was getting now defended him. Danny represented the continuation of a long line of military greatness. The older guys accused the younger guys of being anti-American and of being communists. The younger guys yelled back that they loved this country as much as anyone did, but that didn't mean they should support killing innocent people because President Johnson said so.

The "debate" descended into the younger guys being called communists and the older guys being idiots and just when it looked like a fight would start Uncle Charlie kicked the young guys out. They started to protest that it was unfair to ask them to leave, but Charlie wouldn't back down, and they were outnumbered. When they finally did leave the guys remaining continued their defense of the honor of the United States.

"Nobody's gonna tell me that this isn't a great country. If we're over there it's because we're doing good things for people."

"Imagine that," another guy said. "Criticizing American soldiers while we're at war."

That last part bothered me too. I believed it took guts to be a soldier, so just being there showed that Danny had guts. The men at the bar felt good about themselves, having just successfully defended their country and the soldiers fighting for it. I allowed myself to take comfort in the idea that even the people complaining about all the attention Danny got were still basically in his corner. The Lovely Bit, whatever else it might have been, was a neighborhood bar and a patriotic place, and no one was going to come in there and start badmouthing it. As I got up to leave Charlie was buying a round for them as a way of thanking them for their love of country. I walked away feeling better about the idea that no matter how much people may have grumbled under their breath about all the attention Danny was getting, they still admired his commitment to his country.

The Last Sunday in Ordinary Time

What I failed to realize at that time was that the worst opinions of Danny would come not from people in the neighborhood, but from the other afternoon paper. As much as the Daily News wrote courted the blue collar Chicagoans, the American did the opposite. The two papers saw each other as enemies and often took contrary positions on issues in a sort of tug-of-war for readership. The American seemed to be antagonizing the blue collar workers in neighborhoods like Holy Truth in an effort to appeal to more upscale, better educated readers in wealthier city neighborhoods and the suburbs. Roy Cannon continued to use his Cannon Fire column to give a hard time to the people of Holy Truth and other west side parishes. The Negro march he first suggested weeks earlier was definitely going to happen. Cannon wrote a column introducing the world to the Reverend Torian McAllister, a Negro minister who fancied himself a colleague of Martin Luther King. What King had done in Selma, Alabama Reverend McAllister intended to do in Chicago. He would lead the marchers down Madison on the Saturday before Christmas proving that the Coloreds were neither afraid of walking through Holy Truth, nor afraid of Chicago's cold winter weather. Their cause was bigger than that.

Roy Cannon may have been genuine in his desire to promote extending social equality to Negroes in Chicago, but as far as the people of Holy Truth were concerned, his true intention remained self-promotion. His columns encouraging Negroes to march through Holy Truth made us feel like he was smirking at us, showing us to be inferior to the more liberal thinkers like him. The column achieved its goal. Roy Cannon forced everyone to talk about his column, and he became the subject of hundreds of angry conversations. If we complained about Negroes coming to march through our parish, then we were a bunch of bigots. If we said nothing then we'd have Coloreds overrunning our neighborhood. Holy Truth was enraged, no one more than my Uncle Charlie.

"All that crap about equal rights and selling them houses in our parish may sound good to the snobs in the wealthy suburbs, but this isn't some kind of social experiment. This is where we live, and we shouldn't have to tolerate them marching around like they own it. They don't. We do."

The fury of the parishioners was aimed at three people: Roy Cannon for sticking his nose in our business, Rev. Torian McAllister for organizing this march through our neighborhood, and, most of all, Alderman Mugsy O'Bannion for daring them to march. If he had kept his mouth shut then we wouldn't have the marchers coming. It was bad enough that they were coming, but they chose Christmas Eve, the Saturday before Christmas to march.

The store owners along Madison were furious. That was an important shopping day, but if it were disrupted by a protest march, then they stood to lose a lot of business. Mick and Uncle Charlie were two of the business owners who would be least affected by the march but they were angry anyway. Charlie, because he was the ward committeeman, took several phone calls and had other men stopping in to demand that he do something to stop the march. I don't know what he told them, but the whole parish was on edge.

In the news we started hearing a new phrase about the west side of Chicago, "white flight." The Negroes continued to push for integrating parishes along the Eisenhower expressway, but every place they managed to purchase saw a virtual stampede of White families selling and moving out. With each passing month the Negroes were moving closer to Holy Truth, a reality causing near panic in the parish. With the Coloreds now living so close to us, there began to be confrontations, and a series of violent attacks that were racially motivated on both sides. Watching the news on television we saw a lot of Rev. McAllister, and heard his constant refrain about Negroes only wanting to live peacefully with their White brothers. Increasingly, however, there were also interviews with angry young Negro men who had no interest in the whole Martin Luther King-Gandhi nonviolence movement.

"If we wait for it to be given to us, we'll grow old waiting. This is America, and Americans take what they want. You have to fight to get yours, and were ready to fight if that's what people want. Fighting to get yours is the American way."

We all heard stories about guys being jumped for no reason. While there wasn't too much happening in Holy Truth itself, we kept hearing about guys getting jumped at Kedzie and Lake, or Pulaski and Divisions streets. It was definitely moving closer to Our Lady of Holy Truth. Nobody believed that white guys didn't start at least some of the fights, but the truth was that as Negroes moved nearer to us, the nearby parishes became more violent and less safe. It was an ugly mix of rumor and reality and it caused more and more anger toward the Christmas Eve march that Rev. McAllister planned to make.

As it turned out, Danny Kilnagael had another friend in Chicago, a Colored guy he befriended in the army who happened to be home to

213

attend a family funeral. When Arthur Brown learned of Danny's death he decided to pay his respects to Mr. and Mrs. Kilnagael, something soldiers typically do for their buddies. The young man thought that by paying a visit to the Kilnagaels while wearing his army uniform, he could set an example of racial harmony and also perform a heartfelt act of friendship for his fallen fellow soldier. He believed that his army uniform would keep him safe even in a parish under great tension. He was wrong.

For Roy Cannon it all proved to be the mother lode of material for his column. His next column ran on Tuesday and it told the story of Arthur Brown stepping off the bus on Madison beginning to walk the two blocks to the Kilnagael's house. To prepare for his visit to the parents of his fellow soldier he made sure his shoes were shined, and his uniform neatly pressed. According to the Cannon Fire column, he had been practicing what he would say to Mr. and Mrs. Kilnagael, expressing his love and admiration for Danny, and stressing what a great soldier and good friend their son had been. He never made it. Before he got a block away from Madison, a few guys confronted him, wanting to know what he was doing in our parish. Words were exchanged and within a few minutes the young soldier was badly beaten. The picture in the paper showed his distorted face, two eyes virtually swollen shut, and his arm in a sling. The guys who did it ran from the scene, so no arrests were made. I didn't who actually had beaten him up, but there was a rumor that Eddie Mulroney was one of the crowd.

The column served as a lecture to all of us about how terrible we were for acting so violently toward Arthur Brown and another chance for the columnist to remind us how necessary the Christmas Eve march was.

The Last Sunday in Ordinary Time

He bragged that he was the most hated man on the west side. He wrote that the anger generated by his column supporting the marchers proved he was doing his job. If there weren't truth to the accusation that the people of Holy Truth were racists then they wouldn't be so upset.

The Daily News responded with more stories that were more sympathetic toward the people of Holy Truth. They described the beating of Arthur Brown as an aberrational event that did not reflect the general goodness of the hard working people in the neighborhood. There quotes from residents about a few bad apples not spoiling the whole bushel, and even some talk that the young soldier provoked the attack. And several articles appeared about Danny Kilnagael. By writing sympathetic pieces about how Danny reflected the parish's love of country, and how his devotion to duty showed that Holy Truth was a place where people raised children of character and courage, the paper restored some of Holy Truth's reputation that Roy Cannon tried to destroy. It allowed us to remind ourselves that we were good people no matter what was written about us.

The issue of the impending civil rights marchers may have distracted people to a certain degree, but there still existed a lot of irritation over the attention lavished on Danny's death. None of that irritation was aimed at Alderman O'Bannion, however, so he continued to pursue the hero angle as much as he could. It was a way to get the voters' minds off of the march. The Chicago Park District had a small patch of land near Our Lady of Holy Truth that was roughly half the size of a football field and had one statue and a couple of park benches on it. Word began circulating that Alderman O'Bannion intended to have it renamed Kilnagael Park after Danny. His office received a few phone calls from parishioners who resented this, so he held off on the idea. When Mick heard about it he said normally that would be enough to get the idea killed, but because the alderman was desperate to get people talking about something beside the march, the name change would probably stick. He also said that the mayor's office probably wanted to distract voters from the march even more than Mugsy O'Bannion did, so they were calling the shots. O'Bannion lacked the authority to stop it or allow it to go through.

The Daily News continued to feed off the story of the fallen hero. On Wednesday, November 30th, they ran a story with pictures of his casket being transferred in California from a plane from Japan to a plane bound for Chicago. On Thursday they ran a story with pictures of the casket arriving in Chicago, and of Colleen and her family in tears. The pictures included one close-up of Colleen wiping away a tear as the casket was loaded onto a hearse.

The courageous death of Danny Kilnagael grew in importance quickly, with one development after another seeming to be stitched together. The signs in store windows, the attention from the politicians, the quickly arranged return of his body, the naming of a park in his honor, it all seemed to create an almost mythic story of greatness and patriotism. All this for a guy who once told me he considered himself unlucky. Despite all of the accolades and honors being offered to the fallen soldier, Daniel J. Kilnagael, it turned out that he was right about being unlucky after all.

The Last Sunday in Ordinary Time

On the most basic level, of course, if he had been lucky he would not have died in Viet Nam, but he did. If he had been lucky his friends and family would not have gone to such great lengths to promote him as an instant war hero, but they did. If he had been lucky I would have never asked my Uncle Charlie to make phone calls to get details about the return of his body, but I asked, and Charlie did make those phone calls, alerting both politicians and newspapers. If he had been lucky the Negroes would not have been planning to march through our parish causing the politicians to use his death as a way of distracting voters, making him the most famous Chicagoan killed in Viet Nam, but they did. Finally, if he had been lucky, the two afternoon papers would not have been in a circulation war that caused them to work to discredit each other, but they were. The Daily News adopted the death of Danny Kilnagael as their exclusive story of heroism and patriotism. The Chicago American and Roy Cannon could not let that go uncontested. Even as the Kilnagaels made arrangements for the funeral and burial of their son, Cannon worked his network of contacts within the newspaper business, and sought negative information that would undermine the story of Danny's heroic death. It turned out that was able to contact some reporters who were assigned to Viet Nam, and he put out a call for information about the death of Private Kilnagael. In a column headlined "Not Such a Hero After All," he reported that Danny had not died in battle. On the last night of his life, the young soldier learned that he was being sent on a dangerous mission the next day. At about 2:00 in the morning a gunshot was heard setting off a minor panic among the soldiers. They spent the rest of the night on high alert, wary of snipers hidden in the dark. At daybreak they finally got the opportunity to investigate the area. Only then did they find Danny's body. He was dead from a single bullet to the head. He was, in the words of Roy Cannon, more of a coward than a hero. Afraid to face the dangers his fellow soldiers would face, Danny Kilnagael committed suicide.

The Second Sunday in Advent

December 4, 1966

Not seeing God in the Mud

The Last Sunday in Ordinary Time

In the nearly two weeks that passed since Fr. Connolly gave his big sermon on his intention to hold Holy Truth to the traditional teachings of the Catholic church, I had seen him a couple of times in the company of Mrs. Kilnagael. We were both at the Kilnagael's house on Saturday, December 3rd, and his renewed sense of leadership was obvious to all of us. Everything about him carried an air of authority, his body language suggesting that he gained a new confidence in his possession of Holy Truth. Holy Truth now belonged to him as certainly as it was once belonged to Monsignor O'Brien. Inside the Kilnagael's house he displayed the more empathetic and charitable sides of his paternal role in the parish, while outside the house he showed a pronounced sternness when addressing other parishioners. It seemed like every action was an attempt to become the disciplinarian he promised to be. The only trouble with his new found confidence was that he was the only one who really believed it. I thought of my history teacher who quoted the old saying "Men make plans and the gods laugh." Not more than three days after Fr. Connolly promised a renewed adherence to tradition, the Church made an extraordinary announcement from Rome. The Church was ending the centuries old tradition of meatless Fridays. Now we only had to avoid eating meat on Fridays in Lent, but were free to eat it all other Fridays. Even as our local pastor was promising more dedication to traditional Catholic discipline, the pope was requesting less of it.

Still, Fr. Connolly promised his parishioners that he intended to hold a firmer line against what he called the erosion of traditional Roman Catholic teaching. His promise rose partly from his own conservative views on the way Catholicism should be practiced, but also from his desire to mollify the parish elders who so disliked the liberal, modern turn the Church was taking. For all of his posturing and confidence, those elders felt like they were the true voices of discipline and tradition. Once they realized that the pastor had bowed to the pressure they applied, they decided to apply more pressure. Instead of owning Our Lady of Holy Truth the way Msgr. O'Brien owned it, Fr. Connolly found himself in a power struggle with some of the elders.

At 4:00 Colleen, her sister Maureen and I went to the O'Hagan funeral home with her father to straighten out a few last minute details. At virtually the same time the early Saturday night edition of the big Sunday paper was hitting the streets. There was a blurb running across the front page about Danny Kilnagael, inviting readers to open to Roy Cannon's column on page three. The columnist, it turned out, found the information he sought from Viet Nam. The headline read "Not Such a Hero After All."

A two-day wake for Danny was scheduled to begin on Sunday afternoon, and continue on Monday. A large turnout was expected because in the course of little more than two weeks the war hero Danny Kilnagael had become famous, and people were expected to come from all over the city. There was a rumor that Mayor Daley himself planned to attend. The funeral would be held on Tuesday morning, and all of the local TV stations planned to be there. Our Lady of Holy Truth would be the center of Chicago for a day. At the funeral home there was a deluge of flower arrangements. Veterans groups, politicians, business acquaintances of Mr. Kilnagael, some of the businesses along Madison Avenue and friends and neighbors all sent flowers. The number of arrangements was mind boggling. The Ladies of St. Theresa had sent one, the Boy Scouts, and even the Lovely Bit sent one. Mr. O'Hagan commented on the difficulty they were having finding a place for all of the stands they received.

Mr. Kilnagael and the funeral director discussed a few details about crowd control, and making sure that all of the visitors could be accommodated. Usually at a Catholic wake a kneeler was placed in front of the casket to allow mourners to kneel and pray for the deceased. Mr. O'Hagan said the plan was to have the kneeler in place, but if the line of mourners grew too long, the kneeler would be removed to allow the line to move a little more quickly. Mr. Kilnagael agreed that was a good idea, and, with Colleen and Maureen's help, chose the flower arrangements they wanted closest to the casket. They made the decisions based on a combination of beauty and importance of the relationship to the family. Mr. Kilnagael insisted that the one from his brokerage firm be placed in a prominent area, as well as one from Mrs. Kilnagael's brother and his wife. Colleen wanted the one from the Ladies of St. Theresa to please their mother, and Maureen chose the one from Cook County Democratic Organization. It was a massive explosion of red, white, and blue flowers with American flags interspersed to reflect the patriotic nature of Danny's death. Maureen said she thought it made sure that everyone knew Danny was a great American hero. At that point Maureen started crying and not offering any more opinions. Once the flowers were chosen to be near the casket we got ready to leave. One of Mr. O'Hagan's assistants stopped us and asked us to wait for a moment before leaving, and then asked his boss to come with him to another room. The two left us waiting for a few minutes, a length of time that seemed rude to us. We stood impatiently while Colleen said she thought it was a lousy way to treat a family at a time like this.

When they returned Mr. O'Hagan asked us to come back to his office. We all took seats before his desk and while he moved a box of tissue closer to us and took a deep breath.

"I have been in this business for a long time," he said, "but I have never had a more difficult moment than this one. Have any of you seen the early Sunday edition of the Chicago American?"

We all shook our heads and Mr. Kilnagael said a quiet "No."

"I didn't think so. Roy Cannon, that rather nasty columnist for the American has written something about your son and brother, something I certainly don't believe. Nor should you. Never the less, it is out there, in print, and most people believe what they read in the newspapers. I would do anything to avoid having to tell this to you, but it is important that you know it. Mr. Cannon is reporting that Daniel committed suicide."

"What?" It was Maureen who basically screamed at the man while she shook with anger. "He said what?"

"There must be some mistake." Mr. Kilnagael said.

"I'm sure that there…"

"Danny did not do this," Colleen screamed.

"No. No he did not," Maureen added.

The two of them focused their anger at Mr. O'Hagan who remained calm. I could tell it was not the first time he faced an angry family.

"I assure you…"

"Danny did not do this," Colleen screamed again.

"Oh my God. Do you realize that people are going to read that and believe it?"

The two girls directed their anger at the man across the desk as if he were the one responsible for the terrible news. They acted as if they could change it if they could get him to take back his words.

"Don't you sit there and tell us that our brother committed suicide, because he didn't. Danny would never do anything like that."

The girls quieted down after Mr. Kilnagael basically pleaded with them to do so, and then he asked "Are you sure?"

"I offer you my most sincere and profound apologies. I do not believe the story for a moment, but, it is in the paper. I don't believe that Mr. Cannon is a reputable source, but he did put it in the paper. I'm afraid that tomorrow at the wake, people will be whispering. I imagine that most people will have the good sense not to believe such an outrageous claim, but..."

He hesitated, not wanting to finish his thought.

"I don't believe it," I said, "I just don't."

"All I want is for my son to be remembered as a good soldier, and that he rest in peace. Why would they say this about him?"

"It's a lie." Colleen remained angry. "They can't get away with this, I won't let them."

As far as I could tell, Mr. Kilnagael didn't have any fight in him. His grief already sapped his energy, and this latest news compounded that sadness that had already washed over him. For Mr. O'Hagan it became a time to wait for the anger and the sadness to settle within the Kilnagaels, for them to realize the trouble was not in his office, but elsewhere. Finally Mr. Kilnagael stood up.

"Mr. O'Hagan, thank you for the kindness you are extending to us in this most awful of times." "Come on girls. We have to go tell your mother before somebody else does."

As we headed toward their car Mr. Kilnagael asked me to run to the corner drugstore and buy a copy of the paper so we could read it for ourselves. The headline, "Not Such a Hero After All" blared across the top of the front page, inviting readers to open to page three to read the Cannon Fire column. I didn't dare open to the column as we rode quietly back to their house, as much as I wanted to. Colleen shot me an angry look as if she thought it was a mistake to buy the paper, but they had to find out what it said. I attempted to hold her hand on the way home, but she pulled it away.

By the time we got back to the Kilnagaels' house night had fallen. The lights filled windows up and down the street except for their house. The only light in their house came from a dimly lit window in an upstairs bedroom, Kathleen's room. Colleen and Maureen followed their father up the stairs to the darkened bedroom of their parents. I went into the kitchen and called the rectory. I was surprised when Fr. Connolly himself answered it.

"Fr. Connolly? It's Marty Donovan. We just heard some news about Danny. He..."

"I know, Marty. I already heard. I'm already dealing with it. I can't talk right now."

The Last Sunday in Ordinary Time

He hung up the phone abruptly, but before he did I heard the unmistakable voice of Mr. Lally in the background. It was another one of those moments where I realized how difficult it was to be a priest sometimes. Not only was Fr. Connolly having to deal with the news about Danny, he also had to deal with whatever problem Mr. Lally was having. I figured the thing with Mr. Lally must have been serious or the priest wouldn't have hung up like that.

I stood alone in their kitchen and thought about the day Danny told Colleen and me that he thought he was going to die in Viet Nam. Up until that moment I assumed the news about Danny was a lie, but began to realize that maybe it wasn't. Maybe he was already thinking about taking his own life even before he left for the war. It was hard to imagine that he would do something like that, to give up any chance he had of coming home. After a few minutes the girls came downstairs, allowing their parents some time to be alone in their heartbreak. My presence surprised them, but, like always they greeted me warmly, almost like a brother, each of them except Colleen giving me a hug and thanking me for being there.

"Is that the paper it's in?" Eileen asked.

I nodded and she took it and opened to the column by Roy Cannon. She read only a few words before breaking down.

"Maybe you shouldn't read it," I suggested.

"No," Kathleen said. "We have to. We have to know what he's saying about Danny."

She tried to read it aloud but only managed a couple of sentences before she too started crying.

"Marty, will you read it to us?" I looked at Maureen and then Colleen. Colleen stood off in the corner with her arms crossed and a hard look on her face. She refused to come out and say it, but I suspected she didn't want me to read it.

"I don't know. Are you sure you want to hear it?"

They all insisted that they wanted to hear it so I picked up the paper, but before I began I looked again at Colleen hoping for some sort of permission. She turned away from me without indicating whether or not she wanted me to read it, and I began to read it for her sisters' benefit.

In 1918, just as the First World War was winding down, a young
Englishman named Wilfred Owen was killed in battle. In a moment of
heartbreaking irony, his family learned of his death while the church
bells in his hometown rang to signal the end of the war. Young Wilfred
was an extraordinary young man, possessing the heart of a warrior and
the soul of a poet. I mean both of those descriptions
quite literally.

Consider the heart-wrenching beauty of his poem *Apologia Pro
Poemate Meo.* Wilfred fought the war from the nightmarish conditions
of the trenches where the young men were forced to descend into the
very depths of hell. When the enemy fired at the trench and killed one
of their brother soldiers, that same gun fire made it impossible to

The Last Sunday in Ordinary Time

remove the newly dead carcass. The best the soldiers could do was to

heave the body out of the trench as far as possible, which, as you can

imagine, was not too far. Add to the fear, the pain, and the usual

agonies of war, the sight and the smell of human bodies decaying

all around you. Not just any bodies, but the remains of your friends

and fellow soldiers. They watched as rats appeared to begin eating

at those bodies while the soldiers were pinned down by enemy gun

fire, unable to provide the deceased with any type of burial.

Now imagine those soldiers laughing.

I, too, saw God through mud,-
The mud that cracked on cheeks when wretches smiled.
War brought more glory to their eyes than blood,
And gave their laughs more glee than shakes a child.

Merry it was to laugh there –
Where death becomes absurd and life absurder.
For power was on us as we slashed bones bare
Not to feel sickness or remorse of murder.

Gallows humor they call it, the ability to laugh about one's most

unfortunate predicament. He tells us that he saw and heard God

in the smiles and laughter of the soldiers gamely trying to survive

the hellish nightmare of their surroundings.

I, too, have dropped off Fear –
Behind the barrage as dead as my platoon,

The Last Sunday in Ordinary Time

And sailed my spirit surging light and clear
Past the entanglement where hopes lay strewn;

And witnessed exultation –
Faces that used to curse me scowl for scowl,
Shine and lift up with passion of oblation,
Seraphic for an hour; though they were foul.

Owen confessed that he too lost his fear in the
momentary glee
of men laughing at the death, decaying bodies, and
wretchedness of
war. His spirit, he wrote, soared past the hopelessness
around the
trenches in which he was trapped. His fellow soldiers
were angelic
for that hour no matter how foul they were in reality, or
how much
evil surrounded them.

I have made fellowships –
Untold of happy lovers in old song.
For love is not the binding of fair lips
With the soft silk of eyes that look and long,

By Joy, whose ribbon slips, -
But wound with war's hard wire whose stakes are
strong;

Bound with the bandage of the arm that drips;
Knit in the webbing of the rifle-thong.

He loved his fellow soldiers. Not the kind of love
they refer
to in songs about fair women with soft eyes and softer
lips, but
the kind of love that develops among soldiers fighting to
survive
the barbed wire realities and bloody wounds of war.

The Last Sunday in Ordinary Time

I have perceived much beauty
In the hoarse oaths that kept our courage straight;
Heard music in the silentness of duty;
Found peace where the shell-storms spouted reddest
spate.

In that laughter, that gallows humor, Owen saw not
just
beauty, but God Himself. He and his fellow soldiers found
their
courage in that laughter, heard music in the silence of
duty
performed, and found peace in the idea that the
exploding shells
of war could not defeat their spirit.

Nevertheless, except you share
With them in hell the sorrowful dark of hell,
Whose world is but the trembling of a flare
And heaven but a highway for a shell,

You'll shall not hear their mirth:
You shall come to think them well content
By any jest of mine. These men are worth
Your tears. You are not worth their merriment.

Unless you were there, standing in that hell with
them
as the bombs shook the ground around them, and the sky
offered only a path for more bombs to reach them, you
cannot
hear their laughter. Wilfred Owen warned us not to think
of
them as being in anyway content because of his poem.
Those
men were worthy of your tears. You are not worthy of
their
laughter.

And that, in a nutshell, is why Private Daniel J. Kilnagael is no

hero. As Wilfred Owen wrote almost fifty years ago, you cannot

appreciate what makes a soldier a hero unless you go into battle with

him. Private Kilnagael, upon learning that he would be sent into

battle with his fellow soldiers, quietly crept out of camp, placed his

weapon in his mouth, and blew his head off. No battle fatigue or

hell for him, thank you. Let his "buddies" do the dirty work. To

paraphrase Wilfred Owen, soldiers who bravely march into the hell

of battle are worthy of your tears. Cowards like Private Daniel J.

Kilnagael are worthy of your scorn.

For all of the praise his neighbors, local politicians and second

rate journalists want to heap upon the memory of Pvt. Daniel J.

Kilnagael, it turns out that he wasn't quite the hero they're trying to

make him out to be. Currently in Viet Nam there are tens of

thousands of soldiers who carry their guns into battle with courage

and conviction. Many of these same men die lonely deaths while

clinging to the highest ideals of valor and loyalty to both their flag

and their fellow soldiers. Pvt. Kilnagael was not one of these men."

"They keep talking about him being a man, but he was as much a boy as he was a man. He just attended his senior prom a little over a year ago," Kathleen observed.

It was offensive in the way Danny was used as a tool to poke fun at the rival Daily News, and at the politicians who rushed to praise him when he died. With one column Danny went from being a symbol of patriotic courage to one of shameful cowardice. Cannon made it sound like anyone who loved or admired Danny was a fool, and that he died as a man who wasn't worth loving. I might have cried as I read it if I weren't getting so angry. Actually I think the anger in my voice allowed the girls a momentary shift away from sorrow, and more toward anger. Anger left us feeling a little less helpless than the overwhelming sorrow did. The emotional wounds were still too fresh, however, and the unrelenting sadness could not be swept aside by a flash of anger or defiance. Grief demanded its hour and had no intention of allowing the girls to cling to anger, hope, or even love for their brother as an oasis from the soul numbing bleakness that Danny's death brought to their lives.

As I walked home that night I wondered what Danny thought about that night, that moment when he chose to end his life. Did he end his life out of fear? Out of shame? Out of loneliness? I could hear Br. Kevin, my religion teacher dismissing suicide as the coward's way out. "Sometimes dying is easy," he said, "but hanging in there, facing life's challenges when your back is against the wall, that's hard." It was tempting for me to be angry at him because I could see the pain that he had caused his family, but Roy Cannon was so cruel in the things he wrote about my friend that I couldn't bring myself to agree with the things he wrote. I chose to believe that Danny would not have caused his parents such heartache if he weren't in pain himself.

When I got home my mom confronted me because I had been gone all day. The time I spent at the Kilnagaels continued to be a touchy subject between us, and I had been gone for hours. I told her the news about Danny. If she had any negative opinions about the nature of Danny's death, she kept it to herself, and made sort of an unspoken apology by dropping the questions about my day. The news about Danny's death obviously upset me, so she offered a few sympathetic words and allowed me to remain preoccupied with the Kilnagaels without any further protest. I knew she didn't want me to be so involved with the Kilnagaels, and this drama added to her unhappiness with the time I spent there, but she didn't press the issue.

The Last Sunday in Ordinary Time

The Third Sunday in Advent

December 11ᵗʰ, 1966

An Unforgiveable Act

The following day I woke early and went to church with my parents, just like every Sunday. I went through the motions of the Catholic mass, standing, kneeling, or sitting when I was supposed to, but my mind was elsewhere. At the conclusion of mass I walked to the back of the church and waited quietly in the corner. A suicide was a scandal, and people were talking about this scandal with the energy that a good piece of gossip brings to people. I kept my distance partly to avoid showing my anger at them, and partly to keep from crying in front of them. I heard my mother telling a woman that I was taking it hard. I wanted to correct her, to tell to stop telling people that I was taking it hard, to tell her that it was my personal business, but, she was right. I was taking it hard. I could barely manage to say hello to people, never mind conversing with them or telling them to shut up about Danny.

To avoid talking to the others I stood in front of the bulletin board and turned my attention to the list of the names of men from Our Lady of Holy Truth or relatives of parishioners who were currently serving in the military. Actually there was two lists, one of men currently serving, and another with the names of men who had died in the war. I didn't recognize the names of the men who had died, so I figured that Danny was probably the first actual parishioner to die in Viet Nam. To my surprise, Danny Kilnagael's name had already been removed from the list of active soldiers, but had not yet been added to the list of the fallen heroes. It made me angry to think they were too lazy to update the second list.

When I was with Colleen and her family I was the one who maintained his composure, but away from the Kilnagaels I was always on the verge of tears. I comforted myself by concluding that I was more at home in the Kilnagael's house than I was with my parents at Our Lady of Holy Truth.

While I stood at the bulletin board I heard a couple of men laughing and talking about a man named Kelly.

"Did you see this guy Kelly on the news last night?"

"An Irishman is he?" the second man said in a fake Irish accent.

"More of an Irish jig." With that the two of them started laughing.

"He says 'I'm not a Negro, I'm Black.'"

"I know. And then he starts in about how that McAllister isn't Black enough to be leading this march they're talking about, and McAllister points to his own skin and says 'I'm darker than you, I'm darker than you.'"

"Crazy Coloreds. They don't know what they want."

After mass I read the Sunday papers to learn what they were saying about Danny. To my surprise his suicide was not the biggest story in the paper. Reverend Torian McAllister continued moving ahead with his plans to lead a peaceful march through Holy Truth and other neighboring parishes on Christmas Eve, but he found himself facing opposition from other Negro leaders. I realized that as what the men in church were laughing about. Some of them felt that holding a protest march so close to Christmas violated the spirit of nonviolent protest. Others felt that rather than being too confrontational, the protest wasn't being confrontational enough. A new name, Stokely Carmichael, appeared as a counterbalance to that of Martin Luther King, and he became the spiritual leader of a new sense of aggressive protest. This man the guys at church were talking about, Henry Kelly, apparently modeled himself after Stokely Carmichael. When the city suggested it would simply deny a permit to march in an effort to stop it, Kelly spoke in more defiant terms.

"We're talking about Black power. The days of waiting for someone to open the door for us are over. If they don't open the door, we'll kick the stinking door down."

The tough talk added one more complication to the efforts to find a solution that worked for everybody. Now it turned out that, if the city negotiated with the Negroes through Rev. McAllister, then the Blacks would march anyway. If the city negotiated with the Blacks, the Negroes took offense and promised an even bigger march. The more hard line Black leaders planned to sit out the march because they felt it was insignificant enough to be useless, but they made it clear that if the city of Chicago tried to deny the permit to the marchers, the Black Panthers and other, angrier groups would show up in force to make sure the march happened. The mayor's office declared that no decision had been reached yet, but the threat of an even bigger turn out of marchers caused most commentators to conclude that the mayor would cave in on this issue.

According to the paper Rev. McAllister continued to insist that it would be a nonviolent protest march. Alderman O'Bannion refused to make a public comment, but the unofficial word was that if we ignored them, they would go away. Neither of these two benign opinions was as exciting at the idea of the parish being on the verge of a race riot. There were a number of quotes in the paper daring the Negroes to march through our neighborhood, or daring the Whites to stop the Negroes from marching.

Holy Truth became a much more dangerous place in both our imaginations and in reality. The newspapers seemed to play up the newly aggressive rhetoric coming from Black leaders, and could always find people in our neighborhood who insisting on matching the tough talk word for word. Growing up we all knew that we had to lock our bikes up if we rode them to the store or to the park, but now, whenever a bike was stolen, it was concluded that the Negroes did it. On the other hand, guys who travelled just a little bit outside of the parish had to worry about getting into fights with colored guys who now lived just a mile or two east of Holy Truth. There was a lot of staring going on, and Negro, Black or White, you didn't want to be in a situation where you were outnumbered. There were always a few guys in Holy Truth who insisted that "we oughtta kick their asses back to Africa," but now more people were threatening violence. Increasingly we heard stories that "a bunch of coloreds jumped my cousin" or that some guy had to run for his life, but everyone complained that reporters didn't put that in the newspaper. The response to the idea of Negroes coming to "kick the stinking door down" was defiant oaths to just let them try. The newspapers treated anyone of the Negroes who spoke with anger about marching through our neighborhood as a community leader, and his comments were treated like they carried a lot of influence. I might have been more worried about all of this if I didn't have Colleen and her family on my mind. The march was scheduled in less than three weeks

, but neither I nor the Kilnagaels really paid attention.

Despite my mother's unhappiness with the idea, that afternoon I went back to the Kilnagaels to accompany Colleen to her brother's wake. Visitation was scheduled for 3:00 to 9:00 on both Sunday and Monday because of the large crowds expected to show up, so we left the Kilnagaels' house at 2:00 to give them most of an hour to do any last minute preparations. In an effort to somehow ease the crushing pain their mother felt, the girls kept stressing the extraordinary amount of flowers that had been sent, arrangements that overflowed not just the room where Danny would lie, but also the adjoining room. They were such a real, tangible show of love and support that at least the family could take some comfort from them.

When we got the funeral home, however, there were not so many flowers as we remembered. Most notably to me, the massive red, white, and blue flower arrangement from the Cook County Democrats that Maureen had chosen to be near the casket was missing.

"These are not the flowers we chose," Maureen complained loudly to one of the assistants. "What happened to the flowers?"

"Mr. O'Hagan will be with you in just a moment," he said quietly. "In the meantime, we need you to wait here. He'll be right with you."

In anticipation of the large crowd expected, the room had plenty of chairs, so the ten of us sat quietly, but uneasily. Mr. and Mrs. Kilnagael, their six daughters, Kathleen's fiancée Roger, and I all waited. Before Mr. O'Hagan arrived Mrs. Kilnagael's parents arrived, and the girls all rose to greet their grandparents. A few more minutes passed and we talked about the flowers while we waited.

"Marty, weren't there a lot more flowers here yesterday?" Maureen asked.

"Yeah, I don't know, they must be in another room or something. Why would they move them?"

Finally Mr. O'Hagan entered the room with Fr. Connolly. The priest's presence should have been a comfort to us, but the look on his face was troubling. The girls greeted him as well, and he returned their hellos, but there was an awkwardness to it. He stood before us while Mr. O'Hagan stood off to the side.

"Since I came to Our Lady of Holy Truth I have had the pleasure of participating in the life of a vibrant, devout parish. All of the people here have greeted me warmly and welcomed me into their lives. No family has done more to make me feel at home in Holy Truth than this one, the Kilnagaels that I see before me now. Your love for each other, for your church, and your parish is a joy to behold, and an example that other families would be wise to follow. You made my time here among the most rewarding of life."

At that moment he stopped, took a deep breath, seemed to fight back an urge to cry, and looked toward Mrs. Kilnagael.

"The life of a priest is filled with the great joys of baptisms, first communions, weddings, and other moments of family and individual happiness. Then again we sometimes find ourselves saying prayers with men who learn they have cancer, families who lose a loved one in a car accident, wives who struggle with an alcoholic husband, and other such moments of trauma. We see the best in our parishioners, and the worst.

The Last Sunday in Ordinary Time

"The primary role of a priest, however, is as a defender of the faith, a shepherd who must take steps to protect his flock from the evils that exist outside ourselves, and, perhaps more importantly, from the evils that sometimes attack us from within. The devil is always attempting to catch us in our moments of weakness, those moments when we are most likely to ignore or forget our need to remain strong in our faith. It is the first order of business for every Roman Catholic soul to remain true to our faith, and to always place our faith in God, and our fate in God's hands. When we fail to do these things, when in our weakness we give in to the devil, we are required to confess our sins. God will forgive us as long as we offer a sincere, heartfelt confession.

"In my many years as a priest this is by far my single most difficult moment. As I am sure you are aware, we learned that Danny took his own life."

"That's a lie," Colleen yelled. "He didn't do that."

"I'm sorry, Colleen, and for all of you I am sorry. I managed to contact the Chicago American, and they put me in contact with Roy Cannon. He told me the story, about his sources, and, I'm sorry to say, it is true. There is no doubt that Danny took his own life. That means..."

"We know what it means." Mrs. Kilnagael stared at the priest and spoke in a cold, flat tone.

"Because of this I have made the decision to deny Daniel J. Kilnagael a Christian burial. As you know, when a person commits suicide, he dies in a state of mortal sin, and is no longer qualified for a Roman Catholic funeral."

241

"You're saying that Danny has gone to hell, and we can go to hell too as far as you're concerned."

There was a collective gasp. To hear Mrs. Kilnagael lash out at Fr. Connolly like that ended any hope for a compromise. A finality entered the room with those words. When their mother exchanged those the priest, it meant they could not argue with the news any more. They did not, as might be expected, burst into tears. Instead they sat quietly, more shocked into silence than saddened. The harshness of it all overwhelmed them, not leaving enough space for protest or grief or anything else, the weight of it crushing them into a stunned silence.

I looked immediately to Mrs. Kilnagael. In the time since Danny left for the war, she had become the incredibly shrinking woman. Whenever I had seen her as I grew up, long before I ever dated Colleen, she carried herself with an air of friendly confidence, completely comfortable in the role of neighborhood leader. In the few months I spent with Colleen, Mrs. Kilnagael seemed to lose some of her stride, her stature, and appeared to lose ground in the fight to maintain her sense of purpose. She seemed to completely surrender to the awful fear that her son might die in war, and then the heartbreak of learning that her fear had been realized. Until this moment she looked defeated.

"Father," Mr. Kilnagael pleaded, "there must be something you can do. Danny doesn't deserve this. *We* don't deserve this."

"I'm sorry, Peter, but I think it is in the best interest for all of the Catholics in Holy Truth and outside the parish as well. I will pray for the soul of your son, but I cannot in good conscience allow him to receive a funeral in the Church. Further, I have instructed Mr. O'Hagan to cancel

Daniel's wake. It would send the wrong message to the faithful to allow it to happen."

The details of the tragedy of Danny's death started wrapping around his family, adding one coil after another, like a boa constrictor squeezing the life out of them. First they had to accept his death, then learn that it was a suicide, and finally realize they faced a public shaming conducted by Fr. Connolly himself, the priest in whom they placed so much trust. Honestly, I thought they struggled even to breathe. They were devastated and unable to muster the strength to fight back. The silence in the room compounded the damage being inflicted upon them. No one said a word for a moment or two.

"You son of a bitch."

I screamed it as loudly as I could. Even I was surprised by my outburst, but I couldn't just sit there and watch it happen.

"You son of a bitch," I repeated. "What? Does this make you feel important, making a show out of how tough you can be? Kicking them while they're down?"

"Father, Marty doesn't speak for the family," Mr. Kilnagael said.

"Oh, I think he does," Mrs. Kilnagael answered.

"Father, there must be something we can do."

"Never mind, Peter. He doesn't have any compassion for anybody. He's using our family to his show the parishioners who's the boss."

"This is not about me. It is about what is best for the people of Our Lady of Holy Truth. I did not make this decision lightly." Fr. Connolly spoke in a calm, even tone, but also with a sense of purpose. He would

243

not be drawn into an argument or start defending himself. Nor would he allow anyone to make him appear to be some sort of bully who was treating the Kilnagaels unfairly, or allow the Kilnagaels to be bully him into not adhering to Catholic teaching. "I acted in the best interests of all Catholics. I can't turn aside two thousand years of tradition as a favor to a grieving family." He spoke now to them, and not to me. "You all still have my love, and are in my prayers. In time I hope you will come to appreciate that upholding standards even in the most extreme of times is the best way to honor our Lord."

"I know you're right," Mr. Kilnagael said. "A soldier doesn't do what Danny did. A Catholic doesn't do what Danny did. But, still...we can't know if Danny indeed lost his faith. Surely he was still a believer in Christ. There must be something we can do."

"Don't beg him. For God's sake, Peter, don't beg him," Mrs. Kilnagael said angrily. "It just makes him feel important."

Fr. Connolly ignored Mrs. Connolly's insult.

"No, I'm afraid not. There is nothing that can be done. Daniel died in a state of mortal sin, and is therefore, no longer qualified for a Christian burial. His only role in the Church now is to serve as a bad example to others who may lose their faith."

Mr. Kilnagael nodded and whispered "I suppose you're right."

The Kilnagael girls met his words with a determined silence. Neither they nor I answered back, but their mother's support for my outburst did harden their emotions toward Fr. Connolly. He mumbled a quiet blessing, made the sign of the cross toward the Kilnagaels, then turned and walked out of the room.

"He can take his blessing and stick it up his ass," Maureen whispered angrily after he left them room.

"Maureen." Hearing her father speak her name in such a stern manner was supposed to quiet her down, but it didn't.

"What? Am I supposed to pretend he isn't a pompous jerk? Marty, I'm so glad you said that to him. *Somebody* needed to say it," she answered while giving her a father a defiant look.

"I'd take Fr. Marty over Fr. Connolly anytime," Noreen added.

Mrs. Kilnagael placed her head in her hands and broke down into loud sobs. By my estimation she felt deserted, not just by her son Danny or Fr. Connolly, but even by God Himself. In the time we dated, Colleen sometimes made half bitter, half humorous comments about Danny being her mother's favorite child. At this moment the sentiment seemed true. She gave life to seven children, but now her favorite had taken his own life and left his mother to wonder how it ever came to this. Maybe under different circumstances she could have turned to Holy Truth and God for understanding, but now Fr. Connolly took those options away from her. Even her husband seemed to be taking Fr. Connolly's side. In such a short span of time she lost not only her son, but also seemed her faith.

Fr. Connolly acted as if Danny were a cancerous tumor that had to be surgically removed, or a body part to be amputated from the family in order to save the faith of the rest of the Kilnagaels. Mrs. Kilnagael believed, even in death, Danny remained a vital part of the family. If his place in the family were to be so completely destroyed in this way, then the whole family was being destroyed.

The Last Sunday in Ordinary Time

We remained in an awkward silence for a little while more. Mrs. Kilnagael's parents and her daughters took turns joining trying to comfort her. When Mr. Kilnagael tried to put his arm around her squirmed out of it and said "No, don't." Kathleen put her arms around Roger and cried on his shoulder, but when I tried to comfort Colleen she pulled away from me. If her mother could not be comforted by a man, then Colleen wouldn't be either. They whispered among themselves each consoling one another, and repeating that they thought Fr. Connolly was a jerk for what he had done. They, even Noreen and Doreen, made a point of thanking me for what I said to Fr. Connolly. They spent more time talking to me than talking to Roger. I know because, God forgive me, I was keeping score. One or two at a time they came by me not only to thank me, but to vent their anger, express their outrage, or complain about how unfair it all was. Most of all, they told me they were glad I was there.

Mr. O'Hagan returned to the room we were in. He dressed immaculately in dark suits with red ties, his salt and pepper hair short and perfectly brushed and in place. He wore the shiniest, most well-polished shoes I'd ever seen, and an American flag pin in his lapel. His whole manner was a combination of a professional, a confidant, and a man to be taken seriously. He inspired both an air of friendliness and a firmness that suggested we owed him respect.

"I have no answers for you," he said. "I believe that the Church is being more than just unkind to you, but also going so far as to be a bully. Unfortunately, our business here is so intertwined with Our Lady of Holy Truth that we can't afford to be defiant. I assure you that we don't agree with the decision to prevent your son's wake from being here, but we are in many ways a servant of Holy Truth. The only kindness I can offer you at this time is to assure you that we will hold Daniel's remains until you make other arrangements."

"Mr. O'Hagan," Maureen asked rather meekly, "last night when we were here there was a lot more flowers than I see now. I know I chose a large red, white, and blue arrangement to stand near the casket. What happened to all of the flowers?"

"This is a difficult thing for me to say," he answered, "but this is Chicago. Last night, after the story ran in the newspaper, the alderman's office sent a representative to my home. He requested that I let him in to remove some of the flowers because some of the politicians were afraid that it would look bad to have flowers at the wake. They removed everything that had been sent by the politicians and a few that had been sent by local businesses."

"And you just let them do this?"

"You must understand that we are continually in need of the cooperation of the alderman, the police department, and any number of city services. When city hall decides they want something from you, well...we were in no position to refuse."

"Oh, God, I can't believe it. Everybody's deserting us. Why can't they just leave us alone?"

It was a new wave of pain, and they turned to each other, murmuring about how unfair and unbelievable it all was. By now it was 3:00 and people began arriving for the wake only to be turned away at the front door by employees of the funeral home. A sign was hung on the front door saying that the wake had been cancelled. At this moment the

The Last Sunday in Ordinary Time

Kilnagaels had no fight in them. Each moment brought a new wave of sorrow washing over them, leaving them bewildered and unable to react. I looked at Mrs. Kilnagael, the parish matriarch, the lioness who once struck me as so ferocious as she prowled the streets of Holy Truth, the woman who always knew the right thing to say to provide comfort, welcome, or sense of order in her world. "Mrs. K, I am so glad you decided to strike back, to fight back a little" I thought as I watched her sitting so angry and alone.

"Danny has to have a funeral," I announced to his family. "We can't let this happen without a fight. He deserves a proper funeral even if I have to plan it myself."

"Would you, Marty?"

Mrs. Kilnagael spoke for the first time since we arrived at the funeral home. I honestly never expected her or them to take me up on the offer, but her voice shattered the silence, giving a boost to her whole family. They needed to hear from their mother, needed to see some of the fight that I was looking for. Colleen and her sisters all looked at me with some hope in their red, tear-filled eyes. Eileen, Maureen and Colleen all nodded, urging me to keep talking because it was doing their mother some good.

"Don't be silly," Mr. Kilnagael said dismissively. "Marty is a kid. This is too much for him. We can't turn this over to some high school boy."

"What do you suggest? My son has to have a funeral."

"Did you stop to think that maybe the Church has a point? He killed himself. It *is* a sin. Maybe we should just bury him and prayer for his soul afterward."

"How dare you?" Mrs. Kilnagael glared at her husband. The girls collectively gasped, but remained almost motionless, not knowing whose side to be on. Maureen broke down in tears.

"Stop it. Stop it now. Stop fighting with each other. You're only making it worse."

"Maureen, they both still love Danny," Kathleen said as she tried to put an arm around her sister, but Maureen twisted away.

"Don't go taking Dad's sided on this."

"I'm not taking anyone's side. I just want…"

"Dad had no right to say that," Colleen said in almost a shout. "Danny did not kill himself. Mom's right. He has to have a funeral."

Now the girls started moving. Colleen, Eileen, Noreen and Doreen all moved closer to their mother. Kathleen stood beside her father, and Maureen remained noncommittal, alone in the middle until I stepped next to her so she didn't feel alone. Colleen glared at me. No one spoke now, and the silence compounded the ugliness of the situation. I desperately tried to think of something to say but nothing came to mind.

Mr. O'Hagan, finally spoke, speaking in the slow, measured, almost emotionless way tone that seemed to comfort people no matter how deep their grief was.

"Please, all of you, allow me to say something. There is no use in getting so angry at each other. It neither honors your brother nor offers any solace to your family. You have been put in an unforgivably difficult situation. I have never seen a situation quite like this one. I am troubled by how difficult people have chosen to make this for you, and I want to stress that I maintain that you are being treated remarkably unfairly. But rather than letting things unravel any further, let's deal with the situation as it is. Let me go over the issues with you, and offer some possible solutions."

Even the idea that there might be some solutions to the problems the Kilnagaels faced eased the tension a little bit. They were desperate for some sliver of light to penetrate the darkness of the moment, and Mr. O'Hagan offered it.

"First of all, Fr. Connolly and the church have made it difficult if not impossible for funeral homes like mine, ones that do most if not all of their business with Catholic families, to host a wake for Daniel. I find this decision most distasteful, but as a practical business matter, I cannot afford to defy the Church. In an effort to make things easier for you, I made some phone calls. I found another funeral home that is willing to host the wake in our stead. Steinberg and Cohen, a funeral home about three miles east of here said they would be willing to do it for you on Friday."

"That's a Jewish place, isn't it?" Mr. Kilnagael asked.

"Well, yes, it is owned by Jewish families, but they are not exclusively Jewish in conducting business. They do a number of Christian or nondenominational wakes every year."

"So, they do Catholic ones?" Mr. Kilnagael asked.

"Danny isn't *having* a Catholic funeral. The Church won't *let* him," his wife reminded him.

"I am certain that they do very few if any Catholic services, but the problem is that the Archdiocese has chosen support Fr. Connolly's decision completely. I'm afraid that Daniel will not receive a Catholic funeral anywhere in Chicago, and the Catholic funeral homes, like my own, are reluctant to defy Church authority."

"I don't like the idea of a Jew acting as the undertaker for my son. I don't think..."

"Peter," Mrs. Kilnagael said sharply. "Danny has to have a funeral. It doesn't matter if the undertaker eats ham or not. Danny has to have a funeral."

"But, at a Jewish funeral home? Haven't we offended the Catholic Church enough?"

"We haven't offended the Catholic Church at all," she screamed back at him. *"They* deserted *us*. I don't care how *they* feel about it. Danny has to have a funeral."

Mr. Kilnagael was clearly embarrassed by his wife's outburst. He turned his attention back to Mr. O'Hagan and tried to gain a measure of control.

"Aren't there any Protestant ones nearby?"

Mr. O'Hagan hesitated momentarily before answering. No matter how emotional the situation might get for the Kilnagaels, he was not going to lose his very calm demeanor.

"Not really, no. Chicago is a very Catholic city, and this neighborhood is primarily Roman Catholic in its makeup. Even those funeral homes that are not so closely tied to the Catholic Church are dependent on a steady flow of business from Catholic families, so they worry about being blackballed by the archdiocese. I contacted a few of them, but they claimed to be booked this week, so they say they cannot accommodate another wake. I don't know if that is true, or if it is genuine concern about incurring the wrath of the cardinal. Either way, none of the nearby funeral homes are willing to accept this business."

Mr. Kilnagael looked like a man slowly realizing he was caught in a trap. I thought he was searching for a way out.

"How much will it cost?"

"What difference does that make?" Mrs. Kilnagael said in an angry half whisper.

Mr. O'Hagan diplomatically ignored the comment and pressed on with the details.

"Since you have already paid O'Hagan Funeral Home, we can make all of the arrangements and forward the payment to Steinberg and Cohen. If there are any increased costs, they will be minor. Most likely, it will not cost you any extra."

"Tell me something," Mrs. Kilnagael said. "Could these people take care of the details but still hold the wake here?"

"I'm afraid not. It would have to be held at their location."

"Peggy, please. You can't expect…"

"I can't expect what? This is our home. We live in Holy Truth. I don't want my family to be exiled from here. Danny has to have a funeral, and it has to be here, where his friends and family live. I don't care what Fr. Connolly says or does. Holy Truth is our home, and we're not going to be shoved aside so easily."

"Where do you propose we hold his wake and funeral?" Mr. Kilnagael asked.

"I...don't...know. We will find a place." She turned her attention back to Mr. O'Hagan. "You go ahead call these people. We don't have to think about it, go ahead and make the arrangements."

"Peggy, I want to talk..."

"My son has to have a funeral."

"But where..."

"My son has to have a funeral. Don't say another word. My son has to have a funeral."

"But I don't think..."

"My *son,*" she said in a voice barely contained on the edge of a scream, "has to have a funeral."

"Maybe you could do it at the Lovely Bit. I mean, they have a banquet room right next door."

Everyone looked at me, but this time I wasn't sure if I said the right thing or the wrong thing.

While it did seem to ease the tension a little bit, no one reacted right away. The awkward silence returned for a few seconds more, everyone seeming to wait for Mrs. Kilnagael's reaction.

"Actually," she said finally, "that's perfect. Right there on Madison, right in the middle of Holy Truth where that arrogant priest and his ridiculous followers can watch all of our friends come and show him that he can't push people around."

"A tavern?" Mr. Kilnagael said. "Are you serious?"

"Yes, I'm serious. We will have the wake and funeral at the Lovely Bit, right here in our parish."

Mrs. Kilnagael left no room for her husband to try and save face. She asserted her will over him, and he was left to stew in a quiet anger, humiliated by the fierceness of his wife's scolding. For about thirty seconds, maybe a minute, no one said a word until Mr. O'Hagan pressed on.

"Now, about the service itself. I don't imagine that any local Catholic Church will break ranks with the archdiocese and agree to a funeral. If you know a priest, let's say a family friend who would be willing to lead prayers at the funeral home, you may want to call him and ask."

"I don't know if we do or not. Those bastards are deserting us like rats off a sinking ship. Just when we need them most, they're nowhere to be found."

There was not an audible gasp, but to hear Mrs. Kilnagael refer to Roman Catholic priests as "those bastards" in front of her children was shocking to say the least. We exchanged glances, Maureen mouthing the word "wow" when I looked at her, and Colleen and Eileen looking almost proud, with a kind of you-tell-'em-Mom look on their faces.

"I will leave that to your best judgment."

Mr. O'Hagan continued on, acting as if he heard nothing unusual. As I watched them I could almost hear the bond between Mr. and Mrs. Kilnagael splintering in front of me. Their daughters seemed to be again forced to choose sides, but if this family was in turmoil, Mr. O'Hagan pretended not to notice.

"Finally, there is the issue of the cemetery plot."

"We already have one," Kathleen said in a somewhat hopeful voice, "over at Holy Guardian."

Mr. O'Hagan grimaced.

"I don't think you do. Holy Guardian is a cemetery run by the Archdiocese of Chicago, and I expect they will deny Daniel burial there."

"I don't see why they have to be so mean," Maureen said. "I mean, really, why don't they have to be so extreme about this?" She turned her face so she could wipe away the tears that welled up in her eyes.

"I will call and find out if we can still bury him there," Mr. Kilnagael said.

"No, don't," Mrs. Kilnagael responded. "If they don't want us, if my son is not good enough for their churches, we won't insult them with his presence on their holy ground."

"I will contact Steinberg and Cohen and have them look into purchasing a grave at Union Liberty or one of the other nondenominational cemeteries. When they call you, they will have that information as well."

The Last Sunday in Ordinary Time

What Becomes a Funeral?

Mick stopped by our house on Monday evening wearing a suit, unusual for him, because he spent the afternoon downtown in a meeting with Standard Oil. They gathered all of the franchise owners in Chicago to discuss possible changes in the contract between the company and its station owners. The company decided to buy back as many franchises as possible, and they applied pressure to get him and others to sell their gas stations back to the corporation. He didn't want to sell to begin with, but even if he wanted to sell it, Mick felt the price they were offering was way too low. They informed him that a trial date had been set for Tuesday, February 21st, and a judge would decide if they could force him to surrender his franchise.

The Last Sunday in Ordinary Time

"I don't want to go to court," he said, "but neither do they. They keep insisting that the upcoming march by the Negroes is proof that the neighborhood is changing and the gas station is losing value. They're trying to get us to sell to them in a panic, and some guys are ready to sell. They view this opportunity to get out as a godsend because their neighborhoods have grown violent and unsafe. I told them no, absolutely not. Still, they can make it difficult for me if they want."

"Well, these Coloreds are making it difficult for everybody."

"Who cares if they march through Holy Truth? It's not like they're staying." Mick and both of my parents looked at me like I had two heads. "What?"

"They want to stay, Marty," my dad said finally. "They want us to give them for free the kind of houses we've had to work for."

"What if they're willing to work for the houses? Br. William at school says all they want is a chance. He says we should offer them good old fashioned Irish hospitality."

"Hah! It's all very nice for the Christian Brothers to offer our homes and neighborhoods to other people, but they don't have to live here." Mom looked at Dad and Mick to back her up.

"Marty," Dad said, "It's best for people to stick with their own kind."

"What? Mick's dating a Dago."

"Marty!" my dad yelled. "Mind your manners."

"Listen, Mr. Hotshot," Mick said calmly, like he was amused by my insult, "first of all, she's Italian, not a Dago. Secondly, she's Catholic, so she's more like us than you think. Besides, there's a world of difference between Negroes and Whites. There isn't such a big difference between Italians and the Irish."

My mom acted like she agreed with him, but she didn't. She was appalled that Mickey would actually date an Italian woman. Italians were not our kind, and Mick dating one wouldn't make them our kind.

"Italians are not marching through our neighborhood, Negroes are."

"Well, regardless whether the Negroes are marching or not, I have no intention of selling my gas station. They're trying to make me panic, hoping I'll just gladly accept a low ball offer."

I knew enough about Mick to know that holding onto the gas station was vitally important to him. He loved the idea of being an entrepreneur, of owning his own business, of being a real American. His stubbornness, his independence, and his determination may have put him on a collision course with Standard Oil, but I knew Mick would win.

"That's the way those corporations are," my dad said. "They try to make the other guy panic, take advantage of his worry, and cheat him. Especially a small business like yours."

After dinner I announced that I was heading over to the Kilnagael's house.

"Why are you going over there?" Mom asked angrily. "You don't belong there. It's time you let them be."

"I promised to help plan Danny's funeral."

"You what? Marty, after what he did? He's not having a funeral. Didn't Fr. Connolly decide that he couldn't have one?"

"Mom, Mrs. Kilnagael wants to do one anyway. She asked me to help."

"She has no right to ask you to defy the Church. You have no business getting involved, and she has no business asking you."

"But I want to do it."

"I don't care what you want. It's not your place."

"It is my place. They want my help. They asked me to help."

"Marty," my dad said, "you can't go. We don't want you to go."

"You should have seen the look on Mrs. Kilnagael's face when Fr. Connolly told her he wouldn't allow Danny to have a funeral. And all those people taking back their flowers. People have been cruel to her. What am I supposed to do? Call them and say my parents are against you, too? I'm deserting you too?"

"She shouldn't have asked you to do this."

"If I don't go there and help out, it means I'm kicking them when they're down. Even if what they say about Danny is true, that doesn't mean it's okay for everyone to act like they're lepers."

"Marty," my dad said quietly, "suicide is a grave sin. You can't act like it didn't happen or that it doesn't matter."

"But Colleen and her family didn't commit suicide. Her brother did. Why should we punish them? Isn't hard enough to live with this without having to face the scorn of neighbors? Should I tell them I'll be your friend again someday, after I've ignored you for a while? Maybe I should tell them I can never talk to them again because of what their brother did."

"No, I'm not saying that. I'm not comfortable with you going over there, or helping them plan some kind of substitute funeral. It's not your place. I'm not asking you to ignore Colleen. That would be a terrible thing, but ..."

"I can't stop going there now. If I don't go it'll look like I agree with everybody who's saying nasty things about them."

"Don't be silly. I'm sure..."

"I'm going, Mom."

When I arrived at the Kilnagael's house, Maureen met me at the door.

"I'm so glad you're here. Come on in. Boss Kathleen is in charge in the dining room. She thinks she's the funeral queen or something."

The news that the Catholic Church decided to deny Danny a funeral made the front page of the newspapers again, with both the American and the Daily News giving it big coverage. Roy Cannon used his Cannon Fire column to do a victory lap of sorts, smugly giving the readers a big I-told-you-so. The Daily News, on the other hand, wrote a story about the cancellation, and an editorial about how the Church was treating the "least of my brothers." It used the news about Danny's lack of a funeral to take a not so veiled swipe at the American in general, and Roy Cannon in particular. The editors claimed it was "unseemly" for some to claim the Kilnagael's misfortune as a reason to celebrate. Danny may not have met the full measure of what it meant to be a soldier, but that did not give anyone the license to dismiss the importance of his life.

Danny's death, or at least the memory of his life became the centerpiece of a pair of strange tugs-of-war, one between the Daily News and the American outside the small Irish neighborhood of Holy Truth, and one between Mrs. Kilnagael and Fr. Connolly inside the parish. I had been certain that most people who lived in Our Lady of Holy Truth would be sympathetic to the Kilnagaels, but realized that maybe it wasn't true when I read Roy Cannon's column. He wrote about a Saturday night meeting at the rectory between Fr. Connolly and a number of angry parishioners led by Mr. Lally. I remembered that I heard his voice in the background when I phoned Fr. Connolly, and now I knew why. Mr. Lally led a group of people who insisted that the memory of all truly valiant soldiers who died in battle would be tainted if a Danny was allowed to have a "hero's funeral" at Holy Truth. The column quoted Mr. Lally saying "This is a priest who insisted he would uphold the traditional standards of the Catholic Church, so we made sure he did. A guy who commits suicide is not eligible to have a funeral in a church. I owed it to my son to make sure it didn't happen." Saturday evening, while we were learning the truth about Danny, Fr. Connolly was learning it too. Even if he had wanted to go easy on the Kilnagaels, the priest had been pushed into a corner by Mr. Lally and his crowd. Fr. Connolly made it sound like he chose to hold a hard line in order to maintain Catholic discipline, but Mr. Lally made it sound like the parishioners forced the priest to do as he was told.

The girls were all sitting around the dining room table, with Kathleen at one end, the self-appointed chairwoman. When I walked in they all greeted me and Doreen got up and moved so I could sit next to Colleen, but only after Colleen told her to. Kathleen had a notebook in front of her, and I could see that she had a list on it.

"Let me bring you up to speed," Kathleen said. "Our mission, as we see it, is to turn the Lovely Bit O' Blarney into Holy Truth. We decided, actually Mom insisted, that we can't try to do some kind of imitation mass. There won't be any communion but we'll try to include the rest of it. We're not trying to do our own thing, but it still has to be religious. We are still Catholic."

"Have you picked a Catholic theme?" I asked.

"Yeah, that's what I said," she answered.

"Which one?" They all looked at me.

"You know, there's Christ the King, Christ the Redeemer, Christ the Sacrificial Lamb, Christ the Savior, ...I don't know, the Prince of Peace, the Son of God, the Son of Man, Christ the Servant. There are a lot of them."

"Wow. You really are Fr. Marty."

"Knock it off."

Mrs. Kilnagael, who had been listening from the kitchen, looked in at us and said "I like the Prince of Peace. I can't claim that my son was a great warrior, but I'd like to think it was because he was such a peaceful soul." She grew teary as she finished, and Eileen went over to her.

"Good idea, Mom. We'll make this about peace, and, hopefully, Danny can rest in peace."

Kathleen read the list of things that they had decided should be included in a service to help make it a Catholic funeral:

1. Music
2. Candles
3. A crucifix

4. Reading from the bible

5. Photographs

6. A eulogy

7. Prayers

8. Banners

9. Danny's belongings

10. Group participation

Mrs. Kilnagael added one more thought. She was very moved by the editorial the Daily News wrote reminding people that "whatever you do to the least of my brothers, that you do unto Me." She wanted her daughters to plan this ceremony, but they had to stick to the idea that "less is more." She wanted a humble remembrance of her son, somehow equating the funeral of her son being held in a bar to the birth of Jesus in a manger. With that in mind we immediately dismissed the idea of sprinkling holy water or burning incense, and after some discussion decided that burning candles was not too Catholic, and would be appropriate. Mrs. Kilnagael wanted to put as much distance between her son and Holy Truth as possible.

Kathleen was the one who brought up the idea of group participation. The mother of one of her college friends died, and Kathleen went to a Methodist service.

"It was really neat. They asked people to stand up and say something nice about this woman who had died, and probably thirty or forty people did. One woman talked about how she had broken her leg, and this girl's mom started making dinners for her family while she was laid up. Another woman mentioned that Mrs. Hamlin had watched her other children while she was in the hospital visiting her son who was dying of leukemia. One after the other, people remembered times when Mrs. Hamlin welcomed them to the neighborhood, loaned dresses, all sorts of stuff that helped them through difficult times."

We all agreed it was a good idea.

"But somebody has to get the ball rolling," I said. "You guys all have to think of one or two yourselves to encourage other people to join in."

"Okay, but what do we do first? We can't just start asking people to stand up and start talking. We have to begin with a prayer or a song or something," Maureen said.

"I was thinking about Danny," I said, "and whether or not he was a good soldier. I think it was just the opposite, that he wasn't cut out to be a soldier. Like your mom said, he was a man of peace, not a man of war, and I always loved the prayer of St. Francis. What would you think about opening with the prayer of St. Francis?"

"We could do both with that," Colleen said, "a prayer and a song. The choir used to sing that sometimes, and I'm sure that we could convince them to sing it on Friday."

Everybody loved that idea, so it was decided that we would open the service by singing the prayer of St. Francis. Their mom was pretending to let us do this on our own, but she remained within listening distance in the kitchen. I could tell she was standing near the doorway even though I couldn't see her. When she didn't say anything I assumed she liked the idea.

"How much music do we want to have? How much singing should we actually do?"

"Well, there is still 'Danny Boy'" Colleen said. "I mean, I know that some people got upset last time, but it is a beautiful, sad song. Really, it's perfect for this."

The girls all agreed that it was a perfect song for the funeral, and we thought it would be the right song to end the ceremony with. We had the opening song and the closing song.

"I think we should have one more, in the middle someplace." Maureen said.

Nobody could name a third song, so we moved on the other things. It followed that the theme of the service was now peace, and how Danny was too much of a gentle and peaceful soul to have become a killer in combat. Having chosen peace as a theme, we turned our attention to the idea of banners to decorate the hall. During the teenagers' masses at Our Lady of Holy Truth, kids had met to design vertical banners eight feet tall by two feet wide that somehow reflected a certain holiday or message, like Easter, or "Give to Caesar what is Caesar's, and give to God what is God's." They were made of felt with different pictures made of cloth cutouts depicting a sacrificial lamb, a sunrise, a chalice, a candle, or some other symbol.

"What could we use to depict peace?" Kathleen asked. "The obvious answer is a dove."

"How about," Eileen suggested, "we do two of them. One depicting a tree full of leaves, full of life, and one with bare branches depicting death."

"That's good," Kathleen answered, "but let's put a dove in the life tree, and show the dove flying off to heaven in the death tree."

"I think that would be lovely."

It was Mrs. Kilnagael again, who had been standing in the doorway listening to us. Because she liked it, we approved it right away, and Noreen said she would work on them with her friends.

Kathleen went down the checklist they had made: "Next, candles – Do we want to have candles or not? If so, who's in charge of getting them?"   Kathleen said she would take care of the candles, but if she couldn't find the right ones, they would skip them.

"Number four, crucifix."

"We have to have a crucifix," Maureen said.

"How about the one hanging in the hallway upstairs?" Norreen asked.

They reacted in unison. They had a Celtic cross hanging in the upstairs hallway, and everyone agreed that it was perfect, Irish, Catholic, but not too Catholic. Noreen smiled brightly as her older sisters congratulated her on the idea.

"Number five, the reading. Do we want to have a reading, and who is going to choose it? And, how many are we going to have?"

"They have two readings and a gospel in mass. Maybe we should skip it so it doesn't look like were just imitating the church." Eileen said.

"Oh, we have to have a reading."

"Every religion reads from the bible," I said, "so it's not like it's a strictly Catholic thing."

"So how many do we want to have?" Kathleen asked.

"One, just do one." Colleen answered.

Everybody agreed that one was enough, but nobody knew exactly what we should read.

"Fr. Marty? Do you think you could choose a good reading for Danny?"

"I'll look for one, but I want everybody to think of one, too, in case you don't like mine."

"Good idea," Kathleen said. "Everybody is in charge of trying to think of a bible story or reading they think is right for the occasion. Then we'll choose the one that is the best."

"Number six, photographs."
The girls all wanted to do that, so they agreed to do it together.

"Number seven, group participation."

This was Kathleen's idea, so she volunteered to be put her in charge. She had to introduce the idea to the whole crowd, and act as an emcee for it.

"But everybody has to have something to say about Danny," she insisted. "Now, number eight, prayers."

We knew we were going to sing the prayer of St. Francis. They decided a rosary was too much, but wanted to say at least one prayer, and preferably two. It became everyone's job to think about what prayers they might like to say on Friday.

"Number nine, eulogy."

At first no one spoke up, but then Eileen said she wanted to do it, "if nobody else minds." From watching them I concluded that they all wanted to do it somewhat, but were also afraid to take on such a big job. Nobody else objected, so Eileen would deliver the eulogy.

"Number ten, Danny's belongings."

They all agreed that they would do that as a family.

"Okay," Kathleen said, "we all know our assignments. Remember, everybody needs to think about a possible reading, everybody needs to think about a prayer that might like to include, and we also might add one more song to the middle of the service."

"I have a song I would like to hear."

Mrs. Kilnagael walked in from the kitchen. She moved to where Doreen sat, signaled for her to move over, and sat down so she could share the chair with her youngest daughter. She held a lit cigarette in her hand, took a drag from it, and then seemed to look at all of us one by one as she exhaled the smoke.

"Even before Danny died,…" She hesitated, suppressed a desire to cry, and then continued. "Ever since he went off to this terrible war, I leaned on Mary. I said my rosaries and prayed so hard for her to protect my son, but she didn't do it. Really, when I think about, she was unable to protect her own son from a terrible death, so it wasn't fair of me to expect her to protect mine. Danny's death was God's will; I know that, just as the death of Jesus was God's will. So, Mary was unable to answer my prayers, but she is still here with me, I know she is, and today, when I read in the paper that whatever we do to the least of our brothers, like Danny, we do also to Jesus. Just as I am in pain now, so too is Mary in pain as we watch people attempting to heap scorn on Danny the same way they heaped scorn on Jesus during the crucifixion. Like her I lost a son, and I really like what the paper said about the way people have treated Danny, and him being like the least of my brothers. Since we're this close to Christmas anyway, and as a reminder to everyone that they treated my son badly, I think the song *'What Child is This?'* would be appropriate."

"That's a beautiful song, Mom," Eileen said.

All of the girls we're in agreement, but I wasn't so sure.

"Do you think that some people might take it the wrong way?" Colleen shot me an angry look. "I mean, the song says *this is Christ the Lord.* Some people might think you're comparing Danny to God."

"Nobody will think that," Kathleen said.

"No, that's crazy," Eileen added.

They all murmured support for their mother's idea, and I suggested maybe I was wrong, but I still felt uneasy about it. I conceded that it was a beautiful song, and because we all wanted to please Mrs. Kilnagael, we decided that we would sing *'What Child is This?'* in the middle of the service. It was a couple of minutes past 10:00. Colleen had been given the job of recruiting choir members to sing on Friday, Noreen, and Doreen were to do the banners, and I was to choose some readings we could use. We agreed that we would meet again on Wednesday, this time at 4:00. As I was getting ready to leave Mrs. Kilnagael asked me how many people could fit into the hall, and I told her I thought it was about one hundred. Actually I had no idea, and just pulled the number out of thin air.

"That's not very big, is it?" She made a face to show she was thinking about it. "I'm sure a lot more people than that will show up, but that's okay. If there are people spilling out onto the sidewalk, it'll send a message to Fr. Connolly."

Her question caused me to wonder about it, so even though I was very late already, I decided to stop by the Lovely Bit on the way home and find out. It turned out that when they used the round tables it held only ten groups of eight, or eighty people, but if we didn't have tables, but just lined up chairs, we could put in twelve rows of 10 seats, or about 120 seats in the room with an aisle up the middle. I also figured that if it got too crowded, people could easily spill over into the tavern itself.

Uncle Charlie told me that he had two visitors earlier in the day, Mrs. Kilnagael to reserve the room for Friday morning, and Fr. Connolly later on advising him that he shouldn't do it.

"By then, of course it was too late." I was caught off guard by his irritation with it. "I didn't want to get caught up in the middle of all of this, but I wasn't about to say no to a grieving mother. Neither God nor Fr. Connolly is very pleased with me, at least according to Fr. Connolly. Of course I'm not sure he can tell who's who in that equation."

He eyed me with suspicion.

"I wonder who put the idea in her head to have a funeral here." I shrugged my shoulders as if I didn't know, and he nodded slowly, indicating either he knew I did it or he was at least thinking about it. "Isn't it a bit late for you to be out on a school night?"

I agreed that it was and got out of there as quickly as I could.

The Last Sunday in Ordinary Time

The Gospel Truth Was I Didn't Know

The following day I went to school. I woke up thinking that I might not because I had to work on Danny's funeral, but my parents wouldn't consider it. Once I got to school I started asking guys what they knew about the bible, which, aside from obvious references to Adam and Eve, Moses, and Noah's ark, wasn't much. In religion classes we studied the Baltimore Catechism and learned to be proper Catholics, but rarely read from the bible. I mentioned that to Mick once and he said that was the Catholic way. The priests studied the bible and interpreted it for us. That prevented us from misinterpreting the word of God, which the Catholic Church felt was the biggest problem among the Protestants. Some of my friends joked about me wanting information about bible, but quite a few expressed a genuine interest in helping me find the right bible passage to read at Danny's funeral.

At lunch someone recommended going to the public library because it had copies of the bible and other books that might help me out. Then Tommy Novak said I should go to the library in Oak Park.

"You live in Holy Truth, right? You can take the L straight out west to Oak Park. They just built a new library there a couple of years ago. It's unbelievable. If they don't have the books you need then nobody will."

Oak Park was a suburb that was directly west of Holy Truth, and Novak was right, the L train did go there. It was famous for having several houses designed by Frank Lloyd Wright, and as the birthplace of Ernest Hemingway. According to my eighth grade art teacher, it was also a place where artists like to live, and was where she lived as well. She mentioned once or twice that her husband was an attorney, which, my dad told me later, explained how a school teacher could afford to live there. I decided that I would go there that day to see if I could find an appropriate reading for Danny's funeral.

When I got to the library I asked the librarian where I might find a bible.

"What? A good Catholic boy like you doesn't have one at home?" She smiled and directed me to the section where religious books were, and then asked if I were looking for something in particular.

"Is it a school assignment?"

"Yes," I told her. It spared having to explain myself. "I need to find one that might comfort a family due to the loss of a child."

She nodded and pulled three different versions of the bible off the shelf, which were two more than I realized existed. She then walked over to another aisle and pulled a couple of books about death and mourning.

"I can't help you too much, but these books might help you find something meaningful."

I thanked her and brought the books over to an empty table and opened one of the bibles. Immediately I was lost. The bible, I realized, was a very thick book, and trying to pinpoint one small passage that would be relevant to the Kilnagaels' troubles was like looking for a needle in a haystack. I thumbed through each of the bibles and looked through the other books she had given me, but I sat there bewildered, unable to understand the format of the holy book. I kept looking around but the only other person in that section of the library was a Negro man sitting a few tables away. He had an open bible in front of him, a yellow legal pad, some papers scattered about the table, and a briefcase on the floor. I was a bit embarrassed to ask the librarian for help again, but I kept looking at the Negro. The bible sitting open on the table next to him indicated he knew more about it than I did, so I figured he might be able to help me. I stalled and absentmindedly flipped through the books before me, but I finally I decided I would ask for his help.

"Excuse me, sir."

He wore a black suit with a white shirt and red tie. Coupled with the black, horn-rimmed glasses the suit gave him a somewhat serious look. The man turned to me with a bit of a surprised look on his face.

"Yes, young man?" He spoke with an overly enunciated manner that suggested he was either some kind of English professor, or a man took himself seriously.

"Do you know much about the bible?" He looked at me for a moment as if he were sizing me up.

"What is your name young man?"

"Marty."

"Marty, as in Martin, as in Martin Luther King?"

I smiled and said "Yeah, I guess so."

"Well tell me something, young Martin, why do you want to know if I know anything about the bible?"

He took complete control of the conversation, repeatedly asking me questions and forcing me to earn the information. At the same time, I trusted him, somehow, as he befriended me rather than simply answering. I told him the entire story of the Kilnagaels, and their need to provide their son with a funeral and proper burial. He looked at me intently and made me feel as if he thought every word I spoke was important. He nodded frequently, and threw in small comments like "I see," "Uh huh," and "of course she feels that way," among others. Eventually I asked him if he could direct me to a bible passage that would be appropriate for Danny's funeral, but before he answered me, he asked me a few personal questions.

"You are a Catholic, aren't you?"

"Yes, I am."

"So," he said with a look that suggested he wondered about my motivation, "Do you agree with the Church's teaching that someone who commits suicide is damned to hell?"

"I do, but nobody I ever knew...I mean... it's hard to surrender to such a merciless judgment. Danny was my friend, a guy I actually knew. I'm praying for a loop hole."

"Are you trying to save the young man's soul, or are you trying to ease his mother's pain?"

I had to stop and think about that for a moment. My primary concern was Mrs. Kilnagael, and I remembered her yelling at Fr. Connolly, that he was telling her that her son could go to hell.

"I'm trying to do both. I'm also trying to save our parish. Our parish is Our Lady of Holy Truth, and this decision about Danny is tearing Holy Truth apart. Our priest basically told us that there was no hope for Danny's soul, that, because he committed suicide, he was damned to hell forever. Mrs. Kilnagael is angry that he said that, but also scared that he might be right. I would like to give her some hope, find some kind of a loop hole that would allow her to believe that her son might escape the fires of hell. I'd also like to keep Holy Truth intact."

"That is a tall order, young Martin. Your priest friend might be right. Maybe there is no hope."

"I think her husband, Danny's father, thinks that, that it is hopeless." I put my head down and stared at the floor for a moment. I averted my eyes because saying that aloud was enough to make me start tearing up. "Even the Kilnagael family is falling apart over this."

"What do you believe? Do you believe it's hopeless?"

"I'm not sure, but it's like I don't even care. If I could give Danny's mom a reason to believe that her son might not spend eternity in hell, even if the reason weren't true, I would do it."

"So what you are telling me, young Martin, is that false hope is better than no hope at all."

"Yes."

"Well, for the record, I am not entirely convinced that there is no hope. When a person is caught in something terrible, especially something not of his own making, he can lose his perspective. If this young man, Daniel, did indeed see the horrors of war as a hopeless situation, if he allowed himself to commit the sin of doubting God's love during that dark moment when he was most in need of God's love, I am hard pressed to believe that God would damn him eternally for a such a moment of weakness. My God, our God, is a loving, compassionate God Who understands our weaknesses and imperfections."

"So, are you saying that we can save his soul if we pray for him?"

"Young Martin, I would recommend you pray for his soul whether you can save him or not. If you are asking me if your friend has fallen out of God's favor, I would tell you no, no one ever falls out of God's favor. He loves us all, even the least of our brothers. Remember, Jesus tells us that you whatever you do unto the down and out, unto the powerless, unto the tormented, that you do unto Him. Prayer always helps, and your concern would please Jesus because it makes you a better Christian."

His words comforted me greatly, and made me feel like I was doing the right thing.

"It will also make me a better Irishman."

He leaned back and gave me a puzzled look.

"The Irish have a superstition that says if you don't offer help to someone when you can, the fairies will play tricks on you, but if you do, they will leave you alone." He smiled brightly at that, almost laughing.

"Well young Martin, holy Jesus, the Irish fairies, and a Negro preacher all seem to be telling you the same thing; there is hope."

"So, can you help me? Do you know any bible passages I can show the Kilnagaels?"

The Last Sunday in Ordinary Time

"I believe I do, young Martin, I believe I do."

He began thumbing through his bible, going back and forth, somewhat mumbling to himself, "No, not that one," "maybe that one," and so on, but he interjected a "young Martin" every once in a while to let me know he wasn't ignoring me. Finally he finished, he reached for a briefcase that sat on the floor by his feet and pulled out a business card. He placed the business card face down on the table.

"Young Martin, do you have a pencil?"

I ran back to my table and grabbed pen and paper.

"Alright, young Martin, I will recommend three and let you decide which one is best. Are you ready?"

"I am."

"On the back of my business card I want you to write down these three bible passages. When you go back to your table I want you to look them up. I need to leave and I won't be able to offer you any more help, so you will have to choose one on your own."

I nodded and he continued, pausing at each one to give me time to write them.

"Thessalonians 4:13-18. Romans 8:31-39. Psalm 103: 8—19." He hesitated for a moment before continuing. "Do you have those written down, young Martin?"

"Yes, yes I do. Thank you so much."

"If you have any questions or I can help you in any way, my phone number is on my card. Feel free to call me."

I turned the card over and was astonished to read his information:

Rev. Torian C. McAllister
Living Word Baptist Church

The Last Sunday in Ordinary Time

Pastor

He smiled brightly, enjoying every second of the shocked look on my face.

"You're Rev. McAllister?"

He nodded and said "Surprised?" He then took off his glasses I began recognizing the face I had seen on TV.

"Yeah. What are you doing here? Don't you live in Chicago?"

"Yes, I do, but I work here in Oak Park."

"You look like you could be the mayor of Oak Park."

"Nothing that high falutin', I'm afraid. I clean the streets here in the daytime, and then try to lead people down the road to salvation at night."

"I guess that explains why you wear a suit."

"Well, as you know, I am planning to lead a march down Madison, right through Holy Truth on Christmas Eve."

I nodded but resisted the temptation to say "Yeah, I know, and my friends and family hate you for it."

"If I want my congregation to see me as a leader, then I need to dress like a leader. And if I want your people to respect me, I need to dress like a leader. If I walked around my own neighborhood wearing the uniform of a maintenance man, people wouldn't show me the same respect. If you want to be a leader you have to dress like a leader. I come here after work because nobody bothers me here. At least not until today." With that last line he winked at me.

"I wish you well in your endeavor, young Martin, and if you ever find me in a moment of need, I hope that you will repay me by extending some kindness to me."

"I promise you I will."

He smiled again and said, "It's the least a better Irishman can do."

"Rev. McAllister, thank you. You've been a great help to me."

"Don't be so sure young Martin. Your goal is to keep Holy Truth from changing. My goal is to change Holy Truth."

He studied me to see how I would react to that but I didn't say anything. Honestly, I couldn't imagine Our Lady of Holy Truth changing the way he was hoping it would, but I was too polite to tell him he was wasting his time trying to change us.

With that he told me he needed to leave, so we shook hands and I went back to my table as he packed up his belongings. We waved to each other as he strode out of the room, and I remained behind staring at his business card. In the spirit of the moment I said a brief prayer of thanks that God had led him there to help me. It also occurred to me how different he was from my own father. Dad, like Rev. McAlister, essentially worked as a maintenance man. Dad also held a low level leadership position because of Uncle Charlie, but Dad never worried too much about looking like a leader. The only times my father wore his suit was to church on Sunday, and to the wakes of people closely or even remotely connected to Streets & San. It seemed like Dad's most important management job was to make sure the Daley Machine paid respects to the public employees who worked in Chicago. Rev. McAlister showed much more ambition than my dad showed.

I immediately looked up the three passages he suggested and was amazed at what good suggestions they were. Of the three I thought that the one from Romans was the best one, but I carefully wrote down all three of them. I then spent the next hour or so copying each one of them three more times so I had four copies of each one. I originally planned to make ten copies of each, but it took forever to do just one, so ten was out of the question. When I left the library I was confident that I was ready for the next meeting.

When we got together that night Mrs. Kilnagael was not home, nor was Mr. Kilnagael. Colleen's father thought that the whole idea of a rogue funeral made a bad situation worse. He thought that it was leading his family further away from the Church, and he didn't like it. Mrs. Kilnagael's personality was much more forceful than his, and she would not be denied. Although he didn't come out and declare that he forbid her from arranging a separate funeral, Colleen told me he had been making snide comments, basically stage whispers deriding the work his daughters were doing. After one comment too many there was an explosion between her parents, and they decided to leave the house to avoid arguing in front of the kids. They said they were going out to dinner, but the girls all knew what was going on. None of them believed that their mom would give in, but a small doubt lingered.

As we sat down for the meeting I had a strong sense of confidence. Because the minister had been there to help me find a good reading, my job turned out to be one of the easier ones. Recruiting members from the choir to sing at Danny's funeral was Colleen's job, and we all thought it would be an easy one, but it didn't turn out that way. A

The Last Sunday in Ordinary Time

few of the kids said their parents would not let them take the day off of school, and others said that their parents wouldn't let them do it unless Fr. Connolly gave his okay, but he refused to approve it.

"Connolly's telling people it's sacrilege to attend Danny's funeral," Colleen told me over the phone. "I mean, he's really getting after people not to go. I don't think any of the women from the St. Theresa Society are going to be there. I haven't told my mom yet, but it's really going to hurt her if her so-called friends desert her."

"I can't believe so many people hang on every word a priest says. This is America. We are free to choose. Why are they asking a priest for permission anyway?"

"I don't know," she said, "but they really care what he thinks."

We gathered around the dining room table a second time, and Kathleen acted as the chairwoman again, going the down the list of assignments.

"Okay, first: candles. I went to the religious store over on Division and found the right candles. They're big enough to be seen, but not too big, so we're going to have candles there on Friday.
Number 2: I decided to tell the story about the time Danny broke the head off of Dad's golf club, and then tried to sneak it back into the bag without being caught, but Dad saw him."

All of the girls agreed that was a funny story, and a good choice. Then Kathleen went around the table and asked everybody if they had their stories picked out. Only Eileen knew what she was going to say. The rest of us, including me, hadn't decided what to talk about. Kathleen was aggravated by that.

283

"Look, I'm expecting everyone," she paused and stared at her youngest sister, Doreen, "and I mean everyone, to have something to say about Danny. I don't care if you're nervous or whatever, you have to stand up and speak."

Everyone promised they would be ready, although some of the promises were mumbled more than spoken. Kathleen waited for a few seconds and directed her eyes around the table, taking the time to glare at each one of us enough to make us squirm a little bit.

"Number three: music. Colleen, how is that coming?"

"It's coming badly. So far I've talked to twelve different people, and no one's agreed to sing yet. Patti Dugan said she might, but I'm still waiting. Laura, Alice, and Annie all said their parents won't let them take the day off of school, Bill and Patrick haven't returned my phone calls, and almost everybody else told me that they can't because Fr. Connolly told their parents it was sacrilegious. Fr. Connolly is really determined to stop people from coming on Friday."

"Why should he care?" Eileen said.

"Donna told me that he told her mother that we're trying to defy the Church's authority. She told me that she might not come, it might be a sin," Maureen said. "I was hoping she was the only one, but it sounds like a lot of people are having their doubts."

"Does Mom know?" Kathleen said in a half whisper.

Maureen nodded. "She's heard some things from a few people. The word is out. We are causing trouble and Fr. Connolly doesn't like it."

"The Lovely Bit hall only holds about one hundred people," I said trying to be helpful. "No matter how many people Fr. Connolly scares away, the room will still be full. He can't drive everyone away."

"Marty's right. The room will still be nice and full, but maybe there won't be the overflow we were expecting." Kathleen regained the focus of the meeting. "Everyone relax, it'll be okay. But, Colleen, try to get somebody to sing for Danny, even if they don't normally sing with the choir."

Colleen promised she would, and Kathleen continued going down the checklist.

"Number four: banners. "Noreen, I saw you and your friends working on them. Are they done yet?"

"We got one done, and the other one half-way done. Doreen is helping me, and we'll have them finished, maybe even tonight."

"Good. Good job, Noreen, and you too, Doreen. Number five: prayers. Does anybody have a prayer they think we should say on Friday?"

"I think we should say the Memorare," Maureen said. "Mom said she was depending on the Virgin Mary to help her through this ordeal, so I went looking for a prayer that would ask Mary for help. Plus, a lot of people know it, and it's in the back of the missals, so it should be easy for everyone to join us in saying it."

"How long is it?"

"It's not that long at all. I can read it to you now if you want."

Everybody agreed she should read it aloud so we could decide whether we should use it or not.

The Last Sunday in Ordinary Time

Remember, O most gracious Virgin Mary, that never was it known
That anyone who fled to thy protection, implored thy help, or Sought thy intercession,
was left unaided. Relying on this confidence,
I fly unto thee, O Virgin of virgins, my mother. To thee I come,
Before thee I stand, sinful and sorrowful. O Mother of the Word
Incarnate, despise not my petitions, but in thy mercy hear and Answer me. Amen.

"I think it's perfect. When I was at the library looking for a reading a man asked me if we were trying to save Danny's soul, or ease your mother's pain. This prayer does both."

"What?" Kathleen looked at me like I was crazy. They all did.

"Look. Do you remember when Fr. Connolly stopped Danny's wake, and he told your parents that their son didn't deserve a funeral? Do you remember what your mom said? She screamed at him that he was telling her that her son could go to hell. Remember that?"

"I don't believe that for a second. My brother Danny is not..." Colleen hesitated before finishing. "Danny is not in hell."

They all seemed to turn on me, all of them saying that Danny was a good person, and he wasn't damned. They all spoke continuously, making sure that everyone knew that they were on Danny's side.

"I'm not trying to be the bad guy here, but your mother is worried. The Church teaches that suicide is...it prevents your soul from being saved. Your parents grew up learning that, and now Fr. Connolly is reinforcing that rule. It must scare her to death to think about it."

"As far as I'm concerned, Danny never committed suicide. I refuse to believe that he could do such a thing." Colleen spoke defiantly.

"Marty is right, though," Eileen said. "We're not only praying that Danny rests in peace, we're praying that Mom can live in peace. Some people say that Danny lost hope. We have to make sure that Mom doesn't lose hope."

"The Memorare is a perfect prayer," Maureen said. "It puts Mom, and all of us, in the position of asking Mary to show mercy to Danny and to have her speak to Jesus on our behalf."

"I think it is, too." I said.

Everyone grew quiet for the moment. We had been reminded that what we were doing was serious, and important not just for Danny and their mother, but for all of us. It was hard core Catholicism. The Memorare matched Mrs. Kilnagael's devotion to the Virgin Mary, and also reinforced the idea that Mary would intercede on Mrs. Kilnagael's behalf, and encourage Jesus to answer a mother's prayers for her son. Until then we hadn't talked about the fear that Danny's soul had been damned to hell, but it was on our minds. Now, having talked about it, we decided to add the Memorare to the service. It articulated our purpose, which was to allow Danny to rest in peace.

Kathleen turned to me and said "Marty, did you say you found a reading you thought we could use?"

"Yeah," I said with an obvious enthusiasm. I didn't tell them about going to the Oak Park Library and seeing the man with an open bible. I didn't tell them that I took the advice from a Negro because I was afraid they might think that made his suggestions less qualified or important.

"I wondered whether we were doing this primarily for Danny," (At this point I hesitated to make sure their mom was not within hearing distance even though I knew she wasn't home), "or if we're doing it primarily for your mother's peace of mind. I decided that we needed a bible reading that offered hope for Danny's soul, something that would also make sure your mom was encouraged to believe there was hope for Danny's soul. I have three suggestions, but I like this one the best. Let me read it to you. Romans 8: 31-39:

> What then are we to say
>   about these things?
> If God is for us, who is against us?
> He did not even spare his own Son,
> but offered Him up for us all;
> how will He not also with Him
>   grant us everything?
> Who can bring an accusation
>   against God's elect?
> God is the One who justifies.
> Who is the one who condemns?
> Christ Jesus is the One who died,
>   but even more has been raised;
> He also is at the right hand of God
>   and intercedes for us.
> Who can separate us
>   from the love of Christ?
> Can affliction or anguish

or persecution
or famine or nakedness or sword?
As it is written:
Because of You we are being
  put to death all day long;
we are counted as sheep
  to be slaughtered.
No, in all these things we are
  more than victorious
through Him who loved us.
For I am persuaded that neither death
  nor life,
nor angels nor rulers,
nor things present,
  nor things to come, nor powers,
nor height, nor depth, nor any other
  created thing
will have the power to separate us
from the love of God that is
  in Jesus Christ our Lord!

"That's great," Kathleen said. "It does the same thing. It declares that there is hope for Danny, and if we pray to God, He will answer our prayers, and take care of Danny."

"Good job, Fr. Marty," Maureen said while patting me on the shoulder. "You are such a big help in all of this."

They all congratulated me on an excellent choice, and made a few more of the Fr. Marty comments. I basked in the glory of their approval, allowing them to view me as if I were some sort of biblical scholar. Colleen gave me a kiss on the cheek and showed an enormous pride of ownership, tacitly telling her sisters that she had the best boyfriend.

"Okay," Kathleen said, "just a couple of more things. Ei, are you still working on the eulogy?"

"I haven't finished it, but I know what I want to say."

"Well, you need a deadline. Tomorrow at 4:00 I want to see what you wrote."

"You are not going to take over."

"I just need to make sure you get it done. I just want to see that it has been written. You can let Colleen or Maureen proofread it for you, okay? We just need to know that it's done." Eileen nodded but didn't say anything. "And the rest of you, I want to know what you're going to say about Danny at the funeral. 4:00 tomorrow, know what you're going to say."

"The only other things I have are the pictures, and Danny's belongings. Why don't we do the pictures as soon as we finish this meeting?"

"That's good," Maureen said. "We might see some stuff in the pictures that we wouldn't think of otherwise."

"So, pictures tonight, belongings tomorrow."

"If you guys don't mind, I'll let you take care of all that. I'm going to take off."

They all said that was fine, thanked me over and over, and I got a hug from all of them. Colleen walked me to the door, and stood outside on the porch for a moment until she got too cold. I told her I really loved her family, she smiled and said "We're really glad you here to help us. We kissed one last time, and I left.

I needed to get home because I planned to get up early the next day for mass. Despite all of the harsh words I had said and thought about Fr. Connolly, I was still a Catholic. Tomorrow was December 8th, the day we honored the Immaculate Conception, and a holy day of obligation, meaning we were obligated to go to church. It was going to be a long day for me: mass first thing in the morning, a full day of school, and then working at Mick's until close. Over the past couple of weeks he had allowed me to spend a lot of time with the Kilnagaels, so when everyone else wanted that night off to go to church, it was hard for me to argue that I shouldn't be the one to work. I ate an early dinner at the Lovely Bit so I could be back in time to let the other guys go at 6:00. There weren't too many people at the bar that night, just a couple of men I recognized but didn't know, and Seamus Touhy, of course.

"Well, hello stranger" he called as I walked in. "Where ya been?"

I sat down and told him the latest news about Danny's funeral, and all of the trouble the Kilnagaels were going to in order to give their son a funeral. He already knew we were planning on having the funeral at the Lovely Bit so I asked him if he was planning to attend.

"I suppose so. This is where I do most of my praying anyway so you might as well save me a seat."

"That's the thing. We don't know how many people are coming. We thought for sure that it would be packed wall-to-wall, but Fr. Connolly is telling people it's a sin to attend. A lot of people are backing out, acting like a bolt of lightning will come down from heaven to strike them dead if defy the Church's authority."

"It's not just Fr. Connolly. I hear the people talking here and some of them are genuinely angry at the Kilnagaels. They think they made their son out to be the great hero, but he turned out to be a coward. A lot of people think his family was too pushy and their getting their comeuppance."

"Really? They think that?" He nodded.

"And you have to remember that most people agree with the Church, that suicide is a mortal sin. I'd say the people who plan to attend are doing it just to be kind to his family, but they still think that Fr. Connolly was right. There won't be too many though."

"You think people are going to stay away?"

"Look, Marty: It's a school day, so parents aren't going to let their kids out of school to honor a man who committed suicide. It's being held in a tavern, some people find that disgraceful. He's not the hero he was supposed to be, so that is causing people to shun his family. A lot of them are afraid to offend the Church, so they won't come. You've got the Lally's and that whole crowd who insisted that Fr. Connolly deny him a funeral to begin with. No, my boy, I don't see too many people showing up here tomorrow."

Everything he said was logical but I still couldn't imagine that the room would be empty tomorrow. The Kilnagaels were too popular for people to desert them now. Maybe there wouldn't be as many as I first thought, but there would definitely be more than Seamus was saying.

"No," I said after thinking about it for a moment, "you're wrong. There's going to be a big crowd here tomorrow. They're too well known and well liked for people to ignore them like that."

"How many people are you expecting?"

"I don't know. We're putting out one hundred twenty chairs."

"One hundred and twenty?" He shook his head and said "I bet you won't need half that many."

"How much you want to bet? I know that more than sixty people will show up."

I didn't really want to bet. Saying 'how much you want to bet' was more of an expression than an actual offer to bet. He smiled at me like he was a proud father. There existed a tradition of strange bets that were placed in the Lovely Bit, wagers that were either incredibly stupid, like which glass of ice would melt faster, or tasteless, like betting on the attendance at a funeral. One of the first times I was in the Lovely Bit, they started talking about the cashier at the grocery store down the street. She was a rather fat woman who used to spend her day leaning against the checkout counter smoking cigarettes. I guessed she was about sixty years old, and sometimes her mother, who must have been eighty, would walk from their house a few blocks away to do a little shopping. The guys started talking about how much better shape the mother was in, and suddenly bets were being made on who would live longer, the cashier or her mother. There were quite a few comments about there being a special place in hell for people who would make such a bet, but also a lot of laughing about the tastelessness of it. There was not a high likelihood that any money would actually change hands over it, and nobody was writing anything down, but the guys did enjoy debating the topic. I was not thinking about that when I suggested the bet, I was simply trying to assert my conviction that people would show up.

"I'll take that bet. $1.00 says no more than sixty people will show up."

The Last Sunday in Ordinary Time

I didn't want to make the bet, but what could I do? It would be unmanly to withdraw the offer of a bet, especially in a bar. I felt like I had betrayed the Kilnagaels somehow, and felt dirty because of it. I thought about refusing the bet because it was too personal, which was the truth, but it felt like I would lose my standing in Seamus' eyes. We shook on it.

I walked back across the street to relieve the guys who were leaving to go to church. It had been an unusually warm day for mid-December, with temperatures in the fifties. Even now, at dusk, it was still in the high forties. It had been a slow night and Mick made them run around the gas station cleaning stuff we virtually never cleaned. By the time I returned from the Lovely Bit there was precious little work to be done. Mick had me sweeping all around the gas pumps which was a rather pleasant job in the warm evening air. I asked Mick about Standard Oil, and were they still trying to pressure him to sell the franchise back to the company.

"They are," he said, "and I'm beginning to think more seriously about selling it."

"Really?"

"Well, I spoke to an attorney and he told me that when push comes to shove they can probably force me to sell anyway, so my best bet is to make sure I ask for a lot of money. If they want it bad enough, an extra $15,000 or $20,000 thousand won't even cause them to blink."

"But you would actually sell the gas station? I thought you liked owning it."

"I do, but money talks. Besides, with the Coloreds pushing so hard to grab a piece of Holy Truth, I'm not sure I'll want to stay anyway."

"But this is such a great place to live. I mean, this is such a great Irish neighborhood, why would you want to leave."

"Listen, Marty, if being Irish was the answer I would have never left Ireland. America is where I wanted to be. When I think of the color green I don't think of Ireland, I think of the almighty dollar. I worship at the church of John D. Rockefeller, and I'm more than willing to change my address to increase my bank account."

"Well, I hope you don't sell. I hope you own this gas station forever."

"What difference does it make to you? I'll let you work here as long as you're in school. If you ever quit college you'll be quitting this job at the same time." He hesitated for a moment, and then continued. "And when you become a CPA or an engineer or whatever it is that you study in college, I bet it won't be long before you leave Holy Truth behind. Probably have a wife and two or three little Marty's running around some fancy house somewhere out in the suburbs. So don't talk to me about staying here forever. You won't be."

I didn't say anything but I thought "Yes I will. I'm going to marry Colleen, and we'll buy a house right here in Holy Truth. We will make sure we visit her parents and my parents all the time because they'll still live in the parish. Two or three kids? We're going to have eight or ten kids like a real Irish family does."

The Last Sunday in Ordinary Time

December 16th, 1966

It Wasn't a Military Funeral, but There Were Taps There Anyway

The casket the Kilnagaels chose for Danny was placed at one end
of the banquet room of the Lovely Bit, surrounded by flowers, an
American flag, and a plain Celtic cross crucifix that lacked the image of the

tortured Jesus on it. One of the things Mrs. Kilnagael insisted on was a plain cross. I learned over the past three days that Catholics were big on having crosses with Jesus still on it as if he were still writhing in pain, but Protestants tended to have plain crosses with the body of Jesus missing. In their minds Jesus already died and went to heaven so He was no longer on the cross. The Church, Mick told me, liked to remind people that Jesus endured the agony as a sacrifice to save mankind from sin, so we emphasized the pain rather than the redemption. They chose the Celtic cross that had been upstairs in their house as Noreen had suggested. I knew it sounded weird, but after growing up in such a Catholic environment I came to take comfort in the image of a tortured Jesus. If it had been up to me I would have put a more Catholic crucifix next to Danny's casket, but it wasn't what Mrs. Kilnagael wanted.

In her grief over the loss of her son, Mrs. Kilnagael chose humility as a theme for his funeral. Like Jesus being born in the humble surroundings of a manger, Danny would be mourned in the poorly lit, somewhat dingy surroundings of the rather oddly adorned banquet hall in the Lovely Bit. Unlike most funerals that started at the funeral home where mourners gathered and then drove in a procession to the church, Danny's would start in a tavern. His body remained at the O'Hagan Funeral Home until Friday morning until that morning when a hearse from the Steinberg and Cohen Funeral Home picked it up to deliver it to the Lovely Bit. I travelled to Steinberg and Cohen with the family, where we arrived at 8:30. The funeral was scheduled to start at 10:00, but the Kilnagaels met with the staff at 8:30 to go over a few details.

The Last Sunday in Ordinary Time

The first question was should the casket be delivered through the front door or the back door of the Lovely Bit. Going through the front door meant wheeling it through the tavern itself, a rather undignified image, so Mrs. Kilnagael decided using the back entrance might make that moment a little more private. Mr. Kilnagael remained very quiet, although his discomfort with the whole thing was apparent. Colleen told me that he was serious when he suggested burying Danny without a funeral of any sort. He was ashamed of what his son had done, and this do-it-yourself funeral furthered his sense of shame. He only attended it as an act of loyalty to his wife. Out of her earshot, however, he had been making disparaging comments about it to his daughters.

"When some people are in mourning they go to church and get religion," he muttered to Colleen and her sister Maureen, "and some people go to a tavern and get drunk. I guess we can kill two birds with one stone this way."

The first night we were in their dining room planning Danny's funeral, Mr. Kilnagael had been downstairs, sitting at the bar by himself, drinking. His daughters never said a word to me about it while I was there, and I was too polite to ask where he was. His harsh words of ridicule for the idea of a homemade funeral were tolerated by his daughters because they knew that he how much pain he was in. He attempted to achieve a stoicism bathed in whiskey, but his grief was evident, like light bleeding into a dark room around the edges of a closed door.

We drove in a lonely procession over to the O'Hagan Funeral Home, picked up the casket there, and then proceeded to the Lovely Bit.

The Last Sunday in Ordinary Time

It wasn't until they wheeled the casket into the hallway that we realized there wasn't enough room to turn the corner and enter the banquet hall. The three men from Steinberg and Cohen ended up virtually standing the casket upright to get it through the doorway while Mrs. Kilnagael yelled at them "Be careful, that's my son." They managed to get the casket into the room, but it felt more like movers delivering a couch than an undertaker delivering a the body of a loved one.

By this time the Kilnagaels had roughly forty-five minutes to add their finishing touches to the room. The girls started placing the flowers around the casket and photographs on a pair of tables along the wall. Noreen placed the cross on a stand next to Danny, and Doreen placed mimeographed copies of the songs and prayers to be used during the service. Roger, Kathleen's fiancée, had returned from college to attend. He had not been part of the planning because he had some important classes that he could not afford to miss, so they decided it would be better for him to not skip the entire week of school. She had expected him to join her in front to act as emcees for the event but he begged off. It turned out he wasn't even Catholic, so he was uncomfortable with the prayers we had chosen. At the last minute she asked me to help her in front since I knew everything that was supposed to happen, and she was too upset to do it alone.

As we grew nearer to 10:00 the room became eerily quiet. Colleen's grandparents arrived, aunts, uncles, and some cousins, but not all of them. A few newspaper reporters and photographers arrived and took seats in the back. Our original thought was to ask them to leave when the service started, but so few people were showing up that they

299

made the room seem less empty. Seamus Touhy wandered in from his barstool along with two men who could accurately be described as old drunks. My mother came, and three women from the Ladies of St. Theresa walked in. Four guys Danny used to hang around with showed up, and Kathleen, Eileen, and Maureen all had a few friends show up. None of either Colleen's friends showed, or the friends of her younger sisters came. My Uncle Charlie and Aunt Bridie kept appearing in the doorway to check in on things. That was it. Relatively speaking, nobody showed up. I asked Colleen if there were any people from her dad's work there, and she said no, he told them not to come. It was a heartbreakingly small crowd. We waited a few minutes past 10:00 but when it became apparent that no one else was coming, we got started.

It turned out that Colleen got angry and ugly with her friends when they wouldn't agree to sing at her brother's funeral. That was part of the reason that none of them showed up. Kathleen asked everyone to join in singing the Prayer of St. Francis, but when only Colleen stood in front to lead the song, Kathleen nudged me, and the two of us joined her. We managed to get the song started, and people joined in with more a sense of politeness than anything else. There were enough voices to make it passable, but it lacked conviction. It felt like we were dragging the singers with us, and finishing it was a relief.

When we finished singing Colleen sat down and Kathleen started to introduce her sister Maureen, but she broke down twice, and then attempted a third time. At that point I stepped forward and took over.

"As you know, we are here to mourn the death of Daniel J. Kilnagael. He died…" I hesitated, trying to find a way to be tactful. "… in war, under difficult circumstances. He was too much of a man of peace to allow himself to be the type of cold blooded killer a soldier sometimes needs to be. Because of this *weakness,* as some people call it, it has been suggested that he doesn't deserve to be prayed for. This is not true. Now more than ever Danny needs our prayers, and he needs our prayers to be heard. With that in mind, I would like to ask Maureen, Danny's sister, to lead us in saying the Memorare."

Maureen walked up to the front, shaking from nervousness the whole time, and began to speak. She began to say her piece, but her voice was barely audible. As she fought her way through it I sat there angry at myself. My introduction made it sound like I was desperately begging the people in attendance to participate. I kept looking over at Mrs. Kilnagael to see how she was reacting to it, but she remained stoic, betraying neither approval nor disappointment.

"Please join me in saying the Memorare. You will find it on the mimeographed sheets we left on your chair.

"Remember, O most gracious Virgin Mary, that never was it known
That anyone who fled to thy protection, implored thy help, or Sought thy intercession,
was left unaided. Relying on this confidence,
I fly unto thee, O Virgin of virgins, my mother. To thee I come, Before thee I stand, sinful and sorrowful. O Mother of the Word Incarnate, despise not my petitions, but in thy mercy hear and Answer me. Amen."

Even as Maureen walked back to her seat you could sense the discomfort in the atmosphere. Although everyone harbored some doubts about the legitimacy of the service, our repeated reminders of the humble surroundings reinforced those doubts rather than eliminating them. We had hoped acknowledging that we were unfit for the Virgin Mary's mercy, but asking for it anyway would give the entire preceding a worthiness it may have been lacking. Instead it gave the "ceremony" a feeling of desperation. Kathleen, at least, made an effort to continue. She stood before the crowd and began talking.

"As I look around this room I am struck by how plain it is. It hardly measures up to the greatness of a proper church, but like Mary and Joseph searching..."

At this point there was a commotion in back. Kathleen stopped talking and all eyes turned to the front door of the banquet hall, essentially the back of the church. Rev. McAllister was standing in the doorway trying to get in, and Uncle Charlie was arguing with him and trying to keep him out. The reporters and photographers leapt into action and started and flashbulbs started popping like crazy. I hurried to the back to see what I could do.

"You don't belong here," Charlie told him.

"I was invited to be here," he replied. As I approached he saw me and said "Martin. Young Martin, tell this man that you know me."

I hesitated for just a moment. My first instinct was to tell him that he couldn't come in, that he wasn't welcome. I also knew that my Uncle Charlie was furious that a Colored man was trying to come into his tavern, especially this one. Things were going from bad to worse. I had to make the commotion stop.

"Uncle Charlie it's okay."

"What do you mean 'it's okay?'" he said glaring at me.

"Please, Uncle Charlie. Let him in. We'll talk about it later."

Uncle Charlie looked at the newsmen, and then at me. He surrendered the fight because they were there I'm sure. If not for the reporters he would never have allowed a Colored man to enter.

As the reporters returned to their seats and Rev. McAllister took a seat, the photographers snapped a few more pictures. I returned to the front and heard a few people mention the name Torian McAllister. Even if I hadn't recognized him the day I met him, plenty of people in the hall knew who he was right away. The people in the room were divided, some staring at Rev. McAllister and some staring at me, most notably my Uncle Charlie. I avoided eye contact with Mrs. Kilnagael. I kept thinking that they'd need two graves because when this was over because I was a dead man. Finally, Kathleen started talking again, while I stood off to the side.

"As I was saying, like Mary and Joseph searching in Bethlehem for a place to stay on the night of Jesus' birth only to settle for a humble stable, we have searched in Holy Truth for a place to mourn the death of our brother only to settle for the humble surroundings of a tavern."

As she continued I thought we had the humble part right. I looked around the room and saw three Jews from the funeral home, a Negro, two drunks, a handful of people from Our Lady of Holy Truth, and the unhappy family of Danny Kilnagael. Mr. Kilnagael sat with his arms folded, a look of disgust on his face. Uncle Charlie was standing in the doorway between the tavern and the banquet hall, seething. I noticed Seamus Touhy sitting alone and imagine him saying "It's not a funeral, it's a disaster."

All the while Kathleen continued speaking.

"Jesus warned us that the way we treat the least of His brothers is the way we treat Him. Danny, if you believe what you read in the papers, died as a man unworthy of our sorrow, our mourning, or our prayers. If the world turns its back on Danny that means it turns its back on Jesus. To show that we recognize that we honor Christ by honoring Danny, we ask that you join us in singing *What Child is This?*"

At this point, as if to underscore how dreadful it all was, the three women from the Ladies of St. Theresa stood up and walk out. As they did I put my head down and shook it slightly, in disbelief of how badly things were going. When I looked up I saw Mrs. Kilnagael glaring at me.

Colleen and I returned to the front and joined Kathleen. It was no accident that the Kilnagael girls joined the choir at Our Lady of Holy Truth. They were a very musical family, and the girls sang beautifully, although people might not have known it from the opening song, nor from the way this one started. They were so stiff and nervous that their singing suffered. They started singing and waved their hands to encourage everyone to join in.

> *What Child is this who, laid to rest*
> *On Mary's lap is sleeping?*

From the congregation we heard a new voice, the rich tenor of Rev. McAllister. He sang loudly, beautifully, and with spirit, breathing life into the effort. Clearly this was a man unconcerned about drawing attention to himself, and unwilling to stay in the shadows. Colleen and her sisters reacted to his lead and began to sing with the usual power they brought to the choir. Suddenly what had been a listless effort became something else entirely. The song sung so beautifully and with such

emotion, lifted our makeshift gathering from an ill-conceived attempt to
be spiritual to an actual, meaningful religious ceremony.

*Whom angels greet with anthems
Sweet
While shepherds watch are keeping?
This, this is Christ the King
Whom shepherds guard and angels
Sing;
Haste, haste to bring him laud,
The Babe, the Son of Mary.*

*Why lies He in such mean estate,
Where ox and ass are feeding?
Good Christians fear, for sinners
Here
The silent Word is pleading.
Nails, spear shall pierce Him through,
The cross be borne for me, for you.
Hail, hail the Word made flesh,
The Babe, the Son of Mary.*

*So bring Him incense, gold and
Myrrh,
Come peasant, king to own Him;
The King of kings salvation brings,
Let loving hearts enthrone Him.
Raise, raise a song on high,
The virgin sings her lullaby.
Joy, joy for Christ is born,
The Babe, the Son of Mary.*

When the song ended a momentary pause occurred as we all
seemed to enjoy how beautiful the song sounded. Kathleen and I felt a
sense of relief that at last something had gone right. Rev. McAllister sat
there with a look that suggested he had no idea of the profound effect his

singing had on the room, but I thought he must have known. Kathleen returned to her role as the emcee and introduced her sister Eileen to give Danny's eulogy.

"I know you are expecting me to tell you what a wonderful brother Danny was, but, truthfully, he was actually a pain in the neck. He made a point of daring us to stay mad at him because he was so charming in his ability to aggravate. When we were little we decided that the place of honor at the dinner table was sitting next to Dad. Sorry, Mom, but we all wanted to sit next to Dad. Danny would wait until the table was set and then lick the fork and spoon in front of the chair he wanted to sit in." Eileen had to stop for a moment to smile a little in response to everyone else's laughter. "Mom, of course, would tell him to stop doing that, but since she was laughing while she said it, he paid no attention.

"By the time he got to high school his voice had changed, but his smart aleck tendencies had not. He learned to imitate Dad's voice and would say to Mom, 'Peg, be a doll and hand me a beer.'" She lowered her voice and did an imitation of his imitation. That got a nice laugh, too. "He walked around the house and told us 'Ladies, are you trying to give all my money to the electric company? All kinds of lights on upstairs.' A couple of years ago he ran out of deodorant so he casually used Kathleen's. We know this because Kathleen went crazy when she found an armpit hair on her roll on. It would have been better for her if she had kept quiet, but she made a big show of complaining about how disgusting it was, and he was not to use her deodorant anymore. From that time forward, anytime he needed to relay a message it was always a two-parter. 'Kathleen, Roger called and said he got the tickets to the concert. P.S. I used your deodorant today.' 'Maureen, Patsy called and wanted to know what the math homework was. I used your deodorant today.'

"In my life Danny made me laugh more than anyone else ever did. How sad it is now that he has also made me cry more than anyone else ever did. Danny was a sweet, caring, loving son and brother. We were blessed to have him in our lives. Daniel J. Kilnagael, we all still love you. We miss you. When you get to heaven, lick a spoon if you have to, but make sure you save a place for me. I know that someday we will be together again."

Eileen returned to her seat while we applauded her speech. Kathleen then told her story about Danny, and invited everyone else to do the same. Colleen told one, as did Maureen. Noreen stood to tell hers, but was overcome by a combination of nervousness and sadness, and broke down in tears before Kathleen escorted her back to her seat. When it looked like nobody else was willing to talk I took my turn. I talked about never having a brother of my own, and how good it felt to have Danny make me feel at home in their house. It was an exaggeration since I actually spent very little time with him, and I thought it came across as a bit insincere. I knew Kathleen wanted more people to stand and speak, but it looked like nobody else wanted to. There was, even among his grandparents, aunts and uncles, and even his own father, a sense that they attended this funeral to be polite. There was no great desire to celebrate his life among many in attendance. Kathleen asked if anyone else wanted to speak and an awkward silence fell over the room. Then, just as it looked like we ready to move on, Rev. McAllister stood and walked to the front of the room. He stood there quietly for a moment causing the uneasiness to grow. We were collectively too polite to confront him, and probably intimidated by his brashness. He struck me a man who was always certain of himself, and always ready to exploit the uncertainty of others. He saw our awkwardness as his opportunity.

"I know you all find it strange that I am here. I became aware of this funeral, this celebration of Daniel's life, because young Martin here was brave enough to ask for my help. We met by chance in the public library and he had the courage to ask me to help him, or more specifically, to help his late friend Daniel. I was very impressed by that.

"It appears that, at the time of his death, Daniel had lost hope. You are here, we are here, because his family has been told that the circumstances of Daniel's death meant that he died in a hopeless situation, with no chance of salvation. When young Martin came to me I asked him what he was trying to accomplish by participating in this humble, if I may use that word, this humble gathering. He told me he heard the leaders of the Roman Catholic Church say that there was no hope for Daniel's salvation, but still young Martin hoped and prayed for Daniel's salvation anyway. His exact words were, 'I'm looking for a loophole.'

"The circumstances of Daniel's death are very meager, very humble, and like the birth of our Lord, overlooked and ignored by society at large. Yet young Martin refused to overlook it, ignore it, or to surrender to the idea that Daniel was a lost soul. It is written in the bible that if our faith is great enough we can move mountains. Surely Jesus knows the loving, sweet nature of Daniel Kilnagael, a nature so movingly described by his sisters today. The opinions of all of the priests in the world cannot extinguish the embers of faith that still burn in our hearts. If our faith can move mountains, surely it can sway our loving God, and remind him of the goodness that existed in this young man's heart, even in his darkest hour. I encourage you. I implore you. I beg you. After this brief ceremony ends, remember that the salvation of Daniel Kilnagael depends on us, and our faith that God will hear our prayers. Young Martin went looking for a loophole and he found it. Faith. Faith is the loophole that Jesus offers us all. We all, at different times in our lives, are sinners. We make poor decisions, we lose hope, we turn our backs on the goodness of the Lord. We also have it in our power to forgive those who make poor decisions, to encourage those who lose hope, and to shine a light that leads those who have turned away from the Lord back to Him. Daniel Kilnagael will find salvation if we place our faith and trust in God's mercy. Amen."

Rev. McAllister took his seat again. There a momentary paused in the proceedings as we contemplated his words. He genuinely brought comfort to the Kilnagaels. The timber of his voice, the confidence he showed as he spoke to us, his very presence seemed to counterbalance the harsh judgment of traditional Catholic teaching. It felt like he had single-handedly saved Danny's soul. He also validated what we were doing there that morning.

Kathleen stood up and said "Now, Marty Donovan, a dear family friend, will do our reading."

I stood and walked to the center of the room and proceeded to do with my reading with a new sense of conviction. I not only read those words, I believed them.

"A reading from the book of Romans, 8: 31-39:

What then are we to say
about these things?
If God is for us, who is against us?
He did not even spare his own Son,
but offered Him up for us all;
how will He not also with Him
grant us everything?
Who can bring an accusation
against God's elect?
God is the One who justifies.
Who is the one who condemns?
Christ Jesus is the One who died,
but even more has been raised;
He also is at the right hand of God
and intercedes for us.
Who can separate us
from the love of Christ?
Can affliction or anguish
or persecution
or famine or nakedness or sword?
As it is written:
Because of You we are being
put to death all day long;
we are counted as sheep
to be slaughtered.
No, in all these things we are
more than victorious
through Him who loved us.
For I am persuaded that neither death
nor life,
nor angels nor rulers,
nor things present,
nor things to come, nor powers,
nor height, nor depth, nor any other
created thing
will have the power to separate us
from the love of God that is

The Last Sunday in Ordinary Time

in Jesus Christ our Lord!

Kathleen walked back to the center of the room and hugged me. It was a powerful moment for their whole family, and I could see approval in their faces as I stepped away from the front and took a seat. Kathleen stood there quietly for a moment.

"I must tell you that this is not the crowd I expected to see at the funeral of my brother. I do see several faces that I recognize, but also several that I didn't know before today, but which I will never forget after today. We are in mourning for our brother, and will mourn him for a long time after today. But, the kindness you shared in coming together to pray with us today, the reassuring sense that Danny will still be welcomed into the arms of God will temper our mourning with a renewed sense of faith in a kind and loving God.

"We will close this funeral by singing the song "Danny Boy," a traditional Irish ballad of love and loss in the time of war. You will find the words on the papers we left on each seat. Afterward, we ask that you leave quietly while we gather for one last time, and then proceed to the cemetery as a family. Thank you all for coming."

"Colleen, will you please join me up in front?"

I waited for to ask me as well, but she didn't. The two sisters held hands and again signaled for us to join them.

> Oh Danny boy, the pipes, the pipes are calling
> From glen to glen, and down the mountain side

Like before, Rev. McAllister starting singing in a clear, loud voice. He seemed to put his all into it, and his commitment encouraged us all to do the same. Like before his voice blended with those of Colleen and her

311

sisters, and gave not just the song, but the entire ritual a legitimacy that affected us all.

> The summer's gone, and all the flowers are dying
> 'Tis you, 'tis you must go and I must bide
> But come ye back when summer's in the meadow
> Or when the valley's white and hushed with snow
> 'Tis I'll be here in sunshine or in shadow
> Oh Danny boy, oh Danny boy, I love you so.
>
> And if you come, when all the flowers are dying
> And I am dead, as dead I well may be
> You'll come and find the place where I am lying
> And kneel and say an "Ave" there for me.
>
> And I shall hear, tho' soft you tread above me
> And my dreams will warm and sweeter be
> If you'll not fail to tell me that you love me
> I'll simply sleep in peace until you come to me.

The Kilnagaels, all eight of them proceeded to the front door of the banquet hall and prepared to say good-bye to their guests. Even in this time of their greatest sorrow they maintained the social niceties of playing host, making sure that nobody left without first hearing a thank you from the family.

Standing near the casket I watched the others leave. My mother gave Mrs. Kilnagael a hug and they spoke to each other for a moment. The high school friends of the girls made a point of hugging all of the girls and telling them that it really was a beautiful ceremony. On his way toward the exit Seamus made a point of reminding me I owed him a dollar.

"Like I told you. There were less than sixty people here."

Under any circumstances I would have thought it was a terrible thing to say, but he managed to say it within earshot of Mrs. Kilnagael.

She wasn't looking at me, so I wasn't absolutely certain she heard him, but I assumed she did. The idea that she might have heard it horrified me. Seamus and the two drunks from the bar then left through the front door and then circled back to the tavern through the front door of the Lovely Bit to continue their drinking.

Like everyone else in the room, especially Uncle Charlie and the reporters, I watched Rev. McAllister, wondering what he would do next. He made his way first to Mr. Kilnagael, grabbing the grieving father's outstretched hand with his own two hands, and holding it firmly. Mr. Kilnagael, somewhat taking by surprise, placed his free hand on top of the minister's, and the two of them stood there sharing a rather intimate moment. Flashbulbs were popping as the photographers took pictures of it, and the two men exchanged words, McAllister doing most of the talking and Colleen's dad nodding his head. Then he turned his attention to Mrs. Kilnagael. She surprised everyone by leaning forward and kissing the Negro man on the cheek, a show of affection never seen before in Holy Truth. Rev. McAllister pulled her close and hugged her, saying loudly, "I am so sorry that you lost your son." Again the photographers sprang into action, and flashbulbs went off repeatedly. Mrs. Kilnagael seemed to make an effort to pull away, but he did not let go. He repeated again very loudly, "I'm so sorry that you lost your son." Mrs. Kilnagael nodded and whispered a thank you. For the third time Rev. McAllister said loudly, "I am so sorry you lost your son." This time Mrs. Kilnagael went limp, all the stoicism she had been showing for the last two weeks melted away, she put her head on his shoulder and broke down in tears. All the while newspaper photographers were snapping pictures making sure they had one of the Negro minister comforting the White woman. They remained in that embrace for a moment or two, but it seemed much longer. Finally Mr. Kilnagael stepped forward and pulled Mrs. Kilnagael away from him and began hugging her himself. With a dramatic flourish Rev. McAllister reached into his pocket and pulled out a business card.

"Mr. and Mrs. Kilnagael, if there is anything I can do for you, please call me at any time. I would be pleased to be of service in any way I can."

Mr. Kilnagael looked at the business card extended before him like it was a razor poised to cut him, but his wife reached out and took it, saying "Thank you, Reverend" loud enough for everyone to hear. The men from the funeral home asked everyone except the immediate family to leave and allow the Kilnagaels a moment of privacy. The reporters followed Rev. McAllister out the door, leaving Colleen and her family, Roger and me. Mrs. Kilnagael turned and looked at me. I asked her if there was something she needed.

"Marty, I think this is a time just for family. I hope you understand."

I stood there in stunned silence. After all I had done with them and for them, I couldn't imagine they didn't consider me like family. Finally I answered.

"Oh sure. I'm sorry. Let me get my coat."

I walked out the door and saw my mother waiting outside.

"What took you so long? I was standing in the cold waiting for you."

I looked at her in amazement. I hadn't planned to walk home with her. I planned to go to the cemetery with Colleen. I said as much to Mom.

"I was planning to go with the Kilnagaels."

"Well, Marty, they said only family was invited. You're not a member of their family. You're still a Donovan in case you've forgotten."

We walked home in silence. She could see how hurt I was so she didn't say anything else. I didn't realize how hurt she must have been when I made it clear that I thought I had graduated to a better family I would rather be with them than with her. From a half a block away I could see the Kilnagaels, including Roger, especially Roger, climbing into the cars that would make the drive to the cemetery.

The Last Sunday in Ordinary Time

The Fourth Sunday in Advent

December 18th, 1966

It's not Beginning to Look a Lot Like Christmas

Danny's funeral made the front page of both the Daily News and the American the next day, but the story of what happened differed depending according to the two papers. The Daily News ran the picture of Mrs. Kilnagael crying on the shoulder of Rev. McAllister attached to a very sympathetic story about the beautiful yet humble service conducted in the banquet hall of a neighborhood tavern. The American, conversely, ran a picture of Uncle Charlie trying to prevent Rev. McAllister from entering his bar. Roy Cannon wrote a nasty column about the local efforts made to create a place for a military coward like Danny Kilnagael while also trying to prevent Rev. McAllister from entering the neighborhood. He made it sound like Danny Kilnagael was nothing but a coward who was nonetheless embraced by the whole parish while Rev. McAllister was nothing but a hero who was hated by everyone in the parish for no reason other than race. I hated to admit it, but he was probably right about the race thing.

It angered Uncle Charlie to see his picture in the paper like that not because it showed him as a bigot, but because it showed him at all. He prided himself on being a politically strong but publicly discreet member of the local Democratic Party. Having Roy Cannon accuse him of trying to keep Negroes out of the Lovely Bit or out of the neighborhood actually caused most people of Holy Truth to view him in a favorable light. His customers and others in Holy Truth actually congratulated him for taking a stand on their behalf, so it didn't harm his standing in the neighborhood at all, but it did draw unwanted attention from city hall. The Daley machine resented all negative attention, so he had to apologize to the mayor for his indiscretion, blame the newspapers for distorting what happened, and promise not to let it happen again. When reporters from other papers and the TV news called, his only comment was no comment.

It was Saturday, the 17th of December, and for the first time in months I had nothing to do.   I called Colleen the night before but she said she needed a few days by herself to mourn her brother. My mother remained resentful of my willingness to choose the Kilnagaels over her so she gave me a list of chores to do around the house, but I finished those early in the afternoon. That I finished them quickly and cheerfully didn't appease her. I called the gas station to let Mick know I was available to work but he had scheduled around me because he wasn't sure I'd be available. Mick made it clear he was unhappy that the whole funeral business caused me to miss so much time from work and it was about time I started pulling my own weight. I called Patrick James to see what the guys were up to that night, but he kept asking me to repeat my name. He and my other friends were giving me grief because Colleen had been leading me around by the nose for so long they didn't recognize me anymore. One of the disc jockeys on WLS was emceeing a sold out concert that night, and they had all bought tickets for it. They were part of a big group that was heading downtown, so they wouldn't be around. I was completely alone.

After dinner I the boredom overtook me so I told my parents I was going for a walk. Actually I decided to head over to the Lovely Bit and stick my head in the door long enough to tell Uncle Charlie how sorry I was that the ugly picture of him was in the paper. If I hadn't told Rev. McAllister about the funeral he would never have shown up at the Lovely

Bit. I didn't make it two steps in the door when Charlie told me to get out in no uncertain terms. I stood there with a baffled look on my face, but he kept telling me to leave.

"Out. Now. Go. I'm not going to argue with you."

"Charlie, I'll go talk to him," I heard Seamus Touhy say.

I left and waited outside for Seamus. The December weather continued to be unseasonably pleasant, making it the only pleasant part of my life at the moment. I was crushed to hear Charlie kicking me out like that. I didn't want to stay and wait for Seamus but I knew he was coming and the last thing I needed was someone else to be mad at me. Seamus was still buttoning his coat when he walked out the door.

"Wait up, Marty."

"Hi, Seamus. God, is he that mad at me?"

"Oh, not at all. He's not mad at you at all."

"Sure has a funny way of showing it."

"He told me earlier he got a tip that Roy Cannon planned to do some snooping around, trying to see what kind of bar Charlie is running. He's afraid that every face he doesn't recognize could be a spy looking for things to write in the paper. The last thing he needs is a story that underage kids are hanging out in his bar, so he can't let you in right now. It'll probably be that way for a few weeks."

"Crap. I really like eating lunch at the Lovely Bit."

"Well, you will again in a few weeks. Just be patient."

"It's probably just as well. I dreaded going back into the Lovely Bit because I assume Charlie blames me for allowing Rev. McAllister into his bar."

"How did you ever meet him?"

I told Seamus about meeting him at the library in Oak Park, and asking him for help with Danny's funeral. Seamus listened and shook his head while I spoke.

"He knew what he was going to do from the moment you introduced yourself. Don't worry about it. Charlie said he's seen a lot of politicians in his day, and that guy is a master politician. He knew what he was doing. He wanted to get his picture in the paper, and used you to do it. He played you like a fiddle. That's why you can't trust those people."

"Do you think he planned all that from the very beginning?"

"Of course he did."

I told Seamus how relieved I was that at least one person forgave me.

"My mom is mad at me, Mickey Riordan is mad at me, the Kilnagaels, I think, are mad at me, and a lot of people in the parish act like I invited Rev. McAllister to come to Holy Truth. It feels like everybody is giving me the cold shoulder except winter itself. At least the weather has been warm."

"Don't go believing warm weather in winter, Marty. A stretch of mild weather seems to aggravate Mother Nature, and she exacts her revenge. Mark my words; we're in for some ugly weather ahead."

"So you're telling me that good weather is a bad thing."

"Never mind the smart aleck comments. In winter in Chicago it's supposed to be cold, the wind is supposed to make it feel colder. Mother Nature will make sure things return to normal. We're in for some big storms."

The Last Sunday in Ordinary Time

It felt good to hear Seamus tell me up was down. If I said I was Irish he corrected me. If I called Charlie Uncle Charlie, he reminded me that he wasn't really my uncle. And now, when I said the weather was nice, he told me it meant the weather was bad. His charming cynicism allowed me to enjoy the fact that he never changed. We walked over to the bus stop and continued talking until his bus arrived.

Only one week and one day remained until Christmas and, more importantly, exactly one week until Rev. McAllister planned to lead his march through Holy Truth. The next day I attended mass with my parents, like usual. Mom was in a much better mood, happy that the funeral was behind us, and that she had her son back. Things were going back to the way she liked them, with no interference from Colleen. I, on the other hand, was in a lousy mood. I was upset that Colleen asked not to see me for a few days, and I had to go back to Our Lady of Holy Truth and possibly face Fr. Connolly. The last time we saw each other I called him a son-of-a-bitch, a fact my parents knew nothing about. I worried that he was expecting an apology that I wasn't ready to give. After what he did to the Kilnagaels, he was a hypocrite in my eyes, full of phony compassion and understanding. The last thing I wanted to give him was the satisfaction admitting I was wrong and apologizing. At the same time I was terrified that he would humiliate me by telling my parents what I said.

I spent the hour-long mass contemplating my next move. For a few minutes I kept a lookout in case any of the Kilnagaels showed up, but then I realized it was unlikely that any of them would be here. As mad as I was at Fr. Connolly, they were twice as angry. I asked God to bring an end to the trouble between the Kilnagaels and the Church, to send Colleen back to me, and bring an end to the trouble between us, even if I wasn't sure what it was. I couldn't decide whether I wanted to apologize to Fr. Connolly, but until I knew that until the Kilnagaels came back to Our Lady of Holy Truth I wouldn't feel at home here. More troubling to me was the possibility that I had no reason to expect God to answer my prayers about Colleen if the rift between Fr. Connolly and me continued. I decided that I would express regret for what I had said without actually apologizing to him, if I saw him after mass. That would be the first step in making everything right again.

He was standing at the back of the church greeting the congregation as they exited the church. I took a deep breath, went over my speech one last time, and approached him.

"Fr. Connolly,..."

"Good morning, Marty," he said coldly, and then proceeded to ignore me as he greeted others.

I was willing to say something nice just to make peace, and I wouldn't have minded making a slight apology, but I had no intention of begging him to forgive me. I didn't do anything wrong. His rather dismissive tone of voice surprised me. It actually offended me a little bit. He was angry at me? After what he did to the Kilnagaels? After he denied Danny Kilnagael a funeral? If anything, he should be asking them to forgive him. He should have asked me to forgive him. As I walked away I thought I should be angry with him but I was relieved. I was, no matter what else happened, still Catholic, still believed in God, and I still wanted to be a part of the Church. He was still the priest, and it mattered that he allowed me back in his church.

We may have thought Fr. Connolly was the most important man in Holy Truth, but apparently the newspapers didn't agree. The Sunday papers ran stories about Rev. Torian McAllister, suddenly the biggest celebrity in our parish, or the biggest villain. Charlie expressed a begrudging admiration for the man's ability to draw attention to himself, and to use the press to promote his cause, but he also added the problem was that reporters were lazy.

"They've got to have something to write about, to fill those newspapers, so if a guy like McAllister tells them what to write, they'll write it. It's a whole lot easier than actually working to find the truth."

I remembered Charlie saying those words as I read about the upcoming march along Madison on Christmas Eve, and how the shopkeepers were furious that Negroes were going to ruin the last shopping day before Christmas. I found it hard to believe that he used Danny's funeral because I didn't think he could possibly have known how much attention he would get from being there, but as I read the newspaper I realized how good he was at placing himself in the news.

"Martin told me that Chicago was the toughest place to defeat segregation, but he insisted that Operation Breadbasket must continue. I promised Martin that I would carry on his legacy, and we Negroes in Chicago would not give up our nonviolent struggle for equality until equality was achieved."

Rev. McAllister made a point of referencing Martin Luther King often, occasionally calling him Dr. King, but usually referring to "Martin," making it sound like he was Martin Luther King's right hand man. There was no one in Holy Truth to offer a differing opinion, or to speak out against the march.

Alderman O'Bannion still worried that his political life might be over because it was his careless comment that inspired this march to begin with, so he had virtually become a hermit to avoid further trouble. All of the other elected officials, police department leaders or others who might speak out against the march were under strict orders to keep a low profile, so there was no chance they would say anything. The papers and television newsmen interviewed "average citizens" walking along Madison, but none of them possessed the air of importance that Rev. McAllister possessed, allowing him to have the stage to himself.

The lack of a proper White spokesman caused a growing anger among us in Holy Truth. People started calling city hall and complaining to the mayor, but he had no intention of addressing it. He planned to wait it out, believing that Rev. McAllister's movement, like Martin Luther King's earlier in the year, could not be sustained. People said city hall referred them to the alderman's office, and the alderman was told that if he commented on it at all, he would suffer a self-imposed death sentence. There was a growing panic both in Holy Truth and in me. For most of the parish the cause of the panic was Rev. McAllister. Uncle Charlie was right about him, he was a master politician who knew how to draw attention to himself and his causes. Every day during the week before Christmas he held a press conference, brought a news reporter with him into his neighborhood, or, once, led the local television news crews into Holy Truth, using the free publicity to promote the march, explain the difficulties his followers faced, or to showcase success stories of people overcoming those difficulties. They were honest, hardworking people who only wanted to be treated fairly.

On the other hand the press made the people in Holy Truth out to be cold hearted villains determined to make sure Rev. McAllister and his followers would never even want to visit our parish, never mind owning a home there. Even worse, he made a show of leading television reporters as he walked down Madison Avenue, right through Holy Truth, rubbing their noses in the fact that they were unwilling to confront him while the cameras were present. He got away with it because almost everyone in Holy Truth agreed to follow an "ignore-them-and-they'll-go-away" plan of action. "Besides," my dad complained bitterly, "these news reporters are tripping all over themselves to show that Negroes are good, news reporters are good, and all other White people are bad."

Ignoring him proved to be much more of a challenge than people realized. Since none of the politicians or other high profile neighborhood people was making any effort to defend Holy Truth, the feeling was that this Negro minister was using our parish as a verbal punching bag, and we had to sit there and take it. He could say anything he wanted and no one corrected him. The sympathetic stories he received infuriated the people of Our Lady of Holy Truth more with each passing day. Even the fast approaching Christmas day couldn't soften the negative opinion of him. As the week wore on bitterness grew, and the news people, sensing the mounting frustration, did their best to encourage angry responses on camera. The 10:00 news featured clips of a very calm, thoughtful Negro preacher articulating the hopes and dreams of his followers, contrasted with increasingly angry Irish people lashing out against his presence in their neighborhood. They reacted angrily to all of the positive coverage he was getting, and to all of the trouble he brought to Holy Truth. By Friday more and more parishioners decided that they weren't going to take it lying down, and Christmas Eve or no Christmas Eve, people were intent on defending Holy Truth.

I was too busy with my own problems to get wrapped up in Rev. McAllister. My greatest concern arose from my sudden isolation from Colleen. She asked me to let her have a few days to mourn her brother, so I waited until Tuesday to call her. She told me she wasn't ready yet, and maybe we should wait until after Christmas. Until after Christmas? Alarms bells were going off in my head. I started realizing that I might be on the verge of losing Colleen, and since she wouldn't see me at the moment, I needed to find another way to repair the damage.

On Wednesday I called Patrick James to see if he wanted to go Christmas shopping. While I did need to buy gifts for my mom and dad, I really needed to get a gift for Colleen, and I remembered the Irish sweaters she admired in the Irish import store.

"So, you think it's over between you and Colleen?"

"Don't say that," I said. "Don't even think it."

"Well, I gotta tell ya, when a broad says she doesn't want to talk to you for two weeks, that's not a good sign. If I were you, I'd make sure I bought her a really nice Christmas gift."

"Colleen is not a *broad*."

I knew Patrick too well to be offended by what he said. He never typically referred to girls as broads, so I realized he attempted to diminish my loss by downplaying Colleen's importance to me. I defended her honor and then moved on, almost like he never said anything.

"I keep telling myself it's a temporary thing, that she's upset about her brother. I need to buy her Christmas gift that tells her how important she is to me."

"You need to get her something that says 'Please don't break up with me. I'm desperate to keep you.'"

"Very funny. Actually what I want is something that says I never thought for a moment that you were thinking of breaking up with me, and I already know what it is."

We walked over to the Galway Lady and I walked right over to the counter, looking at the sweaters that were stacked on the shelf behind it.

"Patrick, come here for a second." He came over and I pointed to the sweaters. "So, what do you think?"

"I don't know," he said as if he really did have no opinion.

"You think Colleen would like one of those? She likes being Irish. Her whole family does. It's like they're in a contest to see who can be the most Irish. That's why I think the sweater is a good idea."

"Well, it *is* a nice gift," he said, "but it doesn't strike me as romantic."

"No, actually I think it is. She told me once how much she liked them. I think knowing that I remembered will mean a lot to her."

"Are you getting something for your sweetheart?" the lady behind the counter asked cheerfully.

"I'm looking for a present for my girlfriend. You think she'd like one of those sweaters? Is that a good present for a girl?"

The Last Sunday in Ordinary Time

The lady pulled one of the sweaters down and unfolded it on the counter.

"They're perfect. Any girl would love to have one. Is she an Irish girl? These sweaters are lovely, hand-knitted in Ireland."

She pulled down a second one and unfolded it as well, just like she did the day I was in there with Colleen.

"A sweater like this will not only keep your sweetheart warm, it will always remind her of you."

With that she looked at me and winked. I looked over at Patrick.

"What do you think?"

"It's a nice gift. I'm sure she'll like it, but are you sure you want to spend that much money?"

If I wanted to make an impression on her, to make sure she was still my girl, this was the right gift. I pretty much knew I was buying it before I entered the store, but I was looking for someone to back me up.

"I'll take it."

Patrick let out a quiet "wow" but didn't say anything more. For the first time in a few days I felt like I was at least fighting back, doing something to keep from losing Colleen. I asked the woman if she had a box for it.

"We do have some boxes in back, not specifically for the sweater, but I can find one that will do in a pinch. Would you like me to wrap it for you?"

"Yes, please."

In the final few days before Christmas people began commenting on the continued mild weather, and how it looked like there wouldn't be a white Christmas after all. They also continued to complain more about Rev. McAllister and the march he planned to lead on Christmas Eve. Over my mother's objections Mick scheduled me to work so the guys who had covered for me around Danny's funeral could have the day off. The gas station was closing at six, so I would be there all day with a front row seat to watch the marchers. By Thursday the weathermen on television started talking about the possibility of snow on Christmas Eve, and we started wondering if that would affect the march at all.

Rev. McAllister kept up his publicity campaign in the papers and on the nightly news, causing more agitation among the people of Holy Truth. I heard from Eddie and Brendan that a lot guys who hung out at the Lovely Bit decided to show up and give the marchers an earful. Mick insisted all along that the march would be a minor event and assured Mom that I would be safe working in the gas station. As the week progressed, though, more customers brought up the march and talked about how angry it made them.

People started arriving at the Lovely Bit early the following Friday night because so many college kids had come home for the Christmas break. Because of Danny's funeral, the impending march, and the unseasonably mild weather, it didn't feel very Christmas-y to me. I watched the crowd grow from Mickey's American Standard across the street. Around 7:30 Eddie Mulroney and Brendan Ward stopped by the gas station to say hello on their way into the bar.

"Hey, we heard about Charlie not letting you in because the newspaper guys are sniffing around. That stinks."

"We'll I'm not mad at him or anything. I mean, I am underage."

"Still you're his nephew. It shouldn't be a big deal."

"Hey," Brendan said, "you're not working tomorrow when the march is happening are you?"

"Actually, I am." I told him. "I missed so many days because of the thing with Danny Kilnagael that there was no way Mick was going to give me Christmas Eve off."

"I'm telling you," Brendan said, "we have to ignore them. If nobody pays any attention to the marchers the whole thing will be a failure. They want attention."

"Screw that," Eddie said almost angrily. "I'm tired of watching these Coloreds shooting their mouths off all over the news, and getting away with it. Nobody ever says anything to them. Well, I'm going to have something to say, I'll tell you that. I'm going to tell them to go back to Africa."

While the three of us had been standing there talking Seamus wandered over. He had just left the Lovely Bit and detoured toward us on his way to the bus stop.

I leaned over to Seamus and whispered "Aren't you going to tell him that their not Africans, they're Americans?" Seamus looked at me like that was the craziest thing he ever heard. The conversation, if you could call it that, continued with both Eddie and Brendan trying to talk at the same time.

"So what are you going to do? Stand on the sidewalk and scream at them so you can look like an idiot on the 10:00 news? That's what they want you to do. Don't give them the satisfaction."

"All I know is that if one of them gives me any lip, I'll beat the crap out of him."

"Are you crazy? There'll be more cops on the street that day..."

"So what? They cops hate them, too. They're not going to go out of their way to protect the marchers."

"If anything bad happens, they're going to blame us, you know that."

"No they won't. It's our neighborhood."

"It doesn't matter. Daley doesn't want any trouble. Any cop who gets his picture in the paper doing anything but protecting the Coloreds is going..."

"This is why I left the bar," Seamus said.

Seamus talked about the Lovely Bit. The whole atmosphere in the bar that night was ugly, and he didn't want to listen to anymore of the arguing. Most of the guys in the bar believed that it was better to ignore the marchers, but he figured that about one third of the guys there planned to give the marchers an earful as they marched down the street. Their spit-in-your-eye defiance enraged the people who wanted to ignore the march, causing the resentment to rise on both sides. We could hear yelling back and forth whenever the bar door opened for someone to enter or leave. Eddie and Brendan decided to head into the bar, and as we watched them walk across the street I asked Seamus what he thought would happen in the morning.

"I can't imagine it will get as ugly as the summer marches got because the cold weather will keep a lot of people home. But if people don't stay home..."

331

He shook his head, said good-bye, and walked toward the bus stop while I went back to work. Later that evening a few of Maureen Kilnagael's friends drove into the gas station and asked me about her family. I told them I hadn't heard anything knew, so they started talking about a big argument between Colleen's parents. Mrs. Kilnagael thought her husband wasn't being supportive enough and wanted to stop being Catholic after what they did to Danny. Mr. Kilnagael remained a fully committed and devout Catholic, and had no intention of switching religions.

Others stopped by as well, that night and other times while I worked. Colleen's friends called my house to complain that she wouldn't talk to them, which made me feel better knowing I was not the only one. Other guys stopped by on their way to the Lovely Bit to say hello and get information. Because I spent so much time with the Kilnagaels and everyone thought I knew Rev. McAllister better than I actually did, people viewed me as a sort of expert on what was happening in Holy Truth. Did I think they would really march? Did I expect a lot of parishioners to show up and watch them? How are Mr. and Mrs. Kilnagael doing? I enjoyed being known that way, feeling like a big fish in a small pond. I really felt like I had become an important member of Our Lady of Holy Truth.

The Last Sunday in Ordinary Time

Christmas Eve

Dreaming of a White Christmas

December 24th, 1966

The weathermen were right. After an unseasonably warm December, Christmas Eve Saturday arrived with a definite chill in the air. At midnight it had been forty-one degrees, but by 8:00 in the morning it fell to twenty-five degrees, not brutally cold, but definitely colder than we had gotten used to. By 8:30, when I started walking to work, the first snowflakes were falling. During the 10:00 news the night before, they predicted 4 to 6 inches of snow would fall. By the time I started work at

9:00, the lawns were white, and the snow was starting to stick to the sidewalks and cars.

The air was very calm, and the lack of wind added to the quiet of the snowfall. It was a very gentle snowfall, big fluffy flakes that seemed in no hurry to reach the ground. The effect was hypnotic, muting the usually abundant city noise, and mesmerizing those of us enjoying the peacefulness of it. The first measureable snowfall of the winter always seemed special, somehow, but this time, because it was Christmas Eve, and because so many people were on edge about the impending march, it carried an extra meaning for us all.

People remained uncertain about the significance of the march. It might pass through Holy Truth without causing so much a ripple of reaction from the locals, but it also might cause the kind of race riots that happened in Los Angeles or confrontations like the ones down south in Alabama. One customer came in and said he thought the snow would discourage the marchers and the whole thing would be cancelled. "No," Mick said, "they're still going to come."

Mick schedule Stosh to work until 2:00, but then changed it to 11:30 when Stosh's mom called and insisted her son leave the neighborhood before the trouble started at 12:00. Mick failed to change her mind the way he did with my mom, so I it would be just Mick and me in the gas station when the march started. For the balance of the morning the two of us kept busy with shovels, clearing snow that fell slowly but continuously. Very few cars pulled in, something I attributed to the snow, but Mick insisted people stayed away because of the marchers.

The Last Sunday in Ordinary Time

"People keep telling me this thing won't cost me money, but it absolutely is. I'm having to pay your enormous salaries while you lean on your shovels watching the snow fall."

Between 10:00 and 11:00 Madison was dead. With no one else to talk to, a reporter from the American came into the gas station to ask Mick a few questions. Mick claimed he knew very little about the march, not even which side of the street the Coloreds would be walking on. He wondered if the reporter knew.

"This march is different from the rest" the reporter told us. "The other marches went down side streets, right past people's homes to make sure everyone knew they wanted access to better housing. That was the point. This time they want to make a point about be allowed to walk and shop in any neighborhood they choose, so they're going to spend the entire time marching past stores. Eventually they'll be on both sides of the street, walking west on the north side, and then circling back east on the south side of the street."

"Well," Mick said, "I suppose we can tolerate a few Coloreds marching along the street for an hour or so."

"There'll be a lot of Whites marching too, you know."

Mick gave him a puzzled look.

"I'm serious. There are going to be a lot of White college kids marching, too. It's become the fashionable thing to do on college campuses this year, to be a civil rights marcher. Them, and the usual liberal artists, religious types, and what not. Yeah, you can bet that there will be a lot of White marchers, too."

The Last Sunday in Ordinary Time

Up until 11:00 nobody shopped, nobody walked their dogs, very few cars drove down the street, and half of the ones that did were police cars. After 11:00 though, things started to change. At first only a few young guys, high schools and college age mostly, walked down the street, joking loudly and throwing snow at each other. Mick, Stosh and I watched the reporter approach several different groups of them, diligently recording the parishioners' reactions to the impending march. In time more adults showed up, all ages and as many women as men as far as I could tell. A few young couples even brought their children with them, but I didn't see too many children. As it neared 12:00 Madison became thick with people on both sides of the street. Mick sent me out a couple of times to ask them not to block the driveways in and out of the gas station, and for a while they obeyed, but eventually so many people were on the sidewalk that a wall formed that cut us off from the street.

Across the street I could see Eddie Mulroney and most of the other guys from the Stage Irish team heading into the Lovely Bit. They apparently decided to watch the march while having a cold one. Even at this late hour people argued about saying nothing to the marchers or yelling at them to leave us alone, but Eddie and his group struck me as guys who would have something to say. I wondered how long they would stay inside the bar.

Nobody knew exactly how things were going to turn out, but shortly before 12:00 word started spreading through the crowd that the marchers were starting to line up. When I looked east on Madison I saw the flashing lights on top of a couple of police cars in the distance, but no more details than that. Through it all the snow kept falling, lending a

Christmas card beauty to a scene that many feared would turn ugly. Along the street I heard people mention "They're coming" as the word passed from east to west. Brendan Ward walked toward the Lovely Bit from the east, but when he saw me he crossed the street.

"Do you know who's getting ready to march with the Coloreds?" he asked almost as if it were an accusation.

I thought it was a strange question and put my hands out before me to let him know I had no idea what he was talking about.

"The Kilnagaels. The whole family."

"You're kidding."

"No, the old lady's there, getting ready to walk front and center with that McAllister. And all the daughters are nearby. The whole family's ready to march with them, betraying the whole neighborhood."

Before Mick could stop me I took off running toward the start of the march. In the distance I saw a Negro in a big, wool over coat leading the marchers that I first thought was Rev. McAllister. Actually he was a cop, who, along with two White cops, walked in front of the marchers and cleared the way, insisting that people step back to make room. Since the falling snow muffled the noise, I couldn't tell if anything was being said to the marchers, but it didn't look good. As I drew nearer to them I heard the ugly racial insults hurled at Rev. McAllister and the rest of the marchers and I knew that people rejected the silent treatment. Holy Truth belonged to us and those who turned out to watch the marchers meant to defend their home parish.

I recognized Rev. McAllister walking behind the policemen. The policemen were assigned to protect Rev. McAllister from what might turn out to be a mob, and the Colored cop drew a lot of the ugly attention away from him. The White officers were doing the same thing, but listening to a Negro officer telling them to step back irritated the crowd. If the angry, ugly insults of the crowd scared him, he didn't show it. He spoke loudly, in a deep no-nonsense voice that carried a long way down the street. He was a big man, more intimidating than intimidated, and he, as much as anything else, kept the crowd under control.

"Move back. Give the people some room to walk. You can't be blocking the sidewalk. Move back."

The sidewalk measured fifteen feet wide, but people standing along both the curb and the storefronts narrowed it down to about half that width so that only two or three people could march side by side. In the second row, directly behind Rev. McAllister, Mrs. Kilnagael walked. She stood arm-in-arm with a Negro woman about her same age. Mixed in among the people in front I saw Colleen and her sisters.

"Young Martin," Rev. McAllister called out, "are you here to join us?"

I ran right past him to where Colleen stood, walking slowly behind her mother and looking very scared as far as I could tell.

"What are you doing? Are you crazy?"

A couple of Negro men stepped over to us and asked her if I was bothering her.

"No, he's fine. There's no problem."

They nodded and stepped back, but not before giving me knowing looks suggesting they had their eyes on me.

The Last Sunday in Ordinary Time

"Marty you shouldn't be here," Mrs. Kilnagael said with a tinge of anger in her voice. "Does your mother know you're here? Peter…"

She gave her husband a look, a quiet demand that he do something.

"Marty, you need to go. This is no place for you."

"Marty, please, don't make a scene."

"Don't make a scene? This whole thing is a scene. You could be hurt. This is dangerous."

"Marty! Marty! You can't be here, not without your parents." Mrs. Kilnagael was determined to get me to leave.

"I'll be right back, Mom," Colleen told her, then grabbed my hand and pulled me out of the procession, through the crowd on the sidewalk, and into a narrow gangway next to a dry cleaner. I didn't dare look back toward her parents for fear that they might stop us.

"Look, I'm sorry, but, you can't stay here."

"Are you kidding me? How can you be marching with these people? It's like you're backstabbing Holy Truth."

"We're backstabbing them? Where were they for us? Not one of these people showed up for my brother's funeral. They said horrible things to us, and they're still saying horrible things. Do you know what that's like? Do you have any idea how much that hurts?"

"Colleen, I'm worried about you. You could get hurt. You know I love you."

She nodded. "In my Mom's eyes Rev. McAllister saved Danny's funeral. She decided she wanted to join this march to thank him, but also to be spiteful to Holy Truth, I'm sure. She talked my dad into it as well."

She stepped toward me, put her arms around my neck and pulled me close, and whispered.

"Marty, you're my friend. You've been wonderful to me and my family, but it's over. Maybe in the future we can be friends again, but for now it hurts too much to see you. We don't want to be part of Holy Truth anymore, and you're a big part of Holy Truth. I don't know where we're going to go to church now, but it won't be at Our Lady of Holy Truth. I'm sorry. I don't want to hurt you."

"Colleen...come on..."

"Marty, do me a favor and tell your mother that we all thank her for what she said to Fr. Connolly."

"My mom? What did she say to him?"

"Oh, God, you didn't hear? Connolly goes up to her in front of several people to tell her that you called him a son-of-a-bitch. I think he was trying to embarrass her. So your mom says 'Well, if Marty thinks you're a son-of-a-bitch that probably means you're a son-of-a-bitch.'"

"She said that?"

All of the worry I had about losing Colleen vanished for a moment while I shared one last laugh with her.

"Both of your parents were always so sweet to me. You are a wonderful family. I have to get back now, but I'm sorry Marty, but it's over between us."

She kissed me on the cheek, squeezed me hard one last time, and then walked back to the sidewalk to rejoin the marchers. I was dumbstruck. So sudden and devastating was her good-bye that I never tried to make a defense. I walked through the gangway to the alley in back. I didn't want anyone to see me cry, and I was crying a little. I kept telling myself that I needed to regain my composure before I got back to Mick's, but I struggled to do it. I loitered for a few minutes, and then slowly eased my way back to Mick's. Finally I comforted myself by deciding it wasn't over, she just needed time.

"Where the hell were you?"

"I'm sorry, Mick. I had to see if Colleen was O.K."

"If anything had happened…I told your mother you'd be safe here. I'm responsible for you. Don't leave this gas station again."

There was nothing to do but watch events in the street. The police must have prevented all cars from driving down Madison because there were none. I grabbed a shovel and went through the motions of clearing different parts of the gas station, but mostly watched the crowd watching the approaching civil rights march.

The people on the sidewalk never broke into a group chant. A few called out insults trying to be funny, but others vented anger toward the Negroes, shouting ugly racial slurs. Still other aimed their venom at the White people, screaming that they were traitors. Just like the reporter told Mick and me earlier, a lot of White people came to march along with Rev. McAllister. Because the long, narrow line or marchers extended so far back it was impossible to tell the percentages, but I guessed it was about 60% Black and 40% White. A number of the marchers carried signs, some read "Operation Breadbasket," some carried pleas for racial peace and brotherhood, and some declared "Black Power."

The Last Sunday in Ordinary Time

Despite all of his talk about nonviolent protest, Rev. McAllister could not prevent some of his followers from presenting a more aggressive message by carrying the Black Power signs that included a graphic of a closed fist. The signs and those who carried them sent a message of confrontation that undercut the minister's desire to be a man of peace, like Martin Luther King.

The more strident posing came across as unspoken psychological aggression. Some of the parishioners who had gathered to witness this demonstration saw that aggression as invitation to verbally defend themselves, but they couldn't decide who made them angrier, the Negroes trying to take Holy Truth away from them, or the Whites trying to give it away. I expected to hear a lot of racial slurs, and I heard them. I also heard the words "traitor" and "turncoat" aimed at the White marchers. A few of the marchers tried to calm things down by smiling and wishing a merry Christmas to those watching them.

By now it was almost 12:30 and, although it was very slow progress walking through the throng of angry witnesses, the procession continued westward. They were being squeezed because people stood along both sides of sidewalk, forcing the procession to follow a very narrow path. They were very near the gas station now and I heard all of the ugly things being yelled, especially at the Kilnagaels.

"I'm glad your son died."

I couldn't tell who said it, but a few people went after the Colleen's family, furious that the Kilnagaels had so betrayed them. As far as I could tell they were the only people from Holy Truth who joined the march, and that perceived act of disloyalty provoked extraordinary anger from some of their neighbors. As bad as the racial taunts were, and as emotional and angry as some of the comments aimed at the White marchers were, the really mean things were said to the Kilnagaels.

"I hope your brother burns in hell."

"All the Kilnagaels deserve to die."

It horrified me. I looked at Colleen, but she acted like she didn't see me. I thought about trying to talk to her again, but when I started to move in that direction, Mick pulled me back.

"Where do you think you're going?"

"I want to see if Colleen is all right."

"Nothing doing. I told you to stay here and I meant it. You're not going anywhere."

"But..."

"But nothing. Her mother is there, so she's well taken care of."

At the gas station the space along the sidewalk increased so things loosened up a bit, but people still stood on both sides of the sidewalk, forcing the march to hear the ugly accusations from both sides. I waved my arms to get Colleen's attention as she went by. I saw her look at me. We made brief eye contact, but then she looked away without acknowledging me. I refused to look at Mick, not wanting to know that he knew how hurt I was at her indifference toward me. I didn't know if he saw it or not.

The three cops in front kept calling for people to clear the way, but the procession moved very slowly anyway, getting ready now to cross the street as it approached the corner. While they inched forward, barely avoiding coming to a complete standstill, snowballs started raining down upon them. A number of guys, I guessed about ten, stepped out of the Lovely Bit and started lobbing snowballs across the street, throwing them in high slow arcs. About twenty or thirty flew across Madison in a matter of thirty or forty seconds, including one that made a direct hit on Colleen, striking her on the right side of the face. I saw that it stung her, and I made another move in her direction but Mick stood in front of me again and said "Nothing doing." Among all the marchers at the front of the line the men reacted, stepping in front of the women to protect them. This included a very tall Colored guy who put his arm around Colleen and held her for a moment until everyone was sure the excitement was over.

Uncle Charlie stepped out of the Lovely Bit and screamed at the guys to get away from his bar, followed by Aunt Bridie pleading with her husband to come back inside. He looked like a very old man at that moment, and I heard Bridie saying "Remember your heart, Charlie. Remember your heart." Rev. McAllister and one of the policemen turned to protect Mrs. Kilnagael and the other women nearby, while a couple of other cops standing near the corner took off after the guys who threw the snowballs. The young guys, including Eddie Mulroney and Brendan Ward, who threw the snowballs had too big of a head start on the cops, and were never caught. The policemen started suggesting that the whole thing be ended there, insisting that they could no longer ensure the safety of the marchers, but the minister and his followers refused.

"We will continue, sir. A few snowballs are not enough to prevent us from taking our place in society."

The march continued, and I watched Colleen, her mom, and her sisters continue to walk west on Madison with the rest of the marchers.

The Last Sunday in Ordinary Time

The procession continued past Mickey's American Standard, and the people in it continued to hear insults and angry comments from others on the street, but the number and the volume of the comments diminished as the less important marchers went by. People directed most of their deepest anger at Rev. McAllister and the others at the front, including, to my horror, the Kilnagaels. The snow kept falling gently on Holy Truth, placing the entire scene under a peacefulness that seemed determined to smother any attempt to maintain hate. This message from the heavens coupled with the snowball incident eased the determined anger of the crowd. It was one thing to yell a few harsh words, but to actually throw things at people, especially White women like Colleen, ratcheted things higher than most neighborhood people wanted to go.

They walked another half mile west on Madison, then crossed the street to begin walking back east on the south side of the street. I spent the time waiting for them to return for their second pass in front of Mickey's by shoveling snow again, clearing the areas in and around the pumps. I felt stupid and angry while I did it. I said a silent prayer that enough snow would fall to make the footprints in the snow disappear, creating the illusion that the march had never happened, but there were so many marchers that they trampled the snow on the sidewalks completely. Colleen was going to go marching right past me and the snowfall would never be deep enough to cover up that ugly truth. It was going to keep on falling, she would keep walking away from me, and in both cases I was powerless to stop it. Nonetheless I kept on shoveling and watching for Colleen reappear.

A few minutes later they came back down Madison, walking more quickly now, and wishing Merry Christmas to the crowd still gathered to watch them. Again Colleen refused to acknowledge me, but all of her sisters waved, and I waved back. This show of friendliness drew a couple of sharp comments in my direction, accusing me of fraternizing with the enemy. I didn't care. The friendliness of her sisters gave me a cause for optimism, and allowed me to believe that Colleen just needed a little more time. At times the people of Holy Truth reacted with anger and ugliness occasionally, but for the most part they showed restraint. As they moved past I watched television and newspaper men taking pictures and stopping to interview people on the sidewalk. The mood of the marchers improved greatly since it started. Now they walked more easily, repeatedly calling out "Merry Christmas" to people still watching them. They heard angry responses from some of the people still watching them, but the number of comments continued to dwindle until, in the end, very little drama occurred. The biggest news of the day was that Colleen said she was finished with me and that wouldn't make the newspapers.

Christmas Day

There is no Santa Claus

December 25th, 1966

It never felt like Christmas. It was just another Sunday, no
different than all of the Sundays before I dated Colleen, and completely
different than the ones I spent with her since. In church everyone showed

up wearing their Sunday best or the new clothes they found under the tree. Their faces radiated the joy of the day, and the altar almost exploded red because of all of the poinsettias placed on it. On the way into mass people went out of their way to exchange holiday greetings to each other, including me, but I remained distant in my responses. Until I started talking to Colleen again, I it felt like I didn't really belong to Holy Truth, and that Holy Truth didn't really belong to me.

I returned to listening to my dad talk about the man who never took off his hat until he sat down, to watching other families and their full rosters of children, and felt completely alone. As the very long Christmas mass continued I scanned the congregation, hoping to spot Colleen and her family, but I knew they weren't there. They quit Our Lady of Holy Truth, and they weren't coming back. Instead I took note of the many other families, some with kids squirming in their seats, dying to go home and find out what Santa left for them. Others sat so still I almost thought I they were paintings of families rather than actual living, breathing people. I couldn't quit Holy Truth because I never really belonged, not the way the big Irish families belonged, so I sat in church feeling like an unwanted guest.

After mass we returned home. Christmas morning reinforced the sense of isolation I always felt except when spending time with the Kilnagaels. All of the restaurants were closed so we went back home to eat a quiet breakfast before going to the living room to exchange gifts. No matter how hard my parents tried, watching a sixteen-year-old open presents lacked the excitement and charm that watching a six-year-old offered, and all holiday mornings, especially Christmas morning, found us going through the motions of exchanging pleasantries and wishing each other Happy Easter, or Thanksgiving or whatever. Mom actually went out of her way to make a nice meal because Mick was coming over early for tea and it was the only meal he planned to share with us. Mick usually ate dinner with us on Christmas Day, either at our house or Charlie and Bridie's, but that year he planned to eat with Tina Avelini's family, so we'd only see him in the morning. That meant a Christmas dinner that included Charlie, Bridie, Mom, Dad, and me. We expected them around 4:00.

One of the benefits of being an only child was that I got a lot of stuff for Christmas, but that year they couldn't have bought me enough to improve my mood. I went through the motions of expressing surprise and gratitude for all that I received, but nothing surprised me, and I was not grateful. None of them knew that Colleen had officially broken up with me, but my parents and Mick knew that we hadn't seen each other for two weeks, so they must have suspected it. I assumed that's why they allowed me to remain so distant and unpleasant, and didn't protest too much when I said I was going out for a walk.

I told myself that I wouldn't go anywhere near Colleen's house, and I took off walking west, going as far as Cicero Avenue. The entire city remained blanketed in snow after 7 inches fell the day before. I stopped into the only store I found open, a drug store on Cicero near Lake Street. Despite the snow it didn't feel that cold, so I bought a bottle of orange pop and a package of chocolate cupcakes, and stood under the L tracks both eating a snack I found both repulsive and enjoyable at the same time. I remained lost in a fog of boredom, desperate for something, anything to do. As I started back for home I reminded myself again to avoid Colleen's house, but eventually decided to walk past her street, but not down her block.

I stood on the corner of their block and looked at their big, beautiful house. From where I stood I saw no lights on, so I decided to walk down the block to get a closer look. As I got closer I looked for a tree inside but didn't see one. I knew that they hadn't gotten a tree before Danny's funeral, but it looked like they didn't get one afterward either. The house that I always associated with life and laughter now sat dark and empty. If they celebrated Christmas, the celebration took place far away from Holy Truth. As I approached the house I kept rehearsing what I might say if they caught me walking down their street, how I hadn't realized where I was, or that I was just passing by on my way to somewhere else. I stopped directly in front with alternating hopes of not getting caught "spying" on them, and of being there when they pulled up in their station wagon. I imagined Colleen and her sisters piling out of the car, excited to see me, hugging me, wishing me a merry Christmas, and making me feel like a member of the family again. I stood there for a few minutes and then turned and headed back home. My exile from the Kilnagaels continued.

"We thought you got lost," Mom said as I walked in the door.

I smiled and gave her a hug, holding the hug for a long time. The top of Mom's head came up to my chin, and I knew she enjoyed the fact that her son could swallow her up in a bear hug like that. On the last stretch of my long walk home I finally regained some gratitude that Mom and Dad were waiting for me. I imagined how lonely I would be if I didn't have them to come home to, and so I entered the house with a renewed sense of how lucky I was to have them. Dad sat in the living room reading the paper and watching an old movie version of *A Christmas Carol* on television.

"Well, your picture is not in the paper, but you're the only one. Colleen made the front page."

"She did?"

He handed me the front section and there she was. A photographer captured the moment the snowball hit her the day before, and the shock and fear showed in her face. Inside they ran several pictures from the march, including one of the guys throwing the snowballs outside the Lovely Bit. I thought Eddie and those guys were jerks for doing that to her, but it frustrated me more to remember that she wouldn't have wanted me there to help her. No wonder the Kilnagaels didn't stay home for Christmas; their own neighbors were the ones who threw the snowballs at them.

"You can see Uncle Charlie in the standing in the doorway of the Lovely Bit."

"I saw that," he said. "He hates having his picture in the paper, so he won't be too happy about that."

"And there's Mickey. You're right. I'm the only one who didn't get his picture in the paper.   Did you see Mickey standing behind the crowd?"

"I did," Dad answered, "but you'd hardly notice him behind all the people screaming in front. You can't buy advertising like that."

He smiled at his own joke and I smiled to, partly to be polite, and partly because I enjoyed his amusement. Despite all of the pictures there wasn't much written about the march itself. The columnists and the editorial writers must have written their Christmas columns well before the march ended. When Charlie and Bridie arrived Dad greeted them as the "famous people we read about in the papers." Charlie grunted, smirked and shook his head, a gentle show of anger about having his picture in the paper.

During dinner Dad wondered if the protest ended up hurting the businesses on Madison much.

"I'd say it did," Charlie answered. "By the time everyone went home it was almost 3:00, and the street was busy, but not as busy as the Saturday before Christmas should be, Christmas Eve or not."

"Did it affect your business any?"

"If it wasn't for those jokers causing trouble, throwing snowballs right outside my front door... Anyway, I got my picture in the paper for the second time in two weeks. I'm sure I'll hear from city hall about that."

"It never gets any easier, does it?"

"If they had taken that picture a minute later they would have seen me yelling my fool head off for this one to come in out of the cold," Bridie said. "I was afraid he was about to have a heart attack right there on the spot."

The two of them gave each other knowing looks, almost as if Mom, Dad, and I had dropped out of the conversation. He shook his head slightly, but she responded by raising her eyebrows, a silent argument between the two of them.

"Just go ahead and tell them," she said.

"We go through this every year."

"Well, this year will be the last year we go through it," she told him firmly.

"Bridie is after me to sell the bar. She says it's time."

We were literally speechless. None of us said a word for twenty or thirty seconds.

"Nothing is decided, and you..." He pointed his finger at me. "You are sworn to secrecy. Not a word to anyone. Besides, she's been telling me it's time for the last ten years."

"I won't say a..."

"I'd say it's decided. You know what the doctor said."

Uncle Charlie put his fork down and glared at her.

"Is everything all right?" Mom asked. "You're not sick are you?"

"No, it's nothing."

"It's not nothing. The doctor said you had an irregular heartbeat, and you need to slow down."

"My heart is fine. And the Lovely Bit is good for my heart."

"It's good for your heart when you're not getting into fistfights with Negro preachers at the front door," Dad said.

Uncle Charlie groaned to show his aggravation and gave Dad a whose-side-are-you-on look.

"How old are you, Charlie?" Mom asked.

"He'll be seventy-three in the spring," Bridie answered.

"Not exactly a spring chicken," Dad said and we all laughed.

"I've been doing whatever she tells me to do for forty years, but...let me enjoy my Christmas before I have to make a decision."

The Last Sunday in Ordinary Time

I never took the conversation seriously. Of all the things that anyone said that night, I placed the most faith in Uncle Charlie's words "The Lovely Bit is good for my heart." My dad often joked that he expected to see Charlie carried out of the Lovely Bit by an undertaker, and I grew to believe he never planned to sell it. If I really thought he planned to close the Lovely Bit, I might have panicked. Instead I enjoyed sitting with the adults and getting treated as an equal.

Many of my friends, including Colleen, spoke about the kids' table, the one they sat at with their sisters, brothers, and cousins on Christmas and other holidays. While the adults sat together in one room the kids sat together in another, sometimes even in the basement. No 'kids' table' existed in my house since I represented one hundred percent of the children present at nearly all family holidays, and gained a place at the adults' table by default. It meant something when they discussed the possible closing of the Lovely Bit in front of me, and even though Uncle Charlie pointed at me and told me not to say a word, he didn't ask me to leave the room. Nor did any of them grow uncomfortable because they were talking in front of me. I grew up listening to Mom and Aunt Bridie remind Mickey that there was a child at the table while Dad and Uncle Charlie suppressed laughter. Mick grew bored when social niceties became too prudish, so he made a point of using salty language or making a crude joke as a small act of subversion. I regretted he missed this dinner and the chance to see me in a new light. I lingered at the table a little while longer after dinner, and enjoyed my new status as one of them.

New Year's Day

The Circumcision of Jesus

January 1, 1967

For the first time in my life I found myself asking questions about the holy days of obligation. Why were we obligated to go to mass on New Year's Day? Technically we "celebrated" the circumcision of Jesus, but in

The Last Sunday in Ordinary Time

light of Fr. Connolly's arbitrary decision to deny Danny Kilnagael a funeral it felt more like a made-up reason to force us to go to church one more time. Thankfully January 1 fell on a Sunday so we didn't have to go an extra day. The previous year we went to mass on Saturday, January 1ˢᵗ because of the circumcision, and then had to go again the next day because it was Sunday. Sunday or not, holy day of obligation or not, many people stayed home that morning. "Too many hangovers from celebrating New Years Eve," my dad noted when we took our seats, but it didn't bother me as much as last year because it was Sunday and we had to go to mass anyway. Last year the church was half empty on Saturday and as the mass continued the idea that everyone else stayed home while I was stuck going to church with my parents gnawed at my peace of mind. Afterward Mick told me that New Year's Day was not a holy day of obligation in Ireland, so a lot of the Irish didn't honor it here either, not that they needed much of an excuse to skip it after a hard night of celebrating New Year's Eve. I still felt obligated to attend mass, but knowing that the Irish didn't have to go to mass on New Year's Day made me wonder why Americans had to.

Fr. Connolly forgave me and I attended three other masses there since Danny's funeral, but I still felt out of place sitting in Our Lady of Holy Truth. Just like I doubted the need to be forgiven, I doubted my place there, and observing the anniversary of Jesus' circumcision compounded my growing restlessness with Holy Truth. Maybe my faith belonged outside that parish. I remembered Sr. Bernadette explaining the importance of the circumcision in religion class, how the few drops of Jesus' precious blood were spilled as a pledge of His complete

357

bloodletting later on. I accepted the rationale behind it because I accepted all of the Church's rules and teachings at first, out of respect for Sr. Bernadette and the other nuns who taught me in grade school and because I wanted to be a good Catholic. On that Sunday, as I thought about I contemplated it the more farfetched it seemed, and knowing that the Irish didn't bother with it seemed to justify my doubts about it. Fr. Connolly said our mass that morning, and he gave a homily explaining the meaning and importance of the circumcision, but to me it sounded like he merely wanted justify the holy obligation, and appease the conservative traditionalists with the type of traditional homily they wanted to hear. It provoked in me the same dilemma I faced in thinking about Fr. Connolly's hard line stance on Danny Kilnagael's funeral. In both cases I wondered if he truly believed that the Church's teaching was absolutely correct, or did he have doubts like me, and did he choose to adhere to Church teaching anyway. I changed from a dutiful Catholic to a doubtful one, and it scared me to think that way.

On that day I prayed that God would help me patch things up with Colleen, but I also thought something was missing without the Kilnagaels. Holy Truth belonged to the Kilnagaels as much as it did to me, and if they no longer wanted to be a part of Holy Truth, I wondered if I really wanted to belong to it without them. I also said a prayer for Uncle Charlie so that God would watch over him, and allow the Lovely Bit to stay open. I believed it would stay open but I wanted to cover my bases anyway. I wanted to be anywhere but church, but I knew God watched me from heaven. Was it better to spend an unhappy, inattentive hour saying prayers out of rote habit, or would it have been better to not go to church in such a poor state of mind?

From the earliest moments of my Catholic education the nuns warned my classmates and me to be wary of the devil. The devil, we were told, encourages weak men to question God, and once we started questioning God, we risked losing our way, and eventually our faith.

"The Church knows the recipe for getting into heaven, and you must follow it," Sister Christina taught us. "If the recipe for a cake requires that it be baked for an hour at 350 degrees, then you must have faith that it will be done in an hour. If you question the recipe and remove the cake too early, or you leave ingredients out, or try to bake it at 200 degrees for ten minutes, the recipe is no good to you. Likewise in getting to heaven you must go to mass on Sundays, you must go to confession, you must keep the holy days of obligation. The Church knows the recipe to get your soul to heaven, and you must follow the recipe if you long for salvation. The devil will tempt you the same way he tempted Adam and Eve, but you must keep the faith."

Sr. Christina told the truth as far as asking questions was concerned. Now that I started asking questions more and more of them entered my head. In the first few days after Fr. Connolly refused to allow the Kilnagaels to hold a funeral for their son, a couple of college guys in the Lovely Bit talked about a Church history class. Their professor told them that the Catholic Church always guarded its power jealously. When the United States emerged as a new democracy the Church eyed it suspiciously. If people got the idea in their heads that they should have a vote in electing the president, they might start thinking they should have a vote in electing the pope. What other authority might they want to strip away from the clergy? That nugget of information added to my growing confusion about right and wrong, and my devotion to the Roman Catholic Church. I began looking at Holy Truth differently, questioning a lot of what I saw, from the way they treated Danny Kilnagael to the importance of celebrating Jesus' circumcision.

I reminded myself of my new found sense of maturity, of the way Mom, Dad, Charlie and Bridie treated me on Christmas Day. I needed to draw on that strength, to make a plan for moving forward, and for regaining my religious certainty. If I put my faith in God and thought the problem through carefully, I knew I could win Colleen back. Too much happened too quickly. Colleen overreacted. I needed to be sure I didn't overreact, and to take my time while things with Colleen worked themselves out. After communion I knelt before we rose to say the final prayers, and I thanked God for not deserting me. I needed Him to help me and nothing Fr. Connolly had said or done, nor the things the college guys mentioned about Church history, would prevent me from asking Him for His help again.

With the turning of the New Year the newspapers and television stations moved on from Our Lady of Holy Truth. As far as the rest of the world was concerned the protest march was insignificant, no more than a meaningless snowball fight. Inside Holy Truth desperation gripped the parishioners. Everyone knew that Blacks continued to buy houses in more and closer neighborhoods, and each neighborhood saw a wild reaction of White people selling their houses and leaving in a panic. The newspapers called it "White flight," and now, because of the march, we dreaded that our parish was next. Nobody wanted to be the first one to sell a house to Blacks, as they asked to be called now, but people also feared they could get stuck living in a Black neighborhood if they allowed others to react quicker than they did themselves. People spoke about sticking together, saying that if nobody sold to a Black then Holy Truth would be safe. The Kilnagaels already undermined that idea by marching with Rev. McAllister on Christmas Eve, leaving the rest of the parishioners to view their neighbors with suspicion rather than trust.

In a parish filled with large families, economic realities meant some were in a better position to sell than others. The people who could least afford to sell their houses lived with a greater dependence on others to maintain the neighborhood stability. They feared the changing neighborhood most, and I heard those fears expressed by my friends. They didn't come out and say it explicitly, but I could tell that they knew their parents were in no position to sell their houses. For my part I kept preaching optimism, that I believed that Holy Truth would not change, and that it would remain a vibrant Irish neighborhood. Some of them told me I was crazy, but many of them quietly thanked me for be so positive and reassuring. During that New Year's Day mass I had a lot to pray about.

The Last Sunday in Ordinary Time

The Epiphany

January 6th, 1967

A Wise Man Bearing a Gift

On January 6th I attended early morning mass with my mom. January 6th was the day we marked the Epiphany, the day the three wise men arrived at the manger bearing gifts for the baby Jesus. Although it was not a holy day of obligation in the United States, it was a holy day of obligation in Ireland, and Mom never stopped recognizing it as one. As I had been doing for the past couple of weeks, I spent my time in church praying for God's help in regaining Colleen's affection, and for the general well-being of Our Lady of Holy Truth. For all of my talk about my confidence that Our Lady of Holy Truth would remain a staunchly Irish Catholic parish, I held profound doubts. Nobody but my family knew that Mick faced pressure to sell his gas station to Standard Oil. Nobody but my family knew that Aunt Bridie wanted Uncle Charlie to sell the Lovely Bit O'Blarney Pub. I doubted many people realized that the Kilnagaels never intended on attending mass at Holy Truth again, or how angry they were at the parish they felt deserted them in their time of need. It dawned on me that they were the one family willing to sell their house to a Black family without worrying how the rest of the parish felt about it.

Fr. Connolly said mass that morning. By that time I had accepted his forgiveness and no personal awkwardness existed between us any longer. His homily considered the gifts the three wise men brought for Jesus, and he asked what gifts meant to our savior.

The Last Sunday in Ordinary Time

"Remember that the baby Jesus was born into the most humble of circumstances, in a manger, basically a barn, surrounded by barn animals. Here He was, the Savior, God's gift to man, the very Son of God, and people relegated him to sleeping in a crude shelter. The three wise men arrived to basically set the record straight. Jesus was our King, our Savior, our Redeemer. They came bearing gifts, three kings who set their own importance, their own majesty aside, knelt before the baby Jesus and declared You are the one true king."

He suggested that the only gifts that meant anything to Jesus were love, forgiveness, patience, kindness, charity, and other signs of our devotion to Him. Jesus wanted us to put His teaching into practice, to turn ourselves into tools for use in spreading God's love to others.

"It was up to us," the priest said, "to find a way to make our faith a dynamic faith, a faith that does not just rest in our hearts like a book on a shelf, but rather pours forth from us like water offered to a thirsty world. Our job is to go forth into the world like so many wise men and wise women, and offer our good works as gifts to Jesus."

After mass Mom and I said hello to Fr. Connolly on our way out of the church. He asked about the Kilnagaels and wondered if I talked to them lately. I told him they were still keeping to themselves and not even Colleen would talk to me.

"Well, don't give up on them, Marty. In my eyes and I'm sure in God's eyes as well, they remain an important part of Our Lady of Holy Truth. If you see any of them let them know I asked how they were. I'm still heartsick over what happened, and I would like to mend fences somehow."

"I will, Father."

He smiled warmly.

"I know you will. You may be the one person who can help make things right between us."

As we walked home Mom told me to ignore what Fr. Connolly said.

"You're still a high school boy, and you don't need to be getting in between the Kilnagaels and Fr. Connolly. Just leave it be."

"Do you think they will come back to Our Lady of Holy Truth?"

"I don't know, Marty, but don't worry about it. If they come back, they come back. If they don't, they don't. I'm sure the parish will get along fine with or without them. It's nothing for you to be concerned about."

But I knew my mom was wrong. We needed them to remain a part of Holy Truth. Both the homily and my conversation with Fr. Connolly stayed with me long after mass ended. He was right, I was the only one who could make things better between Fr. Connolly and the Kilnagaels. I was the only who could make things right between the Kilnagaels and the whole parish. I still believed that Holy Truth was a special place, and that the Kilnagaels were an important part of it. I pictured all of the little Irish touches that had in their home, the music, the curtains around the kitchen window, all of it. The Kilnagaels celebrated being Irish, and there was no better place to be Irish than in Holy Truth. I needed to remind them of that if I wanted them to stay.

I needed to reach Colleen, and through her, all of the Kilnagaels. The sweater I bought for Colleen sat in a box on the floor of my closet, wrapped and ready to be given. Until that moment I wanted to give it to her anyway, but now I also saw it as a way to give her and her whole family the kind of gift Fr. Connolly spoke about. I knew she would like the Irishness of it and it would remind them all how much they enjoyed being Irish. It also dawned on me that somebody needed to extend forgiveness to the Kilnagaels the same way Fr. Connolly extended it to me. I knew that the Kilnagaels didn't feel the need to be forgiven, just like I didn't feel the need for Fr. Connolly's forgiveness. In time though, the fact that Our Lady of Holy Truth forgave them would ease the awkwardness that existed between the Kilnagaels and others in the parish. Just like me they would eventually appreciate the kindness, and appreciate the fact that it made reconciliation easier. The special nature of Our Lady of Holy Truth could be saved if we kept the faith, and it started with me.

I saw it as a domino effect, the analogy politicians used to explain the need to stop communism when they justified the Korean War or the Viet Nam War. In my eyes the loss of the Kilnagael family represented the first domino to fall in Holy Truth. The people in Holy Truth worried that as soon as they lost one family, the whole parish could then fall like a series of dominoes until it changed from an Irish neighborhood to a Black one, and the Kilnagaels were the biggest domino. Somebody needed to extend an olive branch to the Kilnagaels, and nobody was in a better position to do that than I was. All those people who called me to find out about the Kilnagaels after Danny's funeral convinced me that others saw I had a special relationship with them. If I could use my influence to make peace between Holy Truth and the Kilnagaels I could save the parish.

I promised God and myself that I would make an effort. Like the three wise men who came bearing gifts for Jesus, I would use the Irish sweater in my closet as the gift I would use to convince the Kilnagaels to remain in Holy Truth. I intended to call Colleen and to keep calling her until she agreed to meet with me one more time. Although I desperately wanted to win her back I vowed to sacrifice my personal desire for the greater good of the parish. I intended to give her that sweater because it was a beautiful Irish work of art, a symbol of how wonderful it was to be Irish, and to remind Colleen and her family that they belonged to Our Lady of Holy Truth, and with the people who lived there. I convinced myself that the Kilnagaels needed Holy Truth as much as Holy Truth needed the Kilnagaels. As the Kilnagaels went, so went the parish.

The Last Sunday in Ordinary Time

The First Sunday after the Epiphany

January 8th, 1967

The Last Sunday in Ordinary Time

The Return to Ordinary Time, and the Feast of the Holy Family

Although we still had only one snowfall so far that winter, the daily temperatures finally fell and remained seasonably cold. High temperatures barely made it into the twenties during the day, and were in single digits overnight. At Mickey's American Standard we remained inside as much as possible and ran out to the cars to pump gas while bracing against the wind, all the while listening to Mick tell us to ignore the wind chill factor the TV weathermen kept talking about. They claimed that if it were 18 degrees with the wind blowing at 15 miles per hour, for example, it actually felt like it was only 5 degrees out. Mick refused to believe it.

"If I put a bucket of water outside and it's 33 degrees, it doesn't matter how hard the wind blows, the water will never freeze. It's all in your head."

The cold weather also seemed to warm Uncle Charlie's heart, and he allowed me to come back over and eat lunch at the Lovely Bit. He must have assumed that the newspapers moved on and were no longer trying to catch him breaking the law. Whatever the reason, I enjoyed sitting in the tavern again, and especially enjoyed talking to Seamus. He asked me how I was doing, and about the Kilnagaels. He didn't know that Colleen and I had broken up, and surprised me by expressing genuine sympathy that it had happened, but he managed to give me a dig at the same time.

"Well, anyway," he said, "it's a shame when a pretend Irish lad with a pretend uncle tending bar loses the pretend Irish colleen with Irish name that isn't a name at all."

"I'm still shocked that more people didn't come to the funeral. You would think that the Kilnagaels had better friends than that in the parish."

"Marty, now, suicide, that's a serious thing. Many people see it as the worst of sins. Even if Fr. Connolly never said a word and allowed the funeral to take place in the church, a lot of them still wouldn't have come. It's like the whole family was somehow dirtied by the event, and the sinfulness of it would rub off on anyone who dared to stand too close to them. The minute word got out about it, the whole family was tainted in the eyes of some."

We talked about the march and their decision to march with Rev. McAllister. He agreed that it was a big mistake.

"In time people may have forgotten about or apologized for not attending the funeral, but marching with the Negroes? That was the true mortal sin committed by the Kilnagaels. Their neighbors will never forgive them for that.

"They say the Irish are good at politics, but that minister, he's as good as anyone, better than most I'd say."

"Do you think the neighborhood will change?"

"Of course it will change. It already has. Take a good look around you, lad, because you won't be seeing this much longer."

"I'm not sure. I hope it doesn't. I want Holy Truth to stay the same as it is."

The Last Sunday in Ordinary Time

"I know what you mean, but it's a lost cause. When I was a kid in Ireland I thought my home was the perfect place, and knew that it would never change. Then my father died suddenly. No accident or anything, just a young man walking in from the field when he fell over and died on the spot. A heart attack we guessed, but no one really knew. My older brother left home to find work in Dublin, then London because we desperately needed the money. He sent home as much as he could, but never enough. My sisters and I never had decent clothes or enough to eat. When I turned seventeen he put me on a boat to America to find a job so I could send money back too. After my father died, God rest him, my worst day in the States was better than my best day there, and I vowed I'd bring all of them here, Mom, my brother and our three sisters. But Mom wouldn't leave Ireland, God only knows why, and my sisters Mary and Nora met the men they would marry so they decided to stay there. My youngest sister, Kitty, refused to leave Mom alone, so they all stayed there. Standing on that pier, kissing them good-bye, it's the last time I saw any of them."

"Did you send money back to them?"

"Every month. Still do. Kitty is an old woman now, living alone, so she needs the money as much as ever."

"So that's why you think it will change here."

"Of course it will change. It's always the same; it always changes. Now if it stayed the same that would be a change."

He enjoyed the cleverness of what he said, and my reaction to it.

"I wonder if the Irish have the discipline to hold the line and not give in to that White flight they talk about."

He shook his head.

"It sounds nice to talk about not giving an inch, refusing to sell and all that, but you have to remember that a few people who panic or who simply don't care are enough to set the whole thing in motion. Besides, if my father hadn't died so young I might never have made it to America. You have to remember that when things change, sometimes they change for the better."

Even after hearing Seamus insisting that the neighborhood would change I still believed that it wouldn't, or at least I could keep it from changing. The foundation of our parish rested on two equally important things, its faith in Catholicism and its understanding that it was special because it was so Irish. I knew that the Church could be counted on to stay so the people in our neighborhood knew they would always find reassurance from Our Lady of Holy Truth, both the physical church itself, and the faith that it represented. The trouble rose from the fact that the Irish half of the equation lacked such an unequivocal physical symbol, so it relied on the reassurance we took from hearing names and seeing faces similar to ours. Because they were so prominent within Holy Truth, I always thought the Kilnagaels were the Irish face of Holy Truth: attractive, successful, charming, and welcoming to all who shared Holy Truth with them. When the people in the parish turned their backs on Colleen's family I wondered how the Kilnagaels fell from favor so quickly. In the weeks that followed it surprised me to learn that not everyone held the family in such high regard. Individually those names and faces might change as people aged, married, and moved in or out, but the overall look, sound and feel of Holy Truth never really changed. The look and sound of the parish still hadn't changed, but the feel of it certainly had. Rev. McAllister's march unnerved us and made us not just afraid that Blacks were about to move in, but suspicious of each other, wondering who exactly would be the first family to sell their house to a Black family.

Maybe in other times they could have moved away from Holy Truth without causing as much of a stir, but now, with the demise of our parish looming, we needed the reassurance that a family like the Kilnagaels wanted to stay. If the most prominent family in Holy Truth chose to stay, why would anyone else need to leave in some misguided panic? It were as if the Kilnagaels and Our Lady of Holy Truth were a married couple now heading for a divorce, desperately in need of someone to stop them before they went too far. As the Kilnagaels went, so went the parish, but I realized that conversely, as the parish went, so went the Kilnagaels. Just as a gardener needed a garden to fulfill his passion to make things grow, the Kilnagaels needed an Irish parish to indulge their love of being Irish, and they would never find another one like Our Lady of Holy Truth. My certainty that I needed to do something grew each day, but first I needed to get together with Colleen and she wouldn't see me.

I called Colleen twice that week and they told me she wasn't home. I decided to wait a few days before calling again, but I chose not to accept no for an answer. I still allowed myself to believe that we would get back together eventually, but that was less important to me now negotiating some kind of peace agreement between the Kilnagaels and Holy Truth. Whenever my friends and I talked about Fr. Connolly or other priests we tended to see perverse motives for their actions, proclaiming that they acted as they did to show off how important they were, to get their hands on more money, to act like tough guys, or simply to placate a group of parishioners who complained too much, like Fr. Connolly did with Mr. Lally and the others who insisted that Danny could not have a funeral. As the weeks passed since the funeral I started to realize that the priest might have chosen to deny the Kilnagaels because he honestly believed he needed to uphold the standards of the Catholic Church. He counted on us maintaining respect for the Catholic Church no matter how we felt about his decision. We both knew that even though I lashed out at him when he first told Colleen's family that their brother would not get a funeral, priests maintained a place of authority in my life. Even though I not only yelled at him but actually swore at him, Fr. Connolly never yelled back. Our 'fight,' if it could be called a fight, lasted only long enough for me to scream at him, and then he walked away. When he did that, he assured that I, like virtually every other Catholic, would hesitate before confronting or embarrassing a priest. His restraint showed that he remained committed to the Catholic faith that led him to Holy Truth. I held no similar assurance that the Kilnagaels were still committed to their faith in the Irish.

They were genuinely angry that more people didn't come to the Lovely Bit to pay their respects to Danny and his family. Rather than walking away like Fr. Connolly did, the Kilnagaels showed their disdain for the rest of the parish by marching with Rev. McAllister. I forced myself to believe they made a rash decision and, if they had to do it over again, they would not have marched. Before I assured one of them that they were still welcome in our parish, I needed to remind them that Our Lady of Holy

The Last Sunday in Ordinary Time

Truth was a wonderful Irish parish, and how much they loved Holy Truth and their place in it. If they chose to leave and join another parish it was unlikely that they would ever find a second one like this one. Eventually they would come to value Holy Truth again but it might be too late. I needed to convince Colleen and her family to remember why they loved Our Lady of Holy Truth so much. Somehow I convinced myself that if Colleen wore the beautiful Irish sweater I bought for her, and if her family saw her in it, they would all remember how they loved being Irish, and living among the Irish in Holy Truth. I had to get that sweater into Colleen's hands. Since the day of Danny's funeral I spoke to no one in Colleen's family except Colleen on Christmas Eve when she told me it was over. I took comfort in the fact that she broke it off with kindness, that she still held some affection for me.

The Third Sunday in Ordinary Time

January 22nd, 1967

A Mild Winter No More

Standard Oil made Mickey an offer for his gas station that they
assured him was their final offer. As much as he liked to put forth a brave

front and spoke of not backing down, the pressure to sell the company placed on him took its toll. He found it difficult to sleep, and you could see the strain of it on his face and in his suddenly muted personality. While normally he never stopped talking, around this time he grew very quiet, sometimes barking out orders for us to get back to work, but otherwise saying very little. I attended mass at Our Lady of Holy Truth with my parents as usual. They reminded me that Mick needed our prayers, and I certainly included him in mine. Thursday the 26th, just four days away, was D-day for him, the day that he and Standard Oil were scheduled to go to court and learn if Standard had the authority to force him to sell or take his franchise away without paying him anything at all.

"My attorney tells me they do," he said, "but it doesn't have to be completely on their terms. They keep telling me they will walk away if I don't accept their offer, but my attorney says they'll make a better one. It may be out of my hands."

I also said a prayer for Colleen and again asked God to convince her to talk to me. I called her house every other day for the last ten days, and even got up the courage to ring her doorbell once, but nobody was home. I actually felt relief that no one answered because during one phone call Mrs. Kilnagael told me point blank, politely but firmly that I should stop calling. I called anyway. I needed to talk to Colleen one more time to try and heal the wounds between the Kilnagaels and Our Lady of Holy Truth.

I worked that Sunday afternoon and finally got a break when Maureen drove into the gas station to talk to me. When the conversation started she spoke in a clipped, business-like manner, trying to emphasize her displeasure at needing to talk to me, but she softened very quickly. The Kilnagaels were not very good at being aloof or rude, or in any way disrespectful to the people they talked to, especially, I thought, not to me. She asked me very nicely to stop calling their house, and stressed that Colleen didn't want to talk to me.

"I know, Maureen, I know. But…" I hesitated for a moment. "I need to talk to her one more time. After that I'll never bother her again, I promise."

"Marty, can't you forget about it? I mean, I know it's harsh, but it's over. Forget about her."

"Maureen, this is the deal. I bought her a Christmas gift that I want to give her. That's all. If she is willing to talk to me for a few minutes, accept the gift…that's all I need, but I do need it."

"You're not going to start asking her to go out with you again, are you? It won't happen. You know that, right? You're not expecting this to change anything, are you?"

"Between us? Colleen and me? No, I don't expect that. I know that she, and all of you for that matter, but especially Colleen, were heartbroken because of what happened to Danny. I don't want to tell you what it is, but I got her a gift that I think will help her mourn your brother. If she would meet me to accept the gift…"

Maureen nodded slowly.

"Okay, Marty, tell you what. On Wednesday afternoon I'll have Colleen meet you, but it has to be some place that can't be misconstrued as a date."

"How about on the steps of Holy Truth?"

"Not a chance," she said. "We don't go there anymore."

"How about Columbus Park, by the golf course?"

Maureen nodded.

"Okay, I'll drive her over there and be waiting in the car, and if you try anything or say something stupid to her, I swear to God..."

"I won't. I promise. Is 4:00 okay?"

"4:00. She'll be there, but you have to promise me you won't call our house or bother Colleen anymore."

I promised her that I'd leave Colleen and them alone, and watched Maureen drive away, a little hurt by how determined they were to be done with me. Even though I assured her that I knew it was over between Colleen and me, I took a little sly pleasure in choosing the spot where we would meet. On our first date we went to Columbus Park and it was there, by the golf course that we kissed for the first time. I wouldn't say anything romantic to Colleen, but I secretly hoped the memory of our first kiss would say it for me.

A couple of days later, on Tuesday, I sat in the Lovely Bit again, talking to Seamus. I still loved having lunch at the bar, talking to Seamus and listening to what the other men talked about. That afternoon the conversation eventually ended up about the weather. Except for the one big snowfall on Christmas Eve we'd seen almost no snow, and the temperatures, while still fairly cold, remained mild for winter in Chicago. Now, for the next day, the 25th of January, the weathermen were predicting temperatures in the high sixties. The men at the bar all said they couldn't ever remember it being that warm in January before, so they consider it a real treat. Of course Seamus didn't agree.

"It's not natural to be this warm. If it gets warm in winter you can bet your last dollar a storm will come after."

"That's what you said in December, and I don't remember any big storms," Mr. Lally said.

"Didn't we have seven or eight inches of snow on Christmas Eve?"

"Hardly a big storm."

"Big enough," Seamus declared defiantly. "And besides, it never got into the sixties in December. It wasn't that warm."

As I got up to leave he turned his attention back to me. He still enjoyed viewing himself as my teacher, and I remained the one person who always took him seriously. For all of his smart aleck comments, he liked that I listened to what he had to say.

"Mark my words, Marty. When the weather gets out of whack like it will be tomorrow, a big storm will follow."

Back at the station Mick was very nervous. His meeting downtown with the lawyers from Standard Oil was two days away, and the pressure they continued to apply was proving difficult to withstand.

"My lawyer keeps telling me not to worry, but that's easy for him to say. He's not about to lose everything."

I knew that Mickey would never sell his gas station so the court date didn't scare me. As far as I was concerned Mick's determination to not sell would be enough to prevent him from losing the gas station. I couldn't imagine Holy Truth without Mickey's American Standard, or without the Kilnagaels for that matter. I convinced myself that when Mickey beat Standard Oil it would be an omen that the Kilnagael's would be staying in Holy Truth as well. Sometimes all it took was a kind word to remind people that they were loved, and even if the Kilnagaels were angry with the rest of Holy Truth, all they needed was a reminder of how special it was to live there. I still believed they were the first domino, and tomorrow I planned to meet Colleen and begin the process of returning them to their proper place of prominence in our parish. My prayers about Holy Truth staying intact were being answered: Charlie had already let me come back to the Lovely Bit, Mickey would beat Standard Oil in court, and the Kilnagaels would remember how much they liked living in an Irish parish like Holy Truth.

"And remember, this is all hush-hush. Don't breathe a word about my court date with Standard Oil to anybody."

I had to hustle to get Columbus Park by 4:00 that Wednesday afternoon, but I made it with ten minutes to spare. Colleen hadn't arrived yet, so I sat on a park bench near the golf course and waited with her present sitting next to me. The wrapping paper frayed a little since the woman who owned the Galway Lady wrapped it for me almost a month ago, and I gave some thought to rewrapping it before I left the house, but decided it still looked neater than one of my typical wrapping jobs so I left it alone. As predicted the temperature reached the mid-sixties that afternoon, allowing me to sit in the park wearing only a short-sleeve shirt. I wanted everything to be perfect, but now realized that had I given Colleen the sweater on virtually any other day that winter, the chill in the air would have made it seem like that much more of a thoughtful gift. Now, in the spring-like warmth it came across like a raincoat on a sunny day, not right for the conditions. I tried not to think about that.

The Last Sunday in Ordinary Time

I practiced what I wanted to say to her several times over the past few weeks, and even more frequently over the last two days, but rather than becoming more polished, my words sounded more desperate to me. I remembered what Colleen said to me in that store months earlier as clearly as I remembered my own name, but now I found myself panicking that she might not remember talking about the sweater at all. If she didn't remember talking owning a cable knit sweater then what? Would she think I was crazy? Would she be glad I at least remembered? What if she still wanted one, just not one from me? I calmed myself down by repeating that I did this not for myself but for Colleen. Yes I wanted to date her again but, even if she didn't want me back ever again, I still wanted her to feel that sense of being "Colleen the Irish colleen" again.

A couple of minutes after 4:00 Maureen and Colleen pulled into the parking lot; Colleen got out of the car and walked toward the bench where I waited with my gift wrapped box. I stood to greet her and she gave me a little smile as she approached. She made an effort to show me just enough affection or warmth to be polite, but she showed a determined reserved in the way she stood in front of me, and in the fact that she made no effort to hug me. She let me know she wanted to keep emotional distance between us.

"Hi, Colleen, it's good to see you."

She nodded.

"You wanted to talk to me?"

Her tone of voice was flat, almost angry, and not very welcoming.

"Yes, I do. I got you a present for Christmas not just because I wanted to give you something, but because I think it's something you need."

"Marty, I don't want anything from you." Her voiced seem to soften in the middle of the sentence. "Marty, I hope you know that I am not mad at you. I mean, I know I wasn't very nice to you after Danny's funeral, and you've always been so nice to me."

"Colleen, it's okay."

"No," she answered softly, "nothing's okay. Everything changed. Everyone, or maybe everyone but you, they turned their backs on us, and, I'm sorry but I can't separate you from the rest of the parish."

"I think you're wrong about the way the parish feels about you."

"Wrong? We're not wrong. You heard what they said to us at that march. You saw how few people showed up for Danny's...for Danny's funeral."

"But they were just doing what Fr. Connolly told them..."

"No they weren't. They told us that they had no sympathy for Danny or for us." She stopped and took a deep breath. "Look, I don't want to talk about this. If this is why you wanted me here, I should go."

"No, Colleen, wait. "There is something I want you to have."

I don't want a present from you. It's over between..."

"Wait. Before you refuse it just look at it. Open it up and look at it."

My answer did not please her. She let out a sigh as if opening the present was too much to ask, and the last thing she wanted.

"Please, Colleen, open it up and look at it."

"I *don't* want to open it. Whatever it is, I don't want it."

"Please?"

I picked up the box and handed it to her. In my imagination I always explained it to her before she opened it, but she would not allow me that much time. The present would have to speak for itself, or at least get the conversation started between us. She held the box for a few seconds, taking the time to give me a look of displeasure.

"Please."

She let out another sigh and opened it. When she saw it was an Irish sweater she picked it up and held it before her. I realized that she did that mostly for Maureen's sake, so her sister could see what it was even at a distance. She looked at it, lowered it, looked at me with kindness, but spoke in a flat, almost bored voiced.

"It's lovely. I don't want it."

"Oh, Colleen, please take it."

"Marty, you're being sweet, very thoughtful right to the end, but you can't seem to accept that this is the end."

"You told me months ago that you always wanted one of these sweat..."

"A few months ago I did want one, but things have changed. Do you remember telling my family about Irish fairies, and how they taught the Irish to be kind?"

"Yeah, I remember it."

"The phrase you used was 'the least of my brothers.' The Irish were the people who were careful to look out for the least of their brothers. Well, what did they do to *my* brother? Why did they stop believing in the golden rule when Danny died? Why were they so mean to us?"

"You're right. The people in Holy Truth were rotten to you, and so maybe you don't want it today. I know you're mad at me, and you're mad at the whole parish but... but you're still the same beautiful Irish Colleen that you always were. You may not want to admit it right now, but I know, I absolutely know, that one day you will want to be a part of this parish again. You told me once that nothing would make you feel more Irish than wearing one of these beautiful sweaters. So, although I know you don't want it today, someday you'll be glad you have it. And when you realize you're ready to wear it, this sweater will be waiting for you, hanging in your closet, a reminder of how proud you are of being Irish, especially here in Holy Truth."

I thought I got it all in, that I said everything I wanted to say. Colleen stood motionless, holding the crumpled sweater in front of her, waiting to make sure I finished. After about ten or twenty seconds she turned to me and spoke.

"The last thing I want to feel right now is like I'm part of Holy Truth. The last place I want to live is in Holy Truth. All of that stuff about how wonderful it was to live in Our Lady of Holy Truth, how great it is to live in an Irish neighborhood, it's all over now. That was a nice thing to believe in, but they're kicking us while we're down. This parish is dead to us as far as we're concerned."

Her tone struck a note of grim determination rather than one of anger, and convinced me that she meant what she said. I tried to think of something comforting to say, something that would soften her a little, but nothing came to mind. She reached out and took my hand.

"Marty, you are still my friend. When I think about the terrible day when Holy Truth deserted us, I look back on that tawdry little tavern and see you standing there. You never deserted us. And your mother was there, too. Of all the families in Our Lady of Holy Truth, it was your family and your family alone that showed us the traditional Irish kindness. The Donovans remembered to treat the least of their brothers kindly, and I'm sure God knows your family was there during our darkest hour.

"Can you keep a secret? Can I trust you to not tell anyone what I'm about to tell you now?"

I nodded and uttered a quiet yes. She hesitated for a moment, considering one more time whether she could trust me.

"Marty, we sold our house."

She stopped there to let that news sink in, and to determine if she wanted to say anything more.

"My family knows there's been a lot of talk about nobody selling their houses to Black families, and everyone was wondering who would be the first ones in the parish to sell to them. Well, we did it. I'm sure part of my parents' thinking is revenge for Fr. Connolly refusing to give Danny a funeral, and I don't blame them. We were treated badly and now the whole parish is going to pay for doing that to us. But we also needed to sell it. We have to get out of this parish. We need the peace of mind.

"So, it's over between us, okay? You didn't do anything wrong, and I'm sorry. But you are like Joe Leprechaun or something, the perfect little Irishman. It's not your fault but you remind me of everything I hate about this parish, and every time I see you I can't help but think about badly the rest of our neighbors treated us. So, I'm sorry Marty. I know it's not fair to you, but it's not fair to me or my family either."

"You're right. What happened wasn't fair to you or your family, and it's not fair to me either. But in time…"

"Marty, we're leaving. It's over. Please don't tell anyone about who we sold our house to until we're gone. I'm sure people will find out soon enough anyway, but don't tell anyone."

"I promise you I won't tell a soul, but I want you to keep the sweater anyway, just in case."

"I can't. Accepting anything that anyone from Holy Truth gives us now feels like an act of betrayal to my parents. I shouldn't even touch it."

"Colleen, please take it with you for my sake. You can get rid of it after you leave."

Colleen nodded and we turned the car together. I reached out to give her a hug that she resisted at first, but then changed her mind. She hugged me very tightly and for a long time before stepping back.

"Give your parents my regards. They were both always so nice to me."

She then reached out and softly touched my cheek with her hand.

"I will always remember how kind you are."

She walked back to the car where Maureen waited for her. As she approached the car I saw Maureen shaking her head. There was a dumpster at the edge of the parking lot, so Colleen veered in that direction so she could throw the sweater in the garbage for Maureen's

The Last Sunday in Ordinary Time

sake. She hesitated, looked back at me, mouthed the words "I'm sorry," and tossed the sweater into the dumpster. Then she got in the car and the two of them drove away. I thought about fishing the sweater of the dumpster but decided not to. I lingered on the park bench a while longer, not wanting to go home, but having nowhere else to go. As it approached 5:00 and the evening darkened, the unseasonably warm weather cooled quickly, forcing me to head for home whether I wanted to or not. As I walked through the parish I wondered if it were dying or already dead.

The Last Sunday in Ordinary Time

January 26, 1967

The Garden of Eden was no Garden of Eden

It started out as just another day. I woke early and went to school in a seemingly minor snow storm. During the entire bus ride to school and then at school I remained in a dark mood, remembering Colleen throwing the sweater away over and over again, and thinking about the fact they sold their house to Black people. While most of the guys at school kept commenting on the snow, I sat quietly, dying to tell somebody about what the Kilnagaels did, but I never said a word for two reasons: I promised Colleen I wouldn't say a word, and I feared that if I let anyone else know, the Kilnagaels would be attacked by their former friends and neighbors. I genuinely worried about their safety.

The weathermen predicted 4 to 6 inches of snow, but by 10:00 it was already obvious more snow than that was falling. As we looked out our classroom windows we saw cars creeping along the street, forcing their way through deeper and deeper snow. Guys whispered that somebody heard the principal talking about closing the school early, and it seemed more likely with each passing minute. I sat quietly and prayed that God would close the school so I could be alone with my sorrow. At 10:30 they made the announcement; due to the increasingly bad weather we were going to be sent home early, at 11:00. A yell went up throughout the school and guys shook hands to celebrate out good luck. I felt only a sense of relief. Now I only had to wait out the last half hour.

At 10:45 they called my name over the loudspeaker and told me to report to the office. The school secretary looked up at me and told me my father was on the phone.

"Hello?"

"Listen. I've got a problem and I need your help. How soon can you get to the gas station?"

It wasn't my father. Mickey Riordan was calling me from a phone downtown. The secretary must have thought he was my dad. It turned out that he had the two off-duty policeman working that morning, but they had been called into work because of the storm. One already left, and the other was waiting for someone to show up and replace him. I told him we were getting out at 11:00 and agreed to go directly to work.

The bus I sat in on the way home from school inched its way slowly down Austin packed with guys from my high school. We already had more snow than predicted and I pictured Seamus sitting at the bar with an I-told-you-so grin on his face as the weather got worse. For the rest of them it was a giddy atmosphere, and they were jubilant in their celebration of school getting out early. Rather than joining in on the noise everyone else made, I sat in a state of mourning. I sat quietly because I was scared for Our Lady of Holy Truth and felt awful about losing the Kilnagaels. I kept imagining scenarios where Colleen and I met in some distant place, on a street in New York City, at the entrance of a hospital emergency room where we came to visit others who were sick, on an airplane where we just happened to be seated next to each other for a flight, and each time we knew we were meant to be together. Somehow the cosmic dice would roll in such a way that fate would bring us together again. Then I would return to my present predicament, sitting on a slow moving bus while trying to hurry to Mickey's American Standard.

When the bus finally reached Madison I got off and started walking east. The snow on the sidewalks was so deep that I chose to walk in the street, but even there it started to accumulate. Cars still attempted to make it down the street but they moved very slowly, and I could see their rear wheels spinning and causing them to fishtail every time they tried to resume after stopping. By the time I got to Mickey's I had at least an inch of snow on my shoulders and head, and my boots were covered white. One of the cops who worked part-time for Mick named Brian Mulvaney greeted me at the door.

"I'm glad you're here kid. They declared a state of emergency and are calling all off-duty cops in. I have to report to the police station."

"Did you hear from Mick?"

"Not a word yet. You're on your own."

I stepped inside the gas station as he took off, finding myself alone in the empty office. Looking out at the pumps I saw only one set of tire tracks, and noticed how quickly they disappeared under newly falling snow. This was not a gentle falling snow like we had on Christmas Eve, but a rather angry one, whipped around by howling winds that made sure every flat surface was covered. The radio ran a continuous weather report saying that Midway Airport was under ten inches of snow already, and much more was expected. "This is the real McCoy, an actual blizzard" the man said and advised everyone to head for home immediately. A path had been cleared from the sidewalk on Madison to the gas station door, but it already began to disappear because the snow fell so rapidly and the wind blew it so that everything got covered quickly. I stayed inside Mick's long enough to warm up a bit, and called home to if Mom was all right. Whenever I left home for any length of time she always insisted that she needed to hear from me, and reminded me to call when I got there. Since that long walk I took on Christmas I made more of an effort to call home when I was out. I needed to hear her voice as much as she needed to hear mine. Dad and Mom were my family and after what Colleen had said about my parents the day before, I felt the need to atone for believing that I deserved a better family than the one I had.

After a while I grabbed a shovel, went back outside, cleared the path from the door to the sidewalk again, and began to clear the driveway into the gas station. All of the times that Mick hounded me to get busy and stay busy proved effective because I felt guilty sitting in the office doing nothing even though I knew he couldn't possibly see me.

I barely heard the phone in the office ring, but when I did, I hurried back inside to answer it.

"Hello, Mickey's American Standard."

"Is this the gas station Mickey Riordan used to own?"

"Mick?"

"Hello Marty."

"Hey, Mickey. How'd things go in court?"

"They went very well, thank you very much."

"Are you coming back today?"

"No, I won't be back today. I won't be back at all really. I sold the station back to Standard Oil."

"You're kidding. Really? What happened?"

"Well, they kept me and my attorney waiting until the last possible moment, and then, just when we were about to go into court, they blinked and gave me everything I asked for. They didn't ask too many questions. They presented us with a stack of papers to sign, my attorney looked them over, and then I signed my life away. They wanted immediate possession and they got it. It's no longer my gas station."

"Wow."

Literally, I was speechless. I never actually believed he would sell it, and now it was done.

"So listen, Marty, they're coming tomorrow to take inventory and change the locks and all that, but right now, my gas station is officially closed. How much money is in the register?"

"It can't be much because I've been here for a couple of hours and we haven't had a single customer. All this snow is shutting everything down."

I opened the drawer and gave a quick count.

"You've got one twenty, five tens, six fives, and a whole stack of ones. Probably a hundred and twenty or thirty dollars."

"Okay, well take all of that cash and put it in your pocket. I'd rather you have it than Standard."

"Really?"

"Really. Go ahead, and if there's anything you want, candy bars or anything, take them now. There's a 50/50 chance that Standard Oil with throw them out anyway."

"Ooookay."

I dragged the 'okay' out almost like it was a question. Did he really want me to just lock the door and go home? He sensed my confusion so he started talking again.

"There are only two things I want you to make sure you set aside for me: the metal sign behind the register, and the American flag. Then you can lock it up and go home."

"Wow, Mick, just like that?"

"Just like that, but don't worry about me, I am a wealthier man this afternoon that I was this morning. But make sure you grab the sign and the flag. Officially none of that stuff belongs to me anymore, and tomorrow morning the boys from Standard Oil won't let me take a deep breath in there."

"What about your tools?"

"They paid me enough to buy new ones if I'm ever desperate enough to want to work on another car. I won't miss those too much."

"So you're not coming back here tonight?"

"I don't think I could if I wanted to in this weather, but I have other plans anyway. Tina is down here with me, and we're going out to celebrate."

The Last Sunday in Ordinary Time

After I hung up the phone I sat in his chair for a while. Holy Truth *was* dying. First the Kilnagaels, and now Mickey. I did what he told me to do. I found an empty box and took two twenty-four count boxes of candy bars, two bottles of windshield washer fluid, some of the Standard Oil bumper stickers and road maps, and even considered grabbing a carton of Viceroys for Mrs. Kilnagael but decided not to. The Kilnagaels made it clear that they wanted nothing from anyone in Holy Truth, not even me. I found the flag sitting on top of the storage cabinet in back because of the terrible weather.

I took a screwdriver and removed the metal sign off the wall, but the screws were so old that they were tough to loosen. It took me a few minutes to get it free, and even when the last of the four screws came out, the sign stayed in place. I had to pry it off the wall with the flat head of the screwdriver. I understood why Mickey wanted to keep it. It was a two foot white square metal sign with thin red and white lines running around the entire perimeter, an inch inside the edge. Just inside the lines in the four corners were alternating American Flags and red, white and blue Standard Oil logos. The sign read *Mickey's American Standard, Established 1953, Michael Riordan, Proprietor* in neat black lettering. After years of hanging in a gas station it looked a little grimy, so I took it in back and washed it off. Once clean it looked terrific, and I understood why Mick wanted it more than anything else in the station. His goal in coming to the United States was to be a real American businessman, and that sign proved that he had done so. If it weren't for the awful weather I would have taken Mickey's tool box, but I had no way to get it home. As it was the box of candy was too big for me to carry all the way home, so I head across the street to see if Uncle Charlie would let me store there until I could pick it up later.

Charlie and Seamus were the only two people in the bar, so I looked at Charlie and said "Even on a day like today you didn't give him the day off?"

"What's with the box?" Seamus asked.

"You two may as well be the first ones to know. Mickey's American Standard is now officially out of business."

"What?"

"Honest to God. He had a court date with Standard Oil today. They tried to force him to sell it back to them on the cheap, but he demanded a big pile of money, and at the last minute they caved in. They own the gas station now. He just called me. He asked me to grab a few things for him before I locked up. I was wondering if I could leave them here so I wouldn't have to carry this box home today."

"Absolutely," Charlie said. "Are you ready to go home now?"

"Yes. That's where I'm going now."

"Well, call your mother and see if Bridie is still there."

I did as I was asked and called home.

"Hi, Mom. I'm over here at the Lovely Bit. I'm about to head home from the Lovely Bit, but Uncle Charlie is asking about Aunt Bridie. He's asking when she's planning on getting home. Is she on the way?"

"No, love. Bridie is here and she's staying here, probably for the night. She's too old to be going out in this weather."

"Hang on a sec..."

I went over and told Charlie that his wife wasn't coming home tonight.

"She's not? Well if she's not coming here, I'll go to her."

"Are you sure? The snow is very deep and hard to walk through."

"I'll be fine. I don't want to be separated from Bridie tonight."

I was mystified for an answer but Seamus pulled on my sleeve and took me aside. He suggested I get Bridie on the phone to talk him out of it. I returned to the phone and asked Mom to put Bridie on the phone.

"Aunt Bridie, I'm over at the tavern and Charlie is insisting he wants to walk to our house in this snow. Do you think his heart is up to it?"

I handed the phone to Charlie. Seamus and I could hear him arguing with her, repeatedly saying "I'll be fine, I'll be fine," and refusing to let her talk him out of it. He hung up, turned to us and said "Let me get my coat."

While he was gone the phone rang again. It was Bridie and she wanted to talk to me.

"Marty, can you talk him out of it?"

"I don't think I can Bridie. He's determined to see you."

"Well you stay with him, Marty. Don't let him go walking by himself."

"We're going to start walking to the house but you better get ready to take care of him when he gets there."

After I hung up the phone I turned to Seamus and asked if he thought we could talk Charlie out of it.

"I don't think so. He's a very determined man even if he's a little confused at the moment."

"My mom thinks I should keep him here, but to tell you the truth, I'd rather take my chances with my parents around than stay here on my own. What are you going to do?"

"I guess I'll catch the bus for home."

"I don't think there aren't any busses running now. Maybe should come to my house, too. Besides, I'll probably need your help with Charlie, so why don't you stay with us and help me with Charlie?"

"Thank you, Marty."

We helped Charlie turn off the lights and lock the doors, and then the three of us walked out into the blizzard. We chose to walk down the middle of Madison but still needed to walk slowly because there were few cars still moving, and we had to make it through at least ten inches of snow even in the street where cars had flattened the earliest part of the snowfall. Charlie actually walked with a little more authority than I expected, but Seamus walked with less. They were two old men in their seventies, and their age showed. Seamus and I walked on either side of Charlie, locking arms to keep him steady, but Seamus depended on Charlie as much as Charlie depend on me. We inched our way down Madison, our heads bowed to deflect the wind and also to watch where we stepped. I tried to strike up a conversation with my uncle but he kept repeating that he had to meet Bridie at the train station.

"Seamus," I called almost in a yell to be heard over the wind, "does it snow much in Ireland?"

"Certainly not this much."

The Last Sunday in Ordinary Time

I could hear the effort in his voice. He was not quite winded, but he was breathing hard. This was a workout for him but he understood what I was trying to do.

"If you added all the snow I ever saw in Ireland it would add up to half of this snow."

We continued making weather related small talk and managed to travel about one city block in ten minutes. At that rate it would take us about an hour to get to my house. We continued edging forward while I continually scanned the horizon hoping to see someone who could give us a hand. The streets weren't exactly deserted, but it was close. I saw a few other people struggling to make their way through snow that was almost up to our knees, but it was nobody I knew. We made it about halfway through the second block before we finally saw some guys we knew, Eddie Mulroney, and Brendan Ward.

"Hey you guys are going the wrong way. The Lovely Bit is back there."

"Seamus, stand here with Charlie for a second would you?"

Eddie, Brendan and I stepped a few feet away so Charlie couldn't hear us. I told them the whole story about getting Charlie to my house to see Bridie and asked for their help. Brendan listened to my problem, studied the situation for a moment and then said he had an idea.

"I'm going to run back to my house and get my brothers and a few other guys, and a sled. We'll pull him to your house on a sled."

"Oh, my God, that would be great."

"Eddie you stay here and give Marty a hand now, and I'll be back in a few minutes."

The Last Sunday in Ordinary Time

"Should we keep walking forward?" Seamus asked when I told him what the plan was. I assumed he wanted to turn around and go back to the Lovely Bit. He must have been exhausted.

"Let's keep going while we wait for those guys to arrive. It'll take us about twenty minutes to get back to the tavern, and probably at least half an hour to get to our house, but Charlie won't stop talking about Aunt Bridie. If we take him back to the tavern he'll want to leave right away."

We changed positions a little bit. Now Eddie took Charlie by the arm helped him keep moving forward. Seamus and I were a few steps ahead of them, and Seamus was holding on to my arm.

"God forgive me, Marty, but I'm afraid of falling. That's why I'm holding on so tight."

"That's okay. You hold on to me as tightly as you need to, but let's see if we can get some kind of a rhythm going. Count off the steps with me. One, two. One, two. One, two."

Seamus joined me in counting right away. On the count of one we stepped with our left feet, and on two with our right. It struck me as very child-like, but it made it easier for Seamus and me. I heard Eddie and Charlie start imitating us, and so we did start walking a little faster. We maintained the counting for a while but eventually we moved without needing to count out loud.

"We should take a good look around, Marty, because Holy Truth will never be this white again."

"Very funny, but I guess you're right. Mick sold his gas station, Blacks will be moving in soon, so I'm sure a lot of us Irish are going to move out, it won't be the same."

"You're not Irish, you're American."

As he spoke Seamus had to stop to concentrate on taking his next step, and to catch his breath a little bit. We made it all the way to the end of the second block and decided to stop for a few minutes to rest. Eddie and I exchanged where-are-those-guys looks. We were ready to turn the corner which and leave Madison for a side street. On Madison the cars had matted down the snow somewhat, but going on to a side street meant that even in the middle of the road the snow was very deep. We really needed the sled.

"Are you all right, Charlie?"

He nodded but he didn't look it. He kept mumbling about seeing Bridie, and now started talking about how cold he was. We hadn't made it too far from Madison when we heard and saw a group of guys running toward us. I recognized three Gallaghers, Joe, Tommy, and Peter, as well as Jack and Tommy McDermott, Patrick Casey, and a couple of guys I couldn't recognize under all of their winter clothes. Peggy Brennan was also with them and a couple of her girlfriends. And they had a sled.

Getting Charlie to sit on the sled was easy because he was near exhaustion, but it was very tippy with just him on it, so we told Seamus to get behind Charlie for stability. Seamus sat with his arms around Charlie and a very serious look on his face. He wanted to make sure he kept Charlie safe, and he was probably a little scared himself. Two guys pulled on the rope at the front of the sled, and two guys pushed from behind. After about fifty yards new guys took over back and front. Simply walking through the snow was difficult, and pulling a sled was that much harder, but everyone showed a genuine concern for Charlie who still looked sickly. To lighten the mood the girls started calling out to the few other people on the street.

"Make way. Make way. Bartender coming through. Precious cargo. Bartender coming through."

As difficult as it was to pull the sled, a jovial atmosphere rose among us. As we starting making progress others joined us. Brendan made several phone calls and this now became a party of sorts. Word spread around the neighborhood and many people who sat inside bored to death now came out to join in the fun. We started out as a group of about fifteen, but as we continued to walk the number rose to about thirty-five, and we needed all of the help. It got to the point where guys were switching every twenty yards or so because it was so difficult to march through the snow.

Although we took the job of getting Charlie and Seamus to my house seriously, all around the sled people were laughing, flirting, and generally goofing off. There were snowball fights and guys were tackling each other in the snow all while keeping a safe wall of protection around the sled. Somebody starting singing *I'm Dreaming of a White Christmas*, and others joined in. About half a block from the house I asked Joe Gallagher if he would run ahead and shovel the front steps to make it easier for Charlie to get in. As he and a couple of other guys got there we could hear them saying hello to my mom. While Mom stood in the doorway more of the crowd ran over and "Hi-Mrs.-Donovans" were repeated, followed by a number of "Hi-Bridie's."

When at last the sled arrived in front of the house people started calling out "Special Delivery for the Donovans" and things like that. We helped both Seamus and Charlie to their feet. Seamus seemed in pretty good shape, but Charlie looked weak, like a very old man. Whatever amusement the women took from the boisterous crowd now changed to all out concern for Bridie's husband. He didn't look well at all and needed my help walking up the stairs. After both Seamus and Charlie got inside I breathed a sigh of relief and went back down the stairs to thank everyone for their help.

"Hey, you guys. Thanks a lot. I really appreciate all of your help."

The guys came over and shook my hand, a couple of the girls hugged me, and I heard a lot of "glad to do it," "anytime," and "It was fun." Then they took off back toward Madison. Watching and listening to them walking, laughing and carrying on as they went, it was, I thought, Our Lady of Holy Truth at it's best; Irish people of the parish pulling together to help out one of their neighbors. It also saddened me a bit to remember that the unity of the parish stood on the brink of collapse because the Kilnagaels sold their house to Blacks. As I listened to their voices and laughter fading in the growing distance between us, I wondered if they were aware how close to the end it all was.

Inside the house I found they all were in the kitchen. Mom put the kettle on and was whirling around the kitchen getting something for the two men to eat. Bridie tried talking to her husband, but he was too worn out to carry on a conversation. She stood behind Charlie rubbing his arms in an effort to warm him up.

"Marty! Run upstairs and bring down some sweaters and blankets for these two."

The Last Sunday in Ordinary Time

I did as asked and entered the kitchen with my arms full. Seamus thanked me for the sweater and put it on quickly while Bridie and Mom struggled while helping Charlie put one on. Then Bridie took a blanket and wrapped it around Charlie's shoulders all the while showing profound concern on her face.

"Aunt Bridie, I wasn't sure what to do, but I thought he would be better off here with you. I hope I did the right thing."

"Oh, you did, you did. Thank you Marty."

"He's better off here where we can keep an eye on him," Mom added.

The kettle and the soup Mom had on the stove both boiled, and she quickly had a bowl of soup in front of both Seamus and Charlie. Not until she made tea and put soda bread and butter on the table did she ask what they wanted to eat.

"I'll put a spud on for you?"

"Oh, no Katie," Seamus said. "This is grand. I've enough already."

"Are you sure? How about Charlie? Does Charlie want a bit of steak and potato?"

We all looked over at Charlie. His hand shook as he raised the spoon to his mouth.

"I don't think so," Bridie answered. "I think he'll finish his tea and we'll put him to bed."

Mom told me to sit down and started serving me. I certainly wanted steak and potatoes, but since nobody else did, I didn't say a word. Bridie looked over at me and smiled.

"You're a man just like your father. Today when I saw Charlie walking in the door with you and bringing Seamus along, it reminded of the day years ago when he brought your father through my door bringing Mickey Riordan along with him."

"He does look like his father, doesn't he? Not a bad thing, if you ask me."

"A right handsome fellow, I'd say," Seamus said.

An awkward silence descended and before everyone became too focused on Uncle Charlie. The effort to feed himself was too much for him, and he looked weaker by the minute. I tried to get Bridie talking some more.

"Tell me, Aunt Bridie, did you and Charlie fix Mom and Dad up or did that just happen?"

"Well, we may have pulled a few strings," she said and winked.

"Did you know you were being set up, Mom?"

"I'd have to be stupid not to know. Charlie got me a job with the city but used to have me come to his committeemen's office sometimes to make phone calls and help get out the vote. He had me come on a day when there was no reason for me to be there and had me making nonsense phone calls asking voters if they needed anything from their alderman, garbage cans or what not."

"That's right," Bridie said, "we did. I remember that now."

"Dialing the phone that much can be murder on your fingers, so I used a pencil to dial. Not ten minutes after I started Charlie sent your father in to make a phone call. I could tell he wasn't more than a day or two in America by the way he was dressed, and he sat down a few feet

The Last Sunday in Ordinary Time

away from me by another phone, but he watched me intently. He had me convinced he was smitten with me. It turned out he had never used a rotary phone so he watched me to learn how to do it. When I finished my phone call he leaned over and said 'Excuse me, miss, can I borrow a pencil to use the phone?' God forgive me I laughed hard. And the poor man just sat there turning beet red.

"In an effort to make him feel better and also because I thought he was a handsome man, I walked over and said 'Let me show you how to do it.' I stood behind him and talked him through it, but I also put my hands on his shoulders while I talked to him. He shook so much from being nervous I thought he might die right there."

"Well, Mom, you little flirt."

She smiled and said "I have my moments."

"So did he ask you out or did you have to ask him out?"

"Don't sell your father short. I felt so bad about embarrassing him that before he left, I walked over and quietly apologized to him. He looked me straight in the eye and said, 'Katie Brennan, was that a nice thing to do to the man you're going to marry?' Now I was the one who was speechless. Then he smiled at me, said good-bye, and walked away. He left me standing there unable to say another word."

"I never heard that story before," Bridie said.

"I was too afraid to repeat it to anyone. What if he was just joking? If I went around blathering it to everyone I knew and he never called me, I'd look like a fool. As it was, he waited three months to call. He said he needed to earn a few paychecks first."

The Last Sunday in Ordinary Time

We stalled as long as we could. Uncle Charlie was fading right before our eyes. Mom suggested trying to get him to the hospital but Bridie refused that idea.

"He's too weak to go out in this weather and...he's better off surrounded by family."

Seamus nodded slowly. I realized that Bridie saw the same thing that he saw. I helped Charlie walk up the stairs and then Mom and Bridie took over. They decided to put Charlie to bed in Mom and Dad's room. Bridie got him ready for bed with Mom's help, and Mom had me carry two overstuffed chairs upstairs from the living room to the bedroom. Charlie went to sleep immediately and Bridie and Mom stayed in the room to pray a rosary and watch over him. Bridie moved her chair next to the bed and held Charlie's hand with her left hand, and my mother's hand with her right. She knew her husband had a weak heart for some time, so his decision to walk through the snow scared her. She shook with fear, but remained determined to stay by his side.

Seamus and I went to the living room. They were showing a John Wayne movie on TV, but we ended up looking out the window and marveling at all the snow. It was still coming down.

"Your mother is a very nice woman, Marty. You're blessed to have a woman like that for a mother."

"Thanks Seamus. You're right, I am. She's great. And I'm glad you were with me when I had to get him here."

He nodded and said "And I'm grateful that you asked me to join you."

The Last Sunday in Ordinary Time

We stood there for a few minutes staring at the snow, marveling at what was buried and how deep it was. Along the street we could see the outlines of cars buried in white, and even the area in front of our house that had been shoveled was under six or seven new inches of snow. Never the less, my mind kept returning to the idea that Holy Truth was dying, at least as far as being an Irish neighborhood was concerned.

"I used to think that Our Lady of Holy Truth was like some kind of Garden of Eden. Now I'm wondering if Uncle Charlie is going to close the Lovely Bit, Mick sold his gas station, Blacks will be moving in... I'm sure a lot of the Irish are going to move out, it won't be the same."

I wanted to say "and the Kilnagaels are moving out" but I had promised Colleen I would say a word. Losing Mickey Riordan's American Standard, The Lovely Bit O'Blarney Pub, and the Kilnagaels were terrible blows suffered by Our Lady of Holy Truth. As far as I was concern, Our Lady of Holy Truth could have survived one of the three losses, but the three of them at one time meant the end was near.

"Well, you have to remember that the Garden of Eden was no Garden of Eden."

He made me laugh. It was such a perfect Seamus thing to say.

"You're going to have to explain that to me."

"Well, if you know your bible you know the snake was in the Garden of Eden the whole time. Adam and Eve were always in danger of being tricked by talking snakes and what not. And you have to figure that any place that had talking snakes is not all that great to begin with. And don't forget, it was a walking, talking snake at that. God punished the snake by making all snakes crawl on their bellies forever afterward."

The Last Sunday in Ordinary Time

"So you're saying that Holy Truth isn't as wonderful as I think it is."

"No, I'm not saying that. I'm just saying that just because you think it's wonderful doesn't mean it's perfect."

We both leaned forward and looked at a lone figure fighting his way down the street. Every step required effort and we could see that he was laboring.

"Hey, I think that's my dad." I walked over to the stairs and called up to my mother. "Hey, Mom, Dad's home, or at least he will be in about three minutes."

"Marty, put the kettle on. I'll be down in a jiffy."

I did as she asked and then opened the front door for him. We greeted him as he got to the stairs, causing him to do a double take when he saw Seamus. He greeted Seamus by named which surprised me a bit, but then I realized Dad had probably been to the Lovely Bit often enough to have met Seamus.

"Hello, Bill," Seamus said. "Your son was kind enough to invite an old man in off the street."

"Well more power to him. Glad to have you."

"How far did you walk, Dad?"

"I got off the train at Cicero and Lake. It must have been two hours ago. I had to stop and rest a few times."

"That's a good stretch of the legs on a warm day," Seamus said.

Mom came downstairs and asked if he was ready to eat. He nodded and said he was, but he wanted to change first.

"I left some clothes for you in the bathroom. Charlie Fitzpatrick's asleep in our bed. Bridie's up there with him."

"Oh?"

"He doesn't look good. Marty brought him home."

He looked at me and said "Well, you're full of surprises tonight."

Before Mom went into the kitchen I asked her if she could make a steak for me too, and she said she'd be happy to. I went upstairs to sit with Bridie. We left Seamus on his own to watch the John Wayne movie, and I looked in on Uncle Charlie.

"How's he doing?"

She shook her head and said "He doesn't look good, the poor thing."

I sat down beside her and put my arm around her.

"You know, when we were at the Lovely Bit he said something about meeting you at the train station. Do you know what he was talking about?"

"I do. It may surprise you to know, but when I was a young woman I was considered quite a catch."

"That doesn't surprise me at all. If you weren't already married I'd be putting the moves on you right now."

She gave me a friendly little slap on the arm and said "Stop.

"My older sister was a nun who lived in a convent in Des Moines, Iowa."

"I didn't know you had a sister living here."

"I did. In fact I had both a sister and a brother. Mary Margaret was her name, and Joseph was my younger brother. She lived in Des

Moines and I would try to go see her every summer for a few days. In 1922 I spent a week there, but made plans to be back in Chicago for a big dance taking place on Saturday night. Everyone was going and I didn't want to miss it. My train was scheduled to arrive downtown at 1:15, and Joseph was supposed to pick me up. At the time there were three or four fellows who were interested in me, not the least of which was Charlie. He already had a city job, and was involved in city politics. He also had access to a car, something none of the other men had. Charlie offered my brother the bribe of a city job if Joseph would let him pick me up at the train station. Joseph agreed and when I got off the train there was Charlie Fitzpatrick waiting for me."

"Was that a big deal, to have a car?"

"Oh, it was, and I was dazzled by it. It was actually a city car, but Charlie was already making connections, so he finagled a way to use it. Anyway, he asked me to let him take me to the dance and I agreed. I'm sure the other guys were shocked when they saw me walking into the dance on his arm, but Charlie was always an ambitious man. He charmed me so much that night that I was a goner."

"So that's what he meant by meeting you at the train station."

"I am a lucky woman. He always makes me feel beautiful. Every woman should marry a man like that."

Dad stuck his head in the door and said hello to Bridie.

"How's he doing?"

Bridie again shook her head and said "He's sleeping as if he hasn't slept in weeks."

The Last Sunday in Ordinary Time

"He looks very pale. Do you think we should try to get him to a hospital?"

"No, Billy, he doesn't need a hospital, just a good night's sleep."

"Well, now Bridie you can't know that for sure. Maybe we should call for an ambulance."

"No. He's here, surrounded by family. This is the best place for him tonight. Maybe in the morning I'll see things differently. And you'd never get an ambulance through in this weather."

"Bridie, if there's anything we can do, anything, you just ask."

"I will, thank you."

I sat with Bridie for a while longer but she insisted I go downstairs. I assumed she wanted to be alone with Charlie and I said as much to Mom when I entered the kitchen. Seamus had a beer in front of him, Dad waited for his dinner to be served while Mom was busy at the stove. I couldn't wait to ask Dad about meeting Mom that first time, so I started right in on him.

"Hey Dad, Mom's been telling stories about you. She told us that you didn't know how to use a telephone when you came to America. Did you really ask her for a pencil?"

"She told you that story, did she? Well, I guess I can't keep any secrets. Yes, my friends that is a true story."

"It's amazing the things we didn't know when we came to this country, isn't it?" Seamus said.

"It is."

"Well, Mom says you knew enough to ask her to marry you the first time you met her."

"Marty..." Mom protested.

"That's a true story, too, smart aleck. I knew a good thing when I saw it."

"It?" Mom asked.

"Oh, pardon me, your royal highness. I mean I knew a beautiful woman when I saw her."

"Much better."

"Way to go, Dad. I didn't think you had it in you."

"Oh? Listen to this one," Dad said to Seamus, "he doesn't realize that once upon a time I had a full head of hair and was considered the Irish Cary Grant."

"I've often heard it said that Cary Grant was no Billy Donovan," Seamus replied.

"Actually, and I've never told your mother this before, but when I was on the ship coming over from Ireland, an attractive woman went out of her way to strike up a conversation with me."

"No. No you never did tell this story to me," Mom said with a tone of mock concern.

"Well, she did. And I, being the girl-shy man that I was, stammered and stuttered and basically made a fool of myself. I remember one smart aleck calling out 'Whatsa matter, Billy, are you afraid of the skirts?' Which, of course, I was. Oh, they had a great laugh at my expense, except, of course, for Mickey Riordan. He didn't say anything that day, but the next day he sat beside me and said 'Don't worry about it. You're going to America, land of second chances and new opportunities. If you don't meet up with that girl again, you'll meet another.

"He was right about that. I wasn't more than two or three weeks here the day I met your mother."

"And I was much prettier than that old Trollope who was throwing herself at every man on the boat."

"Oh, you're definitely and infinitely more beautiful than she was, but how do you know that I wasn't the most handsome man on the boat? Maybe I was the only man she threw herself at. Maybe she wasn't a Trollope at all, but a woman of good taste and refinement and she knew a great man when she saw one."

It was a rare treat for me to hear my parents needling each other back and forth, and I could see that they were enjoying it as much as Seamus and I were.

"So you're telling us that you went from being a girl-shy dork to asking Mom to marry you in three weeks?"

Dad gave me a look like he was offended by the question.

"First of all, I never said I was a dork...."

"You were," Mom said immediately, and we all laughed at that except Dad, who smiled quite a bit but refused to allow Mom the satisfaction of laughing at her joke. By this time she was placing plates in front of both Dad and me, and asked Seamus one more time if he wanted some.

"I have plenty," she assured him.

"Oh, no, Katie, thank you very much."

"But, Dad, you actually told Mom you were the man she was going to marry then and there."

"I did, but not for the reason you might think. Without question your mother was lovely, and being so lovely she made me nervous, but it was Mick who really made me nervous. As you know I brought Mickey with me when I showed up at Charlie and Bridie's door. After he had seen me look foolish with that other woman, and after he told me I'd get another chance, I couldn't very well let him see me looking so foolish again. I was panicked about what I should say to the lovely Katie, and just as panicked about what Mick would say if he found out I said nothing. I had seen a movie where a man used that line, 'Is that any way to talk to your future husband?', and so I said it to your mother. I was afraid that Mickey would find out that Charlie tried to fix me up with her, and I couldn't face him if I screwed it up again. I will always be grateful that your mother was kind enough to apologize to me, and that I, for one brief instant, was bold enough to say 'Katie Brennan, was that a nice thing to do to the man you're going to marry?' Actually, in the movie, the fellow kissed the girl before he walked away. I wanted to step forward and kiss your mother, but I wasn't that bold."

"If you tried to kiss me that day I wouldn't have been the woman you married."

Dad gave Mom an oh-really look while she failed to suppress her laughter.

"Atta girl, Mom. You play hard to get."

"When I went to sleep that night, for the first time I wasn't worried. Whatever qualms or questions I had about coming to America seemed unimportant because I was certain that Katie Brennan was going to marry me. And so she did."

"And so I did."

It was as joyous a moment as I ever remember in that kitchen. While we were delighting in my parents' story of how they met Aunt Bridie walked into the kitchen.

"Charlie is asleep, and I heard so much laughter I had to come down and see what was going on."

"Well come and join us. How's he doing?"

"It's his heart. He keeps trying to deny it, but he can't take the strain of running the tavern in his condition. I'm putting my foot down. It's time to close the Lovely Bit O' Blarney."

"Wow. Mickey's and the Lovely Bit both closing on the same day? Who would have guessed that?"

They all looked at me for a few seconds without speaking.

"Did you hear from Mick? Is he closing his gas station?"

"He is. He told me that his lawyer was right. If he held out long enough then Standard would meet his price. Just before they went before the judge, Standard caved and gave him everything he asked for. He called me this afternoon and told me to lock it up. It all belonged to Standard Oil now, the tools and everything. He and Tina were staying downtown to celebrate."

"Well more power to him," Dad said. "Italian or not, she's the perfect woman for Mickey. She owns her own business. He owned his own business. The two of them are both all business."

The Last Sunday in Ordinary Time

"Do you really think you can convince Charlie to close up shop?" Seamus asked.

"The old fool risked his life walking here in this snowstorm just to be with me. He'll do it because I asked him to."

As the four of them continued talking my mind wandered as I thought about Mickey. If he hadn't pushed my dad maybe my parents wouldn't have gotten married. And he was the one who pushed me to ask Colleen out the first time. Was he afraid that I was too much like my father, and unlikely to gather the courage to ask Colleen out without his help? He said the same thing to both of us. This is America, and Americans believe in the pursuit of happiness. He had no patience for people who didn't act like proper Americans and pursue their dreams or their loves. Even on a night like this, when it seemed everyone was trapped in Holy Truth by the blizzard, Mickey managed to find a way to be celebrating life outside the parish. Not even a blizzard could stop him.

As for Our Lady of Holy Truth itself, I preferred to think of that Thursday as the last day that the parish still possessed its charms. This meal around the kitchen table, full of laughter and warm memories became the last supper of my childhood. The help I got from friends and neighbors to help me deliver Charlie and Seamus to my house reminded me one last time of how much affection I felt for the people of Holy Truth.

The Last Sunday in Ordinary Time

The next morning people emerged from their houses to take a closer look at what the storm left behind. The blizzard buried Chicago under twenty-four inches of snow, and as the neighbors gathered to begin shoveling, the first question was 'Where do we put it?' The atmosphere filled with laughter and good will, adults checking on neighbors, sharing groceries and watching their kids jump off of porches into deep piles of snow. The schools closed down along with virtually everything else. Dad and I joined the other men on the block and we began clearing steps and sidewalks, giving everyone a little wiggle room. For Our Lady of Holy Truth it meant one last gasp of being a friendly, cohesive Irish parish. Other than the people inside my own house, I doubted anyone else realized how much changed in twenty-four hours.

Years later I spoke with old friends who commented on the fact there was a Polish neighborhood on the near northwest side of the city that remained intact. The Polish apparently refused to sell their houses and their neighborhood stayed mostly Polish long after other predominately Polish, Italian and Irish neighborhoods collapsed under the panic felt by White families who refused to live with Black families. I believed whatever chance we had to maintain our neighborhood ended because the Kilnagaels were the first family to move out. If they had stayed, maybe others would have followed their lead, but when the Kilnagaels decided to get out, everyone else figured that if the wealthiest family in the parish left, only the poorest or dumbest would remain. The newspapers called it 'White flight,' and because of it, Holy Truth was doomed. As far as Fr. Connolly was concerned, the sudden change in his parish ended his chances to be an old-fashioned iron-fisted pastor like Monsignor O'Brien. Holy Truth was already one of the smallest parishes in the archdiocese, and as the Irish Catholics moved out, Blacks moved in, very few of them Catholic. As the congregation dwindled the parish became too expensive for the archdiocese to keep open. Within a couple of years Fr. Connolly had been reassigned and a few years later the church itself was closed and sold. It became a Protestant church, the Gospel House of Jesus. Maybe the change would have happened anyway, but it always seemed to me that his decision to deny their son a funeral drove the Kilnagaels out of Holy Truth and eventually forced Fr. Connolly out as well.

Sometime that day or within a couple of days after, a sign appeared in the window of Mickey's American Standard: *Reopening soon under new management.* As for the Lovely Bit, it remained open for a couple of more months, but Charlie and Bridie found a buyer fairly quickly, and by the summer of 1967 the Lovely Bit O' Blarney Pub became the Dew Drop Inn. The Dew Drop Inn lasted a little over a year, but with each passing week, more of the regulars were leaving the neighborhood and the customer base grew too small to sustain it. The new owner also didn't take too kindly to an old man sitting at the bar day after day, nursing a beer or two, so Seamus was made to feel unwelcome. The regulars still remaining felt the new owner was out of line for treating Seamus that way, and that hurt his business as well.

Mickey married Tina Avelini. Dad joked that it was as much a business merger as a marriage. Mick joined her in the real estate business, and they used some of the money from the sale of his gas station to open a bigger sales office. Tina kept her maiden name not because she was determined to maintain her independence, but because she thought it was good for business. With the name Avelini they could more easily pursue business from Italians, and with the name Riordan they could pursue business from the Irish. They called the new business **R**iordan and **A**velini **R**eal **E**state. The sign in the window promised customers would receive a **R.A.R.E.** level of service.

I maintained some contact with Seamus for a few years afterward. He lived by himself in a small apartment that he stayed in even after most of his neighbors moved on. He began coming to our house for Thanksgiving and Christmas dinner, but during my sophomore year in college he went missing. I stopped by to invite him to join us again for Thanksgiving, but there was no sign of him. A neighbor said he may have gone back to Ireland because he once mentioned something about an ailing sister. I found it hard to imagine Seamus would get on an airplane. He remained gone through Christmas, and later in the spring the landlord moved all of his belongings to a basement storage room because no rent had been paid for months and said he would hold them until November 1st. When I asked if I could look through Seamus' stuff, the landlord agreed, and there I found picture of Seamus and me shot in the Lovely Bit. I didn't remember the picture being taken, but I wanted to keep it and the landlord did not object. It was a very warm photograph of two friends wearing bright smiles. It remains the only evidence I know of that Seamus actually existed.

The Last Sunday in Ordinary Time

When I graduated from college Mom and Dad bought me a ticket to Ireland, and the three of us spent a month there. I made a journey to Seamus' home town to see if he might still be there taking care of his sister. In the little town of Moat, County West Meath I met one of Seamus's nephews. Seamus never made it back to Ireland. As I suspected, he was a white knuckle flyer and shortly before the plane landed Seamus died in his seat. In death as in life Seamus managed to keep himself caught between Ireland and America, not really belonging to either place. I visited his grave, said a prayer for him, and left him an unopened bottle of beer that he could nurse in the afterlife.

By the mid 1960's a number of new suburbs and existing small towns began to grow just outside the city. Several of them needed new directors of public works, and my dad began applying to them in hopes of moving up in the world. I was unaware that he was doing this until he actually got one. It was my parents' intention to join the great white flight to the suburbs, but where we might end up all depended on Dad landing a new job. He applied in new suburbs way down south like Tinley Park and Palos Heights, and in older, more established towns like Wheaton to the west and Des Plaines to the North. Eventually he landed a job in Mt. Prospect in the far northwest suburbs. On those nights when my parents told me he was going to attend a wake for a family member of one his coworkers in Chicago, he was actually wearing a suit to go on job interviews. In the smaller towns the councilmen and mayors worked full time jobs during the day, and conducted their meetings in the evening. After countless trial-and-error interviews, Dad finally mastered the interview process and got his job in February, 1967.

The Last Sunday in Ordinary Time

He started working for the City of Chicago on May 7th, 1947 which meant he was just about three months short of the twenty years he needed to qualify for a pension. Uncle Charlie stepped in and got Dad a night shift in Chicago, so for almost four months, until June that year, Dad worked for Mt. Prospect during the day, and then for Chicago at night. I believe his new job in Chicago allowed him to sleep part of the time, but, in any event, he stayed on long enough to get his twenty years in. My parents bought a nice house in Mt. Prospect, and I finished my high school years driving to Chicago from there so I could finish school with the friends I grew up with.

Within such a remarkably short time none of it remained. The Lovely Bit O' Blarney was gone, Mickey's American Standard was gone, and even Our Lady of Holy Truth was gone. Some people might wonder if such a place actually existed, but it did. Like the first kiss from the first girl I ever really loved, Holy Truth and the Lovely Bit O' Blarney linger in my memory, growing more dear to me even as the memory grows more distant.

Made in the USA
Monee, IL
08 February 2021